CHRISTMAS AT LOCK KEEPER'S COTTAGE

LUCY COLEMAN

Boldwood

First published in Great Britain in 2020 by Boldwood Books Ltd.

This paperback edition first published in 2021.

1

A CIP catalogue record for this book is available from the British Library.

Paperback ISBN: 978-1-80280-212-2

Ebook ISBN: 978-1-83889-058-2

Kindle ISBN: 978-1-83889-057-5

Audio CD ISBN: 978-1-83889-054-4

Digital audio download ISBN: 978-1-83889-055-1

Large Print ISBN: 978-1-83889-764-2

Boldwood Books Ltd.

23 Bowerdean Street, London, SW6 3TN

www.boldwoodbooks.com

To Lynda, a beautiful soul who now has wings. x

IMMI

PROLOGUE

I read an article the other day, giving tips on how to manifest the life you want. You begin by writing a letter and... burning it. Whether you want to free yourself of worry, realise a dream, or simply declutter your mind, a well-respected life coach believes that the universe is listening. I'm not sure how I feel about that statement, but I can see how it might be cathartic for some people - assuming they have the guts to do it properly.

What I'm discovering, though, is that being honest with oneself isn't easy. After almost an hour, most of it spent with a pen in my hand hovering over the piece of paper in front of me, it remains blank. Even though I love the idea of releasing negative energy into the ether, or drawing positive energy towards me, I can't do it. I'm not ready to bare my soul to anyone. Least of all, myself.

Maybe I'll write a letter to Santa, instead, and burn that. Start small and work your way up, Immi, I tell myself. As one of my three jobs involves wearing an elf costume every weekend in December, I figure that if I'm not ready to reach out to the universe, Santa is the next best option.

This year I'm hoping Christmas is going to be a truly joyful occasion to make up for the disappointments of last year. When the man you love – your soul mate – is supporting a parent through the big C, life can feel as if it's on hold. I won't lie, it's been tough. My mind and my body ache when he isn't here with me because I'm simply going through the motions rather than living my life.

Anyway, what harm can it do to honour an age-old tradition? After all, I'm one of Santa's biggest fans. They say the act of believing makes things happen and I've seen that with my own eyes. So here goes:

Dear Santa

When I was six years old, I wrote you a very special letter. I handed Dad the sealed envelope and we stood together, hand in hand, as he threw it onto the fire. I watched in fervent anticipation as the wisps of pale grey smoke, tinged with little curls of white, disappeared up the chimney.

Everyone thought I was asking you for a doll's house, but actually, I asked you to bring my mum back home to us. Dad didn't understand why I burst into tears on Christmas morning, after I'd unwrapped the wonderful presents beneath the glittering tree. And, at the time, I didn't understand that I had asked for the impossible.

Every year until I was twelve, when I wrote my last letter, I just asked for toys, books and clothes, as the other kids did. But in my heart there was only one thing I longed to have, because I honestly believed that it would make my life complete.

But I appreciate now how lucky I was, and that the true magic of Christmas was there all along. I was surrounded by love. The love of my dad, my grandparents and our friends. No child could ask for more than that.

This year there is only one thing on my list and it's to be able to celebrate Christmas with the man I love, Gray, by my side. I need it to reassure me there really can be an us and that life isn't going to cheat me, yet again.

Just keep everything crossed for me, will you? That's all I ask. And keep up the good work. A lot of people believe in you, regardless of their age. In today's world that's both magical and inspiring, because what is life without hope?

With much love, Immi

1

DECK THE HULL WITH BOUGHS OF HOLLY

'I'm just about to turn off the main road, Immi. Let the countdown to Christmas begin.'

'At last,' I croak, although the sound of Gray's voice makes me instantly break out into a beaming smile.

In the background, the thrum of the car's engine sounds eerily distant, but it's a relief to know he will be here very soon. The thought of sinking into his arms again fills me with nervous anticipation and yet another part of me hates feeling so... needy. There's an emptiness that gnaws away at me when he isn't around, which nothing else can fill.

'What's wrong with your voice? Please don't—'

The signal drops out for a second or two, and I imagine the car negotiating the bend as he heads away from the village hall, which sits proudly alongside a magnificent green. Originally a farming community before the lock was built and – much later – the marina, Aysbury is rather spread out. There are some large country properties set back from the road behind high walls, before the first cluster of farm cottages signals the approach to the canal. But our community extends both sides of the waterway, with a network of narrow lanes giving tantalising glimpses of a variety of old stone cottages and barn conversions.

Beyond that, the winding lane dips for several hundred yards and the tall swathe of trees are an impenetrable barrier. '... not coming down... something.'

I grip the phone tighter, raising my voice a little as I reassure him. 'No. I'm fine. Really, I'm good.'

There's a short pause and I'm sure we've been disconnected, then the thrumming sound is back, and the engine kicks up a notch as the car accelerates along the open stretch of road. Almost here. He's almost here.

'You're not crying, are you, Immi?'

Drawing in a deep breath, then taking a moment to expel it in a controlled manner, I make a concerted effort to sound bright and breezy.

'The Christmas magic has begun with the most inspiring, heart-warming and tenderest of moments. And it's down to a seven-year-old boy, named Billy.' As I swipe away a wayward teardrop with the sleeve of the new, bright green elf jacket, an overwhelming sense of happiness lifts my spirits.

'Ah, Immi. That's wonderful. This is going to be one a-ma-zing Christmas, I can feel it in ma bones, *ma bones, feel it in my bones bi-ba-bi-ba doo bah doo.*' Gray, being Gray, launches into song. Without any warning my heart misses a beat, as excitement leaps up inside me. It's been six weeks since he was last here; the longest six weeks of my life.

'I've been trying on the new elf costume. I'll do a quick change and then head up to The Bullrush Inn. See you there in ten. Watch out for stray sheep in the lane by Adler's farm. Two are still on the loose after a breakout last night.'

'The boys are back,' he sings and starts laughing. 'Oh, that's baad news, really baad,' he jokes, and I roll my eyes. 'And I forgot to tell

you – I have a new backing track for Tollie's Christmas Tale; it's a surprise and I think he's going to love it.'

He begins to hum it for me, and I realise that's one of the things I miss most when he's not around. Music. The second main man in my life is mad, truly mad, but I wouldn't change one single thing about him.

'I love you, Captain Christmas.'

'I love you, too, Santa's number one elf.'

* * *

Wrenching shut the door of Lock Keeper's Cottage, I head off along the towpath. Every Friday evening there's one place everyone at the marina heads for – The Bullrush Inn. As I push through the door and step inside, the low hum of chatter tells me that most of the regulars are here already. I liberally dispense waves and smiles as I make my way between the tables.

A café and gift shop by day, every Friday, Saturday, and Sunday evening between six and ten p.m., it's the haunt of the Aysbury Junction Marina Anchor Club members.

'Hi, Fisher.' As I walk past the marina manager he jumps up, leaning in to give me one of his bear hugs.

'Hey, darling girl. Where's Tollie?'

'I left him wrapping the kids' Christmas presents. We've been at it all day, but Gray's on his way, so Granddad has given me the evening off.'

Fisher beams from ear to ear. 'Glad he's back, Immi. I know how much you've missed him. Besides, the Christmas festivities can't begin until he's here.' He gives me a second hug before easing himself back down into his seat.

Fisher took over when Tollie retired, a little over twenty years ago, now.

When I first came to live with my granddad, I had just turned fourteen and it was a rough time for us both. Ernest Tolliman – Tollie, as he's known to everyone, including me – struggled to cope with the grief of losing his only son. Throwing a teenage grand-daughter into the mix didn't make it any easier. But the truth was that all we had left in the world was each other. My mother had disappeared when I was only three months old, never to be seen again.

For Tollie, my dad's death brought back the grief he felt over losing Grandma, two years before. I can see that now, but I didn't appreciate that fact way back then. All I could feel was my own loss and an overwhelming sense of anger. My head was screaming 'why me?' as I was forced to say goodbye to friends I regarded as family. Losing Dad broke my heart and I was angry at life, at fate and at a stupid accident that needn't have happened.

Dad worked at the Royal Navy Training Centre in Portsmouth. He promised me faithfully it would be our last move, and we fitted right in, surrounded by a great bunch of people.

Ironically, it wasn't the dangers of the sea that snatched him away from us, but a freak accident when the brakes failed on a coach in which he was travelling. Dad had been away for three days, running an off-site refresher course, and he just never came home. That made it worse, not being able to say a proper goodbye. Nothing prepares you for that and I'm afraid I didn't manage my emotions very well at the time.

Fisher ended up being my listening ear whenever Tollie and I fell out, which was a frequent occurrence in those early days. My frustrations and disappointments in life turned me into something of a rebel and I wanted to fight back. So, I took on the world. Now I can look back and think, poor world and poor Tollie, because it wasn't anyone's fault.

But helping me – us – through that period created a bond. Even today, Fisher is still my go-to man whenever I have a problem or need an unbiased opinion. He's also my boss two days a week, although I spend a lot of time telling him how lucky he is to have me to sort out his piles of paperwork.

I work my way over to the counter. Sarah gives me a wink as she finishes serving a group of *day-raters*, visitors passing through who rent a birth for a night or two.

It's a busy time of the year for us, nestled here on the edge of the Cotswolds. With so many Christmas markets in the area and Egerton Castle putting on a whole month of special events nearby, Aysbury has become a bit of a go-to. Christmas-holics of all ages descend upon us to kick-start their celebrations.

'Hi, Immi, how are the Christmas cruise preparations going?'

'Good. But there's still a fair bit to do. Gray's on his way, though, and the extra pair of hands will be welcome. He should be here any minute.'

Sarah and Kurt Lieberman have only owned The Bullrush Inn for six years and in that time they've turned it from a tired and dingy canal-side tea shop into a buzzing, thriving business. It brings people to the marina in droves. Their twins, Jade and Jude, were just seven years old when they moved here after turning their backs on a busy life in the city.

It took Sarah and Kurt eighteen months to completely renovate the place and it wasn't an easy time, as they did most of the work themselves. While they juggled the demands of two very lively kids and tried to keep the café open with major building works in progress, our little community did what it does best. And that's to support their own. It's what good neighbours do and what Aysbury is all about.

The 'waifs and strays syndrome', as I call it. And I count myself as one of those. People have ended up here in desperate need of something – more often than not without a clue about what exactly that elusive *something* might be. Maybe they come for a sense of community and a feeling of belonging somewhere, especially if that's never been true before; either because they don't have a close family, or they've struggled to conform. 'Round pegs, square holes,' as Tollie often says.

The nature of a marina is that a lot of the boats moored here long-term have owners who appear infrequently throughout the year. Beautiful, expensive boats lying idle for long periods, only getting to feel the wash of a cresting wave against their bows during the peak holiday season. Which is a shame, I always think. The waterways are much pleasanter, in my opinion, during the quieter months when the seasonal changes make their offerings.

Sweltering sunshine brings out the crowds and that spoils it for me, although in a twist of irony it's the Christmas crowds who make the festive atmosphere really buzz.

People are the beating heart of the marina – those who live and work here, and the owners of the handful of residential narrowboats moored alongside the canal.

'Right, what can I get for you, Immi?'

'One of your surf and turf sharing platters and a bottle of something special, please. I don't suppose the Christmas beers have arrived yet?'

Our community is very proud to have a celebrated microbrewery virtually on our doorstep. The Middle Norton Brewing Company have made a real name for themselves and it's become quite an attraction for the marina.

Sarah nods her head. 'This morning. Two Santa's Helpers? Or how about trying the new one – The Bullrush Christmas Brew?'

'You didn't!' I exclaim.

'We did. We put the proposal to Pete and David, and they thought it was a great idea. Ten pence from every bottle sold will be donated to The Santa Ahoy Christmas charity fund. When Tollie pops in later, Kurt is going to tell him the news. And Pete just rang to say they are going to run a promotion on it via their stockists, which will run into January.'

'Wow, thank you, Sarah. I mean, that's simply amazing.'

'What's amazing?'

I spin around and it's as if a cloud of happiness has wafted in through the door. Gray throws his arms around me, lifting me off the floor as he raises me up to plant a kiss firmly on my lips.

'I'm back. What's happening?' He pulls away, tilting his head to peer over my shoulder. 'Hi, Sarah, you're looking good, and busy. Have the Christmas beers arrived yet?'

'It's great to see you, Gray. And yes, Immi just placed your order and it's on the way. Grab a table quickly, guys, I've just cleared one upstairs.' Sarah nods towards the door and a large group about to step through.

'Will do. Catch up with you later, Sarah,' Gray calls over his shoulder. Grabbing my hand, he leads me upstairs.

As my foot hits the last tread and I look out over the canal, I get the familiar thrill I always feel to see the boats. This evening everything is right in my little world and my heart soars. I squeeze Gray's hand and quicken my pace as he strides forward to claim the last table by the window. But before he lets me go, he spins me around into his arms and we stand there for several seconds. Resting my head against his chest and, oblivious to the background chatter, I close my eyes, savouring the moment. Just to feel the solidness of him and breathe in the smell of that lemony aftershave balm he uses is heavenly.

I hate it when we're apart, but since last October, Gray's life has had to revolve around his mother, Rona. She's a lovely woman who dotes on her wonderful son. Sadly, just over a year ago, she was diagnosed with breast cancer. After a gruelling programme of treatment, she began having the most awful panic attacks and became a virtual recluse. Gray and I put our plans on hold because family comes first. But for Gray he has had to struggle to work to keep the bills paid and be her only form of support, so it would be a lie to say it hasn't affected our relationship. True love never dies, but it needs constant care and attention. We've both been miserable and lonely, but as hard as it's been for me, it's been even harder for Gray.

Rona has been on her own for a long time, since Gray's father, Grayson Alexander Adams, returned to the States when his son was five years old. Gray has never been to America, or met his grandparents.

I think that's one of the things that drew us together when we were first introduced, almost three years ago now. Neither of us have siblings and both have just the one parent figure in our lives, albeit mine is a grandparent. There's a sense of responsibility that accompanies that, I've discovered as the years have passed. Granddad worries about me, but now I worry about him – constantly. It's been the same for Gray. He ended up having to move back into his family home, as Rona floundered to cope with day-to-day living. And suddenly, it wasn't just our plans for last Christmas that fell apart, but our dream was put on hold.

I try not to dwell on the seemingly impossible question over whether Gray and I will ever be able to get together as a couple, permanently. Rona won't consider leaving the house she's lived in since the day Gray was born and Tollie, well, the marina has been his life for more than fifty years. He's spent the last thirteen years making sure I'm okay, but as time passes our respective roles have begun to change.

The child becomes the parent, and in a way it's the same for Gray. With Tollie, I try my best to knock some sense into him. He takes on too much, resolute in the belief that nothing should slow him down – even the aches and pains of a body that is beginning to rebel. He's eighty-six now and very active by anyone's standards, but he needs to realise he isn't a machine. If he doesn't learn to pace himself there will be consequences and that thought terrifies me.

'Ahem. Two beers?' Kurt appears and, rather reluctantly, I pull away from Gray.

The guys do their usual manshake, ending with a fist pump as Kurt expertly balances the tray on one hand.

'My, The Bullrush Christmas Brew – that's new,' Gray replies with a smile. We're both impressed as we take our seats.

'Famous at last. You can't say you've made it until you have a brew with your name on it. Are you staying over?' Kurt asks.

The same question has been hovering on my lips, too. The heart-stopping disappointment if he isn't didn't allow me to ask.

On the few occasions Gray has made it here for a visit, the two-hour plus round trip has robbed us of precious time together. Our relationship has become a waiting game, full of brief, exciting highs and then long periods where all we've been able to snatch is an hour on the phone, late at night.

'Yep. And, hopefully, every Friday and Saturday right up until Christmas. Fingers crossed I don't get any rush jobs.' Gray winks at me and I could jump up and down with joy. He does look a little tired, but I can see he's content that things at home are going well.

'Us struggling musicians have to chase the work. You know what it's like. One day I'll be famous and then I'll get to pick and choose. But hey, this weekend I'll be donning my Captain Christmas cap and it will be all aboard *The Santa Ahoy Special,* as we kick-start the festive season. Life doesn't get any better than when I have Santa's trusty elf by my side.'

Kurt chuckles as he walks away to fetch our food. I'm very aware that the other pressure on Gray is a financial one, which means he can't afford to turn down any job that comes his way, even if it involves working at weekends. And that adds to the pressure if Rona isn't doing well. As a self-employed musician and composer who was based in London, the distance has put him at a disadvantage. But even when he isn't working, he's always tinkering about with some little project or other.

As we take our seats, Gray holds up his beer bottle and we chink.

'That's good news... that you can stay over.' I'm trying not to sound as excited as I feel, but my heart is pounding in my chest and suddenly I'm full of the joys of Christmas. 'Let the festivities begin!'

Our eyes lock and I can see how much he's missed me and feel that sense of regret for the time we've lost. Sometimes life seems too complicated and it's hard to avoid feeling a bit depressed. Fortunately, my other part-time job, at the Lockside Nurseries, spirits me away to my happy place. When people, or the world in general, are getting me down, then nurturing nature's bountiful gifts is spiritually healing. I can lose myself for hours in the greenhouses deadheading, or re-potting and watering. It's the only place I can really switch off the emotional turmoil for a while.

Gray is gazing at me and I feel my cheeks begin to glow. 'What?'

'I'm just happy to see you. Is that a crime?' He laughs and I want to hug him all over again.

'That's not a smile, it's a mischievous look you're wearing. It's great to see you so relaxed, Gray.' I reach forward and graze my fingers over the back of his hand.

'Ma is doing well. She's even started driving again. I've left her with a packed weekend planned. So, here's to lovers of Christmas everywhere and to a very special one for us this year Immi.' The optimism in his voice as he makes a toast touches my heart. 'Who is this little boy you were telling me about on the phone, who made my Immi cry, then?'

Taking a quick sip of beer, I'm pleased that it isn't too strong, or overpowering. This is going to be a popular one; Pete and David have done The Bullrush proud.

'A hint of fennel, hmm... I like that,' I confirm, placing the bottle firmly back down onto the tabletop. 'The little boy's name is Billy Davis.'

'And he's seven, you said?'

'Yes. He was nominated by his grandma for a silver ticket. Watch this clip.' I pull out my phone and flick through to find the email.

Mrs Price, Tollie's former housekeeper, is the official contact for nominations for two very special boat trips we run for the Santa Ahoy Little Stars. All the other trips are run in aid of charity, but the silver tickets are for children who deserve a little extra spoiling.

As I click on the attachment, Gray pulls his chair up alongside me.

The picture is dark and a little grainy, but it's just possible to make out a child's bed and the distressed sobs emanating from a heap in the middle. It's a pitiful sound in the soft grey light and it's a wail that comes from deep down inside the poor little mite. The young boy is crouched down on the floor next to his sister, his voice calm and reassuring. He's trying to comfort her, but I don't think she can even hear him above the noise she's making, so great is her distress. Only the odd hiccough breaks the constant sobbing.

'She's lost her Noo-Noo, apparently,' I explain to Gray. 'It's a little blanket, like a comforter, with an animal's head in the centre.'

Rather unexpectedly, the boy lies down on the floor and begins, very softly, to sing. His voice rises up in the darkness hauntingly, with the most beautiful ring to it. It's the voice of an angel. 'Twinkle, twinkle little star—'

At first, it's hard to hear him but gradually the crying begins to subside. It reduces to a heart-rending, intermittent sniffing sound and the boy slowly snakes his hand up onto the bed. When he covers her hand with his she throws it off, unwilling to be pacified in her anguish. He waits a few seconds and then tries again. This time Billy begins to gently stroke the back of her hand with his fingertips. The little girl, who, I know from the email, is three, is no longer thrashing around inconsolably, having run out of steam. She lies there, prostrate and exhausted.

He continues singing for several minutes, the sound of his achingly beautiful voice so soothing and empathetic that my eyes begin to prickle with tears once again. The creak of a floorboard confirms that this is being filmed through the partially opened bedroom door. When it ends my heart feels full, so great is the love and caring in that little boy's actions.

'Ah, that even brought a lump to my throat,' Gray admits.

'I know. The grandmother told me that her daughter unexpectedly went into labour an hour earlier and there was a mad dash to get her to the hospital. The baby wasn't due for another month and, in the panic, they later discovered that the blanket found its way into the overnight bag they'd taken with them. Her granddaughter had been distraught when her parents had left so suddenly, and then losing her treasured Noo-Noo had seemed like the end of the world. They turned everything upside down looking for it, to no avail.'

'Ah. Poor little thing.' I can see that Gray is moved.

'The woman went downstairs to fetch little Maddie a drink of water and when she returned this was the scene she found. Billy finally managed to get Maddie to fall asleep and, a few hours later, a call confirmed that their new baby sister had arrived. Weighing in at only five pounds three ounces, she was tiny, but perfectly healthy. The grandmother said, "I told Billy that he was a little star comforting his sister like that and he is the best big brother in the whole world," and I agree with her.'

Gray tilts his head, leaning in to rest it against mine.

'Has Tollie seen it?'

'Not yet. It came in just before you called. We have some wonderful little stars already lined up this year.'

'Guess it had better be just the one beer for us tonight, then. We'd best be up at the crack of dawn to get Fisher's boat all decked out. Can't have the old girl under-dressed for her first outing of the festive season, now, can we?'

Another thing I love about Gray is that he understood the importance of Santa Ahoy from the outset and even last Christmas, despite juggling the impossible, he was here to captain most of the trips. To some it's just a cruise in aid of charity, down the canal to the marina and back, with Tollie dressed up as Santa. Kiddies come from all over, and it's wonderful to see their eyes shining brightly as we sing Christmas songs and Tollie tells one of his wonderful stories. But when the nominations come in for our *little stars*, kids who have battled through tough times, or are heroes, stepping up when an adult hasn't been around, those are the boat rides that make our hearts soar.

When I met Gray he quickly realised that my world was here and it always would be. Love me, love my granddad, love my friends. And he was keen to do whatever he could to help. Gray volunteered to take over the role of captain when Fisher handed over his cap, and the use of The Star Gazer, his fifty-seven-foot Colecraft narrowboat. It's the love of Fisher's life as it represents a dream, and he spent a year altering the internal layout. After he ripped out the bedrooms, it became a luxury cruiser and his retirement plan. Two years and counting he says, as the magic number fifty-five hovers on the horizon like a beacon.

I think Fisher handed over the reins to Gray as a test, if I'm being truthful. How much did he want to be a part of my life? Gray put his all into it; in doing so, he didn't just grab a place in my heart, but in the hearts of my Aysbury family. It takes a very special man indeed, given his situation at home, to donate his precious free time. From litter picking, to running raffles at our village fairs, the first two years we were together Gray could always be relied upon to help. Last year was different, but he made it here whenever he could, which wasn't easy as Rona couldn't be left alone. Gray would arrange for one of Rona's friends to sit with her and we accepted that staying over was no longer an option.

His life is split into two very different halves and I bet there are a lot of men out there who wouldn't be able to cope with that, but Gray does. I've tried my best to be accepting of the situation we find ourselves in – one where the future seems full of obstacles. But from what Gray said, is that about to change? Could this be our perfect Christmas, at long last?

'Tollie, my man. How are you doing?'

The sitting room looks like a post office sorting centre for Christmas parcels. Tollie is sitting in his armchair with a folding table in front of him. He looks up from the half-wrapped gift he's working on, then quickly rips a piece of tape from the dispenser to secure the paper, before sliding the table away from him. At the side of his chair within easy reach are a dozen rolls of wrapping paper. To his right is a pile of empty jute sacks and two more lean against the wall, filled to the brim with donated toys collected throughout the year.

Gray turns to survey the various piles of beautifully wrapped presents, which cover most of the floor. They're all neatly labelled according to age. Some have silver tags, for girls, and some have red ones, for the boys.

'Good. Great to see you, Gray. I was hopin' our captain was on his way. I can relax now.' Tollie stands and Gray walks over to give him a man-hug. In return he receives a hearty pat on the back. 'It's going to be a busy season,' he adds, looking around him.

'Well, judging by the amount of donations, we're going to do the kids proud.' Gray tips his head, acknowledging Tollie's efforts.

'How's Rona?'

'Doing well, thanks. It's work that's kept me away, this time. I'm on catch up as I fell way behind. I mean... it's good that I've had a big job on and I'm grateful for that, but weekends here are special, and I've missed it.'

Gray turns to give me a knowing smile and Tollie laughs.

'She ain't the same when you're not around, that's for sure.'

'Tollie!'

'Just sayin' it as it is, m'dear.'

I know he has a point. I do try hard not to let Tollie see when I'm really missing Gray, but it's tough always trying to be upbeat and pretending that I can cope with mine and Gray's arrangement. Not least because there have been a lot of days recently when I can't, but it would be unfair of me to admit that. Gray was hoping to move in permanently last Christmas but that was before Rona's diagnosis.

Gray adds that extra something whenever he's here and Tollie feels it, too. For me it's like living on a roller coaster, as my emotions go from extreme highs to the lowest of lows. This year, on the very rare occasion we did get a weekend together, it took a while to find ourselves again. Just as we were slipping into our old, comfortable ways it was time for him to leave. And we had no idea when he'd be back again.

Thankfully, privacy isn't an issue whenever he is here. The 1830s, stone-built lock keeper's cottage only has two bedrooms, but in the sprawling garden abutting open fields, there's a rather size-able barn conversion. It began life as a place to store farming equip-ment and at some point was turned into a storage space to house boats for daily hire and a first floor was added for use as a workshop.

When Tollie bought the property, he gutted it and turned it into a three-bedroom, rather basic but fully functioning holiday let. It was perfect for when Dad and I came to stay four times a year and gave Tollie a small income in between times. Since then it's had a large injection of cash and now 'The Retreat' is a stunning property and I'm lucky to call it my home. It works well, because it means I'm on hand if Tollie needs me, but we both have our privacy too. And when Gray is here it becomes our sanctuary away from our worries, responsibilities and the world outside the door. If only the cottage were as pristine, but Tollie doesn't like change.

'Tollie, you've been at that all day with barely a break. We'll finish off the wrapping. Sarah and Kurt are hoping you'll pop in. Fisher's there and he looks like he's settled in for a pint or two.'

Tollie nods, but I can see he's not happy. 'I could do with stretching my legs, but you two ought to head off to The Retreat to unwind – this can wait until I get back.'

'Well, I think we have time to put in an hour or two's work here, while we catch up,' I reply, trying to estimate how long this is going to take.

Besides, Gray and I have two blissful nights to look forward to and we need that settling-back-in time after such a long spell away from each other. Absence does make the heart grow fonder, but we long to be able to live together like any normal couple. Whether we like to admit it, or not, the fear of it never happening hangs over us both constantly, because you never know what's around the corner.

Tollie heads out and we start clearing the floor, filling the empty Christmas sacks and being careful not to mix up the piles. We carry them through to the big cupboard in the hallway and as we walk back Gray begins to hum. He playfully comes up behind me, placing a hand either side of my hips, and starts to conga. It makes me giggle and I try to shake him off.

'Stop. We have work to do.'

He grabs my hand and I turn to face him as he snakes his arm up above my head and spins me around. Releasing his hand, I bow, looking up at him and shaking my head in feigned annoyance. But now he's in *shoo-be-doo* mode, continuing to sing as I lead him back through to the table.

'That's a new tune,' I remark, taking a seat and reaching inside the first sack. It's a football and I groan; I hate wrapping round things.

'Yep. It's a jingle I'm working on at the moment. It's for a hair shampoo commercial and it's supposed to be lively and invigorating.'

He continues to *shoo-be-doo* beneath his breath, as he begins dispensing tape. The battle with the football begins.

'Rona really is doing well, then?' I ask tentatively.

'The doctor has taken her off the new medication she was on, as Mum said it was making her anxiety worse. She's been seeing a therapist for a couple of months now and I think it's finally beginning to pay off. I didn't want to get your hopes up, Immi, because nothing is guaranteed but there's a real improvement in the way she's handling her panic attacks. Her latest blood tests were all fine and her oncologist is happy. She's started going to her Women's Institute evenings again and her old friend, Hilda, convinced her to join the committee.'

I stop for a moment, my eyes scanning his face. This is brilliant news.

'You engineered that,' I say pointedly.

He sighs, but I can see that it's more tiredness than exasperation.

'Immi, I had to do something. I want a life with you, and it hurts not being able to put you first. I love you, even when you're being annoying. Like now. We could finish off these presents in the morning, you know.'

He sits there grinning at me and my heart melts, once again. I ignore him, of course, and make a start on the next gift.

'Tollie would be disappointed in us if when he arrives back nothing had been done. You know him, he'd take off his coat and sit here until the early hours to finish this off. Tape, please!'

Gray shrugs his shoulders and gets back to work but my heart is pounding. Is the worst really over and can we pick back up where we left off this time last year, looking forward to making our dreams come true?

'You put up with my irregular lifestyle, you understand the pressures and you never moan. I mean, a man can't get any luckier, can he? But we've been living in limbo and it's time to start thinking about the changes we need to make. Mum knows that, too, and she's trying really hard because she wants us to be happy. I confided in Mum's friend, Hilda, and we have a plan.'

I turn my head to look at him. 'Confided what?'

His eyes light up and he starts singing again, softly under his breath. *'Life isn't living without you in my arms, this simple man can't resist your charms.'*

I burst out laughing, shaking my head at him.

'You are seriously crazy, Gray, do you know that? No more distractions – let's wrap.'

'I do love being bossed around,' he replies, making it sound suspiciously like some sort of fetish. 'Rap isn't quite my style, though.'

And that's why I'll wait for him, for as long as it takes to make it all work. He puts the joy in my life and the beat in my heart. The angry, 'why me?' person I once was disappeared overnight when I met Gray. Quite simply, he is my silver lining.

* * *

'Ahoy, skipper, permission to come aboard The Star Gazer?'

Abe's voice booms out from the top of the gangplank. Abe and his wife, Ethel, own The Merry Robin. It's a four-berth, forty-five-foot Admiral narrowboat and is one of the handful of residential moorings here on the canal side. They are like gold dust, as most narrowboats keep moving on because that's the way the system is designed to work. When Abe decided to take early retirement on his fiftieth birthday and managed to talk Ethel into selling up and buying a narrowboat, they struck lucky.

'Permission granted, Abe. Just the man I need to get this stove going.' Gray pops his head out through the cabin doors and I hear the sound of feet being wiped on the coconut welcome mat.

'Hi, Abe,' I call out, angling my head to see over Gray's shoulder. I'm standing in front of the first of the four dinettes, each of which seats six people. Abe steps onto the forewell, a big grin on his face. He's carrying two large sacks of freshly picked greenery, one in front of him and one slung over his shoulder.

'You look a little chilly there, Immi. Ethel will be along shortly to give a hand.' I notice that Abe's eyes stray across to the fire and his eyebrows shoot heavenwards.

'It beats me every time,' Gray moans, shaking his head as he stares at the charred pile of kindling inside the open door of the stove. The cabin is smelling very smoky, it's true, but there isn't even a hint of a flame now. After several attempts, I think it's finally gone out.

Gray moves back towards me, making room for Abe and his sacks to negotiate the two steps down into the hull. That's the trouble with a narrowboat, everything is so compact. Abe places his load in the opposite corner and stands with his hands on his hips, surveying the mess Gray has made trying to get the fire going.

'Oh my. I'm guessing you weren't in the Boy Scouts, then, or went on camping trips when you were a nipper.'

Gray gives an apologetic look. 'No, and no. This is usually Tollie's job, but he's with Mrs Price.' Gray drops his tone, reverentially. 'They're printing out the silver ticket letters today, ready to go out in the post on Monday.'

Mrs Price is about five-foot-two, very slim and is always smartly dressed. She's a dead ringer for the smiley female chef who features on the packaging of my favourite pancake mix. With her hair up in a clip and perfectly made-up, she always makes me wish I glanced in the mirror more often. However, looks can be deceiving because she's not a jolly, 'life and soul of the party' sort of woman. She's rather reserved and I only see her around if it's something to do with her community work. It's not that she's sharp, I muse, it's more that she gets straight to the point.

And it's rare, indeed, to see her at a purely social event – which is a relief, as, if you find yourself next to her, Mrs Price is not the easiest of people with whom to exchange small talk. You instinctively feel personal questions are not permitted and she can be a tad frosty if you unwittingly say the wrong thing.

Before I came to live with Tollie, she was his housekeeper and kept him very firmly in line. Shortly after I moved in she quit, saying I 'wasn't house-trained', as if I were a stray puppy. At the time I thought that was rather harsh and very hurtful, given my situation. But with hindsight I came to see that she had a point. I was a lazy teenager with a chip on my shoulder, and I did nothing except feel sorry for myself and make a mess.

It was the peak of my angry phase and because Tollie, in his grief, didn't know how to address it, suddenly we had to muddle through together. The cottage wasn't always a pretty sight at first, but we learnt as we went along. When you are forced to live in the chaos you create, you soon begin to put things away and wash the dishes, and clothes, before you run out of clean stuff.

So really Mrs Price did us a favour when she quit. She is a

dispenser of tough love. Rumour has it that she's a widow; she never mentions family at all. I'd say she's in her early fifties and I will admit I am a little curious that she appears to have cut herself off from her past. However, you learn to respect the secrets that people choose not to divulge. She's another of the marina's waifs and strays, I suppose. But life here wouldn't be the same without her, despite the way we all tend to tread cautiously whenever she's around.

Abe is already kneeling in front of the stove, moving things around with a poker.

'Right, Gray, take note. If Tollie sees this muddle he'll laugh his socks off! First things first. Immi, my lovely, can you fetch me a couple of pieces of kitchen towel and run them under the tap? Not too wet, ta.'

Placing the box of silver baubles back on the dinette table, I give Abe a little salute, before heading off to the galley at the far end of the boat. It's next to the head and the rain locker. I laughed when Fisher first showed me around his pride and joy, taking time to educate me about the nautical terms. Head for toilet? Rain locker for shower made sense and I rather liked that, but *head* had me scratching *my* head.

When I return, Abe has already re-laid most of the semi-charred kindling that Gray had piled inside the stove. He takes the tissue from me, sticking his hand inside the cavity of the fire to dab it onto the ashes at the very back.

'There,' he says as he rubs the now smutty paper onto the blackened glass in the stove's door. 'Keep rubbing like this and there's enough abrasion to clean this up without scratching the surface. No point lighting a fire if you can't see it,' he declares loudly.

Gray kneels down next to him, a serious look on his face as he takes instruction. I return to my task of dressing the three compact little Christmas trees. One will go on the foredeck, opposite the gangplank, one on the towpath and one in the saloon.

It's quite an art decorating the two four-foot and one three-foot-high potted trees. The smaller one for the saloon requires trimming so it will fit snugly back into the corner. It sits on what is normally a storage locker doubling as a seat. This narrowboat is almost seven-feet wide, but in the saloon area we have the Villager Puffin stove, Santa's bench – which is a double storage locker with a padded cushion – and the tree. Once the fire is lit I'll put down a special mat for the older children to sit on. Little ones often prefer to sit on a parent's lap at the dinette benches until it's their turn to talk to Santa.

I have already entwined lights on the two outside trees, begun hanging the baubles and have moved on to the snowflakes. Thank goodness there are four dinettes, as the fourth table has all the decorations laid out neatly, like a little production line.

Hearing the two men bantering away in the background causes a satisfied little smile to fleetingly cross my face. This is what families do. They pull together and help each other out. Although it's by default, I rationalise that Tollie and I are lucky that we can choose our family; no awkward relatives to placate, just a bunch of interesting characters with whom we love to spend time.

'Yoo hoo! Can I hop aboard?'

'Come on in, Ethel. Join the party!' I exclaim, and as I look up it's as if a rainbow has floated in through the door. Ethel is a colourful lady, both in her actions and the way she dresses.

Today it's a leaf-green hand-knitted scarf that is wrapped around her neck at least three times and trails down almost to the hem of her cherry-red coat. 'I'm just an old hippy,' she's always saying, but she brightens the room whenever she enters.

'Oh, Lordy. Good luck with that, Abe. Ah, Imogen, I thought you might be able to use these.' Ethel places a wicker basket on the bench seat alongside me and I peer inside.

'Ooh. What a gorgeous scent these pine cones have. Thank you so much, Ethel, they're perfect. It's one of my favourite Christmas smells. That and cinnamon.'

She gives me a wonderfully warm smile and if ever I had a picture in my head of what my mother might look like, Ethel embodies it. Energetic, wiry, bubbling with enthusiasm and kind-hearted. Except Ethel cares about people, and clearly my mother didn't.

Ethel is the Mother Earth to Abe's Green Man. I start laughing.

'What's going on inside that wicked little mind of yours, Immi?' she enquires.

'Dangerous question,' Gray butts in and she beams at him.

'I've brought some paper clips,' she adds, lifting a little envelope out of the basket. 'If you open them up you can hook one end around the scales and use the other end to hang the cones from the branches.'

Suddenly Tollie appears, stopping to survey the scene in front of him before stepping down into the hull.

'Well, guess I'm not going to be needed after all,' he comments, casting his eye around appreciatively.

The fire now has a few little sparks of red glinting at us from behind the freshly cleaned glass and the Christmas trees are beginning to gleam with an assortment of treasures. With sparkly silver and red baubles, and white glittery snowflakes, as I hang the first pine cone it's beginning to feel a lot like Christmas.

'We have five hours to go and there's still a fair bit to do.' I look up at him, smiling. I can see how happy he is to see us all here, pulling together.

'Mrs Price will be along later with the gingerbread biscuits and cupcakes. I just popped in to drop off the first of the sacks and then

I'm off to The Bullrush to collect the cartons of fruit juice. Immi, do you want me to rustle up the non-alcoholic Christmas punch?'

I'd forgotten that. 'No, it's fine. Maybe Ethel will kindly finish off the trees for me and I can pop back and get the ingredients prepped ready for later. Is that okay with everyone?'

Ethel nods and Gray stands, stretching out his back and looking with awe at the flames that are now leaping up with increasing vigour. It's freezing on the boat and a part of the attraction for me in heading back to the cottage is in order to warm up a little.

'Absolutely. Abe and I can make a start on the garlands for the outside.' He motions towards the sacks of greenery Abe brought.

'I'll hurry back as quickly as I can,' I promise, and Gray leans in to give me a lingering kiss on my cheek.

'Abe, is there any mistletoe in there?' Gray enquires rather cheekily as he points towards the bountiful sacks.

'You can't have Christmas without mistletoe – 'course there is!'

I roll my eyes as I head off to the sanctuary of a warm kitchen. This elf is going to be donning thermal leggings beneath those new, woollen trousers.

3

THE CHRISTMAS CREW

'Hey, guys, the greenery is beginning to look really good! Kurt just texted to say Sarah is making everyone bacon sandwiches on the house. Is anyone hungry?'

It doesn't take any persuasion at all for everyone to put down their tools and troop off to The Bullrush. Having added another layer of clothing, I'm now feeling quite toasty in my thick navy coat, and burgundy bobble hat pulled down over my ears.

As we walk into the inn, no one fails to spot the big display that has suddenly appeared alongside the bar in the far corner. Pete and David are assembling a sturdy-looking, free-standing shelving unit for the stack of Christmas gift boxes, piled high at their feet. We all head over to check it out. Pride of place in each of the Christmas beer hampers is The Bullrush Christmas Brew, together with an assortment ranging from Santa's Best to Reindeer Hops.

'Great-looking display going on there, just up my street. Who comes up with these names? Sounds like my sort of job. You could pay me in beer...' Abe looks on, amused.

Pete straightens, grinning. 'Good one, Abe. I'm proud to say that's down to us, but we usually come up with them on a Saturday night when we've had a beer or two ourselves. Our team is out setting up all the displays today, but we thought we'd come and get a little hands-on.' He stands back, holding up one last, remaining screw and scratches his head. David turns around, revealing a small metal bracket and frowns.

'Guess we missed one out,' he groans. Pete shrugs his shoulders, sticking the screw back in the toolbox.

'Who's for coffee, who's for tea?' Kurt appears to take our orders. 'You're doing a great job there guys and it's much appreciated. Hopefully there will be a nice little contribution to the Santa Ahoy Christmas charity fund. If it's a success, then maybe we can do it again next year, seeing as it's a *special* special.'

Tollie raises an eyebrow. '*Special* special?'

Sarah has joined us, and she gives Kurt a cutting look, as an awkward silence descends upon us all. He instantly realises what he's done – it was supposed to be a secret.

'Well, judgin' by the way you are all gazin' around tryin' not to look shifty, I think someone should 'fess up.' Tollie is trying to catch my eye, but I studiously avoid his gaze. Ethel comes to the rescue.

'Oh, well, he was bound to find out. You can't really keep a secret when we're in and out of each other's lives on a daily basis. In case it's slipped your mind, Tollie, next year is the tenth anniversary of the Santa Ahoy cruises. A tradition you began and we're all so proud of the way it's grown; it represents what this community is all about and raising funds for charity has become the beat of our collective heart.'

Tollie looks a little taken aback at the tenderness and pride in Ethel's words.

'We thought it might be nice to celebrate the anniversary in style and bring everyone together as an acknowledgement of what has been achieved. So, we're hoping to do a few things, like the special brew here, to raise some money. And we're not just doing that to make it another bumper year, as this one is already shaping up to be, but we also plan to hold a smart dinner to mark the occasion. And you are going to be the guest of honour.'

It takes a lot to shock Tollie; he often says he's seen and done just about everything in his life. But I can see this has shaken him and he's standing there looking decidedly uncomfortable.

'Well, I don't know about anyone else, but the smell of that bacon is seriously making my stomach grumble,' I jump in quickly.

'Oh.' Sarah throws her hands up in the air. 'You must all be starving. Hang up your coats and grab a seat at the long table in the conservatory. We'll start carrying in the platters. Go on, everyone.' She starts shooing people off in the right direction, while I head into the kitchen with Kurt, who is still mortified at his faux pas.

'I am so sorry, Immi,' he whispers as we walk away. 'It just slipped out. Sarah is going to kill me!'

'Well,' Sarah says, hurrying to catch up with us, 'maybe not until after you've delivered the hot drinks to warm everyone up. Tollie was bound to find out and I think we all knew that.'

As we head through the swing doors, I'm delighted to see Jude and Jade standing at the long stainless-steel bench wearing bright blue vinyl gloves and buttering thickly sliced bread.

'Immi!' they chorus, in their twinly fashion.

'Hey, girls. Are you dressing up for Santa's first trip along the canal this afternoon?'

They elbow each other, excitedly.

'Of course. It's a surprise though, so we can't tell you what we're going to be. But it's been a lot of fun as we made the costumes ourselves – well, Dad did help us – using Mum's sewing machine.'

I look at Sarah and she shrugs her shoulders, as if to say it's all down to Kurt and the girls, so beware.

Kurt is already loading up a tray with an assortment of drinks as Sarah begins sandwiching-up a huge stack of bacon rashers.

Between us, it doesn't take long to have two big platters packed with rather rustic, although expertly sliced, sandwiches. Kurt and Sarah carry through the trays of hot drinks, Jude and I carry the platters, and Jade follows with a tray of napkins and little packets of sauce.

As we approach the long table in the conservatory a cheer goes up.

Tollie smooths down his beard, as he sits in the carver chair at the top end of the table, looking very at home. Abe sits to his left, with Ethel next to him. On the opposite side is Gray, next to Pete and David, who are deep in conversation. As soon as I place the platter on the table both Pete and David jump up, insisting I slide along the bench to sit next to my man.

'Thanks, guys. This is awesome. What a way to start the first day of season nine. A bacon sarnie is guaranteed to keep out the chill.'

We raise our mugs to toast and wait for Tollie to do the honours.

'To our Aysbury *family*. Most people don't get to choose theirs, but I guess everyone around this table has chosen to be a part of the clan. Even if it's only by virtue of the fact that they came and never left. One thing I do know for sure is that I count myself lucky to be sittin' here with you all today. Certainly, both my life and Immi's are the richer for your support and friendship.'

There's a 'hear, hear' and a lot of nodding of heads. I believe that every single one of us around the table has a reason to count their blessings. Even Pete and David's story isn't straightforward. The brothers were born in Brighton, but both ended up living and working in London. Pete was in finance and David was an advertising executive. David was only thirty-two when he had a heart-attack. Stress, they think, was the cause, but the shock waves affected his entire family.

Their parents decided that the money they had sitting in the bank could be put to good use if their sons could agree on what sort of business they wanted to set up. A year later, both Pete and David, two keen home brewers, bought out the small microbrewery at Middle Norton, just three miles away. It was a steep learning curve in the beginning, I think they would both admit that now, but they've expanded it way beyond the on-site store.

It's a firm reminder, though, not to take anything in life for granted, because you never know what tomorrow will bring.

'It's a bit late for breakfast!' Mrs Price's voice reflects surprise as she walks towards the table. The hand that was halfway to my mouth stops dead, holding that last, buttery piece of sandwich and dripping tomato sauce onto the table.

There is a moment or two of silence before Kurt speaks up.

'It's brunch, Mrs Price,' he explains, sounding a tad guilty to have pulled us away from the task in hand. 'The team were flagging, and we can't have that. Can I get you a nice cup of Earl Grey tea?'

Mrs Price has a soft spot for Kurt. As soon as her eyes land on him, that iron-rod back of hers seems to relax immediately and her mouth softens, the strained look evaporating away.

'Oh, that would be lovely, thank you, Kurt.'

Sarah immediately jumps up to give her place to Mrs Price, but Tollie is also on his feet and shepherds her around to the top of the table, instead.

'I can't stay long, but then I suspect you are all eager to get back to work,' she hints as she settles herself into the seat.

We last another ten minutes, respectfully waiting until Mrs Price has finished her tea. There's a lot of small talk about the work we have left to do to get everything ready and who is going to do what exactly. Then we disperse, leaving Mrs Price to chat to Jude and Jade as she asks how they are doing at school.

Heading out onto the towpath, I lean in to Gray. 'Do you think she was a head teacher before she came here?'

He shrugs his shoulders. 'I was thinking more along the lines of a sergeant major,' he replies, laughing.

As we walk back towards The Star Gazer, we bump into my boss from the Lockside Nurseries.

'Hey, Immi. I wondered where you all were. I've just dropped off a tray of red poinsettias for the dinette tables. I left it on the gangplank.'

'Ah, thank you, Martin. That's very kind of you.' He's a great boss and he always donates something floral to brighten up The Star Gazer for the Santa Ahoy cruises.

Gray and I stop to chat, the others striding off in case Mrs Price suddenly appears. It's not that she judges people, but more about the example she sets. Mrs Price is always doing something for someone else and I know it makes me feel uncomfortable if she catches me standing around, aimlessly chatting.

'Are you still researching the history of the cottage?' Martin poses the question, while slipping the rucksack off his back.

'Yes, why?'

'Well, I just delivered a vanload of plants to a big house over at Middle Norton. On the way back I dropped into the village hall. There was a Christmas tabletop sale going on, and I saw these and thought of you.'

Martin hands me a pile of aged photographs and a couple of very dusty books, all tied together with a faded blue ribbon. It looks as if it's been hidden away in someone's loft for years.

'The sepia photograph on the top was taken from the other side of the canal. What caught my eye was seeing Lock Keeper's Cottage before any of the hedging had been planted. It looks so naked.'

As I slip the top photo from beneath the ribbon, it's strange to see the stone building without the mass of shrubs and trees that now add to its appeal, as well as lending some privacy from walkers using the towpath. In the photo everything looks sparse, whereas now it takes constant trimming to keep it all under control, with some of the bushes and trees seeming determined to take over. It's an annual battle and another highlighted date on the community action calendar.

'Well spotted, thank you. I'll enjoy going through these. What do I owe you?'

Martin puts up his hand to stop me. 'Call it an early Christmas present. You'll still get a potted something, or other, come Christmas Eve,' he adds. 'Can't break with tradition, or the staff will rebel.' Martin laughs and I smile appreciatively.

'Well, how about popping into The Bullrush and grabbing a bacon sandwich on me? Tell Sarah I sent you.' He looks tempted but shakes his head.

'I'd love to, but I must get back. There are three Saturday lads in helping out today. The second delivery of Christmas trees is due in midweek. We need to move things around in the yard to make sure there's enough space. You did a good job of tidying up the two large greenhouses this week, Immi. It made all the difference when the potted plants arrived first thing. Anyway, I must go – enjoy the first trip of the season.'

'Will do. And thanks, Martin, for the welcome splash of colour.'

He nods his head in acknowledgement.

'Next year, just you wait and see what I've got planned! We're gonna do Tollie proud.' Martin gives me one of his mischievous looks.

My heart is bursting with happiness and it's not simply because Gray is here, but the way everyone is gearing up to celebrate next year's landmark achievement – I can't believe it will be ten years since Tollie started the Santa Ahoy cruises. Over that period, year-on-year the money raised for local charities has continued to grow. It's brought a community together in a way only a good cause can. Next year is going to include an extra-special celebration. We're planning a series of coffee mornings and a few barn dances throughout the summer to fund a special dinner in Tollie's honour.

It's going to be one Christmas none of us will ever forget and just thinking about it is giving me goosebumps. We're all used to pulling out all the stops for the kids, because that's what Christmas is all about. But this tribute to Tollie, and everyone involved, is about recognising the fact that when people join together, their efforts can make a real difference.

I reach out, placing my hand on Martin's arm to give it a squeeze.

'I know we are. The secret is out, but I can tell you that the look on his face was classic. He had no idea what we were planning.'

Martin's eyebrows shoot up in surprise.

'It's a pity in one way, but on the other hand we want this to be special. To do it justice, I think we need Tollie to be involved. Yeah, we'll have a big party – the biggest the marina has seen – but it's important to mark it in a way that makes him happy. I've been worried he might think it was a bit of a waste of money.'

That stops me in my tracks.

'A waste?'

'Well, to be honest, the parties where we all contribute and bring stuff don't cost much. If we did that, instead of some grand sit-down dinner in his honour, the money could be used in whichever way Tollie wanted.'

'Maybe he's right. I'm reporting back to the committee at the Easter get-together. Although, knowing Tollie, he'll already be thinking through his own little action plan and how he's going to get us all on his side.'

4

After another two hours of graft and a quick change, we all head back to The Star Gazer, buzzing with excitement. Finally the first Christmas cruise can get under way. Gray is looking very smart and incredibly handsome today, in his navy-blue suit. With gold buttons imprinted with an anchor, and four shiny stripes emblazoned on the cuffs, his white cap with its navy peak, gold braid and anchor badge, he looks every inch the part of a seafaring captain. He's standing at the entrance to the gangplank, with his legs firmly planted on the towpath and arms linked behind his back, and his smile is genuine. He salutes each and every one of our arrivals in true nautical style; the kids are absolutely loving it.

Mrs Price collects the tickets, warmly wrapped up in a white fur coat that makes her look rather like a polar bear. One by one, the queue of excited children and smiling parents begin to filter on board. The noise level as they descend into the hull is several decibels above the background music, which is a compilation of Christmas carols. Fisher installed a Bose sound system but, with eleven adults and thirteen children quickly filling up the space, we'd have to crank it up to full volume for it to be heard above the chatter.

Captain Gray closes the cabin doors with a flourish and holds up his hands to settle everyone down.

'Welcome, everyone. Please slip off your coats and take your seats. If any of the children would like to come and sit on the rug in front of Santa's chair, please do.'

Abe did a great job of banking up the fire and screwing in the protective guard around it. The glowing coal embers give out a decent amount of heat, particularly at this end of the boat, although with only four radiators covering the whole of the fifty-seven-foot run, the galley area to the back doesn't benefit quite as much.

There's a flurry of activity as the parents settle themselves into the dinettes. Most of the children make their way back to the saloon area to sit cross-legged on the colourful rug. It was handmade by Ethel and Abe. It's an old-fashioned rag rug where small strips of fabric are pulled through the base material, which is a heavy-weight hessian. They spent two winters making it, as it's seven feet by eleven, and the kids seem to love the textures. I often spot them running their fingers back and forth against the various fabrics as they sit watching Santa.

'Now, I hope you're all ready for when Santa asks you that special question.' Gray surveys their expectant, upturned faces.

We have kiddies as young as three years of age, with Jude and Jade being the oldest. But last year was the first time the twins became unofficial helpers, joining in on several of the cruises. To my delight, today they have dressed up as little elves. I'm sporting my own, brand-new elf costume, as the old one was showing signs of wear and tear – a bright green fitted jacket and woollen trousers, black belt, red and white striped hat – and I'm holding a clipboard. The children keep glancing at me in awe. The girls are wearing green elf dresses with red pointy collars and red bobble hats. Their red and white striped leggings are reminiscent of candy canes as the three of us stand in the gangway alongside the dinettes, awaiting Santa's arrival like a dutiful posse.

'Hush!' Gray puts a finger to his closed lips, looking wide-eyed at his excited audience. 'I heard something up on deck.'

The silence is immediate as everyone stops talking to hold their breath and listen. Suddenly there's a sharp rap on the door, which heralds a little chorus of excited shrieks.

Gray waits a moment or two until the backing track changes and suddenly the cabin is filled with the sound of sleigh bells jingling. It's beautiful and a few moments later he swings open the double doors, letting in a blast of chilly air. Seconds later Santa stoops as he steps inside, letting out a loud, 'Ho! Ho! Ho! Merry Christmas, everyone!'

One of the littlest ones throws her hands up to her cheeks, her jaw dropping as she stares in wonderment. Tollie makes the most amazing Santa, even though it's mostly padding, but his naturally white moustache and beard, topped off by a very realistic curly white wig, is reminiscent of a vintage Christmas card. He doesn't just look good, he looks authentic in the eyes of an adult, but real in the eyes of a child.

'I'm so thrilled you could come to see me today. Don't you all look amazing?' His baritone voice is both gentle and jovial. 'We have Christmas jumpers and a whole rainbow of colours that have really brightened my day,' he booms out. 'My chief elf, Immi, will be writing down your requests ready to take back to the North Pole. And her helpers, Jude and Jade, are here to make sure everyone has a really good time. Shall we ask Captain Gray to up anchor and cast off?'

There's a loud chorus of yeses egged on by myself and my little helpers, both of whom put their hands around their mouths as they shout it out. Santa pretends to be blown back in his seat at the raucous chorus, aided and abetted by the parents joining in.

'Well, Captain Gray, we are in your hands!' Santa declares, with gusto.

But Gray doesn't move, instead cupping a hand around his right ear. 'Did you hear that?' he replies in a semi-hushed tone.

He stabs his index finger up towards the cabin-top, and everyone falls silent once more. There's a sharp scraping noise, followed by a succession of hollow tapping sounds. Jade and Jude are now on the mat alongside the children and both put a hand up to their mouths. It's priceless.

'I think it's Rudolph and the sleigh!' Jude declares and the children's eyes widen in anticipation.

Santa claps his hands. 'I wondered when my friend Rudolph would arrive with the presents. Captain Gray, can you do the honours, please?'

Gray swings open the doors to the cabin once more and Abe, dressed in a penguin onesie, waves at the children before handing Gray the first sack.

'Sorry we're late, Santa. A heavy snowstorm descended just as we set off, but Rudolph did us proud. Hi, girls and boys.'

There's a chorus of 'Hi' back, as Gray lifts the sacks over the children's heads to stack them alongside Santa's bench seat. We're full to capacity and there isn't an inch spare, but no one's complaining.

'Right, it's time to get under way,' Gray declares as he disappears out of view.

I change the backing track to fill in the time it takes for Abe to pull up the anchor and cast off, while Gray heads off to take up his position at the tiller.

Jude and Jade hand out printed lyric sheets to the parents as the first of the Christmas songs begins playing.

'Who's going to sing along?' I ask.

Hands fly up into the air as the opening strains of 'Rudolph the Red-Nosed Reindeer' fills the air.

My little elves pass around glow sticks so that everyone can join in, even if they don't want to sing. So, there's a lot of arm waving, much wriggling about and – most importantly of all – a sea of smiling faces. The drone as the engine kicks into life signals the start of our little forty-minute cruise up to the marina and back.

I leave Jude and Jade doing a wonderful job of sitting with the children and egging them on as I head to the galley to begin ferrying around the Christmas punch for the adults.

Santa is doing what he does best and a chorus of unorchestrated voices fills the air; it's a heart-warming moment. Our real-life Father Christmas has the biggest, rosiest cheeks as he laughs out loud in genuine merriment. Tollie is just a big kid at heart and his rotund belly seems to jiggle as if it really is a part of him. He was made for this role and the kids and adults alike are loving it.

But then something happens to change my mood. My eyes alight on a three-year-old little girl I remember is called Hannah; she's rather shy, but I catch her looking directly at me and all she does is smile. For some silly reason I suddenly find myself thinking about Gray and me. If we had a daughter, what would she look like?

A sense of panic and memories of old wounds that never seem to heal begin to overtake me. Questions that I have always refused to acknowledge seem to jump into my head, unbidden. Did my mother walk out because I was a disappointment to her? Or was she the disappointment to Dad and I? But what if I take after her and end up letting everyone around me down?

Something hidden away deep inside me starts to unravel and I realise there's a reason why I'm not putting any pressure on Gray. Yes, I'm sympathetic about his situation, but I'm also scared; scared that I don't deserve someone as wonderful as the man who has captured my heart. And I don't quite know how to handle that.

* * *

Sarah, Jade and Jude are standing on the towpath talking to Tollie as I walk down the gangplank.

'Oh, my goodness, you girls!' I call out, hurrying over to them and giving each a hug of thanks. 'You looked amazing and what a team we made today. Thank you so much for helping out, it was much appreciated.'

'Mum says we can do all the trips this year, if you like. It's fun, Immi, and we love doing it.'

I glance at Sarah and she gives a little nod of her head.

'I would love that. We make a great team, girls,' I admit as Tollie gives me a wink. Their eyes are sparkling with enthusiasm. 'You are both very welcome on board at any time. It's a lot for one elf to cope with, I must admit, and having you there ensured everything went very smoothly indeed.'

They high-five each other and start jumping around, the late afternoon chill turning their breath into little ribbons of smoky whiteness. 'Yay, we get to be the official little elves.'

Shrugging on my hat so it doesn't fall off, I find it hard not to laugh at their exuberance. Like their parents, the girls are doers. They have so much energy and they need to expend it. During the holidays and when they aren't at school they help out in the café. Whenever they are around they bring with them an air of liveliness that is refreshing. Sunny girls, with sunny characters.

'Maybe we should get a Christmas fairy costume and take it in turns to wave the magic wand,' Jade adds, her arm arcing over her sister's head as she sprinkles some invisible fairy dust.

'What a fabulous idea,' I exclaim. 'And Abe's penguin onesie was perfect. That was another little surprise I wasn't expecting.'

The sound of the cabin doors being opened and then firmly shut attracts my attention and I watch Gray as he heads in our direction. He must have walked through from the stern, looking for me.

'You were quick tidying up,' he comments as he strides up to snake his arm around my waist. Without warning he produces a tiny sprig of mistletoe, stooping to kiss me. The girls start to giggle.

Tollie puts his hand up to scratch beneath his wig. 'Well, everyone, I need to get out of this suit,' he declares, looking very pink-faced. 'What with the padding and the hot air we all generated, I need to step under the shower. It was a great first cruise, so thanks to you all. And you did a brilliant job of those new backing tracks, Gray. The one you wrote for story-time was perfect. Not too distracting, but catchy.'

Gray starts to *doo-ba-di-ba-di-ba-doo* and then the girls join in too, as Tollie walks off in the direction of the cottage. His laughter echoes around him as he walks.

'Are you coming back to The Bullrush?' Sarah asks me as she places a hand on each of the girls' shoulders, nodding in the direction of the inn.

I shake my head. 'Maybe later, though.'

'Kurt will be up to his eyes in cream teas and he's only got Maggie there to help, so we'd best get back.'

'Of course. I'm just grateful to have the girls helping out, especially when it comes to joining in with the singing. Sadly, I don't have a tuneful voice, so I tend to mime. I usually leave the singing up to Gray.' I give him a cheeky grin.

He's still trilling his little chorus under his breath and the girls are loving it.

'You shouldn't worry about that,' Sarah replies. 'I don't, even though every other note that comes out of my mouth is flat. A good voice is a gift I envy.'

'There.' Gray turns to face me. 'The reason I do what I do is to bring a little joy into the world. Life without music would be very dull indeed.'

I look at him and as our eyes meet my heart begins to pound in my chest. 'Life is never dull when you're around, Gray. It's only dull when you're not here.'

Oh, dear! I didn't mean to say that, and Sarah shoots me a sympathetic glance, before shepherding the girls back along the towpath.

'If you get a chance to pop in later this evening,' she calls over her shoulder, 'Kurt and I might be able to join you for a quiet drink. Abe and Ethel are manning the bar and Maggie will be in the kitchen.'

'Sounds like a plan. Hope to see you later, then, and thanks, girls, you truly are little stars.'

As we wave them off Gray slips his hand into mine, pulling me close.

'I love it here,' he whispers into my hair. 'Sometimes I wish I had a little camera so that I could see what's happening on board as I man the tiller. I heard the singing and the children were all rosy-cheeked and smiling when they left.'

'Well, it wouldn't be a cruise without our captain.' I tilt my head to look up at him. 'But I forget that you miss out. It was amazing today and Tollie was the definitive Santa. Seriously, he was made for that role. A trained actor couldn't do any better. When he was telling the story, even the most fidgety of the children managed to sit still, more or less throughout the entire time. Then he had them up and dancing, of course, getting rid of some of that excited energy before their parents took them home.'

'And we get to do it all over again tomorrow.'

Instinctively we both turn to look at The Star Gazer. With her beautiful crimson paintwork and the freshly picked greenery draped in swags from the cabin top, she is a showstopper. Tollie and Fisher have made every inch of her sparkle in the run up to today and it shows.

Gray squeezes my hand affectionately.

'Come on, let's go back and put our feet up for a bit. It might be a late one tonight if we head down to The Bullrush this evening. I think it's wishful thinking on Sarah's part hoping there will be time for a quiet drink any time before closing. The car park has been full all day. I doubt there were many spaces free on the main road at the top, either. The canal has been busy this afternoon and the weather couldn't have been more perfect for our first weekend cruises. Granted it's chilly, but, when the sky is so blue and the sun comes out to play, it's a little piece of heaven.'

'We're lucky. Fingers crossed it continues.'

We walk on, Gray swinging my hand as it nestles in his. Music is such a part of his being that it never leaves him and there's a rhythm to everything he does.

'They're a lovely little family, aren't they?' he suddenly pipes up.

He's thinking about Jade and Jude. Sarah and Kurt have done a great job bringing them up, not being overly protective and letting the girls see how hard they both work to build the family business. Something the girls can get more involved with as they get older, if that's what they want.

'Sarah regrets they didn't make the break sooner, as she says she missed so much of those early years having to put the girls in nursery while she worked in an office. But it helped to make the twins more independent, and they are so close anyway that they have always been company for each other. It must be wonderful to have a sibling, someone who knows you almost as well as you know yourself.'

Gray squeezes my hand gently in his, lovingly.

As we take a slow walk back, Gray hums 'White Christmas'. All that's missing is a little sprinkling of snow and maybe a cup of hot chocolate with my favourite marshmallows. Not the teeny-tiny things cafés often dish out, but the big, fluffy ones that go all gooey inside. But I'm one very content chief elf and I'm not complaining. With twenty-four days until Christmas is here there's plenty of time to experience everything this season has to offer...

Flat. Empty. Deflated.

I feel like a balloon that has been floating high up in the sky, soaring above my day-to-day troubles, carefree and optimistic about each new tomorrow. Until it arrived. Suddenly, all of that energising hot air has dissipated and I've sunk slowly and surely back to the frosty, dull brown earth.

'What's up with you this morning?' Fisher looks across at me, frowning. 'I thought you'd be buzzing. That was some start to this year's festivities, and it was great to have Gray back among us.'

'The weekend was amazing,' I admit, doing my best to raise a smile. But I only succeed in lifting the corners of my mouth and it doesn't exactly infuse my face.

Fisher stares at me, his eyes widening as he waits for an explanation.

'I'm being selfish, ignore me,' I mumble, avoiding eye contact.

'Missing Gray isn't being selfish, Immi. It's simply an admission of how you feel. It's okay to admit that and it won't jinx anything, darling girl.'

Sometimes I feel as if my whole life has been jinxed and when things go well, it unsettles me. I'm just waiting for the bad news to arrive. I know he means well, but the sense of emptiness I'm feeling today has put me in a bad mood. Platitudes won't do, even if they are handed out with the best of intentions. Fisher would do anything for me and that includes doing his best to cheer me up.

'Gray's mum is on the mend and he sees that as a glimmer of hope that our situation is about to change. But on a freezing Monday morning here I am again. Alone. The reality of it hits me hard and now, in here—' I tap the side of my temple '—the doubt is beginning to creep back in. His mum can't afford to run that house on her own, having given up work, even if she has turned a huge corner health-wise. So, nothing has really changed, has it? I'm so happy she's doing well but her home is everything to her. Gray is a good son and he'll do the right thing – I wouldn't expect any less of him but that doesn't make it easy to accept. I know that sounds mean-spirited of me, but each parting is getting harder, Fisher, and it feels like we're stuck.'

Fisher sighs, pushing back in his chair as he releases the pen in his hand. It falls onto the desk with a clatter. He's a handsome man, his jet-black hair threaded with enough silver to make him look distinguished. His brow furrows as he stares at me, the sadness in his eyes full of understanding.

'Life is tough, Immi, and we only have to look around to see the evidence of the daily struggles. Remember that it's hard for Gray, too. The truth is that no one knows what tomorrow will bring. When changes come, they often happen quickly, but the period beforehand can feel like treading water.'

Our eyes meet as I acknowledge his words, but there isn't an ounce of positivity in me this morning. There's only that awful depleted feeling of having been robbed of something. I push my shoulders back and shift around in my chair rather uncomfortably. I know I'm being unreasonable because if, and when, the changes do come, it will open up a myriad of different emotions for me. Fear of messing things up being one of them.

'I'm fine, really.' My words sound dejected and I decide to shut up before I make it any worse.

He expels a deep breath and his head tilts forward. Staring down at his hands, he clasps them together reflectively and I feel awful for being such a misery.

'When my wife upped and left me for another man it broke my heart. All my plans for the future involved her and I'd been ploughing on, working towards what I thought was *our* dream. If only I'd taken time out to talk to her, asked her what she wanted out of life... Don't make the same mistake I did, Immi. You need to spell out your concerns to Gray. Knowing you as I do, I bet you simply back off and leave everything unsaid. You can't live your life treading carefully and avoiding the real issues.'

It's as if he can read my mind and he's right. Everyone in my life so far has left me, except Tollie, and, as I could never leave Tollie, I'm as much a part of the problem as Gray.

'If I add to the pressure Gray's feeling, then I'm just another worry for him to juggle. It could end up driving us apart.'

Fisher sits forward, leaning his forearms on the desk as he stares across at me intently.

'Don't let your past scar your future, Immi. Tell Gray how you're feeling. I'm not saying there's a quick and easy solution, but being honest with each other is the first step in determining a way forward that will work for you both. I learnt that lesson the hard way and I'd hate for you to make the same mistake.'

Back in the day, everyone thought Fisher and Wendy were a team. They were working hard to pay off the mortgage on their old converted barn, to give them financial freedom. The future shone bright on the horizon, as Fisher longed to set up his own business. Wendy helped out in The Bullrush and everything seemed fine. Until the day she left, leaving him a note to let him know she had found someone else. What hurt Fisher most was that the affair had been going on for a long time. Wendy had always wanted children, they both had, and as far as I can tell it just never happened for them. The man she left Fisher for was a widower with two children of primary school age.

That was just over eleven years ago now. Buying a grand canal cruiser was supposed to be their dream future together, running special event trips up and down the canals. Instead, they ended up selling the barn to go their own ways. A year later, Fisher bought a small cottage a stone's throw away from the Aysbury Junction Marina. The remainder of his equity he put away until the day he found The Star Gazer and the rest is history. Now he's counting down until he can take early retirement in eighteen months' time. But you can't run cruises on your own. That's the trouble with dreams – they usually involve other people to help turn them into reality.

'Point taken. Thanks, Fisher. I need to steel myself for some tough talking. Or maybe I just enjoy having a moan when I'm in a bad mood.'

'You know that's not true. What does Tollie say?'

Is there anything at all Fisher doesn't notice?

'Nothing. We haven't talked about it.'

Fisher rises up out of his chair. 'That's precisely my point and you must remedy that side of things, too. Now, I need another strong coffee. It's going to be a long day, I think.'

* * *

On Mondays, I finish at four o'clock and I'd promised Mrs Price I'd pop round to have a cup of tea with her. Or rather I was summoned, and, as she's never extended an invitation to me before, I didn't think I could refuse.

It's Tollie's doing, because I'd shown him the old photograph of the cottage tucked into the parcel that Martin gave me, and he must have mentioned it to Mrs Price. Yesterday afternoon when we arrived back after the second Santa Ahoy Special trip for the day, I bumped into her on the towpath. She wanted to know if I had any more photos and I admitted that I hadn't had time to look through the pile. So she decided that *we* could do that task together.

Byre Cottage is a converted cow shed, but from the outside this bijou, reddish-pink brick building is as cute as any cosy little cottage an artist could paint. It's a brisk ten-minute walk to the cluster of farm buildings that were turned into smart new homes back in 2001. As I walk into the central courtyard, I feel honoured to have been invited into Mrs Price's inner sanctum. Few get to see her in her own environment, as she seems to spend most of her time flitting between her various charitable works. Then she disappears for long periods at a time.

As far as Tollie is aware, the only person she ever worked for in Aysbury was him, following the death of Grandma Nell. Grandma and Mrs Price were friends, despite the obvious age difference, both taking an active role in organising many of the community events. Whether she knew anything at all about Mrs Price's past, we'll never know, as Grandma wasn't prone to gossiping and kept secrets very close to her chest. With no evidence of any immediate family, it seems that Mrs Price gravitated here.

Who knows if there was ever a Mr Price from where she hailed originally? The rumour is that she uses a fictitious name, but where that idea came from, I have no idea. Although I was vaguely aware

Tollie had taken on a housekeeper after Grandma died, I can't say I recall Mrs Price ever being around whenever Dad and I visited him.

When I did ask about her once, he said that Grandma hit it off with her from the start. He's not usually one to talk about the past, or other people, so there's little point asking him for information if he doesn't offer it. However, when I pressed him, he simply said that Grandma attracted unusual people like a magnet. He informed me with a wink that he, too, came under that category.

Mrs Price was one of the first people to move into what is known as the Saint Nicholas's Well complex. Byre Cottage is the smallest of the properties, the four other detached barns dwarfing it in size, but, with its own little walled garden sitting inside the main courtyard, it abuts the narrow lane in a very leafy spot.

The rear of the cottage is really the front, and as I stand here looking at the tall double gates I look around for a doorbell, or knocker – some way to announce my presence before I walk into Mrs Price's garden.

The high wall surrounding the property is made from reclaimed bricks and the colours range from a deep red to various shades of dark pink. But it blends in well and looks as if it's been here forever. On the top third of the wall is a brick latticework effect, with a half-a-brick spacing between each one. A whole host of climbing plants, some carrying winter blooms, tumble in profusion over the top of the wall, partially obscuring what's on the other side. It's impossible to get more than the odd, teasing glimpse of the building beyond.

Suddenly a man appears behind me, calling out as he walks across the open space between us.

'Is Mrs Price expecting you?' he asks directly, looking me up and down as if I might be selling something. Well, I do have a plastic carrier bag in one hand and a small potted plant in the other.

'Yes. Yes, she is – I'm, um, Imogen Tolliman. I've walked up from the marina.'

'Oh, right. I thought your face was vaguely familiar. We have tickets for the grandkids on one of next weekend's Santa cruises. Great job you're doing there. They're very excited about it. Here, let me help you with the gate. There's a trick to it, you see. Mrs Price doesn't encourage visitors.' He lowers his tone as he speaks.

Mrs Price has that effect on people, I've noticed.

He reaches up to place his hand over the top of the gate and appears to be releasing some sort of latch. I notice there's an external mailbox on the wall, so I guess for a woman living alone keeping the gate bolted is a matter of security.

'Thank you.'

'I'm Cameron,' he adds, as he slips one of the double gates open for me to step through. 'My wife, Lizzie, and I live in Meadow Barn, over there.' He points to the far corner of the courtyard. Surrounded by its own high walls, it must back onto the fields and I should imagine the view stretches out endlessly.

'What a fabulous barn and an amazing backdrop.'

He gives me a friendly smile. 'Yes. But with that comes the early morning alarm call, as we're in easy earshot of the chickens and the cockerels. You don't get many of those living in the city, but we're used to it now. It's a great place to live.'

I nod, thinking that this is the best of both worlds. Rural and private, but not isolated.

'Do you need a hand with that?' he asks, offering to take the bag from me.

'No, I'm fine, thank you. I'll look out for your grandchildren next weekend. All of the trips are fully booked already and we're thinking about running a few extra excursions next year.'

He gives me a nod, his eyes sparkling. 'My wife and daughter will be bringing them along. You ought to think about doing a

Santa booze cruise for the parents.' He's serious. 'I'll be buying up a few bottles of The Bullrush Christmas Brew to do my bit for the fund,' he adds. Word is obviously getting around.

'Every little helps,' I reply enthusiastically.

'What helps?' Mrs Price's voice rises up out of nowhere. 'If you're coming in, come in. Good afternoon, Cameron. The tea is stewing, Immi, I thought you were late.'

Cameron and I both jumped the instant we heard her voice and he turns on his heels with a quick, 'Goodbye, ladies. Enjoy your tea.'

'It's half-past four, you know,' Mrs Price informs me as I step through into her garden. She swiftly snaps the bolt across before marching up to her semi-opened front door. 'The cat has knocked the door ajar and now I'm losing all the heat.'

It's merely a mumble of complaint and I know it's not really directed at me personally, but I'm beginning to wish I'd said I'd drop off the parcel but couldn't stay.

Stepping inside, I quickly shut the split stable door behind me.

'Well, don't just stand there looking awkward,' Mrs Price admonishes. 'Slip off your coat, and is that plant for me?'

I thrust my hand forward and she does a double take, but after a moment of hesitation she tilts her head in a thank-you gesture.

Placing the carrier bag on the floor at my feet, I take off my coat and hang it on a peg next to the door.

'Right, follow me. I hope you like Earl Grey.'

We're standing in the kitchen area. It isn't huge, but it's plenty big enough and the centre of the single-storey section of the former cow shed. To my left is a latched country-style door but it's closed, and I have no idea what's on the other side. As I follow Mrs Price, we walk through into a very charming sitting room with patio doors to the garden on one side and a large window looking out onto the lane, on the other. Ahead of us is a flight of stairs going up to the first floor. I assume that leads to a bedroom and maybe a bathroom.

The table situated next to the long window is laid out with a rather posh tea. A cake stand is loaded with slices of sponge sandwich and some scones lathered up with butter, jam and cream. There are also some tiny sandwiches and I'm rather touched that Mrs Price has gone to this much trouble for me.

The teapot is sporting a tea cosy; I haven't seen one of those in years. Tollie always throws a teabag into a mug and doesn't stand on ceremony.

'This is lovely, Mrs Price. Thank you.'

'Well, don't just stand there. Take a seat and I'll pour the tea. Help yourself. The scones were freshly made about an hour ago.'

There's nothing at all chintzy about Byre Cottage, which comes as somewhat of a surprise. It's very contemporary country style, with gorgeous white shutters to the windows and doors, allowing the maximum amount of light to filter in, while giving a sense of privacy. The garden is full of mostly evergreen shrubs and the climbers rising up over the walls are a mixture of deciduous and winter-flowering plants. There are some gorgeous, deep pink climbing roses with tight little buds and a beautiful winter-flowering jasmine.

It's rather nice sitting here, munching away and being able to turn my head to gaze at the garden and then turn back to look out over the quiet country lane.

'This is such a delightful surprise, Mrs Price. It's a beautiful cottage,' I remark, without thinking.

Thankfully, she looks rather pleased, but I always feel a little anxious around her, and when I'm nervous I have this awful tendency to say the first thing that comes into my head.

'Thank you, Immi. It's my sanctuary. That's why I don't invite many people to visit. We all need a little space of our own. I am rather excited to take a look at that package of yours, though, I will admit. History has always fascinated me and coming to Aysbury felt very much like coming home.'

I swallow the last mouthful of a scone, wiping my fingers on a paper napkin.

'You had family here?'

Mrs Price raises an eyebrow, suddenly looking rather put out. A little pink glow begins to add a touch of colour to her cheeks.

'I was born and grew up in Middle Norton, but moved away many years ago,' she replies, a little curtly.

I sit looking at her apologetically.

'Sorry, I... um... wasn't being nosey, Mrs Price.'

'Of course,' she acknowledges, her face relaxing a little. 'There's something so very tranquil about a canal setting and I could sit and watch the boats travelling up and down all day. But it's more private here and I couldn't put up with the constant stream of walkers on the towpath. So, it suits me just fine.'

Goodness, we're actually having a conversation. In between taking careful mouthfuls of a meltingly gorgeous slice of sponge sandwich, I try my best to make small talk.

Eventually we're finished eating, and Mrs Price begins to clear the table. I jump up to help ferry the dishes through to the kitchen. We stack the dishwasher and when we return, she suggests we move back to the sitting room. There are two two-seater sofas, each facing a large low-level oak coffee table. She clears a couple of small ornaments off the top and indicates for me to spread out the contents of the carrier bag.

'Ah.' She immediately reaches forward to pick up the sepia photograph of Lock Keeper's Cottage. 'This is what Tollie was telling me about. How delightful!'

Mrs Price takes her time scrutinising the photo as I open up the package for the first time. Sorting through the contents, I find a journal with tiny, faded, but very neat handwriting. It's rather flowery and hard to read so I put it to one side. There are two well-worn volumes covered in a pitted red leather that over time has become brittle but is still intact. Opening up the first one, I'm surprised to see that it contains pressed flowers, separated by thin leaves of tissue paper. Sadly, most of the contents are now a rather bland fawn colour and some have crumbled, sending little pieces falling onto the coffee table.

'Oh, I'm so sorry. I wasn't expecting dried flowers.'

Mrs Price looks across at me, but she's clearly delighted by the contents.

'My goodness, what a find. I don't suppose there's any indication of a date written anywhere?'

'Not inside the cover and there's nothing on the individual pages. Some of the flowers are intact, but you need to turn them over carefully. This one has a tinge of colour left to it.'

'That's a flag iris, I think,' Mrs Price points out enthusiastically. 'I remember pressing flowers when I was a child. My grandmother taught me how to do it. I had a special wooden press and we mounted them in scrapbooks. Nothing as grand as these leather-bound ones and I have no idea where they are now.'

I place the volumes on top of the journal and begin to sift through a pile of photographs. Most are dog-eared, some are so faded that the sepia has become merely a series of blots against the backgrounds. I slide a pile across to Mrs Price, and she immediately begins sorting through them.

'Well, this view of the towpath is incredible; how very different it was way back then. I'm guessing this is roughly where The Bull-rush Inn is now. How strange to see the open fields extending so far into the distance. You can hardly glimpse them these days, what with the trees and the hedges. Ah, here's another shot of your cottage. It's taken from the side angle. It must have felt rather isolated in those days. You can just catch the stern of a boat on the far right as it sails by, but it's a small one. Look, the man is smoking a pipe as he waves out.'

She offers me the photo and I squint, trying to make out the detail.

'You have good eyes,' I remark. 'It's a shame some of the very old ones are so faded.'

'I wear contact lenses,' Mrs Price informs me. 'But this is such a delightful find, Immi.'

Her tone is different somehow. She seems, not only genuinely interested, but enthralled by this little piece of history laid out in front of us.

Well, what an eye-opener this visit is turning out to be.

'Lock Keeper's Cottage and The Retreat will always be special to me, Mrs Price. That's why I'd like to know more about its history. It's the one place that I've known all my life; a place that always felt like home whenever Dad and I returned. I never dreamt, of course, that one day I'd be living here permanently.'

I spread out the remaining photos across the centre of the table and focus on the newer ones. Sadly, some of them have a curious pink tinge, which makes them a little fuzzy.

'These were probably taken in the sixties – that's when colour film became more affordable.' Mrs Price points to the photo in my hands. 'Even if they are well stored, they tended to lose their colour over time. I discovered that while researching my own family history. It's such a pity though. Ironically, the black and white film from the same period usually fares much better.'

We spend a while looking through them together. It's not always easy to identify from what point a photo was taken, as many of the present-day landmarks simply aren't there. No marina, no car park, but a series of old metal sheds and a handful of small dwellings that are long gone. But it's fun and Mrs Price is in her element. I fleetingly wonder if she was a history teacher before she came here.

There are some portrait photos, but none of the ones I turn over have anything written on the back to give us any clues.

'What a shame these ended up at a tabletop sale,' I reflect. 'They probably came from a house clearance and there may well be relatives still living in the area who would connect with these. The couple Tollie bought the cottage from, almost fifty years ago, only owned it for two years, curiously enough. Maybe it was too out on a limb for them. It would be fascinating to discover when the old barn was converted into a boat-hire business and who ran it.'

'Yes, it would be interesting. It was a good thing your granddad had all that work done on it after your dad died, Immi. I guess it was obvious at some point you would need your own space.'

I catch her looking at me sympathetically. Did Tollie take Mrs Price into his confidence, or even ask her opinion about it? He obviously values her input, as her role in sorting out the candidates for the Little Stars Specials is so important.

'When I look back now, I can see that I drove you away, Mrs Price, and I'm so sorry about that. You were good enough to take on the job of looking after the two properties while Tollie came to terms with his grief. And there was I, just two years later, angry and unable to handle my feelings; striding in and disrupting everyone's lives.'

She shrugs her shoulders. 'It was the right thing for me to leave you both to it. And you survived. Nell would have been thrilled to think of you living in The Retreat.'

'Yes. Tollie thought it was a good investment for me for the future. He said Dad would have wanted me to do something meaningful with my inheritance. And he was right. When he finally decided I was old enough to move into The Retreat, things became a lot easier between Tollie and I. And in the interim years, the rental income during the lucrative summer months gave me a nest egg, too.'

Mrs Price nods her head in agreement.

'I left because the two of you needed to establish some rules to allow you to come to terms with two very different ways of grieving. The best way to do that was to be forced to cope with the day-to-day things. Bit by bit you found a way through it together, and that strengthened your bond.'

It's touching to hear a side to it that I could never have guessed at.

'If you let me have a copy of what you've discovered so far and are happy to leave this with me, I'll enjoy looking into what's here. I have a couple of books I found in a car-boot sale about the area going way back. And there might even be something in the library worth taking a look at. It could potentially throw up some names of the families living here back in the mid-eighteen hundreds. What do you think?'

Mrs Price is really beginning to let down her guard, but maybe that's because I'm actually taking the time to have a meaningful conversation with her, rather than simply passing the time of day. She must have missed the company of Tollie, so soon after losing a dear friend.

'Well, if you're happy to do some digging, that would be great. I doubt I'll have much time on my hands now until after Christmas. Weekends will be non-stop and I'm going to be working long days at the nurseries. Martin really needs me there full-time, as the orders for fresh wreaths and swags are mounting. We still have a huge pile of frames to prepare. It's quite time-consuming to attach the pine cones and baubles ready to add the fresh greenery. But Fisher relies on me working two days a week at the marina, sorting paperwork, and I can't let him down.'

'Oh, my dear! It must be difficult for you, juggling two jobs.

Especially when it's coming up to one of the busiest times for Martin. You only have one pair of hands, after all. I might not have any artistic talent, but I'm good with paperwork. As long as someone shows me what needs doing, I could cover your days at the marina. I pick things up quickly and it would allow you to focus on the Christmas orders at the nurseries.'

It's all I can do to keep a look of surprise from flashing over my face. I'm shocked that Mrs Price is offering to step in and cover for me.

'I... um, well, that's a very generous offer. Thank you, Mrs Price. I will talk to Fisher and check he's okay with that – I'm sure he will be – and then I'll tell Martin the good news.'

As I walk back home my phone pings; it's a text from Gray.

Missing you like crazy, Immi. All good here – Mum had a brilliant weekend. Roll on Friday. How was your day?

Getting better by the second, I can't help thinking. It's time to relax a bit. Things are going to work themselves out – I simply need to be patient.

Good. Just had afternoon tea with Mrs Price and it seems I have a new best friend.

A second later I'm laughing at his response.

Really? You and Mrs Price?

Tapping away, I realise that my Monday mood has lifted.

Yep. Best scones, jam and cream I've ever eaten. Jealous?

He sends back a video clip of him singing and playing on the keyboard. He's messing around and doing his thing, but he ends it by making a love heart with his hands.

Crazy guy!

But you love me.

I do.

Throwing my arms around Gray's neck, I sag against him. Friday seemed to take forever to get here this week.

'Hey, what's this all about?' he asks, pulling away to look at me, rather puzzled.

'I told her not to worry.' Tollie's voice filters out from the kitchen. 'The frost was bad this mornin' and took a while to melt. We're expectin' black ice tonight. I told her they'll be gritting the roads, but you know what she's like.'

I look up at Gray and he gives me one of his goofy grins.

'Hmm... I did wonder about the pinging text messages.'

'You didn't respond!'

'I was driving, Immi. I assumed, given the racket my phone was making, that it was to do with work. I've been putting out feelers as it's a bit quiet right now. But this is *our* time and I just wanted to get here as quickly as I could. The roads aren't too bad and the gritters are out in force. Fingers crossed it doesn't affect travel tomorrow, though, as we have our first Little Stars Special cruise.'

The same thing had crossed my mind, but that was the lesser of my two concerns. The cruise could always be rescheduled.

'Earlier in the week a car ended up in the ditch as it was headin' down towards Aysbury Junction,' Tollie explains.

'And that was at lunchtime,' I point out. 'The recovery guy who towed the vehicle to the garage told the driver that the temperature had suddenly dropped after warming up a little and black ice can form at any time of the day.'

Gray nods, frowning. 'No one was hurt, though, I hope?'

'No, but the car will probably be a write-off. Tollie was in The Bullrush having lunch when someone from Adler's farm drove the guy down to have a cup of tea to calm his nerves. His wife came to collect him while I was there.'

'He told us that all four wheels skidded on the ice. An hour later the road was fine. It was crazy, but he was really shaken up. The poor guy said his life flashed before his eyes as he struggled to control the vehicle. And he wasn't even drivin' very fast, as he didn't know the road,' Tollie explains. I realise he was every bit as relieved as I was to see Gray walk through the door.

Tollie disappears back into the kitchen.

'I don't drive fast, I drive safely, Immi,' Gray replies forcefully.

Having let me go, he suddenly reaches out again. Gray's hands grasp my waist, pulling me into him so he can rest his chin on my head. As I sink into his chest, suddenly everything in my little world is fine, just fine.

'You need to stop worrying,' he speaks softly. 'I've got too much to lose to take any unnecessary risks now things are on the up.'

Was there a little catch in his voice as he spoke? But then he's singing under his breath and that Friday feeling begins to consume me. Is it wrong to live my life counting down the hours to the weekend? I wonder. How would it feel if every single morning began with breakfast together? And if every single night we slept side by side? It's something I daren't even dream about right now.

Tollie reappears in the doorway and Gray stops singing into my ear. 'If you two 'ave finished, I want to run somethin' past you.'

We head over to the sofa and Tollie eases himself into his armchair.

'I've been thinkin' about this celebratory dinner party to mark the tenth anniversary next year. It was a surprise, I will admit, and a nice thought. I'm touched that people are willin' to raise funds to make a thing about it, but to my mind it's a waste of money. Let's do something that benefits the community and will be a lasting reminder.'

Oh dear, Martin said more or less the same thing when we discussed it. But having only had two short meetings out of earshot of Tollie, everyone was sold on the idea of a posh do in his honour. The very smart Linden Hotel has already stepped in and offered a special rate to host the dinner as the plans progress.

'Well, I understand what you're saying—' I'm not even sure it's worth trying to convince him, as my gut instincts are telling me he's going to dig his heels in.

'What did you have in mind, Tollie?' Gray glances at me, giving the slightest shake of his head to warn me to sit and listen.

'I'm not sayin' a gatherin' wouldn't be a fine thing to do. But we've done that before and when everyone mucks in to bring a little food and drink with them, it's a neighbourly thing. I'm up for that, but wearin' a suit... and speeches. Too formal for me, by far. Instead what I'd like to do is try to raise enough to build a kiddies' playground.'

'Where?' I ask, totally surprised by his suggestion, although it is a great idea and so typical of Tollie.

'Well, I'm not averse to fencin' off a bit of land the other side of The Retreat and I wondered how you feel about that, Immi.'

I look at Gray and he stares back at me, frowning.

'Tollie, it's your garden. You can do whatever you like with it,' I point out, but Tollie simply shakes his head.

'It might suit me, but the long-term future of Lock Keeper's Cottage is in your hands and it's time we did a swap.'

I freeze. Both Gray and I know what Tollie is hinting at, but how on earth did talking about a celebratory dinner turn into me moving into the cottage? I'd bet money on the fact that Fisher and Tollie have been talking. And plotting, by the sound of it. Gray looks decidedly uncomfortable, as we both know what Tollie is hinting at. Gray isn't in a position to start making firm plans for the future and I have no idea how to reply to that remark. It was aimed at me, but I can see from the expression on Gray's face that he thinks it was aimed at him, too. This is so embarrassing and totally out of order.

'Of course, I wouldn't just hive off that land if you thought it wasn't a good idea. Bein' that you might have different plans for this place.' Tollie looks directly at Gray, before his eyes return to me. 'Oh, before I forget, David and Pete sent up a complimentary box of six Bullrush Christmas Brews. I think a beer would go down rather nicely right now, don't you, Gray? I'll leave you to mull over my suggestion.'

And with that, Tollie disappears back into the kitchen, leaving Gray and me sitting there speechless.

* * *

'He's right, you know, about next year's celebrations.'

Gray looks across the table at me as I sit toying with a plate of Sarah's signature dish, spaghetti with chicken and mushrooms.

'I understand Tollie doesn't want a formal dinner and he'd feel more comfortable with one of our usual community get-togethers. It is special when everyone pitches in and it means the expense is shared. And I agree, a playground for the kids is a brilliant idea. But why on earth he then dragged me into this, I have no idea. Except that—'

I find myself hesitating. Is it time to come clean and say the things we never talk about, but simply skate over?

'What?' Gray stops twisting pasta around his fork and sits back in his chair expectantly.

'Um. Well. I think Fisher said something to Tollie and he decided to interfere.'

'Interfere?' Gray gives me a blank look.

I sigh. 'When you're able to stay for the weekend... well, Mondays are hard for me. Suddenly you're gone and the week ahead seems to stretch out forever. Last Monday I was down. It had been such a long time, you know, since you were able to stay, and I couldn't hide it from Fisher. The minute I walked into the office I dragged him under my black cloud, and it was wrong of me. But we had such a brilliant weekend and, well, it was just one of those days.'

Gray's elbows are now on the table and his chin is resting on his hands. His expression is pained.

'I hate the drive back on Sunday evenings. It's even worse, in a way, than the days I can't stay. We're together, having fun and living like a couple and then it's back to reality. Tollie and Fisher only want what's best for you, Immi. You deserve more than a part-time relationship.'

He sounds glum.

'Listen, Gray, I wasn't a party to this, and I think it's wrong of them to try to—'

'What? Bring it to a head? Make me realise I can't keep stringing you along like this?'

He sounds defeated, as if he's done something wrong.

'I wouldn't have fallen in love with you if you were the sort of man to walk away from a person you care about when they need you the most, Gray. Rona needs you. As Tollie needs me in his life. This isn't just your problem, it's mine too.'

Two half-eaten dishes of food are sitting there, rapidly going cold.

'It's obvious we can't go on like this forever, Immi, I'm well aware of that. It's not fair on either of us, is it? For you, it isn't just about being here for Tollie, but this community has given you the stability you always longed for. I understand that and why it's so important. Believe me, I'm doing everything I can to get Mum to the point where she has her own little network around her again. She's so close to being able to stand on her own two feet again and hopefully pick up the pieces of her life. She knows how hard it's been for you and me, and that's been tough for her to bear. Mum prides herself on being strong, but getting sick made her feel vulnerable and afraid. It takes a while to let those feelings go.'

He hasn't smiled once since we left the cottage and as he pushes his plate away, a little wave of pity washes over me. Life isn't fair, I know that only too well. I understand the situation he's in and, as time goes on, the sense of frustration and impatience that comes with it. Some things simply can't be hurried, as exasperating as that may be.

I reach out across the table for his hand, and we intertwine our fingers.

'You don't need to explain, Gray, really you don't. I'll have words with Tollie and Fisher; it's wrong of them to get involved in our business. They aren't looking at the bigger picture, which is what is making me so damned annoyed. If it were the other way around it would be an entirely different story. If I suddenly decided to move away, they would be floored. It would leave a hole in their lives, as it will for Rona, when you move out again.'

Gray's frown is deep and it's a look that doesn't suit him.

'I should never have moved back in, I suppose. But having to give up work because of her health issues hit Mum hard. Financially, she can only afford to continue to stay in the house if I can pick up some of the bills. Well, until she can return to work, or is eligible to take her private pension early. Maybe then it will be time to move into something smaller and less expensive to maintain.' This is the first time Gray has opened up to me about this and I'd been labouring under the impression that she didn't want to move home.

'Hey, guys, are you done? Was there anything wrong with the spaghetti?' Kurt looks from one to the other of us questioningly.

We unlock our fingers and I give Kurt a forced smile as I push the plates to the end of the table.

'No, it was great, Kurt, really it was. We're both tired, that's all. It's been a long week,' I explain.

'Sorry to hear that. How about dessert on the house?'

One glance at Gray and it's obvious we both want to head back to The Retreat.

'That's a lovely thought, but we're up early tomorrow. Some of the greenery on The Star Gazer will probably need replacing; plus, we have the first of the Little Stars trips tomorrow, as well as the regular cruise. It's going to be all go,' I add brightly.

'Well, the girls are excited about it, that's for sure. There's nothing wrong with Tollie, is there?'

I shake my head. 'No, he's good. But he doesn't want to go with the big celebratory dinner next year. He has other ideas.'

Kurt grimaces.

'Uh-oh. I had a feeling it was going to be all change and that's my fault for letting it slip. He would have gone along with it if all the arrangements had been in place.'

Kurt looks annoyed with himself as he stacks the dishes and settles them into the crook of one arm. I shoot him a consoling glance as I stand and begin pulling on my padded coat.

'I doubt we could have kept it a secret, Kurt, so don't worry about it. The important thing is that we're honouring Tollie's wishes, not forcing something on him that he's not happy about. As long as everyone is included, there'll be some sort of party going on – it might be a little less formal than we'd planned, that's all.'

Gray and Kurt exchange a guarded look. People will be disappointed, and we know it.

'Well, Sarah still hasn't forgiven me, so if you get a chance and could put a good word in for me, I'd be extremely grateful. Especially if the weeks of planning are about to fall apart. I'm not going to be Mr Popular around here.'

I nod, giving him a reassuring smile, but before I can answer him, Gray interjects.

'I don't think you're going to be alone there, Kurt.'

'Hey, guys, neither of you have done anything wrong and I'll be having a couple of very pointed conversations, don't you worry.'

As I stomp off, Gray tries to keep up with me but he's no match. Starting off what promises to be a wonderful weekend feeling angry because of other people's interference is tarnishing the highlight of my week. And that's not fair.

'Slow down, Immi,' Gray calls out above the general background noise. But I beat him to the door. As I step out onto the towpath and take a couple of paces forward, without warning my right foot suddenly slips from beneath me, sending me hurtling to the floor.

'What...? Argh!'

As Gray strides forward, leaning over me with concern etched all over his face, the door behind us slams shut. Suddenly, he too slips and ends up in a heap next to me.

Then I begin laughing as I collapse against him.

'Ow!' I declare, nursing my right arm.

Neither of us moves, we just stare at each other and realise how ridiculous we must look right now.

'Are you all right? Nothing's broken?'

His voice is tinged with apprehension.

'Only my pride if someone else steps through that door before I'm back on my feet. Thank goodness I wore a padded coat as it softened the fall. How about you?'

'I'm okay. Don't try to stand, Immi. This whole section is a sheet of ice. Crawl over to the grass on all fours and I'll shuffle back inside to alert Kurt, so he can throw down some rock salt. I think we're lucky – we both seem to bounce rather well.' However, I notice that he winces a little as he inches backwards.

Rolling over onto my knees and shuffling forward very gingerly, I call out over my shoulder, 'Gray?'

There's a groan as he pulls himself upright using the door handle.

'Yes?'

'Tollie and Fisher are right. I was wrong to be angry with them because they were only looking out for us.'

Reaching the grassy strip, I ease myself back around to face him; he's poised, waiting until he can see I'm okay.

'I know. It's time to formulate a plan; we need to make this happen.' And then he waggles his index finger at me. 'Don't move a muscle until I get back – that's an order!'

Unable to suppress a grin, I call out, 'Yes, boss.'

As Gray disappears back inside I sit there getting soggier by the second, finding myself thinking about my dad. It's so easy to take everything for granted, even the fact that there will be a tomorrow.

I'm done waiting. Life can end up being one big excuse if you let it and that would be such a waste. There are always options to consider if everyone is prepared to work together to find the best solution, and it's time Gray and I did just that.

LET IT SNOW, LET IT SNOW, LET IT SNOW

'Good morning.'

I'm drifting in and out of sleep. Gray's voice seems to float on the air. I roll over, willing myself to sink back into my dream, where I was idly strolling along a beach. Mere moments ago, the sand beneath my toes felt so real that my hands were trying to brush it off and now the vision is no more. Easing open one eye, I see Gray is propped up on his elbow, leaning over me.

'I have a surprise,' he whispers.

'What... at six-thirty in the morning?'

'You'll like this one.'

With that he jumps up and walks over to the window. Rather reluctantly I drag myself out of bed and saunter over to stand beside him. My eyes spring open wide as I stare out.

'Snow!'

'Admittedly it's only an inch, but doesn't it look beautiful? Come on, let's get dressed. It won't be slippery like last night and let's enjoy it before it melts.'

We're like two big kids, wrapping up warmly and creeping out, mindful not to disturb Tollie as we take the path along the side of the cottage and pull the heavy front gate shut very gingerly behind us.

When I stop to draw in a deep breath, the air is chilly on my teeth, and as we begin walking the snow is satisfyingly crisp underfoot. The sky is a rich, azure blue, without a cloud in sight. As the day warms up, this winter wonderland will disappear, so we want to enjoy it while we can.

'What a bonus,' Gray says, wrapping my arm in his and giving it a squeeze as we walk towards the marina. 'How are your bruises this morning?'

'Not too bad. I have one the size of an egg on my arm, but my rear took the brunt of it.'

He laughs. 'Mine, too. Fortunately, you had a little padding.'

I half turn to give him a withering look.

'I meant your coat,' he explains apologetically, and I flash him a cheeky smile.

We walk on in silence and Gray steers us across a grassy bank, helping me over the wooden stile onto the pastureland.

In front of us a pristine white blanket stretches out as far as the eye can see. The pretty and serene setting is only broken by the green of the hedgerows, where the fine powdery dusting is already melting. It's peaceful until some raucous blackbirds fly overhead, giving chase, no doubt, to tiny insects carried on the light breeze.

'This is heavenly.' Gray stops and I sidle up to him, grabbing his hand.

'Life doesn't get much better than an early morning walk like this.'

'Immi, we sort of take what we have for granted, don't we?'

'What do you mean?'

'Well...' He pauses, casting around for the right words. 'We're a couple, an odd couple given our circumstances, admittedly. But—'

He turns to face me, planting a kiss on the tip of my cold, and probably rather pink, nose.

'You will marry me, won't you?' He asks the question rather hesitantly.

Staring up into his eyes, I throw my arms around him. Well, as far as they will reach given that we're both wearing thick coats.

'Of course, I will, crazy guy. Why wouldn't I?'

'No, I mean...' Gray steps away from me and drops down onto one knee. 'Imogen Tolliman, will you marry me?'

As I look down at him, the smile on my face stretches from ear to ear. It's enough to know he's serious about our future together, but the timing isn't right.

'Stand up, you fool! Look at your jeans – one knee is now muddy and wet. There's no rush, Gray, really.'

I offer my hands to help pull him to his feet and we both utter a little groan. It seems that bouncing isn't quite as painless twenty-four hours after the fact.

'Putting it off, I've realised, is making us both miserable, Immi. When you long to be with someone, every single day you spend apart is a day lost. One you will never get back. I knew from the start what I hoped would happen between us. I couldn't take my eyes off you. There was something so magnetic – I felt as if I already knew you, somehow. It was crazy and exhilarating at the same time. The buzz has never left me.'

'Hmm. Crazy is the perfect description for us, isn't it? I haven't allowed myself to really believe that something this wonderful can happen, in case it goes wrong. Every time you leave me, it feeds my fear. I try so hard not to cling to you, when in reality that's exactly what I want to do.' My heart is heavy to admit my insecurities, but it's time to be honest with him.

Gray pulls on my hands, dragging me into him.

'Ah, Immi, it breaks my heart to hear you say that. I know how hard it was for you, losing your dad and being uprooted. It's time I proved to you how important you are to me and I'll sit down with Mum to talk about her options. She'll understand, although I won't pretend it's going to be easy. Like it or not, things can't go on as they are forever. Aysbury is going to be home for you and me, and maybe she should consider living close by. Selling up and buying something smaller will be a big adjustment, but it will take away the financial worries and make her independent again. And we'd be on hand if she needed anything.'

I don't quite know what to say to Gray, as it sounds as if his mind is made up. However, an uneasy feeling in the pit of my stomach begins to stir. Laying out a plan is one thing, making it happen is another.

'So, what's your answer?' Gray is looking at me intently as he awaits my response.

'Yes. Of course, it's a yes. But—'

'No buts. Not any more. As for what Tollie was saying about the cottage, it is your inheritance for the future, but we're happy enough in The Retreat, aren't we?'

I look at him, still trying to take in his words and what this means.

'We are, but you know what Tollie is like when he makes his mind up about something. He often talked about extending the cottage and bringing it up to the same standard as The Retreat. It's his dream, really.'

'It doesn't matter to me where we live...' Gray's voice softens '... as long as we're together. But I also wouldn't like to upset Tollie in any way.'

I can see that it's awkward for Gray, as most couples get to choose their first home together. Shrugging my shoulders, I don't know what the answer is, and I let out a sigh. He looks at me, pointedly.

'I have a nest egg from the sale of my flat. It's enough to cover the cost of renovating the cottage, as it stands. New bathroom, replacement kitchen and total redecoration. Maybe we can convince Tollie to stay put, if we do the work gradually. You know, so it doesn't overwhelm or inconvenience him. Whoever is going to be living there, the fabric of the building, too, requires a little TLC. But more importantly, I want to contribute something. Not because I need to prove anything to you, but to feel that I'm a part of this. And I want to show Tollie that I intend to look after you and keep everything ticking over.'

Gray cradles me in his arms as we stand together, peering out over the wintry landscape. There is such a mix of emotions swirling around inside my head – joy, fear, excitement, hope and sadness, all mixed into one. Tollie is fit and healthy, I tell myself firmly, and there's no need to be maudlin, or change our living arrangements. We simply need to take things at a pace Tollie is prepared to accept. With Gray here by my side life is going to sparkle and, hopefully, Tollie will finally be able to relax a little.

'That means a lot to hear you say that, Gray. And it will mean a lot to Tollie, too. If we both put in some of our savings, then between us we'll make it all happen. Anyway, first things first. When will you break the news to your mum?'

'As soon as we get back to The Retreat.'

'Really?'

'Really.'

'Then it's time to encourage Rona to pop over for a visit, so we can introduce her to everyone. I think she'd get on well with Mrs Price. What do you think?'

Gray laughs softly.

'Actually, I think you're right. If we can keep everyone happy, hopefully everything will slot into place rather nicely.'

As we saunter along, he begins to hum the tune to 'Walking In A Winter Wonderland' softly under his breath.

Making a life-changing decision isn't difficult if you approach it in the right way. Although I will admit that my heart is thudding in my chest at the thought of what's to come. Happiness, I'm beginning to see, is all about having hope and not giving up on your dreams. The idea of finally settling down and being a real family is exciting. To think of Tollie sitting back contentedly in his chair, watching over his – hopefully – growing family, fills me with joy. And if Rona is prepared to think about moving, then maybe Gray and I can make it happen.

* * *

The noise is deafening, as the kids all vie to have their voices heard above the crowd. Santa is holding up the cutest little elf – the newest addition to the team – and he's asked the kids to name him. Standing about fourteen inches high, the soft toy has a cheeky grin and is a miniature version of the twins. Right down to the red-and-white-striped legs.

The screeching continues as a flurry of names floats on the air. Santa jiggles the elf about and the sound of the bell on the end of the green pointy hat is lost amongst the noise.

'Peter... Elliot... Finn...' The names keep on coming.

Suddenly, Tollie points to a little girl sitting cross-legged in the front row.

'I think we have a winner!' he declares as a hush descends.

Cupping his hand around his ear, he indicates for her to stand up.

'Ely the elf.' She twizzles the hem of her top around a finger, nervously.

'Ho! Ho! Ho! Ely the elf it is, then. Now, let me see... what do we have in here?'

Tollie places Ely on the seat next to him, then reaches across to grab one of the three sacks.

In true pantomime fashion, he undoes the twine bow and peers inside. His face is a picture as he looks back at the children, his jaw dropping.

'Well, I never. I bet you can't guess what Rudolph has delivered!' His voice booms out.

The kids are transfixed, watching every move as he gingerly places a hand inside and withdraws it slowly. Holding aloft a smaller version of the newest member of the team, he starts to chuckle.

'It seems Ely has brought along some of his friends for you to take home. Perhaps my little helpers can pass these around.'

The first of our two Little Stars cruises is going brilliantly well, and the boat is packed with five very special guests, their siblings and parents.

Tollie hands the sack to Jade and Jude, who each grab a side and begin dipping in. The kids are buzzing as they each receive one of Ely's friends.

As soon as they settle back down, we start handing out the little snack boxes to keep them occupied, so that Santa can begin talking to each of the children individually. As I usher forward a little girl named Laura, she steadfastly refuses to let go of her Ely and it makes me smile.

'Well, hello, Laura. It's lovely to meet you. I hear you've been a very brave girl and you helped your mummy.'

She nods her head, rather shyly, and Tollie waits for her to reply.

'We were getting ready for school one day and Mummy fell down, bumping her head. She showed me once how to use her phone and I rang the police to get some help. It was scary but she's fine now.'

Laura's mum is diabetic. For a five-year-old, it must have been a terrifying experience as her mum slipped in and out of consciousness, and yet this little girl remained calm, sitting with her until the paramedics arrived.

'Well, I have a twinkly little gold star here for you, as you were such a brave and helpful girl. I've heard a whisper that there's something special you've always wanted.'

Laura beams at Tollie, nodding her head. 'A tiara. Ballerinas wear them and I want to be a ballerina when I grow up, Santa.'

'What a wonderful thing to bring pleasure to people by dancing for them. It takes lots of practice, of course.'

'I go to classes, Santa,' she replies, her eyes sparkling.

'And what would you like to find beneath the Christmas tree this year, Laura?'

She chews on her lip for a moment, deep in thought. 'Well, a tiara, some new ballet shoes and I'd love a jewellery box. A musical one.'

She looks pleased with herself.

Tollie withdraws a present from one of the sacks with Laura's name written on the tag. It's about the size of a shoebox.

'This is a very special present for you, Laura, and my number one elf, Immi, has made a note of what you'd like for Christmas. My team of elves will do their very best.'

He leans in as he hands her the present.

'Thank you, Santa,' she half whispers, taking it from him with her free hand, but with no intention of letting her little Ely go. As she sits back down on the rug, her face is a picture of joy.

And the box? Well, this brave little girl deserved something fit for an aspiring ballerina. A local bridal store very generously donated the most beautiful gemstone tiara, a keepsake that maybe one day Laura will wear as a bride, who knows? But in the meantime, it will be a treasured possession, of that I have no doubt.

There are special gifts for all the children, because often what affects one child in a family impacts upon their siblings. One example is Joe. He's autistic and has an older sister and brother who keep a constant eye on him. They help to keep him safe at times when he launches himself into something without stopping to think, especially given that he's a climber. He's such a vibrant boy, and very loving, his mother told Mrs Price.

When he arrived on board, he wouldn't sit on the mat but wanted to stand in the aisle. As Tollie carries his present over to him, Joe grabs it with an excited shriek and runs off. I follow to check he's okay and find him tucked away in a little space underneath one of the tables, opening his present. He's sitting there quite happily, playing with his box of sensory toys and investigating each one. He laughs out loud as he presses a long green pod and some little peas pop out from the side, like jelly bubbles.

'Joe loves things like that.' I didn't realise his sister had crept up next to me. 'His favourite toy at the moment is an eyeball. It's squidgy and pretty gross, but it makes him laugh.'

I smile down at her. 'Have you opened your present?'

She holds up her wrist, shaking it so that the hearts on the silver bracelet twist and turn.

'I've never had a real, big girls' bracelet before. Only plastic ones,' she replies excitedly. 'I came to show it to Joe.'

In the background, Tollie is now leading a singalong before we clear away the snack boxes and story time begins. As I gaze out of the window much of the snow has disappeared in the mid-afternoon sun. This morning seems like an eternity away, already. But since we had a chat with Tollie after our early morning walk, the change in him is noticeable. I even caught him whistling away to himself earlier on. He said our news was better than any Christmas present he's likely to find under the tree.

It's going to be a wonderful Christmas, I know that, and next year will be even better. By then, the plan is that I will officially be Gray's wife. My head is buzzing at the thought of what's to come and, even though we don't want a big fuss, it's still going to take a lot of organising to bring it all together. I'd love to kick it all off with an intimate Christmas Day lunch at The Retreat, to formalise our engagement, and then I hope Gray and Rona can come and spend Christmas with us, here in Aysbury – as we'd planned last year.

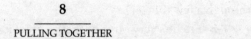
'You're not a tea drinker then, Mr Fisher,' Mrs Price observes dryly as the kettle clicks off.

We're standing in the small kitchen next to the main office at the marina on a chilly Monday morning. I convinced Fisher that, beneath that sometimes rather cool exterior, Mrs Price has a softer side, but we're off to a bit of an awkward start. The conversation so far has been rather stilted, to say the least. Yet with the flu doing the rounds, Martin is struggling to keep everything running at the Lockside Nurseries. It's their busiest time of the year and I knew Fisher would understand my dilemma. With Mrs Price offering to step in and cover my two days a week, it was the perfect solution. Besides, he's been friends with Martin long enough to know that he's not the sort of man who takes advantage of any situation just for the sake of it.

'No, I'm a coffee man, Mrs Price. I'll leave you ladies to it, then.'

I pass him his giant mug and he takes it, giving me a grateful nod as he heads back to his desk.

I brought in a teapot and some good quality teabags today, especially for Mrs Price. The mugs here are mostly freebies from sales reps and I chide myself for not bringing in a nice one to make her feel more at home.

'Sorry about the mug sporting that rather large logo. But they do sell the best engine and gear box controls.' That raises a smile as I stir in a little milk, then place the mugs on the tray. 'Shall we take this up to the viewing deck so we don't disturb Fisher while I run through a few things?'

'I'm sure he's very busy, so that's a great idea. Lead the way.'

Once we're out of earshot it's time to talk in confidence.

'Actually, Fisher is a bit quiet first thing in the morning. Once he's had his second mug of coffee he perks up and he's fine after that.'

'Ah. Thank you for the heads up. My goodness, that's some view.'

I pop the tray down and we walk over to the windows; a half-wall of glass runs the full width of the top floor of the marina building. From here the view over the canal extends in both directions and in front of us, on the opposite bank, it's possible to see over the treetops, way into the distance.

'I keep telling Fisher that they should open this to the general public. I could stand here for hours because there's always something to catch your eye. Even when there aren't many boats cruising along the canal, there are people out walking, and from that small side window you can see them working on the boats in the dry dock.'

Mrs Price saunters over to take a look, while I grab the teas and join her.

'Thank you, Immi. I think I'm going to enjoy my little stint here. I don't know Mr Fisher that well, I will admit, but I'll be mindful of the fact that he's not an early morning person. Once I know what I'm doing, I'm happy enough to just get on with it. Small talk isn't really my style, anyway. It's just nice to have something a little different to do for a couple of weeks.'

When Mrs Price flatly refused to remain as Tollie's housekeeper shortly after I arrived here, I felt she was being unfair and simply didn't like me. After that I guess I avoided her whenever I could and maybe the same was true for her.

Of course, I was rather an obnoxious, angry teen and it must have been a trying time for everyone around me. I was messy, thoughtless and moody. It also never occurred to me the effect that giving up her little job might have had on her. Did she feel lonely at times? She no longer had a reason to walk down to the canal five mornings a week and for a while I didn't really notice her absence. As time went on, she began volunteering for some of the committees and now I can appreciate why.

'Sarah and Kurt are always looking for people to help.' I throw the idea out there, in case it's not something she's considered.

We sip our tea, watching as a visiting narrowboat heads off up towards the next junction. It chugs along, leaving behind a trail of wispy wood-smoke from the log-burner. A woman walking her dog along the towpath waves out; strangers in passing, but there's something about a canal that makes even normally reserved folk feel relaxed enough to smile and wave good-naturedly.

'They've never approached me,' Mrs Price replies. 'Maybe I'm not congenial enough.'

I lower my mug, studying her face, and to my surprise she breaks out into a rather disparaging smile.

'You think I don't know that people find me a little abrupt?'

'Well, um... I wouldn't say abrupt, exactly.'

Oh dear, I wish I hadn't said anything at all now.

'I take after my mother, who was the headmistress – as it was in those days – of the village school over in Middle Norton. She was a no-nonsense lady, who believed in speaking her mind.'

'Ah, so that's your connection to the area, then. Did you end up following in her footsteps?'

Mrs Price nods her head, finishes her tea and then walks over to place the mug back on the tray.

'Yes. I taught history and French. Well, I still teach French, but these days it's from the comfort of my own little study.'

I glance at her, unable to hide my surprise.

'The company I work for, Linguispeak, offer packages for clients who need to improve their conversational and written skills. It's mainly business people that I teach, although I do support a few couples who've moved to France and need help when it comes to communicating with builders.'

'Wow. I bet that's quite interesting.'

She gives a little laugh.

'Hmm. Interesting is one word for it. Sometimes it feels more like being in the middle of two warring parties, or hard work when students have no aptitude at all. But the hours are flexible, and it suits me well enough. Right, what else do I need to know in order to keep on the good side of Mr Fisher, then?'

* * *

'Have I ever told you what a star you are?' Martin is working opposite me, the wide expanse of the workbench between us piled high with all manner of things.

'Yes. Repeatedly.'

I'm at the point where I feel I could do this in my sleep. As I twist wire around the pine cones and attach them to the natural willow wreaths, the bench is filling up fast.

'Only another twenty-six to go before we can make a start on the next order.' He grimaces.

The Lockside Nurseries service all the big manor houses in the area, as well as more than a dozen local hotels. Most of them begin trimming up as soon as Halloween is over, and we do a brisk trade in replacement lights, artificial decorations and trees. Once that rush is over, we're on to getting the wreaths set up for the fresh greenery.

If you own a lavish home, or you're paying a lot of money to enjoy a festive break in a luxurious setting, then it's all about the real thing. But in an indoor environment, particularly where there are log fires and central heating, flowers and even sprigs of greenery need constant attention. So, Martin provides a service where once a week someone goes in to remove any dead foliage and generally freshen everything up. That includes topping up the water reservoirs for the real Christmas trees to avoid the dreaded needle drop.

Often, it's quicker to put up a new wreath rather than fuss around replacing bits and pieces. But that means having a production line going here and this year, for whatever reason, it seems he's becoming the victim of his own success. Not least because the husband and wife team he employs who normally do the rounds are both out sick.

'Martin, this is crazy, you do know that?'

He wipes his sleeve across his forehead, and I can see from his flushed face that panic is beginning to set in.

'I do. And I promise, Immi, that next year will be different. We're under-staffed and if you hadn't talked Mrs Price into covering for you in the marina's office, I'd be well and truly stuffed. I've been in the business long enough to know that this time of the year there's always some sort of lurgy doing the rounds. It's just sod's law it's hit us so hard this year, at a time when we've never been busier.'

'Be careful what you wish for, as they say, Martin. I feel sorry for the pressure you're under. The orders just seem to keep on coming.'

He looks at me and the bags under his eyes tell me that he isn't sleeping well.

'Seasonal work is a nightmare. I might have to begin looking further afield for some additional help.'

My mind is going into overdrive. I wonder if... I mean, Rona is handy with her hands. She knits and she uses a sewing machine, as I recall her showing me some curtains she'd made. This is easy work that can be done sitting down and only needs that little bit of artistic flair, which she most definitely has. If Rona ends up moving to the area...

'I know that look. You're planning something.'

I give him a wide-eyed, *what me?* expression.

'Come on. Spit it out.' He isn't one to give up easily.

'This is in the strictest of confidence. Gray and I are making plans and, hopefully, by next Christmas he'll be living here at the cottage permanently.'

Martin immediately stops what he's doing.

'Immi, that's wonderful news!' he exclaims.

'Well, we're hoping that his mum, Rona, will consider moving to the area. I have no idea how amenable she'll be to the idea, but if she does come, well – she's a lady who is really into arts and crafts.'

Martin expels a big sigh.

'Goodness knows we could do with a couple of people like that. But they're thin on the ground. Look how many temporary staff we've had come and go. They don't last, Immi, do they? The only people you can really count on are the locals. People who live on the patch.'

He's right. Look at Mrs Price. She's juggling her own workload in order to help out.

'That's what I love about Aysbury, Martin. We take care of our own and I really think Rona would flourish here.'

'I also need an assistant manager, someone who can make decisions when I'm out in the van. It's not going to be easy to find someone to whom I can safely delegate that level of responsibility.

It's a real pity you can't work full-time on a permanent basis, Immi, even if it was just Monday to Friday.'

He's right, it would solve his problem, but I shrug my shoulders. I could never leave Fisher in the lurch and Martin knows that.

* * *

'Can I call everyone to order, please?'

Kurt raps on the table with his knuckles, but even so it takes a few seconds for the general chatter to die down. We're all assembled in the conservatory of The Bullrush Inn for the monthly Residents' Meeting. Everyone is free to come along and tonight it's packed. First on the agenda is some damage done to the village sign, by one of the huge lorries delivering Christmas trees to the Lockside Nurseries.

Martin is apologetic and confirms that he has it in hand. Next up there's a discussion about a few fund-raising ideas in the run-up to Christmas, to support next year's tenth anniversary dinner. Instinctively I look across at Tollie, because up to now, any discussions on this topic have been kept very separate from the general meeting.

'Whilst we're on that topic,' Tollie begins, and heads start turning in his direction. 'I know and appreciate a lot of work has already gone into this, but there's no point in me beatin' about the bush. I didn't even realise it was an anniversary; at my age you don't count the years, you count the blessings.'

Tollie has this enviable way of looking at life. It's cut and dry, very to the point and he isn't swayed by outside influences. Looking at a situation and usually managing to see it from differing perspectives, he's a fair man. He doesn't care about what people want to hear, he tells them how it is, whether that's palatable or not, because it's the truth.

'I'm not against a party, but I am against wastin' money. Let's do what we always do and that's to chip in and come together as neighbours, to raise the roof at the community centre. We'll have a dance, a bite to eat and celebrate what is a marvellous achievement all round.'

One thing Tollie is very good at is eye contact and as he scans around no one makes a move to interrupt him.

'Everyone here is involved in some way, either directly, or by spreadin' the word. And many of you are kind enough to approach your employers, and businesses far and wide to donate toys. Each year we end up with a bigger kitty to distribute amongst our featured charities and that keeps us going year after year. But if people are going to put their time and energy into raisin' funds to mark the anniversary, then we owe it to ourselves to use it wisely. What I'm proposin' is that we look at buildin' a playground alongside the canal. Somethin' with a fence and a gate, where the kids can run off a little steam while the parents sit and keep an eye.'

There's some general nodding of heads, but the truth is that no one will disagree with Tollie. He's merely pointing out the obvious – that we got carried away and lost sight of what's important.

'Show of hands?' Kurt calls out and it's unanimous.

'Do you think the local council would go along with this, Tollie?' Fisher is ever the practical one, because that's how his mind works.

'Well, you know what these things are like. It would be more likely to involve the Canal and River Trust. Negotiations can run on for months and we need to make this simple. I'll have a strip of land on the south side of Lock Keeper's Cottage fenced off; it runs adjacent to The Retreat. The only cost involved will be that of installin' the playground equipment and the correct surface, so it's compliant with current regulations.'

Abe immediately pipes up.

'The primary school at Little Hampton have just had a new play area installed. I know one of the guys who worked on the job. He owns The Sea Sprite, up at the marina. I could ask him about it and see if he can get us a discount, if you like.'

Tollie looks delighted.

'Nice one, Abe. As for general maintenance, Gray has stepped up, as has the lovely Immi. There are going to be a few changes in this next year at the cottage and, all going well, Gray will be settlin' in with us on a permanent basis.'

I can feel my cheeks glowing as all eyes are suddenly on me. I know Tollie is really happy about our news, but I had no idea he was going to blurt it out like that. I won't feel happy until I've seen Rona's reaction for myself and I don't know how soon we can make that happen.

'You kept that very quiet, Immi,' Sarah responds, looking a little miffed.

'Um... well, it's not official just yet. That's why I haven't said anything, but Gray and I are working on it.'

There's a bit of a buzz now around the table. I steal a glance at Fisher and clearly Tollie has already spoken to him, as he isn't showing any signs of surprise. In fact, he looks a little smug.

'Seems likely there will be two big parties going on next year, then,' Abe declares, and I'm just glad Gray isn't here to be put on the spot. We were supposed to be easing ourselves into this, one step at a time, not making a big announcement.

'Right, next on the agenda, if we can all settle down again, is the problem of graffiti in the public toilets at the marina.'

'Morning, Mrs Price. I thought I'd pop in on my way to the nurseries just in case you had any questions. Is Fisher about?'

She smiles at me warmly.

'He's had his two cups of coffee and he's out in the boat yard at present. I'm glad you called in. It's not urgent, but when you get an odd half-hour if you could go through the damaged stock return procedure with me, I'd be grateful. There are two items to go back and Jack simply shrugged his shoulders at me.'

Jack? No one calls Fisher Jack – in fact, I'd almost forgotten what his first name was.

'No problem. I'll arrange with Martin to leave a bit early on Friday and pop in here around three-thirty?'

'Perfect. I hear congratulations are in order, too. I was so sorry I didn't make it to the meeting, but I was teaching. I can't believe I missed such an interesting one.'

Mrs Price sounds genuinely delighted by the news. All those occasions when she hasn't been around, I thought it was because she didn't want to join in. It turns out she was working and would love to have been involved.

'Thank you. I... um, well, there's a fair bit to organise first, of course. Gray's mother, Rona, has never been to Aysbury and he's hoping she'll be free to drive over at the weekend. I'd love to introduce you to her; she's a charming lady, and it's going to be a bit daunting for her at first. She used to teach, too; infants, I believe, so you have something in common.'

'Yes, of course – that would be delightful. I'm free all weekend, in between clipping the Santa Ahoy cruise tickets, of course.'

'Perfect. I'm hoping we can fit in an afternoon tea at The Bullrush Inn and introduce her to a few of our friends.'

I feel so guilty now, for thinking of Mrs Price as rather aloof. And it looks as if Fisher is happy to have her around, too, because if he wasn't, he'd be on the phone to me in an instant.

'Right, I must get off. Martin was panicking yesterday, and I'm keeping my fingers crossed everyone turns up for work today. We were three down again and I ended up having to go out in the van with him to give a hand with some deliveries. Actually...' I lean in, lowering my voice '... I enjoy freshening up the floral arrangements. But don't breathe a word to Fisher. He's already annoyed that I give Martin more time than I give him.'

Her mouth twitches.

'Jack told me you're like a daughter to him, Immi, and he meant it.'

'Yes, well, I'm a bit annoyed with both him and Tollie, to be honest with you. But I've managed to cool down a little. Sometimes they forget that I'm a grown woman, perfectly capable of organising my own life.'

Mrs Price's eyes open a little wider in surprise as I head off, muttering to myself. It seems that everyone is now aware that Gray is going to become a permanent member of our happy little band.

I'm pretty sure that Tollie knew what he was doing at the meeting; it wasn't something that simply slipped out. He was making sure Gray and I don't drag our feet. I don't know whether to feel cross that Tollie is still trying to steer me along my path in life, or touched that he's so convinced Gray and I are right for each other.

As I exit the marina, it's time to step up the pace – I'm running behind. I spot Fisher coming towards me.

'Everything okay?' he asks, a slight frown etched on his forehead.

'It is, thank you. I'll pop in on Friday, but I can't stop now. I'm late.'

His frown deepens as we pass by, but I keep walking. He turns to call after me, but I don't look back.

'You're cross with me, I can tell. No harm meant, Immi.' His voice gets louder the further away I get, as he tries to make amends. 'It's going to be a great Christmas, though.'

I nonchalantly wave my arm in the air, while breaking into a jog. It doesn't hurt to let him stew for a bit. It's time to put a halt to the meddling.

My phone starts to ping, but I don't have time to stop and see who it is; I bet its Fisher telling me to be careful I don't trip and fall into the canal, or something equally ridiculous. And overprotective.

I glance up at the sky. It's another beautiful day and several degrees warmer than yesterday. The early morning frost is almost gone, already. I'm praying that it stays like this through to the weekend and Rona is able to drive herself over. How could anyone not think of this as a little slice of heaven, and the perfect place to move to be close to family?

* * *

'You've been glued to your phone for the last twenty minutes,' Martin complains as he polishes off the last of his sandwich.

I nod, munching as fast as I can in between texting Gray. He still doesn't have anything firm lined up for work and there are no more cheques in the pipeline. He had high hopes for a big project, one that would really take him in the direction he longs to go, but communication has gone ominously quiet. After a little back and forth, he suddenly changes the subject.

Mum's definitely up for driving over on Saturday. I suggested she join us for the second cruise. I think she'd enjoy that. She's looking forward to afternoon tea at The Bullrush.

Does that mean he's told her everything and had *the* chat about moving?

Great. I've invited Mrs Price along. I'll book a table in the conservatory. How is Rona doing in general?

He'll know I'm fishing.

We had a talk about the house, and I pointed out that it needs a fair bit of work doing to it now. I sowed the seed. Hopefully Saturday we can build on that.

I let out a sigh. It would have been better to sit her down and tell her exactly what's happening and the fact he'd be happier if she was nearby. But I can't interfere, and I don't want to upset him.

Great. I must go. Lunch is nearly over and Martin is waiting for me. We're off to the Linden Hotel. We're decking out the big function room for a corporate Christmas party on Thursday. No expense spared. Speak later. x

Martin and a couple of the guys are already loading the van.

'Is Gray alright?' he enquires as I walk past him with my arms clutched around an oversized box containing a garland for a mantelpiece.

'He's good. His work tends to tail off at Christmas. He's always writing tunes, so he keeps busy, but he worries about cash flow.'

'When you're self-employed it's always a concern. I've had my tough years, wondering whether I could keep afloat, and now it's going the other way. I've just swapped one load of worries for another, it seems. Right, I think we can head back to get the rest of the boxes now.'

He half turns, calling out over his shoulder.

'Grab your coats, guys, we have a long afternoon ahead of us.'

* * *

'I owe you an apology for blurtin' out your news, Immi.' Tollie at least has the decency to look genuinely sorry. 'I just got a tad carried away, I'm afraid.'

There's a little sparkle in his eye that hasn't been there for a while. He's been worrying about Gray and me, and now he feels he can finally relax. Which makes me feel guilty, so how can I be annoyed with him?

'I don't believe a word of it, but I'll forgive you, all the same. We are determined to keep the engagement celebration small, though.'

Collapsing down rather gratefully onto the sofa, I'm exhausted from a long afternoon climbing ladders and trekking back and forth to the van.

'I'll happily foot the bill if you want to hold it at The Bullrush. Everyone will be expectin' an invitation, Immi.'

My phone pings and it's an excuse to avoid eye contact. It's a text from Gray.

'Tollie, that's very kind of you but we don't want to make a big fuss. There's too much going on in the run-up to Christmas. We were rather hoping to have some quality family time together, rather than a party.'

'This is about Rona, isn't it?'

I shrug my shoulders as I push the phone back into my pocket.

'That will need some sorting, admittedly. Which is why we want to take it slowly. But this is the quiet time of the year for Gray, work-wise, which means he's worried about money, too. With the hours I'm working I can pay for a party, but he's a proud man; you know what he's like.'

Tollie looks at me rather glumly. 'I said the wrong thing, at the wrong time – that wasn't fair. I shouldn't have meddled, Immi, but – well, I didn't stop to think about the implications.'

'It's not your fault, it's just the circumstances. I suggested to Gray that we wait until the spring to celebrate our engagement, but he wouldn't hear of it. He's so happy now the decision has been made that he just wants to make it all happen. But we both agree that we keep the celebration small and no one gets carried away. The fact it's all being arranged at such short notice is the perfect excuse, to be honest. I'll get my head around it somehow.'

'Fair enough. I'm sure folk will understand. I'm assumin' the weddin' bash will make up for it, though?'

I let out an exasperated tut. 'Tollie, please! Yes, we'll have a big party and all the locals will be invited. However, I'm warning you now that the wedding itself is going to be a very simple, and small, affair. The last thing I want is Gray worrying about what it's all going to cost. If Rona isn't able to find herself a nice little job, then she's reliant upon him to help her out.'

I can't let Tollie know that Gray intends adding his own little nest egg to mine, so we can pay for the renovation work to bring the cottage up to date for him. And I certainly don't want Tollie frittering away his life savings on things that aren't necessary, like an over-the-top wedding.

'Well, I might as well say what's on my mind, then. I've been waitin' for the right moment and it's been a long time comin'.'

Tollie raises his eyebrows, a little tic suddenly flickering away at the side of his eye. He's emotional and I need to sit quietly and hear him out.

'When your grandma knew she was dyin', being the type of woman she was, I was given my orders. So, you can't argue with this, Immi, because it was her wish. Whatever your weddin' costs, the money has already been earmarked. You have what makes you and Gray happy, because it's sorted.'

He pauses and I resist the temptation to interrupt him, thoughts of Grandma making my eyes prickle with tears.

'There's one more thing. Well, two, as a matter of fact. The first is that she wanted me to give you her engagement ring when the time was right.' Tollie eases himself up out of his chair and walks over to the carved wooden box that has always graced the mantelpiece. Lifting off the lid, he dips inside and turns, holding out a small velvet pouch to me.

I stand and walk towards him, as our eyes meet. The look we exchange is one of uneasy sadness, and we both have tears in our eyes as I undo the string. Pulling out Grandma's ring, I lay it flat on the palm of my hand.

'It's beautiful, Tollie. I always thought that. And I'm grateful to you both. I will treasure it always.'

He takes a moment to compose himself, but when he starts speaking again his voice is uneven.

'It's likely you'll want your own ring, of course, but she was insistent that I waited for this moment to give it to you. She said it would remind you that her love is around you always.'

I stare down at the vintage, eighteen-carat, white-gold ring, which I admired even as a very small child. The octagonally cut aqua stone is stunning, with a small baguette diamond on each shoulder of the setting. Grandma told me the story many times over, of how Tollie insisted on taking her ring shopping. When she looked in the window, he saw the aqua stone catch her eye, but she instinctively turned and pointed to a much less expensive ring. He'd had to almost drag her inside to get her finger measured, as she was loath to see him spend his hard-earned money. She told him a ring wasn't necessary to win her heart.

On the day of their engagement when she opened the box, she said she almost fainted when she saw the aqua ring. She told him off and, apparently, everyone burst out laughing. He had to talk her out of returning it. Grandma gave in when she realised Tollie wasn't simply trying to impress her, but it was a mark of his love for her.

I place it back inside the pouch and step forward to accept Tollie's embrace.

'This is the ring I want, and I know that Gray will understand. It means so much, Tollie. Besides, I'd rather he helped sort his mum out financially and this feels like a gift to us both.'

Standing back, I can see his relief at my reaction.

'Well, m'dear, she'd be proud, for sure. With regard to Rona, houses here aren't cheap, but it would be nice for her to be close by. As we get older, every memory we make is precious. That's why I want you and Gray to take over the cottage. It's time it had a facelift to see it through its next stage in life. Think on it, Immi. I'm just being practical. There's little point in me fixin' this place up, as the pair of you will have your own ideas. It needs extendin' in my opinion. Do it once and do it right for the future. When I'm gone The Retreat will be a way of earning a little extra and you'll no doubt be glad of it.'

'Oh, Tollie – let's not make any hasty decisions; we can talk about this after Christmas. And as for the engagement party, well, I had an idea which I put to Gray and he just texted a thumbs up. What do you think about having a small gathering on Christmas Day? I know that's a bit unusual, but it gets around the problem of not inviting every single person we know in Aysbury.'

I give him a pointed look and Tollie puts his head back, chuckling.

'Christmas Day?'

'Yep. Fisher's on his own and so is Mrs Price, so I'm sure they'd be delighted to come along. With Rona, Gray and the two of us that's six, but I also thought it would be rather nice to invite Ethel and Abe. Sarah, Kurt and the girls will be at her mum's, of course, so they won't feel left out. Can I cope catering for eight people, do you think?'

'You bet. Sounds perfect to me, if that's what will make you happy.'

'Oh, I'm so looking forward to Christmas Day now. It feels like a turning point, Tollie. Anyway, that's enough planning for now. It's been a long day and I'm shattered, so I'm off to bed. Sleep well and thank you – Granddad.'

He tips his head, leaning in to plant a kiss on my cheek. It's been a long time since I called him that – he'll always be simply Tollie, to everyone who knows him, as he was to Grandma Nell. But he's touched to see me feeling emotional, as I recall Christmases when I was too young to use his nickname.

'I've waited a long time to see a smile like that on your face, m'dear. Everyone will welcome Rona, don't you worry – she's a kind-hearted lady. And there's a bit of money left in the pot to help with doin' up this place properly for the pair of you. Right, I'm off to The Bullrush to grab a pint with Fisher. See you in the mornin'.'

As I close the back door of the cottage behind me, I'm not sure how I feel about the thought of Tollie not living here any more. It doesn't feel right, somehow, and I know that Gray will feel awkward about it, too. Maybe once Gray is here permanently we can talk Tollie into staying put but suggest we all pull together to put in a new kitchen, to start with. It would certainly be nice if we could freshen things up. Doing it ourselves, we can make excuses about being settled in The Retreat and carry out the work on the cottage at a pace Tollie is happy to accept. With Gray's things around us, The Retreat will soon begin to feel like our home together, I'm sure of it, and we wouldn't feel we were pushing Tollie out of his.

'I love it when a plan comes together,' I whisper into the darkness, swinging open the front door to The Retreat and stepping inside. 'It's payback time, Granddad,' I murmur aloud.

It might take until next summer to get Gray here, but there's so much to look forward to. Turning on the lights, then sinking down onto the sofa, I grab my phone when it kicks into life.

'Did you get my text?' The sound of Gray's voice makes my heart skip a beat.

'Yes. I was talking to Tollie, so I couldn't respond.'

'Oh. Did you put forward the idea about Christmas Day lunch?'

'I did. And he thought it was a good idea. And Mrs Price is going to join us for tea at The Bullrush this Saturday. I told her your mum used to teach.'

Gray starts humming the strains of 'Hallelujah' and I burst out laughing. Do I spoil his mood and ask if he's heard anything about work? On reflection, I don't have the heart, so I tackle him about the other issue.

'Tollie knows the cottage needs attention. The kitchen and bathroom are well past their sell-by date, let's be honest. He wants us to have the cottage, but it doesn't feel right, Gray. It was his home with Grandma. He's jumping too far ahead, intent on handing everything over, as if we're swapping roles. Which is ridiculous.'

'I totally agree with you, Immi.' Gray responds instantly.

'I hoped you would. There's one other thing we need to discuss;

something that means a lot to me.'

'Uh-oh, it sounds like you've already made up your mind about whatever it is.'

'Before Grandma died, she told Tollie that she wanted me to have her engagement ring. It's truly beautiful, Gray, and I really hope you understand that it's her gift to us. She might not have met you, but she knew that one day I'd find my Mr Right, and this would make her a part of our celebration.'

I take a deep breath and hold it in, anxiously awaiting his response. I don't want Gray feeling undermined in any way.

'Well, I will admit it's taken me by surprise, as I was looking forward to going ring shopping together. I mean, I don't want to upset you if your mind is made up, but you deserve a bit of spoiling and this was going to be my moment.'

Finally expelling my breath, I screw up my eyes in the semidarkness, keeping my fingers crossed this doesn't turn into a thing between us.

'I'm grateful for that thought, Gray, really I am, and there will be lots of little moments to come when you can spoil me. But this means a lot, more than any modern piece of jewellery ever could. There's also a wedding fund she left for me. Oh, I've told Tollie straight that we don't want a lavish affair, but that we will have a big party afterwards. He says whatever we want is fine, but he and Grandma put aside a pot of money for this occasion. Out of respect I think we need to accept it graciously. There's no arguing with Tollie, at times.'

Gray is ominously silent.

'It's very generous, but that hardly seems fair on him, Immi. I mean, hopefully I'll get some cash together to share the cost of it. Admittedly, Mum doesn't have much, but I was thinking we could involve her in the arrangements, so that her contribution really counts for something. And I'm still adamant that what I have in the bank goes to fixing up the cottage. That's something Tollie is going to have to accept.'

I was concerned this was going to be a little awkward but I'm glad to be addressing the issues in one fell swoop.

'Of course. And that's a wonderful idea about Rona, Gray, as we'll need all the practical help we can get. The thought of having to organise a wedding is a little daunting, so I'm perfectly happy for her to take charge if she wants to do so. But please let's not make this about who pays for what. Tollie wants to do this for us. If it means that leaves you in a better position to help your mum get settled here, then that will make everyone happy, won't it?'

Another silence. I sit, my fingers nervously skimming over the cushion next to me. Money and property are two such emotive issues. I don't want Gray to feel he's being forced into doing something he's not happy about.

'Immi, is this what you really want, or are you doing it to make the best of the situation we're in? I don't want you to compromise for the sake of it and end up harbouring regrets.'

'Gray, I just want us to be together and for everyone to be happy. That includes Rona, and Tollie – of course – and all our friends. Grandma's ring is a celebration of love and does it really matter who pays for what? We can repay Tollie and Grandma's kindness, by sorting out the cottage. That doesn't mean we'll move in, but he's not to know that.'

An affirming 'okay' comes back a few seconds later.

'We're lucky, aren't we?' Gray continues. 'I only have one request and it's that I buy your wedding dress. It's your choice entirely, but it's my gift to you.'

'Oh... you're not expecting some silly ball gown, are you?'

He laughs. 'Surprise me. Will I be doing the suit thing?'

I frown, giving it some serious consideration.

'Let's do it in the summer and dispense with the jackets. I'm thinking of a cornfield with poppies... a floaty knee-length dress and you in a casual white shirt, and trousers. What do you think?'

'Okay... sounds interesting, if we can talk the vicar into it, of course.'

When you truly love someone, anything is doable. Stumbling blocks are rarely insurmountable, they are simply detours that end up taking you in the right direction.

'You, me, the vicar, Rona, Tollie and Fisher in a field. Then later in the day, a big party at the village hall, catered by Sarah and Kurt. What do you think?'

A loud 'hmm' filters down the line.

'It's fine by me if that does it for you. But good luck getting that past Sarah, Kurt and the girls, Martin, Mrs Price, Abe and then there's my crowd from London. I daren't leave anyone out and choosing a best man is going to be a tough decision. You'll understand once you meet them all.'

'Okay. That guest list for the ceremony might need a little tweaking. Just the teensiest bit.'

'I'm staying well out of it. You tell me what you want done and I'll do it.'

Gray is beginning to sound a little overwhelmed already.

'Your task is to focus on Rona. You won't be happy unless you know she's settled and happy. We all know she can't stay where she is because it's not practical. She wants you to be happy, but we want her to be happy, too. So, you concentrate on that and leave the rest to me. Is that a deal?'

'Yes, boss. And I'm looking forward to doing up the cottage for Tollie – at least that's something I can do. Mum won't let me loose on her place because her heart isn't in it any more, so the sooner she cuts the last of her emotional ties with it, the better. I love you, Immi. You've made our wedding about everyone and not just about us. And that's precisely why I fell in love with you in the first place.'

As I'm packing up to head over to see Mrs Price, Martin suddenly reappears after being absent for a couple of hours.

'I'm glad I managed to catch you before you left, Immi. We were stuck in traffic and the deliveries seemed to take forever. At this rate we're going to run out of Christmas trees, can you believe it? I wanted to say a huge *thank you* for everything. Not just the extra help, but you've worked tirelessly this week and it's appreciated. More than you know. I will admit I woke up on Monday morning wishing I could just roll over and go back to sleep. That isn't me, as I'm not a quitter, but I had no idea how we were going to get through what needed to be done. And now it's Friday, our customers are happy and we survived. I owe you, big time.'

I shift from one foot to the other, feeling a little embarrassed.

'It's my pleasure, Martin, and it was teamwork. We had a laugh and I think I've probably lost a few pounds climbing ladders and running back and forth to the van. So, it's all good. I'm equally relieved that we managed to get everything done. Fingers crossed, next week will be a little less frenetic if everyone is finally back to work.'

He holds up his left hand, doing just that.

'When you see Fisher, tell him I owe him a drink next time I'm in The Bullrush. How's he been getting on with Mrs Price?'

Martin looks at me, hesitantly.

'Better than I expected. I promised I'd call in as soon as I finish here today, but Mrs Price has been a great help and she's a quick learner.'

His face brightens. 'And you're good for next week, too?'

'Yes. That should see you through the busiest period. We haven't even trimmed up at home yet, so I'm hoping to take off the last few days before Christmas to get things sorted.'

'Of course. And whatever you need from here, you just help yourself. Word is that you're having a quiet engagement celebration.'

Obviously Tollie has continued spreading the news.

'Yes. It all happened so quickly and with the Santa cruises wiping out the weekends, there just isn't time to organise a big party. I don't suppose you and the family are around on Christmas Day?'

This is uncomfortable, and I do feel bad, as I know they aren't.

'No, sadly. We're away as usual. This year it's the in-laws' turn, as we alternate it with my parents. Why on earth they're happy for us to descend on them for three days with the kids and a dog in tow, I have no idea. It would have been nice to have popped in for a quick celebratory drink with you all, just to mark the occasion. But we'll definitely catch up with the two of you as soon as we get back, I promise.'

As I head off in the direction of the marina, I am a little bit sad not to be able to get everyone together. But the problem with Aysbury is that it's all, or nothing.

'You've made Tollie's Christmas, you do know that?'

I spin around to see Abe striding out to catch up with me.

'Yes, so it seems. Has he mentioned Christmas Day lunch to you?'

'You bet.' Abe beams. 'I'm off to tell Ethel now. She'll be thrilled to bits. We'll come loaded up with a home-made Christmas pudding and Christmas cake. You know what she's like. That woman loves to bake.'

'Well, the kids adore her gingerbread men and the star cookies. Last Christmas was rather quiet, so it'll be nice to have a little gathering this year. Say hello to Ethel from me and I'll see you tomorrow. If she needs any help with the baking in the morning, just shout.'

'Will do, but she should be fine as Mrs Price has already offered – bye, lovely!'

Abe takes the right fork to cross over the bridge as I trudge along the winding path. There's a bitterly cold wind today and it's a battle to keep the hood of my coat covering my hair. I really hope it isn't like this tomorrow, but maybe it will at least blow away those ominously heavy rain clouds.

By the time I walk into the office I'm so cold that I head straight over to the radiator, making no attempt to take off my coat.

'You look like you need a hot drink,' Fisher says, pushing back on his chair.

Mrs Price indicates for him to sit back down. 'I'll make it.'

'Thank you, Valerie. There's a box of mince pies in the cupboard.'

My jaw drops in surprise. Valerie? Mince pies? I snap my mouth shut as Fisher looks at me, a tad sheepishly.

'You've had a tough week, Immi. I bumped into one of Martin's guys in The Bullrush last night. He said it's been non-stop.'

'Since when are you on first-name terms with Mrs Price?' I whisper, keeping an eye on the door.

Fisher strides over to stand next to me, pretending to look nonchalantly out of the window.

'It surprised me, too. Did you know she teaches French?' He keeps his voice low.

I nod. 'Yes, she told me on Monday. I didn't even know she had a job.'

I listen out but can still hear her moving around in the kitchen.

'I was a bit nervous when you first suggested the idea of her coming in, but she's been a great help. Do you think I should offer to take her out for a drink, to say thanks? I mean, she did step in at short notice and the pay isn't overly-generous.'

The door suddenly opens, and we spring apart.

'Fisher just suggested that we all meet up for a drink in The Bullrush tonight, Mrs Price, as a thank you. What do you think?'

'Oh, that would be lovely. What a nice thought, Jack.'

He hurries over to make room on the desk for the tray. I sneak a look at them and there's a little flirting going on there, for sure. Slipping off my coat and grabbing a mince pie, I turn towards the door.

'Right. I'll go and find those return forms, then.'

I leave them to it for a few minutes, and when I walk back into the room they're laughing, so much so that I hang back a little. The moment they spot me they immediately stop, and Mrs Price gives me an apologetic look as she carries across two mugs of tea.

'Right. Let's do this, then, Immi, so you can get off home.'

Fisher doesn't look at me as he grabs his coat off the hook, but the vestiges of his smile are still etched on his face. 'I'll take mine out with me. It's almost locking-up time and I want to grab the work sheets before the men leave for the day. See you later.'

As soon as he's gone, I turn to Mrs Price, raising my eyebrows.

'Well, Fisher's in a happy frame of mind.'

'Is he? He's been like that all week. So, these are kept in the stationery cupboard, then? I did have a good look but wasn't sure what was what.' She points to the small stack of forms in my hand.

'Yes, but, as they're not used very often, I always kept them on the very top shelf, on the left-hand side. We're a bit low on a few things, I notice, so I'll run through a stationery order with you, too. If you can fax it across on Monday, that will tide us over until the middle of January. They'll be shut for two weeks over Christmas and New Year. So, how has it been?'

She nods enthusiastically, finishing off a mouthful of pastry.

'Good. Enjoyable, actually. How about you?'

'Tiring. But Martin is a lot happier. I can't believe what we managed to get done. He built his business from scratch and if anyone deserves to succeed, it's him.'

'He has two girls, doesn't he?'

'Yes. Sadly, his eldest daughter has Crohn's disease and arthritis. She was diagnosed about a year after he started the business. She was very ill for a while, constantly in and out of hospital. It was a tough time and adding money worries into the mix meant it was a hellish period for him. Finally, she's doing well and so is the business, but being short-staffed during his busiest season has been a headache.'

Mrs Price is watching me with interest.

'You care about everyone here, don't you?' she asks, pointedly.

I shift a little in my chair.

'I arrived here a moody teen with a chip on my shoulder and they welcomed me into the community because of their love for Tollie. They put up with my antics for a good few years, as you're aware, much more graciously than I deserved. Now they are my family too.'

'That's a lovely way to look at it, Immi. My family are scattered, some long gone. I grew tired of being surrounded by people who turn everything into a drama. Life is simpler for me here, but I'm beginning to see that loneliness is an awful thing. Shutting people out might make for a quiet life, but it's not fulfilling.'

For a moment, the look on her face is one of intense sadness and maybe regret. It makes me catch my breath.

'I'm sorry to hear that, Mrs Price.'

'Please, call me Valerie. I think it's time I stopped pushing people away.'

In the midst of my surprise at this unexpected turn of events, I remember some information I came across while I was at the Linden Hotel.

'Before I forget, if you let me have your phone number I'll send you some photos you might find of interest. I think it could be a clue about the family who originally owned Lock Keeper's Cottage.'

I can see her interest is piqued.

'Well, that's unexpected. I do love pulling random clues together to solve a mystery. It's so important to learn from the past, even if it's simply to avoid repeating the same mistakes. I'll look forward to seeing what you've discovered and where it might lead.'

* * *

Gray messages to say that the car has broken down and it's a real shame this should happen tonight. I text Fisher to explain that I might need to go and fetch him and it's unlikely we'll be able to meet up for a drink later. It would have been rather pleasant for Gray and me to while away an hour or two in The Bullrush with him and Mrs Price. I mean, Valerie. A text alert pings and it's another update.

Recovery are here and are going to give me a jump-start. I'll head off to try and get a replacement battery. There's a late-night garage a few miles away and the guy is going to ring them to see if they can help. I might be a couple of hours yet.

I glance up at the clock. It's already gone seven and Gray must be shattered. He had to drive back from London, and it involved a very early start.

Why not come straight here? We can get it sorted in the morning. There's no point driving around in the dark when you don't know the area.

'Is he on his way?' Tollie calls out from the kitchen.
'Not yet.'
Ping.

Okay. You're right. I'm hungry and cold. And missing you. I'll be there in about an hour and a half unless the car cuts out on me again.

Every mile he drives brings him a mile closer to me.

In which case, I'll come and collect you.

'It's going to be a while, Tollie. I'll wait and eat with Gray when he gets here.'
Tollie walks back into the sitting room.
'The pies are done; you'll just need to reheat them. I might as well pop to The Bullrush, then, and catch up with Fisher.'
I give him a knowing little smile and he does a double take.
'What?'
'Nothing. Enjoy your pint.'
He pulls on his waterproof. 'It's tippin' down out there. Still, at

least it's warmed up a little. See you later, then. Text me when Gray arrives, just so I know he's all right.'

I nod, settling back on the sofa to while away the next hour or so. Having sent Valerie the photos I took at the Linden Hotel, I decide to go online and do a little digging myself, using Tollie's laptop.

It was a real surprise when I took a careful look at the framed photos in the lobby. I've been there a few times in the past and never really stopped to check them out. But on one of the many trips back and forth to the van, one of them caught my eye. On closer inspection, I was convinced I'd seen the man's face before – in the pile of photos I'd looked through with Valerie. It bore an inscription: Henry Smythe, Aysbury 1946. What was even more interesting was the fact that he was standing in the garden of Lock Keeper's Cottage.

The Smythes – or what became the Harrington-Smythes some time in the nineteen eighties, from the little I've unearthed – are major landowners in this area. But I have no idea why his photograph was among that random collection we sorted through, which were mainly views of the canal and the surrounds.

Tollie bought the place from a Mr and Mrs Carter, but that was almost fifty years ago. Annoyingly, the original deeds were lost – as many were, back in the day. I bet they would have made for fascinating reading. Often an historical parcel of deeds didn't just contain documentation regarding ownership of the property, but all manner of things: death certificates of former inhabitants, copies of wills, as well as old receipts relating to parcels of land being purchased, or sold, and any work carried out. They could tell a story in yellowing documents, some on parchment bearing official seals, even personal, handwritten letters.

Kurt once showed me a folder of documents he has for The Bullrush, some going back to the early eighteen hundreds. There was even a document requisitioning what was The Anchor Inn at the time, as a temporary hospice. It was following an outbreak of cholera among the boat people in the eighteen thirties. It was believed to have been spread when a skipper brought his laundry ashore to be cleaned by a local washer woman. The disease spread quickly and there were seventy cases in total; nineteen people died – including the woman who took in the washing.

When we buy a property, we become a part of its living history; the history of a building that often stands for generations to come. But we're only passing through, merely temporary custodians in a long line of owners.

I can understand Rona's attachment to the only house she's ever lived in since Gray was born. In the same way that Tollie could never sell the cottage, because his memories of Grandma are here and passing it on to Gray and me is important to him. My future here with Gray is going to feature in the history of this place and I wonder if that is selfish of me. I know Gray misses the friends and colleagues he left behind in London, but that didn't change because of me. But now he's back with Rona, will she understand, or will she feel I'm being unfair? After all, I suspect a part of the reason she's still in her marital home are the wonderful memories she once experienced there, as a happy young bride. No one marries expecting their relationship to fall apart, do they? Having Gray there again is a comfort and one she might not want to give up.

'Morning, Immi. All alone?'

Ethel appears, with her wicker basket packed full of home-baked goodies for the kids.

'Yes. Gray's car battery is dead and Fisher took him off first thing to get a replacement.'

She heads down towards the galley, talking as she walks.

'Another change in the weather, I see. It's pleasingly mild today and that's one beautiful sky.'

'I know I shouldn't say this, having already slipped on the ice once this winter, but it's not quite as Christmassy when it's like this, is it?'

Ethel laughs. 'You can't have it both ways, lovey.'

There's a loud tapping sound on the glass and I look up to see a hand waving back at me. Then I realise it's Rona and I leap up.

'You found us all right, then?' I say, ushering her in. 'Mind the steps as you come down. I thought Gray said you weren't coming until later this afternoon.'

Rona's face lights up. 'I thought I might be able to help, if that's okay. And Gray told me about the plans for Christmas Day – I'm so excited I couldn't sleep last night. My, isn't this cosy?'

I lean in to give her a hug and she pats my back affectionately – lingering a little longer than usual. Her delight is lighting up her face, adding that touch of colour she's been missing the last couple of times I visited her.

'I'm still taking it all in. Anyway, I'm so glad you found us all right. Ethel,' I call out, 'this is Rona, Gray's mum.'

Ethel gives a wave. 'I'm up to my elbows in biscuits and mince pies, so excuse me for the moment. It's nice to meet you, Rona, and welcome to Aysbury.'

'Thank you and if there's anything I can do, just let me know. My, the cinnamon hits your nose and together with the greenery it smells delightfully Christmassy in here.'

I haven't seen Rona for a couple of months and the difference in her is incredible. I almost did a double take when I first set eyes on her. Maybe it isn't just our news that has brightened her spirits, but she really is feeling a lot more like her old self. She was looking a little frail at one point, but she's regained some weight and it suits her. Rona's hair has regrown and, while it's very short still, she's had it styled and it's very flattering.

Ethel finally makes her way towards us to shake hands.

'Why don't you two go off in search of Tollie? I'll sort out the galley and then set things up on the tables, Immi. Abe will be here soon enough; he'll keep an eye on the fire.'

I give Ethel a grateful hug, slip on my coat and Rona follows me out onto the towpath.

'You look very well, Rona. Sorry it's been a while, but I've been stretched thin, lately. Juggling two jobs and getting everything set up for the cruises means it's hard to get away.'

She turns to look at me, obviously delighted to be here and

showing no signs of concern over my absence. Or upset that her son will, at some point, call Aysbury *home*.

'Oh, I know how hard you work, Immi. Gray talks about you all the time. I've told him he has to stop worrying about me now. At my last check-up everything was fine.'

'Gray said you were seeing a therapist to help with the anxiety?'

'Oh, I am and that will continue for a while longer. But moving to six-monthly check-ups is a landmark when you've had cancer and it's a turning point. It means they have confidence the treatment has worked.'

It's really good to hear her sounding so upbeat and the relief is very evident in her tone.

'Things are finally getting back to normal and, while my hair may never be quite the same again, I'm feeling strong and positive. They do say when your hair grows back the texture is different and I still struggle to style it – that's why I keep it short, rather than growing it out.'

I can't even begin to imagine what Rona has been through in the last eleven months. Longer, even, as she was unwell for months before she was diagnosed.

'The anxiety made me nervous driving for a while there, I will admit,' she continues. 'But Gray arranged for me to have a few lessons until I regained my confidence. It made all the difference and, now I'm feeling more like my old self again, there won't be any stopping me.'

Does that mean Rona will be going back to work, so she can keep the house? Gray and I both hoped she'd be close by so we can pop in on her. How will he feel if that isn't going to be the case?

'I'm so glad to hear that, Rona.'

Her eyes are darting around everywhere and today it's busy so there's a lot to see. We stop to admire the steady stream of boats passing by and Rona leans in to inform me that today will be her first trip on a real barge.

'They're referred to as narrowboats,' I explain.

'Tollie!' I wave out as I spot him just about to head over the bridge on his way to the marina.

He turns, smiling broadly as soon as he catches sight of Rona. Tollie immediately strides forward and we increase our pace to meet him. They've only met once before and that was last summer, but he takes the obvious change in her appearance in his stride.

'Rona, how lovely to see you.' Tollie stoops to kiss her cheek. 'And we have a cause to celebrate.'

She scrunches up her face in a beaming smile and inwardly I groan. If these two put their heads together who knows what the outcome might be?

'I know. At last. It was tough having to rely so heavily on Gray, but now things can really begin moving forward for these two. It's exciting. Gray is so happy when he's here. He returns relaxed and ready for the week ahead, which isn't easy for him right now with his work being so quiet. His life in London was very different and he misses being a part of that, but this is where he longs to be.'

Tollie frowns. Gray doesn't say a lot about work in front of him.

'Are the problems a temporary blip?'

'He doesn't like talking about it. Work is such a constant worry for him, though. I really don't know what he's going to do about it. It's a tough industry and very competitive. It's as much about who you know to get your foot in the door, rather than how talented you are. Which is a real shame, as he's running out of options. He's talking about applying for a job in a sound studio, but I know he'd get bored. Gray is creative and composing is his dream, not just writing little jingles, or playing backing tracks on someone else's work. He sees rhythm in everything around him. When he's not at home, I will admit that I miss constantly hearing him playing those little tunes he keeps coming up with.'

They exchange pleasant smiles. Tollie misses that, too, when Gray returns home – as I do.

I know he's been under pressure, but Rona's words are a real cause for concern. Gray should have been sharing his worries with me, but he's been sparing me the worst, it seems. I knew he was missing his mates, but I didn't quite realise how important his trips to London were in terms of reminding people he's still available. The fact that this might not be just a temporary dip for him comes as quite a shock. I find it hard to believe he's about to give up on his dream, though.

'I'm sure the new year will bring with it lots of fresh opportunities,' Tollie replies, doing his best to sound upbeat. 'It's bound to be quiet on the run-up to Christmas.'

The three of us are trying hard to be optimistic, but I think we're all feeling the same level of concern. It must be bad for Gray to even consider working for someone else again.

'We're heading back to the cottage, Tollie. Can you join us?'

He shakes his head, sadly. 'Fisher just rang. He asked me to pop into the boat yard. There's some sort of problem and he's still at the garage with Gray.'

'Oh, right. Well, we'll sit and have a cup of tea and see you back onboard The Star Gazer a little later, then.'

'Will do. Enjoy yourselves, ladies.'

He strides off and Rona catches my arm in hers, giving it a squeeze.

'Gray will sort something out, Immi. You two have so much to look forward to and I can't wait to hear about the plans. I wanted to ask if there's anything I can do to help with the Christmas Day lunch celebration? He said you weren't keen on having a big party.'

I steer her towards the cottage, and she lingers for a moment at the gate, taking it all in.

'This is a beautiful old building. I was expecting a rather plain stone cottage. Lock keepers weren't paid a lot, were they?'

'No. That's why the cottages usually came with a fair bit of land, as they often needed to grow their own vegetables to supplement their income. Most had families to feed and some would sell produce, too. It gave them a roof over their heads and a basic living. This one is a little special though, so whoever built this had money. It's unusual, I agree, as it wasn't a position that carried any social standing with it.'

'Well, I can fully understand your attachment to it, Immi. No wonder Gray is happy here.'

Any fears I had about Rona being unsettled by our news is fading fast. She's happy for us both and, having been through a hellish time, maybe she will find the choice about her own situation easier to handle. It puts everything into perspective, that's for sure.

I unlock the front door and indicate for Rona to step inside.

'It's bigger than I thought it was going to be. And so charming.'

Slipping off my coat, I give her a knowing smile.

'Charming, but rather tired and worn out. Everything works – just – but the kitchen and bathroom are tiny. Tollie is keen to extend on the side and have a wall of glass doors looking out over the pastureland and the woods to the east. He had plans drawn up to extend it into a three-bed, two-bathroom a few years ago, but says he can't face living on a building site.'

'But Gray says that there's another building?'

'Yes. I've lost count of the number of times I've tried to talk Tollie into moving into The Retreat with me while we make a start on the cottage. Stubborn doesn't even begin to describe it. My granddad has a mountain of excuses, but the cottage grows shabbier by the day. It won't be long before things stop working and I'm dreading that happening.' He has the money but not the motivation and, in truth, who can blame him at his age? Living through the disruption wouldn't be easy when all he wants is a quiet life.

It's time to take the tour and we walk across to The Retreat.

'Oh, who doesn't love a barn conversion when it's been done so well?' Rona stands looking out across the fields from the patio doors in the sitting room. 'And such a gorgeous view.'

'Aysbury is very picturesque. We're very lucky and the sense of community here is like turning back the hands of time. When neighbours were neighbourly.'

She nods, her eyes scanning the fields and taking in the landmarks. Gazing out at the hills far in the distance and the way the light plays across the landscape as a passing cloud obscures the sun's rays, I can see Rona is captivated.

'I'm rather glad we have a little time together on our own, Immi. There's something I need to show you.'

Rona walks back to the coffee table where she left her handbag. She unzips it and pulls out a rather bulky envelope.

'Gray hasn't seen this. I've been sitting on it for a couple of weeks, but time is running out and I can't ignore it any longer.'

Taking it from her, I sink down onto the sofa.

'I'd like your opinion on what you think I should do for the best, especially given your future plans.'

Rona doesn't take a seat but wanders back to take in the view as I glance over the contents.

There's a sheet of paper folded in half and a laminated pouch. When I flip back the cover and slide out the contents it contains two airline tickets. I glance across at her, but she isn't looking this way.

The flight is from London Heathrow to Los Angeles, flying out on the twenty-eighth of December. Placing the tickets back inside the envelope, I turn my attention to the letter.

My dearest Rona

It's such a huge relief to hear your good news. I couldn't bear to think of what you were going through and am only thankful Gray is such a comfort to you.

There is one favour I need to ask, as I extend an invitation I hope you can find it in your heart not to refuse. I promised I would never interfere with your lives, as I have no right to do so, but one of my mother's biggest regrets in life was the way she came between us. It was only at the very end that she could bring herself to admit her wrongdoing.

You know about my own regrets, as I've expressed them many times over the years, but I've always respected your strength in choosing to bring up our son alone.

But that's in the past now. Knowing that you are well again, nothing would make me happier than to spend a little time showing you the delights of California. There are no strings attached and while I understand that it would be awkward for you to stay at the house, some dear friends of mine are away until the end of January. They live a few doors down and there is a four-bedroom house with a swimming pool entirely at your disposal.

Please think of this as a little holiday and an olive branch. I expect nothing in return, other than the chance to chauffeur both you and Gray around and make your stay enjoyable.

My mother's death has made me realise that Gray will never feel a personal connection to me – how can he, when I've been absent from his life? But in adulthood I owe him the chance of meeting me face to face. I can't change the past, but there will be things he no doubt wants to say to me. Even if it's just a chance for him to tell me how much he despises me, I owe him that at the very least.

But he is also the only beneficiary in my will and, having recently had to go through probate for my mother's estate, there

*is a practical requirement attached to my offer too. Introducing
Gray to my appointed executor will mean that I can then forget
about the matter and get on with the rest of my life. And, so can
our son.*

*One meeting will suffice, and I have no intention of putting
any emotional pressure on Gray, whatsoever. This isn't about
making amends. I know it's too late for that. It's simply about
ensuring that, when the time comes, Gray can be assured that
any input from him will be minimal.*

*I will wait for your decision, whenever you are ready. If a visit
in person is too painful, then I will of course understand, but it
would simplify matters all round. And give me a chance to thank
Gray for being your tower of strength.*

With my best regards,

Grayson.

I look up, unsure of how long Rona has been standing there
watching me.

'Poignant, isn't it? It sounds as if he never got over losing us, his
only fault was in accepting it. I wish I'd realised his approaches
weren't aimed at trying to take Gray away from me.' Her eyes reflect
regret and sadness.

'And you're sure his intentions are good now?'

Rona nods, lowering herself down onto the sofa next to me. She
sinks back into the cushions and I can tell from the way her body
sags that she's torn.

'Yes. We never lost touch completely when Gray was growing
up, you see. Every couple of years he'd write, asking how we were
doing, and I'd send him a little update. Then about a year ago, he
wrote to me to tell me that his mother was dying and asked if he
could phone me. She was putting her affairs in order and wanted

him to let me know how bitterly she regretted interfering in our marriage.

'When Grayson and I first met, he was over here on business. He flew back and forth for a while then eventually brought his mother over to meet me. I gather that she told him straight that I wasn't good enough for him. We married eighteen months later and on our wedding day, he admitted to me that she'd tried to talk him out of going through with it. In hindsight, she probably couldn't bear the thought of letting him go, even though his father told her she was being manipulative. It broke her heart when he came to live here and she gave us six years of hell, aimed at trying to undermine our relationship. And she succeeded in getting to him. So, Grayson began trying to sell me the idea that we should move to the States.

'I honestly think she thought I'd give in and it was only a matter of time before the three of us flew off and she could take control of Gray's upbringing. At the time, Grayson believed her motives were for the best and he would have loved that, but I couldn't face it. Her hatred for me grew for what she saw as stealing her son away from her and then her grandson. She was never going to forgive me for those lost years.'

'I'm so sorry to hear that, Rona. What a terrible thing for you to bear. It's both sad and tragic. Gray hasn't mentioned his grandmother's passing.'

She stares down at her hands, looking agitated.

'He doesn't know. It's always been a taboo subject in general, because even the mention of anything to do with his father makes Gray angry. Oh, this is such a mess now and I don't know quite how to handle it. I could have been a peacemaker all those years ago and I wasn't. My pride was hurt and, well, I took it out on poor Grayson. I gave him an ultimatum and that was wrong of me.'

Poor Grayson? That's not quite the picture I'd imagined from the little Gray has told me.

'You were put in an awful position, Rona, and that wasn't your fault.'

'No, it wasn't. But I became bitter and angry, retaliating in the only way I knew would really hurt him. I told Grayson I no longer loved him and that's why he gave up trying and left. We never got divorced, you see. Gray doesn't even know that.'

I'm stunned. 'Goodness, Rona, that isn't going to be an easy conversation. My heart goes out to you.'

'Gray was nearly five when Grayson and I decided it was over and he flew back to California. It was a difficult time. He insisted on supporting us until Gray was old enough for me to work full-time. I begrudgingly accepted that, although in fairness he'd offered a lot more. But I wasn't interested in his money, as I saw it as a form of control – and that reminded me of his mother. However, I had to be practical for the sake of my son. Once I had an income, I paid half of the mortgage and the arrangement I agreed to was that I'd remain in the house until Gray left home and then we'd sort things out. It was all handled through a third party and when the day came and I informed them of the change, I'd assumed the house would be sold and all ties cut.'

She glances at me, trying to assess my reaction, and her embarrassment is plain to see. This is a lot to take in and, as for Gray, I can't even begin to imagine what his reaction is going to be.

'But that never happened?'

'No. He said that after all these years I had a right to live in the house as long as I wanted. When he rang to inform me that his mother had passed away, I felt it was only fair to tell him that I had breast cancer. I had no idea what was going to happen and facing up to that meant he had a right to know. I couldn't even bear to think about the two of them being left to sort out the mess I'd allowed to continue.'

Poor Rona, this is the last thing she needs right now. 'Well, given the time you two have been apart, hopefully a solicitor can sort this out fairly easily.'

'I believe Grayson when he says this isn't about making up for lost time. A close death rams home the fact that the only inevitable thing about life is death. If anything happens to Grayson, or me, as it stands, we're still technically husband and wife. I have absolutely no idea how that complicates matters, or the problems it presents. This trip would allow us to begin the process to put that right. As for leaving everything to Gray, well, that comes as a real surprise. It saddens me to think Grayson has never had someone else in his life. I assumed he just chose not to marry again.'

I refold the letter, placing it back inside the envelope, and hand it back to Rona.

'That's the real reason why you can't just sell up and move, then. Oh, Rona, what a tough situation you're in. And I know that Gray plans to try his best to convince you to look at a property close to the marina.'

She shakes her head, sadly, indicating that she has no idea what she's going to do.

'I need to make a decision rather quickly and I simply don't know where to begin to explain all of this to Gray. He's so happy right now and who knows how he'll react when I tell him? I feel awful having to be the one to upset him, but I'm partly to blame, so maybe that's karma. The only person I can ask for their opinion is you, Immi. I've put my son through enough and now all I want is for the two of you to be able to grab the happiness you both deserve.'

Instinctively I cup my hand to my mouth, pressing my lips against my curled fingers. I wonder if it's a subconscious warning to say nothing, but Rona's eyes are seeking mine out, appealing for help.

I let out a rather jaded sigh. 'I think that whatever you decide will come with its own set of problems. But ignoring it is just postponing the inevitable.'

As a new wife, how awful to be made to feel you aren't good enough. Sometimes events overtake decisions and it sounds as if Grayson's mother was backing Rona into a corner, so her gut instinct was to cling onto her son and push her husband away. Is she worried that Gray will see it differently when she tells him everything?

'You're right, there's no way you can anticipate Gray's reaction to this. But my take on it is that you need to separate the two issues. Just stick to the facts. You're being asked to pass on a message from his father. Let Gray read the letter and decide for himself. If he doesn't want to go, then clearly his father holds no meaning for him. If he agrees, then there's unfinished business here for him. Just because we don't speak about something, doesn't mean we've let it go – does it?'

Rona leans forward, placing her hand on my shoulder.

'You're thinking about your mother. I hope I haven't made you sad. And as for my other problem?'

Rona has no choice.

'You can't think about moving on until it's resolved, can you? If you do nothing and ignore the letter, the problem won't simply go away. Gray and I want you to be a part of our lives going forward, on a daily basis. He will eventually know something isn't right if you cling onto the house for the wrong reasons. I'm sure he'll understand if you explain it all to him. When the deed is done, if there's anything at all I can do to help, then I'm here.'

'Thank you, Immi, for putting it into perspective and giving your honest opinion. I feel so awful that in the midst of your good news, this has suddenly reared its head. The last thing I'd ever want to do is to upset either of you. After all, you are Gray's future and my stupidity at letting this slide means it could risk upsetting any New Year's plans the two of you have made.'

It's awful to think that Rona has had this hanging over her, when she should be celebrating the good news about her health.

'Missing a couple of parties isn't the end of the world, Rona, if Gray decides this is something that he has to do. And I hope he does, for both your sakes. It's the curiosity, you see. Wondering what your biological parent looks like and if they truly regret the past, not simply saying they're sorry. Sorry doesn't cut it. You say *sorry* if you accidentally knock into someone in the supermarket. Missing out on being a part of someone's life, and even shaping it, is life-changing. My mother was young when she left and maybe she couldn't cope, I don't know – but I'd still like to find out what exactly happened. The fact that Grayson never remarried might mean he found it harder to walk away than it appeared at the time. Who knows?'

Rona looks upset, but more than that – I can see she is carrying a heavy load of guilt and has deep regrets. I find it hard to believe this gentle woman could ever do, or say, anything to cause an irreparable hurt, if she wasn't convinced she was doing it for the right reason.

'What if I was wrong? Maybe I wanted to punish Grayson because I felt he didn't stand up and fight for us. Pride is an awful thing, Immi, but perhaps I was too young to be able to appreciate that fact.'

Is it simply human nature for most people to blame themselves first? Time and time again I wonder if my mother walked away because she was disappointed in me. I can empathise with the emotions welling up inside Rona as she faces one of the toughest tasks any mother could. The decision she made changed both her and Gray's lives forever, but the events leading up to that weren't of her choosing.

'Love shouldn't be about fighting, Rona. Love should be about nurturing, not making your loved ones choose – that's just selfishness. Grayson's mother put herself before her son. You have always put Gray first, and that's why he'd do anything for you.'

She looks at me with the sadness in her heart reflected in her eyes.

'I know it's a lot to ask, but if the right moment presents itself, would you... could you... warn Gray that I need to talk to him about his father? For several years now, he's refused to talk about anything to do with the past. I need him to listen to me, even if he has nothing to say in return.'

I stare back at her, feeling her pain, and I know I can't refuse her request.

'I promise I'll try.'

'That's all I ask. Thank you, Immi.'

12

JINGLE BELLS ALL THE WAY

Rona decides she will sit down with Gray on Monday to have the talk and tell him everything. For the sake of her health she can't ignore this for much longer, because the last thing she needs in her life now is stress. For the rest of today, however, I decide to make sure Rona is surrounded by laughter and gaiety to take her mind off a task she isn't relishing.

Watching Rona and Ethel in the galley, assembling the kids' little snack boxes and chattering away like old friends, I send up a silent prayer of thanks.

'It's good seeing her here, isn't it?' Gray sidles up to me. I tilt my head, looking across at that handsome face, and reach up to tweak his captain's hat.

Sometimes he's just too darned cute-looking for his own good.

He starts humming the tune to 'I Wish It Could Be Christmas Every Day' under his breath, grabbing me by the waist and sashaying me around playfully.

'Stop, or you'll end up with a crooked cap again. Yes, they're getting on very well indeed. Valerie is going to join us for the cruise today, too. I never thought to ask her before, but she was delighted.'

'Valerie?' Gray wrinkles his brow.

'Mrs Price – our ticket lady.'

'Valerie? My goodness. Who would have guessed?'

He draws me even closer, giving a quick squeeze before planting a kiss firmly on my lips, regardless of who might be watching. I pull away, laughing.

'Behave yourself, captain. Anyway, I think it suits her. Let's keep a special eye out for her in future, Gray. I know she only lives a short walk away, but we mustn't forget to involve Valerie in everything. It never occurred to me before that the reason she probably doesn't come to The Bullrush Inn after dark is that she has to walk home alone along quite a stretch of a badly lit, narrow country lane.'

He purses his lips. 'Hmm. I see what you mean. Good job you have Captain Gray here on hand, then. Just give me a nudge whenever you need me. And soon, well, pretty soon, I'll be a permanent resident here, too.'

'Where's the music, then?' Abe eases past, as we're blocking the gangway.

'I'm off to sort that now,' I reply.

'Immi, how many boxes do we need today?' Ethel calls out.

Gray rests his forehead against mine for a brief second.

'Go on, I'll stop distracting you. Nothing functions right unless you're directing us. Have I ever told you that you're the best thing that's ever happened to me?'

'There are only eleven boxes here, Immi. There aren't any more in the cupboard. Please tell me we have a stock somewhere else,' Ethel continues.

I turn on my heel and start humming 'The Holly and the Ivy'.

Gray joins in, then Abe in his raspy, baritone voice and before I reach the galley to search for boxes, everyone is singing in unison.

* * *

As The Star Gazer chugs along, the kids are sitting cross-legged on the rug while Santa tells one of his stories.

'When I began to slide down the chimney...' Tollie pauses for a second, glancing from face to face '... I came to an abrupt halt. Rudolph's face peered down at me from the top and I called out, "I'm stuck, Rudolph, get help," and off he dashed. I wriggled and wriggled, but nothing happened. I breathed in, but it made no difference. I swung my legs back and forth, kicking my boots against the bricks, trying with all my might to free myself. But I was well and truly stuck.'

He places his hands on his padded belly, giving it a jiggle. The children are listening to every single word, enthralled, as Santa shakes his head in dismay.

'And the clock was ticking. I looked up at the chimney pot and saw the stars twinkling in the darkness of the night sky. I thought of the huge pile of sacks in the sleigh, still waiting to be delivered. And then I saw something glinting, way above me.'

Not one of his audience moved a muscle.

'I caught the tiniest sparkle, as the moonlight bounced off something far in the distance. It came closer and closer, until I was able to reach up. It was a rope, and on the end...' he pauses for maximum effect '... was a bottle of washing-up liquid.'

The kids all start laughing.

'I flipped open the top and squirted the liquid all around the edge of my big black belt. It was rather sticky, but it wasn't long before I began to slide, very slowly, down towards the open fire grate. When my boots hit the ground, I shouted up, "Lower the sacks!" and my trusty elves got to work in double-quick time.'

One little boy raises his hand impatiently and Santa bids him to stand up.

'How did you get back up the chimney, Santa?'

Tollie's eyes sparkle. 'Well, young man. It wasn't easy. My number one elf, Immi here, found a big rope. I squirted lots and lots of washing-up liquid around my middle and when Immi told me they were ready, I grabbed the rope very tightly with both hands. She tied it to the sleigh and the reindeers began to pull. "Heave," she called to them. "Heave." And inch by inch I rose up, until I was safely at the top.'

The little boy frowns, glancing in my direction and then back at Santa.

'What about the milk and cookies. And the carrots for the reindeer?'

Tollie's eyebrows shoot up and he sits there for a few seconds considering the question.

I walk over to stand next to Tollie, placing my hand on his shoulder and giving it a gentle pat.

'Well, Santa asked me to pop back to collect them, of course. There was milk, a packet of star cookies and a bag full of carrots. And now, whenever Santa is about to climb down a chimney he always checks first to see if he will fit. But sometimes...' my voice lowers, conspiratorially '... there isn't even a chimney.'

I gaze around at the eager little faces staring back at me. Some with mouths open still, at the thought of Santa getting stuck. I lean forward, continuing to talk in a whisper. 'I'll let you into a little secret. Santa has a big bunch of front-door keys, just in case he has a problem.'

Today's little group are mostly five and under, but two older children at the back simply sit and smile. The little ones look relieved and Santa gives me a beaming smile.

'It's all about teamwork,' he booms out and the kids start giggling.

I look across at Rona, Ethel and Valerie, standing in the

gangway just beyond the dinette tables, where the parents look equally amused.

It doesn't matter how young or how old you are, the festive time is all about traditions. Christmas is a time when if we aren't making our childhood memories, we're remembering them. Tollie didn't always look like Santa. For many years he only had a moustache and it was almost black in those days. Most Christmases, Dad and I came back to Aysbury, and Tollie has always been Santa to me, as even in the days when he needed a fake white beard, he represented that jolly spirit. A man who opened his house and his heart to many over the years, and made sure everyone was fed.

We are about to wipe away the disappointments and doubts of last Christmas, as Gray and I make a commitment to each other. Looking forward now, it's exciting to think that next year is going to be another amazing one, too. Nothing cements relationships like a party and we're going to have two. One to celebrate our wedding and one to mark the ten-year anniversary of Santa Ahoy. Now all that needs to happen is for Rona to sort her dilemma out and then it's full steam ahead.

Simple. Ish.

* * *

The Bullrush is packed with visitors. Children are milling around everywhere, still buzzing from the second Santa Ahoy cruise of the day. Parents are tucking into cake and drinking tea, while Jude and Jade – still, rather charmingly, dressed in their elf costumes – ferry plates to and from the kitchen. Maggie waves out, directing us upstairs. She calls one of the girls over and says something to her, as I wave back.

'We're upstairs, guys,' I inform the happy little troop following me.

Christmas carols are playing softly in the background, but with the level of chatter around the tables you have to strain your ears to hear them.

After negotiating our way through the narrow walkways between the tables, avoiding the little ones running around and the servers carrying platters of cake, we climb the stairs. It's packed up here, too, but against the back wall in the far corner, two of the small tables have been pulled together and a reserved sign graces the middle of it.

'That must be ours.' I point, heading towards it. Walking around to sit on the other side, I slide along the banquette seat, leaving a space either side of me. Indicating for Rona to sit opposite me, Valerie slips into the seat alongside her. Gray engineers it so that Ethel sits the other side of Rona, and then he takes a seat next to me.

Bringing up the rear, Abe, being a tad portly, looks at the narrow space between the table and the window alongside and starts laughing. Gray immediately jumps up, grabbing hold of the edge of the table.

'Hands in the air, everyone. We'll all need a little extra space if we're going to be tucking into a cream tea,' he muses.

Abe laughs. 'I'll make sure I don't go overboard, or I'll be giving Santa a run for his money.'

I look around, but there's still no sign of Tollie. He was popping home to change, then heading off to track down Fisher, so he could join the party.

The twins arrive to take the orders and we put our hands in the air for teas and coffees.

'There will be another two for tea, girls,' I inform them.

'Coming up,' Jade replies, sounding every bit like a professional waitress. Jude hands out a pile of plates and napkins.

'Mum said to say sorry, she was hoping to get everything laid up ready, but it's been very busy again today.'

'Tell her it's fine, Jade. We're not in a hurry and I bet she really missed having you two around to help. We're lucky to be able to borrow you. It's not easy finding elves, these days.'

That makes her smile and a little ripple of laughter goes around the table. She gives us a cheeky little elfish grin, before heading back downstairs.

'Lovely girls, aren't they?' Rona remarks. 'And what a wonderful trip it is along the canal and around the marina. The children were enthralled. I bet the Little Stars Specials are quite something, too.'

Valerie turns in her seat to look at Rona, whose face hasn't been without a smile all afternoon. 'It's hard to read some of the emails we receive without feeling a little tearful, Rona. Of course, this was all Tollie's idea in the first place.'

'Did I hear my name mentioned?' Tollie's voice booms out above the general background noise. Striding up to the table, he's now wearing his old brown corduroy trousers and his favourite bottle-green padded jacket. 'I rounded up the missin' party.'

Fisher is close on Tollie's heels, scooting around him as he stops for a second to glance around the table. Fisher manoeuvres himself into the seat next to me, while Tollie slips off his coat and sinks down into the carver chair at the head of the table.

'Well, what a treat this is. Ho! Ho! Ho! I'll be needin' more than a few squirts of washin'-up liquid this Christmas Eve.' Tollie's booming Santa voice puts a grin on everyone's face, including some people sitting at neighbouring tables.

Maggie, Jude and Jade appear, each carrying a large tiered cake stand, and behind them Kurt and Sarah hold trays of hot drinks.

'You've done us proud,' Tollie says as we reposition ourselves around the table so everyone has a little elbow room. 'Nothin' beats a cream tea.'

It's a bit of a squeeze, but it's good to see business booming and what's good for the café is good for Aysbury. Maggie begins shifting things around on the table to accommodate our feast and my mouth begins to water.

Valerie looks across at Fisher. 'Jack, I don't think you've met Rona, Gray's mum. It's her first visit to Aysbury.'

Heads turn to stare in Fisher's direction.

Everyone is trying to disguise their surprise, but it's plastered all over their faces. They're all sitting there like startled rabbits, in total disbelief. I doubt whether anyone, aside from me and Tollie, even knew his name was Jack.

'No, I haven't, Valerie. It's lovely to meet you, Rona. I also go by the name of Fisher; it's a nickname that started when I came to work at the marina.'

I feel the need to break the silence and what is now a whole bevy of awkward, questioning glances, as it's obvious Fisher and Valerie have a new-found rapport.

'He's being modest, Rona. Not only is Fisher in charge of the marina, but he's the owner of The Star Gazer,' I inform her.

Rona inclines her head as she smiles in Fisher's direction.

Valerie leans in towards her. 'The Santa Ahoy Christmas charity cruise will be celebrating its tenth anniversary next year, Rona.'

'Oh, that's wonderful! What an achievement, everyone. I do so love the community spirit here. It reminds me of the old days, when I was a young girl. Nowadays people are always so busy. I rarely see my neighbours. They leave early and arrive home late,' Rona replies, sounding more than a tad nostalgic.

As everyone begins tucking in to tea, there's a lot of general chatter about how things used to be and the consensus is that some things haven't changed for the better.

What is obvious from Gray's demeanour is how delighted he is to see Rona feeling so relaxed and comfortable. She seems to have slotted into our little group so easily and everyone has taken to her.

If we had any fears about selling the benefits of living in a small community, they've melted away. It's ironic that now we are facing an entirely different sort of problem, except that Gray isn't aware of that – yet. But given what we've all been through, each problem now seems a little less like the end of the world.

With Christmas only ten days away I refuse to let anything take the shine off that thought. Good things happen to good people, and it's our turn.

'Thank you for today, for making sure Mum felt at ease with everyone.'

Lying in Gray's arms in the darkness, I'm buzzing. Not from the two glasses of red wine we enjoyed with Sarah and Kurt after the restaurant closed, but from the warm glow of happiness that is rising up from the pit of my stomach. To end a wonderful day spent in the company of family and friends snuggled up with the man you love is a blessing.

'I was a bit anxious, I will admit, as she must have felt a little daunted to begin with.'

Then I remember the conversation I had with Rona earlier today. She can't simply sell a house that she only partly owns, even if the thought of living in Aysbury is appealing. As the warmth of Gray's body warms the chill of my own, I'm feeling torn. I made a promise to her, but Gray is so happy right now and I know it's a topic that will bring him down.

Oblivious to my train of thoughts, he begins talking about today's cruise and how well it went, but my mind is in overdrive. Gray is so used to stepping up for those he cares about, whenever the occasion arises, and now I want to be here for him. Rona is the only one who can answer his questions, but she's right. She can't simply launch into it without some sort of warning that it's coming. Rona feels I'm the one best placed to do that and I can't let her down.

'And as for Fisher and Valerie... you do know what everyone was thinking, don't you?' Gray sounds rather incredulous and it occurs to me that I was the only one privy to this week's rather surprising turn of events.

I try my best to switch off my swirling thoughts. Problems always seem bigger at night, as darkness closes around us.

'Yes. There's definitely some chemistry going on between them, isn't there? And I think it's wonderful. In fact, I wanted to ask your opinion, as I'm thinking of asking Fisher if he would like to offer Valerie my two days a week on a permanent basis. Martin is talking about employing an assistant manager, as he desperately needs some support. Especially if he's going to be taking on more part-time staff, even just for the peak times. He can't manage a rota and be out in the van at the same time. He's a salesman and front-of-business kind of boss, rather than someone who pores over work schedules and ordering stock.'

Gray inclines his head to rest up against my own.

'I never thought I'd hear you talk about leaving your job at the marina. I mean, you and Fisher are so close.'

'I know. Me neither. But nothing will change in terms of my relationship with Fisher. Mrs Price – I mean, Valerie – has simply blossomed this week and he's like a different man when he's around her. He smiles more, and they have this easy banter when they think no one can overhear them.

'I'm not saying either one of them would jump into anything quickly, because neither of them are like that. But there's no denying there is a mutual attraction. And one I don't think anyone could have anticipated, so why not encourage it and see what happens, right?'

Gray's foot gently rubs up against my toes and a feeling of well-being washes over me.

'When it's real there's no denying it, is there?' I don't need to see his face to know he's smiling as he speaks. 'Assistant manager, you say? Is that what you want?'

'What I want is to support Martin. He took me on as a temp when no one else would. It gave me my first taste of independence, earning a few pounds stacking shelves and cleaning every Saturday. He did it as a favour to Tollie, of course, but it was good of him and he was patient with me. Martin took time out of his busy day to show me how to tend the plants and I'm grateful for that too. If Fisher's happy to let me go, then I'll tie it up with Martin and leave Fisher to approach Valerie.'

'Okay, I'll make sure I don't let anything slip, then. What else is going around in that head of yours, Immi? Something tells me there's more.' Gray slides his arm around my waist, giving me a loving squeeze.

Pausing for a moment in the silence of the inky blackness, I'm torn about what to do. This is my chance to broach the topic Rona asked me to raise. But it's such a delicate subject that I need to think carefully about how to tackle it.

'That's an ominous silence, Immi.'

I roll away from him a little, easing myself up onto my elbow. He rolls over onto his back, placing his hands behind his head as he stares up at the ceiling.

'Hit me with whatever it is, Immi. If something is worrying you, then it's also a concern to me.'

Just tell him, the little voice in my head whispers to me.

'This is awkward, but I made a promise.'

Gray clears his throat anxiously.

'Is this about Mum?'

I place my free hand gently on his chest.

'There's nothing to worry about; she's doing well. This is something different.'

He lets out a long, slow sigh.

'You're sure?'

I trace my fingers up over his T-shirt, letting them linger against his cheek.

'A trouble shared is a trouble halved, Gray, and that's what being together is all about. Rona reached out to me today, as if I were already her daughter-in-law, her confidante. This is about your father and there's a message she needs to pass on to you, but she's finding it difficult to raise the subject. Your mum asked me to forewarn you, as it's important you understand that and are at least prepared to hear her out.'

Gray immediately sits upright, scooting back a little to lean against the headboard. I shift position, sitting up to look at him. Half of his face is in darkness, only the left-hand side is visible, as the moonlight shines through a gap in the blinds. Gray's expression is fixed, his jaw angular, and I watch him bristle at the mention of his father.

'I knew something was going on. I didn't think it would be about *him*, though.'

His tone is dismissive, but I can't back down now. I'm doing this for Rona, but I'm also doing this for Gray. I'd rather be the one on the receiving end of his initial, possibly angry, reaction and hopefully by the time he sits facing Rona he will at least be able to listen to her calmly.

'It's not about making amends. He's written a letter to her, which Rona allowed me to read. But it's about you, well, in a manner of speaking. I appreciate the reason why you refuse to have anything to do with your father, or his family, but life moves on,

Gray. Your grandmother died recently, and although you never met her it has made him think about putting his own affairs in order. That's what they say, isn't it?'

Gray's eyes are closed, but he's listening to every word I say, while showing absolutely no reaction whatsoever. I let it sink in, looking instead over his shoulder and out through a chink in the blinds, at a twinkling star.

When I look back at him what I really want to say just seems to pop into my head, unbidden.

'Do you ever feel that sometimes it's too coincidental how events simply slot into place? As if there really is a master plan and we're merely adhering to it, without even appreciating that's what is happening.'

Gray's laugh is dismissive.

'A man ditches his family and then has the right to be heard, just because he writes a letter. Sounds like a flawed plan to me.'

At least he doesn't sound angry – it's more of a couldn't-care-less attitude.

'I understand that. Can I just ask that when Rona gets up the courage to talk to you, you let her say her piece, because she's only the messenger? Like it or not, there is unfinished business – things that need to be resolved. Read the letter and know that whatever you decide I'll support you one hundred per cent.'

His groan is dismissive, but he says nothing.

'The hurt is something I understand, Gray – believe me. And yet I'd love the chance to meet my mother just once, even if she rejected me. I carry her genes and yet I don't have any photos of her, because my father burnt everything. It's not about forgiving someone who doesn't deserve to be forgiven, but about the need to finally let go – as an adult – of the curious inner child. You can only do that face to face.'

I move closer, allowing myself to sag against Gray's chest, and he encircles me with his arms. His muscles are firm against my body, no longer relaxed, but tense and angry. Not at me, or Rona, but at the man who hurt his mother.

'It took a lot for you to tell me that, Immi. And you're right. You have no idea how grateful I am that Mum was happy to take you into her confidence like that. This can't have been easy for her, or for you. I will be a good son and will bear in mind what you have said. But there's nothing wrong with having just one parent and it's infinitely better than having two, if one of them feels trapped.'

It takes me a long time to drift into sleep as Gray's words sink in. My arrival in the world made my mother want to run away. But at least it means that I can be empathetic when it comes to Gray's situation, and that's all that matters, not a past I can't change.

* * *

Even though both Gray and I are flagging as he packs up the car to head back to Rona's, we're both on a high. Today's cruises were a huge success and the second of the Little Stars Specials was a delight.

We had everyone singing at the tops of their voices after Gray and Abe moored The Star Gazer and joined us on board. Abe played guitar and Gray acted as conductor. It was hilarious, as he split the kids and adults into two groups to sing different backing sounds, then he proceeded to do a voice-over.

One half were sleigh bells, singing 'jingle jingle', and the other half the sound of Santa's sleigh as it 'whooshed' through the snow.

'I love you,' I declare as I stand on tiptoe to place a lingering kiss on his lips. Thoughts of last night pop into my head, making my stomach do a little flip. 'Thank you for the singalong today. It was amazing. You are amazing!'

'And next you are going to remind me to be nice and listen to Mum when she ambushes me tomorrow.'

'Hey, I wasn't trying to manipulate you. It's not an easy situation, but somehow you have to work through it together.'

We're in the big car park and I follow him around to the boot of his car. I wait patiently while he stows away his holdall and computer bag, sadness festering away in the pit of my stomach.

'It's horrible saying goodbye, isn't it?' Gray whispers as he steps back to take me in his arms.

'Ring me if you want to chat. Any time of the day, or night – I'm here for you, Gray, always.'

His grip around me tightens as he hugs me even closer, gently rocking me back and forth. Then he lets go with one hand and spins me around, pirouette-style.

'Don't worry. Everything will be fine, Immi. Only people you love can really hurt you. Everyone else... well, the worst they can do is be annoying.'

As I wave him off I wish I could be by his side tomorrow, but it's something he has to sort out with Rona, and I can't influence his decision. I trust, and hope, that he'll see this as a positive step, tidying up loose ends that should have been sorted a long time ago. Every ending signals a new beginning and that, at least, is a positive outcome.

As Gray's car disappears out of view, I spot Valerie walking down the lane towards me and wave out.

When she draws alongside me, we both head back in the direction of the canal.

'Ahh, I was hoping to catch Gray before he left. Goodbyes are tough, aren't they?' She sounds tired and somewhat dispirited.

'It doesn't get any easier, I will admit. But it's been a good weekend and we've suddenly made an enormous leap forward in the right direction. I guess we needed a bit of a shove to just get on with it.'

'It's often an intervention that's a triggering factor. We're all guilty of glossing over life's problems when we're not quite sure how to handle them.'

Valerie's pace is slow, and she seems upset, maybe even a little depressed. I glance sideways at her, questioningly.

'Problems?'

She tips her head back, looking up at the sky and letting out a deep, heartfelt sigh.

'It's nothing. I thought a walk would clear my head, that's all.'

Whatever it is, Valerie is struggling with it. Gray's words come back to me... 'Only people you love can really hurt you.'

'Loving someone isn't easy. Everyone comes with their own set of problems, it's just a case of finding some middle ground and hoping it all works out in the end. I always find that sharing a problem helps, even if it's only to stop me bottling things up.'

Valerie looks at me, scanning my face.

'There's so much wisdom in your words, Immi. But I don't deserve any sympathy over this; it isn't about me, or my feelings.'

There's a bench up ahead of us, set back in a nook on the side of the towpath, and, although the late afternoon chill is a little bracing, I incline my head towards it. Valerie gives a nod and we make our way over, sinking down and settling back to stare out over the water.

'This is about my son,' she begins. 'It's been a few years since we've spoken. And now an old friend has phoned to say she bumped into him in Dartmouth and that it wasn't an accident. He asked her if I was still living in Aysbury.'

I fleetingly wonder what the connection with Dartmouth is, but I don't feel I can ask.

'It could mean he's ready to get back in touch. That's good news, isn't it?'

Her mood is sombre, so I doubt it's a simple case of making up and putting the past behind them.

'My family were originally from here, but my parents ended up running a little tea shop in Dartmouth Harbour and I lived there for a while. You are very kind to listen to my woes, Immi. I only ever wanted the best for Liam, but I seem incapable of getting it right.'

It's sad to see how distressed she is about this.

'I'm sure you're being too hard on yourself, Valerie. I often made my dad despair at some of the things I said and did, but none of it was his fault. It was simply a part of growing up. Kids instinctively want to push the boundaries and challenge the rules. They tend to take their frustrations out on those around them, too.'

My words as least seem to make her stop and think for a moment.

'He sees life in a very simplistic way. Right or wrong, black or white – but it never is as cut and dried as that, is it? People make mistakes all the time and end up having to live with the conse-quences. Following the divorce, in trying to shield him from the harsher things in life, I stifled him. I see that now. At the age of fifteen he grew restless. Jeffery was running a restaurant in Portugal at the time and Liam made contact with him. I had no choice but to let him go. That's when I moved here. Like his father, the travelling bug was in his blood. I knew that as soon as he was old enough he'd be off on his own adventures And I was right, he constantly moves around from place to place as his funds allow.'

Divorces are never easy. I fleetingly wonder whether Mr Price was Valerie's first and only love. It's natural that she should cling onto her son in that sort of situation. I had my suspicions that Valerie and Rona might have a lot in common, but that wasn't quite what I was expecting.

'Perhaps it's time for him to come home,' I reply.

She shakes her head sadly.

'I doubt it. And I doubt he will ever forgive me. When my father suffered a massive heart attack and died, six years ago, it was a shock to us all. Liam and I lived with my parents for nearly two years after the divorce, so he was very close to them. Liam took it particularly hard as he couldn't make it back in time for the funeral.

'Less than six months later, my mother caught pneumonia. I packed a case and after she was discharged from hospital, I stayed with her while she recuperated. She was getting better and Liam rang every day to talk to her. And then she had a funny turn and was readmitted. I was so sure it would be all right that I told him not to worry, that they would sort her out. We were laughing as I kissed her cheek before I left that night. In the early hours of the morning I received the call – she was gone, just like that. Liam blamed me for not making it clear how ill she was.'

'Some bonds are very special, and I can imagine how awful he felt. But it wasn't anyone's fault, Valerie. Who can predict something like that?'

'It broke my heart when I rang to break the news. He simply couldn't take it in at first. It was too much grief, so soon after losing his granddad, and he couldn't cope with it. Liam managed to get a flight home for the funeral in Dartmouth, but he was angry and when he left, he just went – he didn't say goodbye.'

'Coping with the loss of loved ones is a very personal journey for each of us, Valerie. Some manage that better than others. My life would have been very different if it hadn't been for Tollie and Grandma – they were like parents to me. It's a blessing, but when they're gone it leaves yet another gaping hole in your life that can never be filled.' I'm speaking from the heart and trying not to feel overwhelmed by the sadness welling up within me. Old feelings, old hurts, old regrets.

'It made me realise that I'd spent most of my life running away from my own emotional turmoil,' Valerie confides in me. 'Grief can do that to you, and it's only recently I faced up to the fact that I'd turned myself into a bit of a recluse.'

This rather proud, introverted lady my grandma Nell befriended must have mourned the loss of her friend. If Grandma was the only person she was able to really talk to, it would have been yet another blow. Agreeing to become Tollie's housekeeper would have been a comfort to them both after Grandma died, I should imagine.

'You're so well regarded here, Valerie. Everyone admires the way you get things done and you are an important part of our community. But people—' I pause, casting around for the right words. 'People see you as a very private person and they hesitate, only because they don't want to cause offence.'

A little smile tweaks at the sides of her mouth.

'Being aloof is something I learnt from my mother and it has its advantages. But this last week has shown me that it's easier than I thought to stop hiding. I didn't really know Jack at all but working with him he made me so welcome, and he's funny, and kind. I saw the way everyone responded when we were sitting around the table having tea together, yesterday. But, Immi, it's more than I deserve after the mess I've made of things.'

I raise my eyebrows. 'We all make mistakes. Look at the upset I caused when I first moved in with Tollie and everyone forgave me for being self-centred and downright thoughtless at times. All you need to do is to join in the fun. It doesn't always have to be about giving something of yourself,' I impress upon her. 'And if you need someone to walk you back on an evening, whenever Gray's here he told me to tell you he's more than happy to escort you back to the complex. If not, Tollie is your man. But I think Jack might beat them both to it!'

The twitch turns into a satisfied little smile.

'You think?'

My enthusiastic nod leaves her in no doubt at all. 'I do.'

I really need to make it a priority to grab a few minutes alone with Fisher and get things sorted. Something tells me that handing in my notice isn't going to be a problem at all, as this could just be the start of something truly wonderful.

'Any news on the work front?'

It's nine o'clock and I can't hold off any longer. Even though I was rushed off my feet at the nurseries today, I can't possibly climb into bed until I've spoken to Gray.

'None. Nada. Not even from the other leads I've been pursuing. Every single friend I have, who has a contact in the business, has been asking around on my behalf. Phil, Reece and Dharma came up with a couple of names, but Nathan and Kerrin both said the same thing. It's going to be mid-January now before I'm likely to hear back, as everyone is gearing up for the long Christmas and New Year shutdown. No one is thinking about new projects, they're too busy clearing their desks.'

He sounds maudlin.

'You've done all you can, Gray. It's brilliant they're all looking out for you and you're obviously missed.'

'I keep promising to take you up to London for a long weekend to meet everyone. We're such a diverse group, but they are all London-based. Since I moved back in with Mum, it's been difficult only heading back up when I'm involved with one of the joint projects. I miss the socialising and the jobs that materialise over a pint in the pub after a session in the studio. I feel I'm becoming invisible.'

'I know, but now your mum is on the mend you'll get up there more often and the work will start coming in again.'

Gray doesn't need to be dwelling on this right now and I decide to change the subject.

'I had a lovely chat with Valerie after you left yesterday. And on my way back from the nurseries today, I met up with Fisher. We went for a quick drink in The Bullrush. I broke the news about Martin needing help and Fisher accused me of matchmaking.'

Gray bursts out laughing, which is good to hear.

'Well, you are. How did he take it?'

'Fisher is smitten, but then I think we could all see that at the weekend. He also realises that, not only would this be a promotion for me, but it will take a huge worry and weight off Martin's shoulders. And it means more money in the pot for us to sort out the cottage, so it doesn't matter so much if your work is quiet for a while. We'll manage between us, Gray, and that's the whole point about being a couple – we share everything.'

The silence when I stop speaking is heavy. Gray is never this quiet when we're on a call. He's always fiddling, humming, or tapping with his fingers, but tonight he's preoccupied.

'That's a plus, then,' he replies after a few awkward seconds have elapsed. 'And I know you love working at the nurseries. It indulges that creative streak of yours, as well as the need to organise everything and everyone.'

He says it in jest, but there's a hint of truth in his words. I do like organising everyone and we both know that.

'Well, I think it's a perfect solution all round, but it's been a tiring day.'

He clears his throat and I strain my ears, as when he starts speaking again his voice sounds distant. Something is wrong – that's very clear. What I wish more than anything, is to be there with him to be able to offer the comfort he obviously needs.

'I did as you told me. I listened, but heck, Immi – that man has some cheek. I don't want his money. I don't want anything from him.'

Ah, now I understand. Gray doesn't sound angry, he simply sounds adamant that he's not going to play along.

'That's understandable, Gray, given the situation. But think of it like this: you are his flesh and blood. It's no different from Tollie wanting us to swap with him and take over the cottage as if we're already the owners. I guess there comes a point when we all want to tie up the loose ends. My dad wasn't able to do that, and we had no idea what his wishes were. It isn't just about money, or possessions, but making sure we don't cause a dilemma for the people we leave behind. Well, that's what Tollie said to me, only last week.'

There's a rather reluctant 'hmm' down the line.

'Point taken. But I was hoping we could all be together in Aysbury to see in the new year. I don't want to be thousands of miles away from you, Immi.'

'Aww... Gray, me neither. But we have the rest of our lives to celebrate each new year together. Get this sorted for Rona's sake, even if it doesn't hold any meaning for you.'

I'm holding my breath. How honest was Rona about the situation? I wonder. Once again, the seconds roll by; I should say goodnight now and leave him in peace.

'They're still married,' he blurts out, sounding indignant.

Rona is a strong woman, but I know how hard that must have been for her to admit. It's such a relief, though, as it wasn't my place to share that information with him.

'It's only paperwork, Gray. When people are on two different continents it can be a long-winded and costly thing to sort out. If neither party remarries, then it must be easy to let it slide.'

Another, distinctly jaded 'hmm' travels down the line.

'I'm going to have to man-up, I suppose, and pretend I give a damn. Which I don't. I'm doing it for her, and not him. But only if you are in agreement; I mean, we're celebrating our engagement on Christmas Day – the man has no sense of timing.'

'Does he even know?' I point out.

'I don't suppose he does, and it's none of his business, anyway.'

'You would do anything for your mum, and rightly so – she managed single-handedly to raise one very caring, responsible and kind-hearted man. And that's what I love so much about you, Gray. Get this done and we can get back to planning our wedding.'

Suddenly, he's humming again and it's Mendelssohn's wedding march.

'Sleep well, my lovely Immi. I'll call you tomorrow.'

Lying back, I close my eyes, grateful to Rona for the gutsy and stoic man she raised. The loose ends are about to be tied up and while Gray's away my mission is to focus on Valerie and Fisher. Two people I really admire, who deserve to find happiness, too.

There's a tap on the door and I pop the phone down on the coffee table as I shout out, 'Come in.'

Tollie appears in the doorway and I jump up, walking across to greet him with a kiss on the cheek. It's unusual for him not to just burst through the door and it's evident that he has something on his mind.

'You ain't gonna like this, Immi, but you'll have to suck it up, m'dear. When I was in The Bullrush just now, they were all talkin' about the kitty.'

I stare back at Tollie, blankly.

'What kitty?'

'The engagement kitty.'

It's hard not to show my exasperation, but out of love and respect I simply shrug it off.

'No party, no presents. Just a cosy Christmas Day lunch for a few people to raise a toast after Gray has officially slipped Grandma's beautiful ring onto my finger.'

'I'll pass that on, but I doubt you'll win this one, Immi. Folk want to club together to get you both a special gift, and me, too. So, I'll be givin' you a sum of money towards the new furniture.'

That stubborn streak of his can be trying at times. It irks me, because it reminds me of when I first came here to live.

Unable to restrain myself, I burst out laughing.

'Oh, my goodness. I hope I'm not as stubborn as you, Tollie,' I reply shaking my head. 'You might as well know that Gray and I don't want to push you out of your home.' My voice is firm, but the look in his eye is one of bloody-minded determination and his stance confirms that.

'Most of the furniture in the cottage has seen its best years,' Tollie continues, ignoring my input. 'There are a few mementos aside from my personal things, which I'll move into here when we swap over, but I don't intend hangin' onto stuff for the sake of it. I want my remainin' years to be about enjoyin' every single day as it comes, not buryin' myself in the past. The memories I need to keep me goin' are all in my head, where they don't gather dust.' He taps the side of his forehead with his forefinger.

'Like you worry about dust.' I give him a rather disparaging stare.

'I'm countin' on the two of you to make me proud, Immi. I want to see the cottage turned into a real family home. You two are goin' to be makin' new memories for us all, so remember that, because it's quite a responsibility.'

His little speech is heartfelt and honest. Tollie is right and I understand where he's coming from, even if I don't feel comfortable about it. Gray and I have been very happy in The Retreat and I can't see why that has to change. I, too, don't need to look at old photos to remember Dad, or Grandma. I will admit that I wish there were a photograph of my mother. She's never seemed real to me because I have no memories of her, but if I could see her as she was when she married Dad, then after she had me, maybe I would be able to look at her face and instantly know why she didn't want to stay with us.

'Oh, Tollie!' I step forward, throwing my arms around him for comfort, while my emotions continue to swirl around inside me.

I know that I have no choice in the matter, because he's just doing what Gray's father is trying to do. Tollie is setting his life in order, so he can get back to enjoying each and every day as if it's a bonus. As if he can hear my thoughts, Tollie continues.

'Don't dwell on the past, m'dear. Let's focus on the future and makin' the cottage as wonderful as The Retreat. At my stage in life I don't have the energy to do that, or live through the mess, but I am willin' to help you and Gray. There's nothin' to fear when change comes – you need to learn to relax and go with the flow. Your grandma would have been so excited about this next stage in our lives.'

'You won't throw anything away though, will you, Tollie?'

He takes a step back, his eyes flashing over my face with concern.

'Whatever you want of your grandma's is yours, 'course it is. The rest can go to the charity shop – she would have liked that. Nell didn't attach any meanin' to things, only people. I had me instructions about the ring and there are a few other bits of jewellery in her trinket box that are yours, anyway. It's just that I would like to have the pleasure of seein' you and Gray settin' up home in Lock Keeper's Cottage. Then you can get on with buildin' your new life together.'

The look on his face is a picture. He's happy; happier than I've seen him for a long time.

'Relegating you to the house in the garden, as you did to me, a wayward teenager who was driving you mad.'

It's his turn to laugh out loud.

'The Retreat is just that, isn't it? But it's not too shabby. It gave us the distance we needed. To be honest, I'm bein' selfish. Spendin' time in my armchair lookin' out over that view of the fields is rather appealin' at my time of life. You and Gray will be far too busy workin' to turn the cottage into your perfect home, to sit and gaze out at that view – but I'll be in my element. The cottage is too beautiful a place to let fall into disrepair and we would be lettin' your grandma down. The bonus is that I'll be well away from the buildin' work. But I'd like to think at some point the two of you will buy a boat and spend a bit of time cruisin' up and down the canal, as we did when you were a nipper.'

I might not have had a mother, but I had a brilliant dad and two truly special grandparents.

* * *

'Morning, Abe. Need any help?'

I'm on my way through to the sales desk with a box of Christmas baubles that are on special offer. Abe isn't a frequent visitor to the nurseries and, judging by the way he's standing there, with one arm folded across his chest and rubbing his fingers up and down his chin, he has a dilemma.

'It's our wedding anniversary, my lovely,' he replies, giving me a wink. 'I usually buy the old girl an ornament or something. There's not a lot here that isn't Christmassy, this year.'

'Ah, that's nice. How many years?'

He looks at me, screwing up his face. 'I dunno. Lots.'

It's hard not to laugh as I stand next to him, box pressed firm against my chest, gazing at the display. He's right. This year it's a Christmas explosion for sure, as Martin has really ramped things up and it's paying off.

'What sort of thing were you looking for?' I ask him.

'Last year I bought one of those crystal paperweights. It had a butterfly etched inside. Beautiful. She loved it.'

'Follow me. Let's see what we can find.'

Abe looks at me quizzically but does as I ask. After dropping off the box ready to set up the new display, I lead him on past the staffroom and into the stockroom.

'It's a bit of a squeeze,' I admit as we negotiate the narrow gangways between the racking.

There are boxes stacked everywhere and it's a sharp reminder that this lot has to go back on display once the festive period is over. But before that will be the big sale, which will hopefully mean fewer Christmas things to box up and store until next year.

'Mind out for Bert.' I turn on my heel as I warn Abe not to catch himself on the antlers of the large cast-iron stag I have affectionately named as he squeezes past.

'My, he's a big one.'

'Yes,' I call over my shoulder. 'We use the heavy-duty sacktruck to move him in here so we can make way for the Christmas trees. It's a shame, as he's so regal and Christmassy. I hate to think of him being hidden away in a dark room like this, when he should really be outside. But people are more likely to buy trees, trimmings and small gifts than large, very expensive garden ornaments.'

'Can I take a peek under the sheet?'

I turn around, lifting up the cover with both hands. Abe gives Bert a nod of his head.

'What a fine fellow. Nice to meet you, Bert.'

Abe turns over the little white tag hanging from Bert's neck and his eyes widen as he sees the price.

'He's a statement piece. Martin is very attached to Bert, though, as he sees him as a good-luck omen. It's funny, because Martin isn't usually one to make an impulse buy and I wonder if Bert will ever find a true home. There aren't many visitors who can stump up fifteen hundred quid just like that.'

'If I had a garden, I'd be tempted, but the old girl would probably veto it.'

I shake my head at Abe, raising an eyebrow at the reference to *the old girl*.

'I rather like the fact that Bert has been here as long as I have, Abe. He's one of the staff, too,' I joke. 'Never mind, Bert. Not long now until we get you back out into the fresh air again.'

I reach out affectionately to pat Bert's majestic neck.

'You have a friend there, Immi.' Abe laughs.

Carefully tucking the sheet back around the mighty beast, I head off in the direction of the racking at the back of the storeroom. As I scan the shelves, Abe stands alongside me with a slight frown on his face.

'How do you know what's what?'

'Well, everything has a supplier code and this stack is mainly angel statues, then it's glassware, and this is... what I'm looking for.'

I grab one of the boxes and carefully lift off the lid, offering the dark blue box with the padded white silk insert to Abe.

'My, that's pretty.' He studies the handmade, crystal glass hummingbird and a smile creeps over his face.

'It's a sun-catcher, Abe. When you hang it up this little cut-glass crystal attached to the tail acts like a prism. When it reflects the sunlight, it will really bring out the beautiful purples and blues in the wings. Rather special, isn't it?'

'Spot on, my lovely. Knew you'd sort me out. Ethel is going to love it. How are things with you?'

I pop the lid back on and we retrace our steps out through to the till.

'Good. I'm really looking forward to Christmas Day and having what, for us, will seem like a house full of people. That doesn't happen these days and I do miss the old times. Ethel's Christmas pudding will, no doubt, be the highlight of the meal, but I'll be glued to the cooker doing the very best job I can with the turkey and trimmings.'

As Abe walks alongside me he turns his head, giving me a knowing glance.

'It's the thought that counts, Immi, so don't let it be a pressure on you. And besides, it's a doubly special occasion this year. We're honoured to be a part of it; that means a lot to Ethel and me. It was nice to meet Gray's mum, Rona, last weekend. Big changes coming for her, next year, that's for sure.'

Involuntarily, I find myself frowning.

'Well, hopefully things will work out.' I'm not sure it's a comment as much as it's wishful thinking.

'I'm sure they will. He's a lucky man, is Gray, but he knows that.'

'What's this all about?'

As Gray swings open the hallway door and steps into the open-plan area, I can't hide a self-satisfied grin.

'Surprise!' I call out from behind him.

He stands with his back to me, dripping a little from the heavy rain as he surveys the dining table laid out for two in all its finery. I even managed to get Tollie to go digging around in the attic to find Grandma's prized silver candelabra.

We slip off our wet coats and I go off to hang them up to begin drying out. When I return Gray is sniffing the air appreciatively, turning to me with his eyes full of mischief.

'Please tell me that's Sarah's beef in red wine.'

I nod and he walks around the holdall he dumped on the floor to wrap his hands around my waist. Planting a noisy kiss on my lips, he swipes a few raindrops off my cheek, but they're quickly replaced as droplets are still running off his hair.

'If you don't let me go it's in danger of burning.' I smile up at him. 'And you need to dry your hair.'

He catches me up in his arms playfully, walking me backwards into the room.

'Well, we can't waste all your hard work, and you have one hungry man here.' Gray deposits me next to the cooker, looking happy and relaxed. The weekend starts here.

'I figured you've had a tough week and we're overdue a romantic evening together. Sarah sends her regards.'

'It's just what I needed, Immi, and it's the thought that counts. But where's Tollie?'

'Him and Fisher have taken Valerie off to an open night at the Middle Norton Brewing Company. We were all invited, and someone has to show local support, of course.'

'Ah.' He beams at me. 'That's an invite no one can refuse, so I'm astounded I won the toss-up. I wonder if Valerie is going along just to keep an eye on them; who's the designated driver?'

'Valerie insisted.'

'Ah. That makes sense, then. But you got us out of it?'

'I did. I wanted to start the weekend off in a relaxing way.'

I wriggle out of his grasp to check the oven, calling out over my shoulder, 'Five minutes, no more.'

Gray heads off to the bathroom as I ferry plates and dishes across to the table. When he returns, he lights the candles then switches everything else off so we can sit side by side, staring out at the garden. Surrounded only by the soft, flickering light, this is bliss.

'It's rather dramatic in the rain, isn't it?' Gray reaches for my hand, clasping it tightly in his.

The garden up-lighters illuminate little patches of shrubs right down to the boundary and it makes the slanting rain glisten in places. Beyond that it's impossible to see any detail of the vast expanse of fields, but the backdrop of a light, opaque thread of sky on the horizon melts into the graduated darkness of heavy black clouds. The contrast is stunning; one of those dramatic skies that don't look real.

A sudden clap of thunder overhead makes me jump and my hand flies straight to my chest.

'It's like looking at a painting, seeing the sky like that, but I hope the storm passes quickly. Anyway, fingers crossed this tastes every bit as good as it smells.'

Gray reluctantly releases my hand, but I can see from his expression how much he's looking forward to eating.

'Great-looking roast potatoes,' Gray remarks as I pass him a serving spoon.

'These are all my own work,' I inform him quite proudly.

'Well, I'm glad there's plenty of them. Anything happened this week that we haven't had time to talk about yet?' he enquires, piling roasters onto his plate.

Next, he lifts the lid on the casserole dish, holding up his plate so I can dispense a generous ladleful. Wafts of beefy goodness make even my stomach begin to grumble.

'Well, Fisher has spoken to Valerie and she will officially take over my role after Christmas. I'll go into the office for one final day to do a formal handover. To be honest, it isn't really necessary, but Fisher and I are both a little sad about it. It's the end of an era and we need to mark it in some way. Doughnuts and lunch at The Bullrush, I think, so not a lot of work is going to get done.'

Gray's mouth is full, so he nods his head in acknowledgement. I find myself toying with a cube of beef on my plate. It's time to tell him about the conversation with Tollie.

'Apparently, in The Bullrush on Sunday evening they were talking about clubbing together to get us an engagement present. I told Tollie to put the damper on that, as we don't want a fuss – that's the whole point of doing the ring thing on Christmas Day and not having a separate celebration. But—'

I pause and Gray puts down his fork, sensing my apprehension.

'He's adamant, Gray.' My tone is one of acceptance as I know it's useless fighting Tollie on this one. 'We're doing the swap once you come to live in Aysbury.'

Gray shakes his head, sadly, half turning to reach out and cover my hand as it languishes on the table.

'I know we both feel awkward about this, Immi, but it's a big deal for Tollie. He doesn't see it in the same way that you do – it's not about clinging onto the past. He's passing on the baton and he's counting his blessings that he's still fit and able to see you run with it. Our job is to make him proud and to bring his dream for the cottage alive.'

Gray's eyes seek out mine and we sit for a moment, in silence. We both know that I'm the one here with the problem and I'm projecting that onto Tollie.

'Funny, he said more or less the exact same thing. Okay. We're doing it. I can't say it will be easy, as Tollie is going to begin clearing out all the old stuff. It will be hard on us both, Gray. And I still don't like the thought that he wants to pass everything on to us now, as if there's some sort of rush. There's a lot of living left in him and I don't want to think about the future in that way.'

Gray shifts slightly in his chair.

'You can't look at it like that, Immi. He wants to experience it all alongside us, the joy of setting up our new life together. Tollie is eighty-six and a young eighty-six, at that. He's fitter than a lot of men twenty years his junior, so let's just be grateful and start making plans.'

Gray cups my chin in his hand. 'Now, cheer up. This food is getting cold and that's a waste. And I want you in a happy mood for later.' The look I receive is decidedly flirtatious.

He picks up his fork again and I sit watching him eating with relish. Nothing knocks him for long; he has an indomitable spirit. I notice the fingertips of his left hand are tapping away lightly on the tabletop the other side of him. In his head there's a melody playing and it's what I love so much about this man.

I begin eating too, resolving to stop hankering over the past – what was and what might have been. It's time to focus on creating a new reality. I know Grandma would simply tell me to pull myself together and get on with it.

'Country chic is a good look for the cottage,' I begin. 'What do—'

Suddenly, everything goes black and, aside from the flickering candlelight emanating from the centre of the table. The room around us seems to get sucked into the shadowy garden outside.

'Uh-oh,' Gray moans, shovelling up the last forkful of food on his plate, then wiping his mouth on a paper napkin. 'You finish yours, and I'll check the distribution board. There's nothing in the oven still, is there?'

'No. I made the New York cheesecake this afternoon.'

Even in the softly flickering light, I can see Gray's eyes lighting up at the mention of his favourite dessert.

Eating alone in the cosy shadows and listening to Gray banging around in the under-stairs cupboard as he grabs the small stepladder, I know that I'll miss this place. Even though it reminds me of my journey from being a petulant teenager into an adult, it really has been my retreat from the world through some very tough years. A part of my reluctance to move has been as much about me as it has been about Tollie, I finally admit to myself. But tonight, I feel at peace with what's to come. And grateful.

'Thank you for giving me Gray,' I say out loud to the emptiness around me. And then immediately feel rather silly.

'What's that?' Gray calls from the hallway, as I savour a last mouthful of tender beef. 'It's not the board. It's a power cut,' he adds.

Well, there's nothing we can do about that, so I carefully pile up the plates and carry them across to the sink. Swilling them off, I stack them in the dishwasher as Gray returns.

'It's going to get rather chilly, very quickly,' he points out and I groan.

A huge fork of lightning sees us both running to the patio doors. Instinctively, I grab Gray's hand and he wraps his arm around my shoulders.

'I think there's only one thing that will help take our minds off this storm.'

I gaze up at him, smiling. 'I'm thinking hiding in the cupboard might be the best option.'

'A big helping of cheesecake. Preferably in bed, so we can stare out and watch the display.'

Gray is already corking the wine bottle and stowing it under his arm, as he grabs the half-full wine glasses off the table.

'I doubt this will last for very long before they get the power back on. It probably shorted something at the sub-station. I'll be back to carry the tray.' He throws the words over his shoulder as he begins to make his way upstairs.

I do hope this storm eases off before Valerie has to drive back from the brewery. It seems winter just can't make up its mind what it wants to do this year. It's not looking good for a white Christmas, though.

* * *

We're in bed by eight-thirty, so it's no surprise that at just after three in the morning we are both wide awake.

'I feel like I've had a full night's sleep,' Gray whispers in the darkness. 'I wonder if the power is back on.'

When we jump out of bed to stare out of the window, it's clear that we left the lights on. 'The garden lights are back on. So, it's all good. The heating hasn't kicked in, though, and it's freezing. Do you fancy a cup of tea?'

Gray eases his legs over the side of the bed.

'I'll go and reset the boiler, while you pop the kettle on.'

Grabbing one of my thick jumpers from the chest of drawers, I tug it over my head, reappearing to see Gray staring at me.

'What?'

'Very fetching,' he replies.

Even in the gloom, Rudolph's bright red nose seems to glow as if it's lit up.

'He's cuddly. I've had him for years.'

Grabbing the tray from our evening feast, I make my way down to the kitchen and brave putting on one of the side lights.

I'm so used to living here alone that it's still strange, whenever Gray sleeps over, to hear someone banging around upstairs. But it is comforting and being one of a couple means that a lot of things are about to change – it's time to start getting used to that.

'Heating's on. It won't take long to warm it up. Do you have any biscuits?'

I look across at Gray as he approaches and burst out laughing. He brings his usual T-shirt and shorts to sleep in, but it is icy cold in here and he's grabbed my winter dressing gown. He looks like a hobbit with the hood up and his hairy – admittedly, very muscular – legs exposed, as it barely reaches his knees.

'Fetching,' I remark, not even trying to hide my reaction. 'It's a *no* to the biscuits, sorry.'

Instead, he swings open the fridge door, reaching his hand inside.

'Would you think it awful if I had another slice of cheesecake?'

'Not if we share it,' I retort.

'Ah, a woman after my own heart. Shall I pop up and get a blanket so I can take off this teeny dressing gown and we can snuggle up on the sofa?'

'Please do and I'll try my best to wipe the image from my mind.'

I wave him off while I sort everything out. There's something so decadent about being awake when the rest of Aysbury is fast asleep. A feeling of exhilaration courses through me. It's not simply the fact that Christmas is looming, we're engaged, and Gray and I will soon be living together, but the feeling that my life is finally falling into place.

Carrying the tray into the sitting room, I find Gray is now assembling an array of candles on the coffee table. The moment our eyes meet my heart begins to thud in my chest. He is my soul mate, there's no mistaking that. And I'm his.

'You spoil me,' he says.

I hold out a plate and he grabs one of the two forks in my hand.

'Everyone deserves a little spoiling now and again. You surprised me this last week.'

I sink down next to him and he covers us both with the blanket, tilting his head to look at me and give me one of his loving, radiant smiles.

'How?'

'I thought you'd be angry about this thing with your father. Poor Rona was so anxious about it.'

His smile fades away and his discomfort is tangible as he shrugs his shoulders.

'We fly out on the twenty-eighth of December, which is annoying to say the least. I wanted to be around to savour our engagement celebration and spend a little time here with you. Plus, Valerie invited Mum to stay with her for a couple of days over the new year period, which was very thoughtful of her. It would have helped to cement their friendship. Now, instead, we'll be heading off to sunny California and it's not exactly going to be a holiday, is it?'

He sounds gutted and I feel for him.

'No. It's not, Gray. But you're lucky, in a way.' The look he gives me is one of empathy and guilt. He knows I'd give anything to meet my mum face to face. Even if the result was that it made me realise my dad and I were nothing to her. At least I'd know for sure.

'I'm sorry, Immi. You're right. Do you know something? You make me a better person just because your take on things is honest. Your gut instinct isn't to be resentful, but to live in the hope that eventually even the worst of us will do the right thing. But some people don't deserve a second chance, or even forgiveness for what they've done. I don't ever want anyone to take advantage of your good heart, my love. That's why Tollie worries about you and from here on in it's my job to be your protector so he can relax a little.'

Am I that fragile? I feel like a warrior most of the time, but inside – well, Gray is right. There's that piece of me at the core that I keep hidden for fear it will break as easily as shattering a glass.

'How long will you be gone?'

Gray expels a deep breath, which indicates reluctance, more so than resigned acceptance. He just wants it to be over.

'Ten days. Ten lonely, wasted days without you. I have no intention of interfering between Mum and Grayson. I'll just do my bit as requested and leave them to sort themselves out. It's utterly ridiculous that a few forms are stopping Mum from moving on. This is where she needs to be. Aysbury is the perfect place to encourage her back out into the world and she's crazy if she allows him to stand in the way of that.'

'Let's hope for the best, Gray. I doubt that either of them are happy with things as they stand,' I reply encouragingly. His frown reflects his annoyance.

'It's my father's fault that they're still in this situation after all these years. Considering that Mum talks in rather reverential tones about him being an astute businessman, he's demonstrated a total lack of responsibility. Mum might not have had the money or the access to a solicitor to help her sort it out, but he most certainly would have done. But why on earth did she let him get away with it? It was a big mistake letting it slide and now he expects everyone to jump because the timing is right for him.'

I scoop up a large forkful of cheesecake, placing my hand beneath it as I offer it to Gray. He rolls his eyes and duly opens his mouth.

'Well, all you can do is be there for your mum if she needs a little support. I feel rather useless not being able to help you at all on this. But I'm here to make you cheesecake whenever you need a bit of cheering up, as at least that's one thing I know how to make.' I brush off the guilt of whipping the box straight into the bin as I empty out the two sachets to make him his perfect treat. 'And before you jet off, we have what promises to be one awesome Christmas Day engagement celebration. This time next year everyone's troubles will, hopefully, be a thing of the past. And you and I will be living in the cottage. Keep holding onto that thought and grit your teeth while you're in Los Angeles. Just savour the sunshine while you're there.'

Gray stares down at the plate, impatiently awaiting another forkful.

'Maybe I'm being a little unfair,' he reflects, sounding rather mellow now as the sugar kicks in. It's amazing what cheesecake can do.

'It's easy to look at things as an outsider and be both judge and jury, isn't it?' I conclude.

Loading up the fork once more, I pop it into my own mouth and Gray feigns a look of disappointment.

'All right, I'll try my best to be a little more understanding. And now I think I'd better grab another forkful pretty quickly, before this is all gone.'

16

CHRISTMAS PANIC SETS IN

First thing in the morning, Tollie and I head into town to do a special food shop for the Christmas Day party. It means leaving our trusty crew to get everything set up for the last day of Santa Ahoy cruises, but with less than three full days now until Christmas Eve, I'm beginning to panic. Tollie usually does most of the cooking and I have no idea why I told him he could leave it to me. What was I thinking?

'You're drivin' a bit fast, m'dear,' Tollie points out.

Easing up on the accelerator to appease him, I know I'm distracted. There's still so much to do. The spare bedroom in the cottage needs a good clean ready for Rona's stay and I have so many different lists with things still to be ticked off that my head feels as if it's about to explode. And I'm already stressing over the thought of taking delivery of the turkey. It's the first time I've cooked a full Christmas dinner, let alone catered for eight people.

'Um—' Out of the side of my eye, I notice Tollie is staring down at the fistful of paper I thrust at him before we jumped into the car. 'Is there any particular order to these lists?'

My hands grip a little tighter around the steering wheel.

'I'm not sure. I can't remember. I just keep writing things down.'

Tollie drops them into his lap and reaches forward to turn on the radio.

'What are you doing?' My tone reflects a sense of irritation. I need peace and quiet to process my thoughts, not a cacophony of sounds.

'Immi, you seriously need to relax, m'dear. Do me a favour and turn the car around.'

Immediately jumping on the brakes, I pull into a little passing area off to the side of the narrow lane. Is Tollie feeling unwell?

'What's wrong?'

'Nothin'. We're goin' back to pick up Valerie.'

I look at him, unable to hide a sense of confusion. Did he offer her a lift and he simply forgot?

'Valerie? Why?'

'Just do as I say. Trust your old granddad. If we're goin' to avoid major stress we need someone with a cool head who knows what they're doin'.'

I breathe out slowly. He's right. It's time to take a little diversion.

* * *

'What on earth? Did you buy up the entire supermarket?'

Gray stands in the kitchen, surveying the mass of carrier bags and looking most concerned. I notice Tollie giving him a warning glance, accompanied by a little shake of the head. I went too far, and I know it.

'It's all under control,' Valerie replies calmly. 'We could do with a little space, though, to get this lot sorted.' Her voice is firm, and the two men quickly disappear, throwing me a rather sheepish look.

Leaning back against the countertop, I feel myself sagging ever so slightly.

'Thank you, Valerie.'

'Look, Immi, that got a little out of hand. As Tollie and I tried to tell you, it's one day, that's all. You picked up enough stuff to feed the entire village. There really is no need to panic. But it's simply too much for one person when they aren't used to entertaining.'

She's right. I swear I'm seconds away from hyperventilating and now tears are beginning to sting my eyes as I try hard to blink them away.

'Come here.' Valerie stands in front of me, holding out her arms. I step forward to accept her hug. She's not quick to hug people, but it's nice to see she's feeling a lot more confident about getting closer to people who are her friends.

Suddenly, I'm sobbing my heart out.

'What's brought this on? It isn't like you.'

I'm a blubbering mess and as I step back, she grabs a handful of kitchen towels, which I accept gratefully and use to blot my face.

'I want it all to be perfect, but what if I mess up? It won't just ruin our engagement celebration, but everyone's Christmas dinner,' I blub.

Valerie places a hand on each of my shoulders. This diminutive woman certainly has a strong grip.

'Listen to me, Immi. It's going to be fine. Perfect is what you expect from a hotel, or a restaurant. A dinner for family and friends is about food cooked with love, burnt bits and all. It's about the laughter around the table and guests feeling special because they appreciate the effort involved. And the fact that they will be here to raise their glasses in honour of two very special people making a firm commitment to each other. There will be a lot of love around the table on Christmas Day and that's what's important, not serving up a five-star, gourmet meal.'

I nod, still hanging my head.

'You are putting undue pressure on yourself, Immi. And no one wants that. It's time to delegate. Get out those lists and we'll run through them quickly.'

Rather miserably, I dip into my handbag and thrust the sheath of crumpled notes in Valerie's direction.

'Okay. It's time for some straight talking. We've more than covered the shopping lists.' She gazes down at the mountain of shopping and then glances heavenwards.

As I pulled things from the shelves my lists were the last thing on my mind, and it was like a supermarket sweep. I kept insisting that I needed... everything.

'Yes, well, it's time to calm things down a little now and get this lot put away.'

I'm embarrassed by the inordinate amount of time it takes to find room for everything. We always stock up for winter, but this is crazy.

'Right.' Valerie begins folding up the empty shopping bags. 'Let's sort out those to-do lists next. I'm guessing that you're fretting over the fact that, in your eyes, the cottage isn't ready for guests. As it will be Rona's first time staying in Aysbury, I understand you want everything to be just right.

'However, what did strike me was whether she'll feel a little awkward sharing a bathroom with Tollie, when they don't really know each other that well. Rona is also unlikely to want to stay in one of the two spare bedrooms in The Retreat with you and Gray, is she? So, what if I invite her to mine? I'd enjoy the company and my study has a folding bed, which is very comfortable indeed. I've already extended an invitation to stay with me over the new year period, but Rona says she's going away. I didn't give the Christmas Eve arrangements a thought.'

I flash her a grateful look as I search around for a pen. Valerie throws the shopping lists into the bin and then straightens the remainder of the crumpled papers. She takes the pen from me, with an encouraging smile.

'Iron the new bedding for the spare room – tick. No longer necessary. Right. Starters. Tick. I'm sure Rona and I can cope with that. We can make up platters and bring them with us on Christmas morning. What did you buy?'

'Mushrooms, garlic and herbs for crostini and the ingredients for goats' cheese and shallot tarts.'

Valerie raises her eyebrows and begins laughing.

'Okay. I think the two of us will be able to get our heads around that. What if we also prepare a large dish of cauliflower cheese and red cabbage with chestnuts? Those can be quickly reheated in the oven on the day.'

Already I can feel the pressure beginning to lift a little. Valerie is turning out to be a saviour.

'You'd do that?'

'Of course. You can focus on the turkey, gravy, stuffing and roast potatoes. You were sensible enough, thank goodness, to buy frozen peas and sprouts. To be honest, they're the best option, anyway. What else is there on these lists?'

She trawls through the various sheets, randomly crossing things out.

'Did you say Ethel is bringing Christmas pudding and Christmas cake?' Valerie asks, getting me to focus.

'Yes.'

'Well, I have a big batch of mince pies sitting in the freezer. They're fine from frozen and much better than the shop-bought ones, anyway. But cheesecake? Is that really necessary?'

A little smile creeps over my face.

'It's Gray's favourite.'

'Oh. Fine. That's a priority, then. One piece of advice, if you don't mind me poking my nose in.'

I look at her, shaking my head. 'No. Please do; I can't pretend I'm not a little overwhelmed right now. Christmas just seems to have snuck up on me quicker than I anticipated.'

'Well, you've been rushed off your feet, Immi, so that's understandable. Anyway, have a back-up plan for the turkey. Things go wrong, they always do. Not least the odd power cut. Ring the farm shop and ask them to deliver a joint, as well as the turkey. Cook it on Christmas Eve and, whatever happens, you're covered. And, Immi, don't forget that you will be surrounded by people who care about you and the last thing they want is for you to be worrying unduly. Right?'

'Noted. Thanks, Valerie. Appreciated.'

Valerie has become a friend, one who really cares, and maybe, with what we've both been through, we recognise in each other some common ground. A little help in times of need goes a long, long way.

* * *

It's the final cruise of the year and it's been a fabulous day. As Tollie and Gray do their parting goodbyes at the head of the gangplank, our visitors form an orderly queue to take their turn to express their thanks. One little girl hangs back. Her mother is busy chatting and laughing with several other parents as the line creeps forward very slowly. Everyone is in high spirits after raising the roof with some very exuberant renditions of a whole raft of Christmas favourites.

The little girl's name is Phoebe and she keeps glancing down at me, as I'm rolling up the Christmas rug.

'I know Santa needs a lot of help, so why doesn't he have a

Christmas angel? Angels can make anything happen.' Her little voice is so soft and yet her question is insistent.

'It takes a whole team of elves and helpers to make the toys and get everything sorted. That would be an awful lot for one angel to manage, wouldn't it?'

'Yes, but an elf doesn't have a magic wand.' Her little frown is forlorn.

'Hmm. Well, I guess that would be useful, but magic wands are for special things. Besides, the elves love making toys as they know how much the children look forward to playing with them.'

Her frown continues to deepen as she stares back at me.

'But if Santa had an angel helper, she could make everything right.'

I freeze as I realise where Phoebe is going with this. She's one of the families invited here today on our final Little Stars trip because she recently lost her father in a tragic accident.

'I want my daddy back – just for Christmas.' And with that she bursts into tears. Her mother appears behind her, placing a hand on Phoebe's shoulder as she kneels down to comfort her daughter and wipe her eyes.

My heart feels as if it's being torn in half as I look at those worried little eyes desperately seeking an answer. I have no idea what she's been told, so I don't know what to say and I glance at Phoebe's mother, earnestly.

'Daddy will be watching us from heaven, darling, so he won't miss a thing. He wants us to try very hard not to be sad and to make everyone else smile. We can do that, can't we?'

Phoebe swallows hard as emotions continue to swamp her. Her mum wipes a stray tear from her little cheek.

'I don't want you, Grandma, or Granddad to be sad, Mummy. Even if it hurts to smile.'

Her mother glances at me and what I see is a broken-hearted

woman who is trying so hard to hold it all together. I cast around, desperately wanting to be of some help.

Two pairs of eyes are focused on me as, sitting back on my heels, I begin speaking.

'I believe there is a little angel inside all of us, Phoebe,' I tell her gently. 'When people are sad, we might not have a magic wand to wave, but we can do something really magical to help. And that's to share our love by being strong. It's a time to give people lots of hugs and remember all the happy times. And it's okay to cry and let your feelings out. But being brave and cheerful is important, because your daddy wouldn't want you feeling miserable all the time. When you make new, happy memories, that will make him smile, too.'

Phoebe's mum reaches out to place a hand on my arm, giving it a grateful squeeze.

'We've had a lovely time today, haven't we, Phoebe? We've sung, and laughed, and it's been a blessing. And we will have lots of smiley times this Christmas, in between our tears.'

'We can be like angels, can't we, Mummy?' Phoebe casts an enquiring glance, her forehead wrinkled as she waits for confirmation.

'We can, my darling girl. We can be angels for Daddy. Thank you, Immi. Thank you so very much.'

As they stand and hurry across to catch up with the others, my own tears start to fall. I bend my head, shaking them off as I continue rolling the rug. I feel stupid for obsessing over the minutiae of life, when all around me there are families facing the biggest hurdles of their lives. There is nothing more humbling than witnessing other people's pain and loss.

It's time to start putting things into perspective and focus on my blessings.

The next morning we're all up and out early. Tollie, Gray, Abe and Fisher are tasked with taking down the decorations on The Star Gazer and giving it a good clean. Why Fisher feels the need to join in cleaning his own boat, when he's good enough to let us use it, I don't know. But when the guys are all together there's a lot of banter going on and I think he'd hate to be left out. Besides, Valerie will – no doubt – spoil them throughout the day. Everything from bacon sandwiches, courtesy of The Bullrush, to mugs of hot chocolate and a bottle of the special Christmas brew at some point later in the day.

As for me and Ethel, we're helping out in The Bullrush's kitchen, because it's their busiest day of the year. I'm last out of the door and am conscious I need to up my pace as it's already seven-thirty, so I'm running late. The final Sunday before Christmas is a special day here on the canal with the much-celebrated Bullrush Inn Christmas dinner and an all-day pop-up Christmas market. The stalls are laid out in the communal car park and it's very popular. People come from miles around, as it's a tradition that's been upheld for as long as I can remember.

Thankfully, Aysbury Manor allows the use of a large gravelled courtyard the other side of the lane as a visitors' parking area. There are a few old farm buildings that are no longer in regular use, but store farm machinery that hasn't been moved in a long time. Most of the manor's farmland is now leased, and worked, by Adler's farm.

Up ahead of me I spot Bernie Williams with his clipboard, standing on the edge of the towpath as he directs stallholders to their pitches. I wave out as I stride towards him.

'Hi, Bernie. How are you? It's been ages. How is The Great Escape?'

'Now you're a sight for sore eyes, Immi – that's put a smile on my face. She's good, thank you. The old girl is due to hole up in the boat yard to have some work done to her hull in the spring, so I'll be staying put for a while and giving Turnpike Cottage a bit of attention. Other than that, she's shipshape and the old girl has done me proud.'

Bernie has been around forever and is one of Tollie's oldest friends. He owns a small cottage a mere stroll away and used to have a permanent mooring here at the marina. His wife, Claire, died a few years ago and since then he spends more time on his boat cruising the canals than he does on dry land.

Rumour has it that he has a temporary job at every place he stops, and he works his way around them. I know for a fact that he lends a hand at one of the pubs further up the canal and in summer is often found in the Wennington Lock Tea Gardens, about half an hour from here. He cuts the grass and generally potters, as he's a keen gardener. But he always heads back to run our two pop-up markets. One in mid-summer, which is more of a fête, and the Christmas one, which is very much for food lovers.

'I hear you and Gray are engaged, Immi. Congratulations and about time, too! Tollie is over the moon.'

Bernie leans in to give me a warm hug.

'Tell that man of yours if he doesn't treat you like the princess you are, then he'll have me to answer to.'

I stand back, shaking my head and smiling up at him.

'Bernie! He already has Tollie and Fisher bending his ear. I think poor Gray needs an ally, to be honest with you, as it's tough trying to please them both. Have you heard about next year's celebration – ten years of Santa Ahoy?'

'I did hear a whisper, but I haven't been around much lately. I have plans to catch up with Tollie tonight, though. I've been doing some work for a widow who lives the other side of Wennington. Back in the summer she wanted some bushes pruned and we've sort of struck up a friendship, I suppose you could say. I've been helping her out with a few jobs around the house, in between my usual little jaunts.'

I try to maintain a straight face, as this is obviously a big deal for Bernie but he's trying to keep it low-key.

'Well, that's rather nice to hear. What are you doing Christmas Day?'

'I was hoping to invite her back to the cottage for a couple of days. To be honest, it's been a blessing living on the boat, but I'm not getting any younger and I'll be talking to Fisher about a mooring for The Great Escape.'

'Permanently?'

'Maybe.'

'Well, why don't you join us for Christmas Day lunch? There's only eight of us, so it might be a nice introduction for your lady friend. It will be Tollie, me, Gray, Gray's mum – Rona – Abe, Ethel, Fisher and Valerie.'

'Valerie?'

'Mrs Price. Everyone calls her Valerie now.'

The beam on Bernie's face is heart-warming. 'Oh. Well. That would be smashing, thanks, Immi. I bet Yvonne will love it.'

'Great. I must dash. I'm kitchen hand today and the potatoes won't peel themselves.'

I leave him chuckling away as my fast walk turns into a sprint.

'So sorry I'm late,' I gasp, as I finally head into the kitchen. Having slipped off my coat, I grab one of the aprons and walk over to the sink to wash my hands.

Jude and Jade are cutting out small circles from the largest tray-baked sponge sandwich I've ever seen; and there's a stack of similar trays on a trolley awaiting their turn.

'Great job, girls. Is this one of the desserts?'

'Yes, it's the base,' Jade replies.

Jude jumps in. 'We have vanilla cream and strawberries to—'

'—sandwich in between. And white chocolate nests to go on the top,' Jade continues.

'Well, it sounds amazing.'

'And thank you for the bracelets,' they both say, in unison. 'We love them!'

I knew they would, and I wanted Tollie to be the one to give them to the girls.

'You two make amazing elves and we wanted you to know how much we appreciated your help. It's a wonderful thing to put smiles on people's faces and you are both twinkling little stars.'

They are beaming ear to ear and, behind me, I suspect that Sarah will be looking on, every bit the proud mum. The silver bracelets with tiny little stars hanging from them were the perfect gift.

'Right. It's time to peel and chop.'

There's a clatter behind me and I do a one-hundred-and-eighty-degree turn to see a rather stressed-looking Sarah basting a huge turkey.

'Do you want me to do that? I can keep an eye on it if you tell me how often I need to do it. The practice will come in handy, as that's probably about the size of the one I've ordered from the farm shop.'

Sarah raises her eyebrows, giving me a brief but decidedly hesitant look. I'm not known for my cooking skills, and maybe a huge turkey isn't the best place to start, but I'll manage somehow. I take the basting tool she hands to me, making a mental note to dig out the one I'm pretty sure Tollie will have in his kitchen – somewhere.

'You are an angel. Set the timer for every thirty minutes. Just make sure you put the foil back over the breast each time. I need to start work on the beef Wellingtons. Kurt and Ethel are laying the tables and they'll be joining us as soon as they've finished. Thanks, Immi.'

It's going to be a long day.

* * *

When Tollie, Gray, Abe, Fisher and Valerie arrive, they find The Bullrush Inn team sitting in the conservatory, looking shattered. Jude and Jade are sprawled along the banquet against the side wall; opposite them, Sarah, Kurt and I are each nursing a large glass of wine. The trusty Maggie, who arrived ten minutes ago, places a small glass of port in front of Ethel, who reaches out for it immediately, taking a large gulp.

'Judging by the look of you all it was a busy one this year. Poor dears, you're done in.' Normally she'd have been here, but today her sister's birthday happened to fall on the day of The Bullrush Inn Christmas dinner and Maggie had a fancy lunch of her own to attend.

'Sixty-four covers. But who's counting?' Sarah exclaims. 'I'm sure I said never again, this time last year. It seems I have a short memory.'

'You did,' Kurt confirms, rather soberly. 'But wasn't it a great day? I mean, all that buzz and chatter, all those smiling faces. Well done, team. We did it.'

He sounds elated and the girls sit up, reaching across the table to high-five everyone. However, as we lean forward, Sarah, Kurt, Ethel and I do so with a groan.

'I'm so sorry I couldn't help out,' Maggie says. 'But I'm here now and I'm taking charge. I bet you are all starving.'

Maggie is wonderful; she drives over from Middle Norton and works most weekends and some evenings. She'll turn her hand to anything.

'Sorry, Maggie,' Sarah replies, sounding weary. 'The plan was to do a big pot of stew, or maybe Bolognese for us all, but we ran out of time. There's some cold meat wrapped up on platters in the fridge and a few uncooked beef Wellingtons. Best ones I've ever made, if I say so myself. If you pop them in the oven, they'll only take thirty minutes. I'm not sure what else we had left over.'

Maggie holds up her hand to stop Sarah.

'Worry not, I have it.'

'I'll help.' Valerie suddenly speaks up, and heads turn in her direction. 'We'll rustle up something between the two of us, I'm sure.'

We all nod in appreciation as people start moving up to squeeze everyone around the table. Kurt jumps to his feet, in a surprising burst of energy.

'I'll add another table. No point in squashing up when we have all this space.' Abe immediately follows Kurt to help carry across another four-seater table.

'And I'll put on some music,' Abe says, heading off in the direction of the bar area.

Sidling up behind me, Gray leans in to whisper into my ear. 'Guess I'd better join the kitchen detail, then. I'm a man who is used to taking orders.'

With that he stoops down to plant a kiss on my cheek.

'I'll sort some drinks,' Tollie says, doing a cursory check of the glasses around the table.

The rest of us continue to sit, unable – or unwilling – to move. Even the girls have settled back down, albeit they are poring over an iPad, playing a game that sees them stabbing their fingers at the screen in a frenzy. Every few seconds one or the other of them squeals and it's funny to watch.

'I was so worried about cooking Christmas dinner for eight.' I incline my head in Sarah's direction, to the left of me. 'Now the figure has increased to ten and after today I'm wondering why I was being so silly. Seriously, that was an experience and a half.'

Kurt, who is the other side of me, laughs out loud and Sarah's face breaks out into a smile. 'You did brilliantly, Immi. Those were the best roast potatoes I think we've ever served.'

As we chatter away Fisher, too, disappears into the kitchen and, with one of the Christmas CDs playing softly in the background, my stomach moans hungrily. All that food we served up, plate after plate, and there wasn't a moment spare to think about feeding ourselves. What I learnt was that even a commercial kitchen feels the pressure and if everything turns out perfectly, then it's little short of a miracle. We had crumbly sponge, burnt gravy that meant starting again and Yorkshire puddings that ended up taking over the plates. But the diners were more than content, and eager to let us know it.

One thing I now know for sure is that if I ever need to look for a new career, it certainly won't be in catering.

'Guys,' I say to Sarah and Kurt, 'when you cater for our wedding next year, I don't want you two missing out on the fun. We'll sort a menu that can be prepared in advance and bring in a team of waiters and waitresses to serve us. If I thought you two worked hard before, I now have an even greater respect for what you've built here.'

We do a team toast, including the girls, who raise their glasses of blackcurrant juice.

When Gray appears bearing a large catering platter, there is a round of applause. Raising it aloft, as if he's a professional, he places it in the middle of the long table.

'Napkins? Plates? Forks?' I prompt, as realisation dawns and he does a double take at the table. He smacks his forehead with his hand.

'Right. Give me a minute – I'm new to this lark and it isn't as easy as the girls make it look.'

We all start laughing.

Maggie has toasted thin slices of ciabatta and topped them with slivers of turkey, adding a generous dollop of the leftover, freshly made cranberry sauce. Fisher is next out with a platter of pinwheel sandwiches, filled with roast pork and stuffing, secured with cock-tail sticks.

Gray returns with a platter of thin savoury biscuits, topped with various cheeses and garnished with a gorgeously gooey, homemade red-onion chutney. Fisher is behind him with the plates and napkins. And it isn't long before Maggie appears with a platter full of sliced beef Wellington.

'You'll need a fork for these, guys, because they're really hot but, Sarah, they smell so good. And don't forget to save some room for dessert.'

Ethel brings up the rear with the best platter of all – a mountain of sweet-potato fries – and a cheer goes up.

'What a feast!' Kurt declares, eagerly tucking in.

'Who says leftovers are boring?' Maggie adds, grabbing a plate for herself and gazing at the spread with a sense of satisfaction on her face.

It's funny how one minute you may feel so tired you can hardly move and the next you have the ability to jump up to grab just one more thing to eat. Then another. And another.

Tollie lifts his bottle of The Bullrush Inn Christmas Brew and the chatter subsides for a moment.

'Well, everyone around this table was instrumental in makin' this a bumper year for our charity fund. Whether that's sellin' bottles like these—' he tips his head to acknowledge Sarah, Kurt and Maggie's sales efforts '—or helpin' out on the The Star Gazer. And a special thanks has to go to our wonderful elves – Jude, Jade and Immi – Santa couldn't have had a better trio to back him up. It isn't money that makes the world go around, but kindness and love. And that's somethin' that Aysbury has a lot of, so here's to the most amazing group of people. I feel blessed to call you my friends – merry Christmas, one and all. Ho! Ho! Ho!'

It's a fitting wrap-up to the pre-Christmas festivities. Once everyone is so full they can't manage another bite, Fisher heads off to get another round of drinks, while Ethel, Abe and Maggie insist on clearing the table. Tollie makes his excuses and heads off with Bernie to begin getting Turnpike Cottage ready. He has a regular cleaner going in, but like Tollie, he finds himself surrounded by old furniture and things cluttering up the place. For Bernie, returning home will be a huge change and I know Tollie has really missed his old friend of many years. They went to school together and there are few people who can boast of a friendship spanning so many decades. These two men have lived in, or close to, Aysbury all their lives.

Next, Sarah and the girls march off to organise the desserts, leaving just Valerie, Gray and me to sit back and relax.

It's dark outside now and inside is lit only by the diffusers overhead, and the strings of Christmas lights. Cosy, warm and inviting, this has become a home from home for us all.

'While we're here on our own, I'd like to thank you, Immi and Gray, for... oh, how can I put this into words?' Valerie sits quietly for a moment, twisting her hands anxiously in her lap. 'I... I've always felt on the edge of things and I know that was entirely my own fault. Who isn't affected by what's happened in the past and the disappointments we have to endure? But I've been touched by the way you've taken the time to include me in your little inner circle. It's not been easy to lower my guard but now I have, my life feels different. So, I'd like to propose a toast to the two of you, and the exciting developments the new year is going to bring with it.'

Valerie's little speech obviously comes from the heart and Gray shoots me a rather poignant look as we clink glasses.

'Valerie, you are such a great organiser and I know Tollie appreciates that. And my mum, well, she's relieved to feel she has a friend here – someone who understands what it's like joining an established, tight little community. It means a lot to us all that you've invited her to stay over Christmas. This year is going to be a little up in the air and, no doubt, a little disorganised, but next year, well, we're going to have the party of all parties.'

My heart leaps in my chest.

'And in helping me out, so that I can be there for Martin, you're putting a huge smile on Fisher's face, too, Valerie. One that hasn't been there for a long time.'

She looks down, studying her hands as they lay still, now, in her lap.

'He's a very special man, Immi. Our paths rarely crossed in the past, but I think maybe – on reflection – he was avoiding me. We've become firm friends and we're discovering that we have so many things in common. That's been such a surprise. It really has.'

We've all noticed the change in her. Gone is the barrier Valerie always put up, making it difficult for people to get close to her. But now, well, she's speaking from the heart.

'All I can say is that every time your name comes up it puts a smile on Fisher's face. And that's good to see.'

Is Valerie blushing?

'Strawberry Dreams coming up!' Jude and Jade call out in unison, carrying a large platter between them. The proud look on their faces tells me that Sarah and Kurt have inspired two would-be chefs.

'Perfect!' I reply and Gray, Valerie and I exchange a look of contentment. Sometimes life brings things together rather nicely and all the hassle and problems of the past begin to dim.

The holidays are finally here.

18

THE HOLLY AND THE IVY

It's Monday. But a Monday with a difference, because Gray is here now until he's due to leave, on the twenty-seventh of December, to take Rona home to pack.

Quickly grabbing a jute sack, I follow Gray out of the door. This morning the sky is a silky, vibrant blue. Without a single cloud in sight and the sun still low in the sky, it could be the start of a glorious summer's day. However, everything around us is covered in a feathery, bone-chilling hoar frost.

The scarves wrapped around our faces help to diffuse the sharp, icy intake that comes with each gulp of air. Venturing out without a hat, gloves and sturdy boots would be madness on a morning like this and yet the contrast of brightness and cold is exhilarating. There's something so satisfying about the crispness and beauty of a winter scene that looks as if someone has sprayed everything in their path with hair-like white crystals.

'This is a real winter wonderland, but my eyes are smarting with the cold and keep watering, even with my sunglasses on. I suppose the drop in the temperature means we're unlikely to get snow on Christmas Day, which I suppose is a good thing.' Speaking my thoughts out loud, I figure nature is doing me a favour. 'Imagine cooking for ten and it turns out no one can get here.'

'Are you still stressing about the meal?' Gray grabs hold of the empty sack I'm carrying. Lifting up my gloved hand, he presses it against his cheek. 'We'll soon fill these sacks and then we can get back to the preparations. I'm here to help, remember.'

'I want tomorrow to be a relaxing Christmas Eve, the calm before the storm. Whatever I can do in advance of the day after will be a bonus. I know we are going to make the cottage and The Retreat look festive and inviting. It's just that—' My voice tails off as I cast around for the right words.

'Don't worry so much. We'll get everything done in time, Immi, I promise. Every year won't be like this one; it's just been a bit disorganised because life's been rather hectic for us both.'

I know Gray is trying to be helpful, but that wasn't what I meant. A little sigh escapes unheard, muffled by my scarf as he searches my eyes with his own.

'Come on. At least the muddy ground has frozen over, so it's not boggy, but take care you don't slip on the icy bits.'

We weave our way along the well-trodden path, which veers away from the canal side, and a few minutes later we're facing open fields. Gray extends his arm to help me over the old wooden stile and we head in the direction of the copse.

'Did you get any further with your research on the stuff that Martin gave you? I wondered if there was anything in amongst the documents that related directly to the cottage, or The Retreat. It would be nice if we could find a photo to have framed and give to Tollie as a house-warming gift once the swap is done.'

I'm touched by Gray's thoughtfulness.

'I keep meaning to ask Valerie. I left everything with her because I knew I'd have little chance of sifting through it. She did mention that her mother was from this area. But as Valerie has been covering for me at the marina and, what with the cruises, I doubt she's had time to do much digging, either. I'll check with her, though, as that's a brilliant idea. Then after Christmas I'll have time to get back into the history project myself.'

The path we're treading is wide enough for us to walk side by side now, and I loosen my scarf. Despite the cold penetrating my snow boots and thick, woollen socks, my body is already glowing from the exertion.

'Now that the decision has been made, I'm actually getting excited about doing up the cottage.' Gray certainly sounds enthusiastic this morning. 'How do you feel about opening up the old fireplace to see if we can get it working again?'

It's funny how a tiny thing can trigger an entire memory, one that I haven't thought about for years. Grandma Nell sitting in her favourite chair next to the fire, watching Tollie as he places a tray of chestnuts on a metal grid to toast. He forgot to pierce one of them and it exploded with a bang, a while later. It was like a pistol shot. I screamed and Grandma nearly jumped out of her chair, while Tollie looked on apologetically as he scrambled to shovel up the hot pieces.

'That would be amazing. Tollie had it swept before it was boarded up, because I remember the chimney sweep coming. He couldn't be bothered lighting it after he had the central heating replaced. There was no longer a need to use it, anyway, as the new system was so efficient. But it's not quite the same ambience on a cold winter's night, that's for sure. I have fond memories of sitting around the fire every time Dad and I spent Christmas here in Aysbury.'

It's funny that I didn't realise how much I missed the smell of woodsmoke until Gray mentioned it. But I do. It wasn't the same taking the note I wrote to Santa outside to burn it in a little dish. It would be wonderful to see smoke billowing out of Lock Keeper's Cottage's chimney this time next year.

'I thought you'd approve of the idea. And I have a lot more ideas up here.' Gray taps the side of his head with a gloved finger. 'Now, this holly hedge looks like it could do with a bit of a trim. What do you think? Enough berries for you, boss?'

The swathe of trees and bushes here are exposed, sitting in the middle of flat pastureland. As Gray retrieves the secateurs from his pocket, I stare in admiration at nature's work. The glowing red berries have little feathery strands radiating off them like angels' wings. So fine and yet detailed, as intricate as any snowflake. And the leaves look as if they have been dipped in icing sugar, which sparkles as the sun's rays filter through the skeleton trees.

'Give it an hour or two and the sun will melt all this.' Gray is now holding out the sacks to me and I tuck one under my arm, opening the neck of the other. 'Right. I'll cut and you catch.'

He begins snipping, not indiscriminately but with care, and as he works he hums softly to himself. I follow Gray further into the wooded area beyond, and we stop every few feet to gather holly, ivy and clippings from an overgrown laurel bush. It doesn't take long to fill the first sack and Gray gathers the neck, tying it with some twine and hanging it from a branch.

'We'll leave it here and collect it on the way back.'

'I'm hoping we can get some fronds from the large Douglas fir and maybe some pine cones. A few longer lengths of ivy would be great, too.'

Gray responds by giving me a short, sharp salute. 'Yes, m'am. This way.'

The further in we go, the tighter packed it is and there are areas where the frost is minimal. To my delight the lower branches of the fir are easy to reach and Gray pulls one down for me, so I can gather some cones and take a few cuttings.

After tying up the last sack he turns to face me, suddenly scooping me up into his arms as if I'm as light as a feather.

'This is the start of making our own traditions for the future, Immi, isn't it? I always want us to surround ourselves with family and friends. And to fuss over the tiny details like making the Christmas table look festive and coming here together on a day like this, grateful for what nature can offer. Decorations are fine, but this is the real thing and a reminder of how good life can be when you have the love of your life by your side.'

Looking up into his eyes, I see a depth of happiness that seems to spill out of him. And it washes over me very gently as he draws me even closer and his lips touch mine.

When the words come, I'm slightly breathless as I gaze back at him. 'Finding you is the best thing that has ever happened to me, Gray. Just never leave me, as it would break my heart.'

'Silly. I know a good thing when I see one. Although there is a lot hanging on your skills with that turkey. Admittedly, I might not be much help in the cooking department aside from stirring the gravy, but I'm your man when it comes to clearing up. I can make a messy kitchen sparkle in no time at all.'

'Well, that's an offer I won't be refusing. Everyone has to earn their Christmas dinner in our house.'

He's chuckling as he releases me and hoists the sack over his shoulder.

'I like the way you said that. *Our* house – it sounds good, doesn't it? Come on, let's pick up the rest of our bounty and head back.'

* * *

We place the jute sacks on a sheet of polythene in the hallway as the melting frost soaks into the rough fabric.

'I'll get the kettle on. Hot chocolate?' Gray asks and I nod.

'Great. I'll pop in and see if Tollie wants to join us. Give me five minutes.'

Stepping back outside, there are slippery patches on some of the stepping stones as I make my way across the lawn, and the large flagstone patio leading to the back of the cottage. Even in the depth of winter there are still flower heads on the climbing roses, which ramble over the arbour set back against the old brick wall. It runs around the entire property and, in truth, the various climbers are a nightmare to trim each year, but old stock is the best and the perfumed flowers keep on coming. When the cottage was built it was rather grand for a lock keeper's home and it's puzzling. Whoever built this had money. How much it will cost now to extend it in line with Tollie's vision for us and bring it bang up to date, I don't know. But it's going to be a lengthy project, anyway. I stop momentarily to gaze back at The Retreat, and I wish there were photos of it through the years.

The sound of a door opening makes me turn around expectantly and Tollie pops his head out of the back door.

'It's freezing out there, Immi. I've just made a brew. Are you comin' in, or simply takin' in the view?'

Beaming at him, I stride forward, stepping over the doorstep as he stands aside, eagerly shutting it after me.

'I should have popped my coat back on.' I stand rubbing my hands as Fisher and Bernie gaze at me. 'Hi, guys. Sorry, Tollie – I didn't know you had company. We're just about to have a hot chocolate to warm up after raiding the copse ready to trim up.'

'We're reminiscing about the days when we'd all get an invite up to the big house. Usually, about a week before Christmas. These days not a lot seems to go on up there.'

'These days—' Fisher labours his words '—the Harrington-Smythes spend most of their time in London. That's where everything is happening.' We all turn to look at him questioningly.

He shrugs his shoulders. 'I speak to Stephen and Lucinda's son, Anthony, from time to time. Even Anthony hasn't been back to his childhood home for several years now, as he works mainly in Europe, but he still owns three rental boats moored at the marina. We're about to overhaul one of them for him. He's all right. Easy to get on with and rolling in money, of course.'

Tollie and Bernie exchange disapproving glances.

'Well, my memories of him when he was younger is that he was a bit of a party animal. We had a near-drowning here, after one of his weekend parties got out of hand. Course, his parents weren't around at the time. Stephen wouldn't have stood for it, but it was hushed up. Don't think they ever knew.' Bernie doesn't sound at all impressed.

Tollie shakes his head, sadly. 'Too much freedom, and money, at too young an age. They're down for Christmas because Abe has been up at the house helpin' the groundsman.'

Although a lot of the land around here is a part of the estate, the house isn't visible from the road or the canal, as it's surrounded by extensive woodlands.

'Is it a big house?' I ask, my curiosity piqued. I've seen the odd photograph, but I can't imagine what it's like up close.

'Immense. It's a beautiful old buildin', as you would expect, but it must cost a fortune to run considering they hardly use it. Folk like that tend to go abroad in search of the sunshine when they want a break. Not like the generation before them. Now Stephen's parents, Philip and Elizabeth, they were pillars of the community back in the day. But they rarely strayed from home and they knew how to throw a party. Good old days, for sure,' Tollie reflects nostalgically.

The back door suddenly swings open and Gray pops his head in, surprised to see the gathering.

'Morning, guys. Well, I was wondering what was keeping Immi

but now I can understand why. I can't compete against her three favourite men all under one roof.'

He shrugs his shoulders and gives Tollie a mischievous smile.

'Just talkin' about old times. Fisher, can you sort Gray out with a drink and I'll go and find some photos to show Immi what the manor house looked like in her party days?'

Gray insists on helping himself, while Bernie, Fisher and I grab our mugs and take a seat around the small kitchen table.

'When do we get to meet this mystery lady of yours, then, Bernie?' Fisher enquires. Bernie immediately looks a little flustered before answering.

'I'll be fetching Yvonne over tomorrow. It's the first time she will have stayed at my place, so I'm planning a quiet dinner together. Bit of a step forward for us and I know Claire would understand.'

We all nod in agreement and I can see that Fisher feels embarrassed now, having raised the topic.

'Sorry, Bernie, I didn't mean... of course it's going to be a big deal for you both. But it's good to have you back and you know we'll welcome her with open arms.'

Fisher knows what it's like to live in the community as one of a couple and then to suddenly find yourself changing status. Divorce isn't quite the same as the death of a loved one, but it's still a long process of coping with change. He leans across to pat Bernie firmly on the back and the look of empathy the two men exchange is touching.

'Life goes on, but it's taken me a long time to find a reason to come back home and think about staying. The truth is, I'm not good on my own. I lack direction and that's what Claire always gave me. But I've enjoyed living on The Great Escape and it's been an adventure. Turnpike Cottage is looking tired and neglected, but I've told Yvonne it won't take long to get it fixed up. She likes a challenge, does that lady.'

As Tollie reappears clasping a handful of photos, I glance at Fisher and he's deep in thought. Loneliness is an awful thing and my gut instincts are telling me that he, too, is tired of being on his own. I'm so glad now that Bernie and Yvonne will be joining us the day after tomorrow and, when we're all sitting around the table in The Retreat, maybe Fisher and Valerie will be inspired. It's a brave thing to take that next step but maybe they'll find the courage to take it.

'Success, I found a few. Some with your grandma in them, too, Immi.'

As Tollie lays the photos out in the middle of the table, Bernie stabs a finger at one of them.

'There they are. That's my Claire and there's Nell, all dressed up and with Ayesbury Manor in the background.'

Leaning forward to take in the detail, I'm sure I've never seen Grandma looking quite so glamorous, wearing a long, sparkling evening dress.

'When was this taken?'

'That would be what... December 1993. Everyone was invited, includin' the local kids, as it was a joint celebration – Christmas and young Anthony's fifth birthday on Boxin' Day that year. Thinkin' back, I'm pretty sure it was the last of the big parties. They'd bought this place up in London a few months prior, as Anthony was being schooled there. For the first few years they often came back at weekends, but that gradually tailed off.'

Tollie grabs his coffee mug to join us at the table.

'The house is much bigger than I'd realised,' I reply as Bernie picks up one of the other photos and leans into me.

'This is young Anthony.'

The little boy in the photo is surrounded by a group of other children, but he stands out because he's the only one not wearing a knitted jumper. He's wearing a pair of dark trousers and a white shirt with a tie. Oh dear, the poor lad. Anthony looks ill at ease, when he should have been the carefree birthday boy.

'Are any of these his siblings?'

'No. He's an only child and heir to the estate. I doubt he'll ever come back here to live permanently, even when it falls to him. Everything is run by their agent now, who manages the estate and the house.'

As I gaze at the group photos, both Tollie and Bernie point out people Fisher and I might know. Except that none of the names mean anything to me. Gray just looks on, bemused.

'So, they don't put their hands in their pockets when it comes to raising money here at Christmas for charity, then?'

Tollie shakes his head. 'They all live a different life now. The old days are long gone.'

He doesn't sound sorry about that and I know that while Grandma might have enjoyed dressing up for the occasion, Tollie most certainly wouldn't have done.

'Well, maybe if we spot one or other of them over the holidays, we ought to mention it. And point out that next year there's going to be a big party to celebrate the tenth anniversary of Santa Ahoy. After all, it's on their doorstep while they are still the owners of the biggest house in the area.'

Tollie stares at Gray, a slight frown creasing his lined forehead at that thought. I suppress a sigh, as I compare him now to the vibrant man he looks as he stands next to Grandma in the photos.

'It's worth a shot, I suppose,' he replies. 'That money does a lot of good and not a penny of it is wasted. Maybe it's something I should have thought about. What do you think, Fisher?'

Fisher nods in agreement.

'It could be a nice little boost. All the local businesses make donations in one form or another. And the playground idea of yours to mark next year's event will require extra fund-raising on top, so every little bit will help.'

'Guess I'd better keep an eye out, then, and dig out a shirt and tie from the back of the wardrobe in case the opportunity presents itself.'

At that, we all begin laughing. I hold up one of the photos showing Tollie with his arms around Grandma, either having just kissed her or about to. They smile at the camera, eyes bright and happy.

'Bet that was the last time you wore a dress tie, Tollie.'

'You could be right, Immi. But didn't I look dapper?'

Some memories will always raise a smile, even though there is a sense of sadness attached to them that never quite goes away.

The day after tomorrow my engagement to Gray will be official. Tollie will be there wearing a happy, and no doubt somewhat relieved, smile and I like to think that Grandma, too, will be looking down on us as Gray slips her beautiful, and much treasured, ring onto my finger.

After the impromptu little gathering, Gray and I finally make our excuses and get back to The Retreat to begin the makeover. It isn't long before Valerie arrives with a car boot full of boxes, after a run up to the nurseries. She kindly offered to collect the list of items I gave Martin over the phone yesterday.

'Crikey, Immi,' he'd remarked after I'd finished reeling off more than a dozen items. 'Are you sure you need everything on this list? Who's giving you a hand to pull it all together?'

'Don't worry, Valerie has volunteered.'

I know that if he weren't heading off with the family to his in-laws for the Christmas holidays, then he would have dropped off the order himself and insisted on helping out. The upside is that I've cleared out some of his seasonal stock and he's given me a big discount to save putting the items in the end-of-December clearance sale.

'I'll bring the boxes in, Valerie,' Gray insists, and she duly hands over her car keys. It's a fair old walk down from the car park, even if you aren't lugging boxes.

'Martin put in a few extra things he thought you might be able to use. We ended up having to lay the back seats down, as he had some small potted Christmas trees left over, and he thought you might want to put them out on the patio.'

'Why don't you see if Fisher is still around, Gray, to give you a hand? It sounds like Martin has gone overboard, but it's very kind of him. I really want everything to look magical and if we aren't going to have real snow, then six cans of the fake stuff should at least set the scene.'

I noticed that when I mentioned Fisher's name Valerie's eyes instantly lit up, but she says nothing as Gray nods his head on his way out.

'Right, what can I do?' my more-than-willing volunteer asks, slipping off her coat.

The dining table is covered with a dust sheet and on it is a huge mound of greenery from the first of the sacks of cuttings.

'We're making a garland to string along the wooden beams. Gray rather cleverly suggested buying this drum of jute rope. The span is too great to have garlands made up entirely of greenery, so we're tying bunches together with this florists' wire and hanging them at six-inch intervals.'

I hold up one to show Valerie and it's the size of a small posy. With a collection of holly, trailing ivy, and an assortment of evergreens including sprigs of fir, it looks – and smells – gorgeous.

'We have another large sackful once we've worked our way through this lot.'

Valerie picks up a small pair of scissors, as she begins working away alongside me.

'So, Fisher was here this morning?'

'He was visiting Tollie earlier on. Bernie was there, too.'

'Ah. I don't really know Bernie to talk to, although I know him by sight. He lives on his boat, doesn't he?'

'Yes, but he's coming back to live in Aysbury with his lady-friend, Yvonne. We'll meet her for the first time on Christmas Day, as I've invited them to join us. He owns Turnpike Cottage.'

Valerie nods, her fingers nimbly assembling a handful of stems, and she holds them up to me for approval.

'Perfect! Hopefully Martin found a suitable country-style ribbon we can tie around these. Some of the Christmassy ones are a bit too gaudy for my liking, but maybe I shouldn't have left this to the last minute.'

'Hey, you guys have been rushed off your feet. Judging by the size of the boxes, I'm sure there will be something in there you'll love. That's wonderful news about Bernie and I'll look forward to getting to know them both a little better.'

Goodness. I get moments where I'm unable to see any of the old Valerie in the new version standing alongside me.

As I reach out to grab a piece of ivy some prickly holly hiding behind it sinks into two of my fingers. 'Ouch! Maybe Gray and I should have gathered the holly separately,' I comment, wiping away the little pinpricks of blood that are forming. 'Take care, Valerie, that stuff is lethal.'

The door behind us opens and we both turn around as Gray appears, half hidden by a large box, and behind him, to my delight – and, I'm sure, Valerie's – is Fisher. The smile on his face just keeps on growing as the two of them catch sight of each other.

'It seems we have a production line going on here,' Gray comments. He dumps the box back against the wall. 'This is going to take a few trips, Immi.'

'Just stack them up and I'll sort them out in a moment. Thanks for helping out, Fisher.'

'My pleasure, Immi. I'm at a loose end today, anyway, so I'm delighted to lend a hand.'

I think what he's really delighted about is the thought of

spending some time with Valerie, but I'll take any offer of help I can get, as the clock is ticking.

'Well, there is a little task you could help with. There's a stack of boxes with china and cutlery in them from the days when this place was rented out. Tollie did a bulk-buy and it will mean I don't have to worry about washing dishes up in between courses. They can be stacked in the utility room until I can run some of it through the dishwasher.'

Fisher gives me a thumbs-up. 'I can do that, too. It's one job less on that list of yours.'

'In that case, I'll pop the kettle on,' I call out as they both disappear out through the door.

'Leave it to me,' Valerie insists. 'It won't take a minute and then I'll empty that box. We can use it to store the bunches of greenery. It should clear a bit of space on the table.'

It strikes me that both Valerie and Fisher are people who prefer to be kept busy. I think it's the company they enjoy, as much as anything. It must be difficult going back home at the end of the day when you live alone.

As I plod on, Valerie soon has a tray loaded with mugs and I direct her towards the cupboard and a box filled with home-made mince pies. Not made by me, I hasten to inform her, but the lovely Ethel.

By the time the guys have done another three trips, everything is ready, and Valerie and I pop on our coats to join them out on the patio. It's time to place the miniature Christmas trees and there's a lot of 'left a bit, back a bit, to the right…' before we are all happy.

'These are lovely,' I remark. 'It was really kind of Martin, because I'm sure they would have been snapped up in the sale.'

'Yes, well, having lured you away from me, he's keeping you sweet. Turns out your replacement is equally capable, so I won't hold it against him.' Fisher inclines his head towards Valerie, hardly lowering his tone. 'That sounded convincing, right, Valerie? You're much better, in my opinion, and there's no Monday-morning moaning to put up with.'

Valerie purses her lips together, trying not to laugh out loud. I give him my best attempt at a disparaging frown. Valerie's cheeks are glowing.

'Well, I didn't intend leaving you in the lurch. Anyway, fingers crossed I can find some small outdoor lights to make these trees look festive once I've sprayed them with fake snow. I'll leave you to sweep the patio clean, then.'

Even without lights, they certainly brighten up the patio, which is sheltered by a large concrete canopy. It juts out about ten feet from the back wall of the property. The large dark grey rattan chairs are the sort you can comfortably lie back in or sit in with your legs curled up.

It is a little warmer than first thing and the frost has melted, but it's still chilly and already I'm thinking about going in search of my gloves.

'Fisher, fancy giving me a hand to carry the fire pit across?' Gray turns to look at him.

'Great idea! Afterwards I'll sort that little task for Immi to keep in her good books. Never cross a busy woman,' Fisher jokes.

As I root around in the box of lights, I glance up as they ease the large circular metal base down onto the patio.

'We could have lunch out here, what do you think, Immi?' Gray enquires. Glancing at my watch, I had no idea that it was already half-past twelve.

'Hmm. We could do.'

'I'll get the fire going, if you can pop something in the oven, then.'

Gray leans in to plant a kiss firmly on my mouth and as he looks down at me there's a sparkle in his eyes. He's happy and that makes me happy, too.

'Breakfast already feels like a dim and distant memory. I do love a woman who knows how to rustle up something appetising just like that.' He clicks his fingers and stands there grinning at me.

Handing him a huge ball of tangled lights soon wipes the smile off his face and I leave him to it. But not before I catch him scratching his head in dismay.

Heading indoors, I'm relieved when Valerie grabs her half-full mug of coffee and follows me inside. As soon as she slides the glass doors shut, I turn to her, frowning.

'What on earth am I going to rustle up? I'm not a rustler-up of food. I'm more of a "take the cellophane off a pizza and slap it in the oven" type of girl. Gray doesn't even know the cheesecake I make him is from a packet mix,' I admit, shame-faced.

'I saw the look that came over you out there. Well, your fridges and freezers are brimming with food, so there must be something that won't take too long to prepare.'

We quickly slip off our coats and I swing open the fridge door to peer inside. It's so stuffed full of items that it's a nightmare to see what's in here.

'I picked up some thick-cut fillet steaks, but I've never cooked them before. I'll read the instructions and see how long it takes. There are some wholegrain rolls in the cupboard over there, if you can grab them, Valerie.'

Gingerly extracting the vacuum-packed steaks, I begin reading the label on the back as Valerie comes up behind me.

'In my opinion, the best way to cook those is to make up a rub and quickly fry them off, then ten minutes tops in the oven will do. Wrap them in foil to keep in the juices and they will melt in the mouth.'

I look at her, gratefully.

'I know you bought onions and garlic, if you can dig some out,' she adds.

'The intention was to buy a little of everything, just in case,' I declare, swinging open a door beneath the island unit and pulling out the plastic veggie box.

'It's not just nerves over hosting your first ever Christmas dinner, is it? This runs deeper than that.'

I close my eyes for a second, trying my best not to dissolve into tears.

'The truth is that I'm trying hard to take all this in my stride, but I have no idea what I'm doing. I've never taken care of anyone, not really. And now I'm supposed to step into the role of cook and homemaker, as if it all comes naturally – which it doesn't.' My chin slumps down onto my chest as I heave a sigh.

'I didn't realise, but now the mad dash around the supermarket is beginning to make a lot more sense. It was rather bizarre, as you're usually so calm and organised. You poor thing, you should have said something.'

'I was too embarrassed. Red or white onions, does it even matter? Because I have absolutely no idea.'

'Not really. Either will do. I'll get chopping and you can make up the rub.' Valerie rolls up her sleeves, ready to do business.

'Have you explained to Gray how you feel?' she asks. As I watch, Valerie expertly peels the onion and begins chopping. She's acting as if she isn't shocked, but I'm feeling uncomfortable now. I can't suddenly clam up and ignore her question, as that would be rude.

'No, because what would I say? That I'm scared?'

'Of what?'

Even formulating the answer in my head, it sounds pretty pathetic. 'That grabbing my dream will make it all fall apart, as it did for my dad.'

Valerie stops what she's doing, her face stony. 'Immi, you more than deserve to have everything you want. Gray is so obviously in love with you, we can all see that. You're not saying you have any doubts, are you?'

I shake my head, miserably. 'No, no. But what if when we're together all the time he discovers that I'm not the person he thinks I am? What if I'm not enough?'

I can see Valerie is visibly shocked by my reply.

'Why would you even think like that?'

'What if I take after my mother and not my dad? Dad and I muddled through, which was fine because it's all we knew. But Rona is a loving and capable mum, and Gray is going to expect me to have the same qualities because that's normal, right? I can't cook, and what do I know about family life and raising kids? I can clean and decorate, but it takes a lot more than that to turn a house into a home, doesn't it?'

Valerie stops what she's doing and turns to face me.

'You are a very capable young woman. What is it you're really afraid of, Immi? Gray loves you the way you are and together you'll work it all out, one step at a time. It's new territory for him, too, remember.'

'Gray has coped with everything life has thrown at him in this last year, without flinching. Physically I'm strong, but emotionally it's another matter entirely. What if I, too, end up running away because I can't cope?' My words seem to shake us both, as my tone makes it sound like a confession.

'Oh, my dear. Your mother let you down and that's her failing, not yours. Those around you see a strong, vibrant person who attracts people to them because you are caring and giving. Don't turn your back on your chance to grab a happy future with the man you love because you are afraid something might go wrong. There are no guarantees, Immi, for anyone. Life isn't a rom-com, it's full of ups and downs, and tears and laughter – but loving someone means you face things together, whatever happens.'

Our eyes lock for a few seconds as her words sink in. The thought of a life without Gray is unimaginable and that's what scares me.

'You're right, of course you are. I guess I just needed reminding of that. I've been constantly on the go and I think the tiredness has gotten to me. Rona's on the mend, but there are things that still need to be sorted out between her and Gray. I didn't want to add to his worries, I suppose, so thank you for listening, Valerie. And for your advice – it means a lot. Tollie isn't good with the emotional stuff and it's hard without Grandma around to talk some sense into me when I need it.'

'My point, precisely. We each have our own strengths and weaknesses, but teamwork always wins the day. Now, come on. We have two hungry men waiting and, believe me, they'll eat anything we present them with.' Her words make me laugh, because I know that's the truth and it's time to stop making pathetic excuses.

It doesn't take long to heat up the oven, make up a mix of pink Himalayan sea salt, pepper, and chopped rosemary, freshly picked from the garden. While Valerie minces a couple of cloves of garlic to go with the onions, she tells me to rub the dry mix onto the steaks.

'Goodness, that was simple,' I remark. Maybe I need to experiment more with fresh ingredients, rather than ready-meals, or making a dash up to The Bullrush.

Quickly frying the meat off in a little olive oil to give it some colour, Valerie then slides the steaks onto a tray and pops it in the oven, while I sweat the onions and garlic.

By the time we have filled the rolls with the meltingly tender steaks and caramelised onions, the fire is lit, and the guys are patiently waiting. We wrap the rolls in foil, and I carry the tray as Valerie opens the door.

'Take a deep breath, Immi,' she whispers. 'You'll figure it all out over time.'

'Ta da!' I announce, stepping forward and looking rather smug at the result of our efforts.

'Well, it smells good, whatever it is.'

Isn't it funny how good food and wonderful company instantly seem to lift the spirits? Or is it that everything tastes better when you eat it outdoors?

Even after the first mouthful, it's obvious the guys are impressed, too.

'We need beer with this,' Gray says, jumping up to go back inside.

'Here you go.' Gray comes back and hands around the opened bottles. 'Can't get a better beer than The Bulrush Inn Christmas Brew.'

We all raise our bottles to chink.

'Here's to a wonderful Christmas surrounded by some great friends we've come to regard as family.' As Gray makes the toast I can see that both Fisher and Valerie are touched.

'How did you manage to get the fire going so quickly?' I ask, sitting back to savour the remainder of my steak roll as I watch the flames licking up around the sides of the pit.

Fisher taps the side of his nose, giving me a wink.

'Old trick from my camping days. We found a disposal barbecue in the garage and put that in the bottom, then kindling on the top. Gives out a fair bit of heat, too.'

It's cosy sitting here all wrapped up, despite the chill, and for the first time in a couple of days I'm finally feeling relaxed.

'Is there much still to do?' Fisher asks.

'Quite a bit,' I admit. 'If we can get all the greenery sorted and store it overnight in the outhouse, then we can put it up first thing tomorrow. I don't want the berries falling off because the temperature inside is too warm, but we're going to need the heating on if it's as cold tonight as it was last night.'

Gray peers up at the sky.

'Well, if the temperature plunges again tonight the gritters will be out in force, that's for sure.'

'You might have to go and fetch your mum in the morning. I don't like the thought of her driving over if it's icy. It's so kind of you to put her up, Valerie.'

We turn to look at Valerie, and her cheeks begin to colour.

'I'll be very glad of the company. Only one of my neighbours is home for Christmas, so Saint Nicholas's Well is going to be rather quiet this year.'

After our little chat the other day I did wonder if she'd invite her son to stay, but maybe it's simply too soon.

'Don't forget I'm always around to walk you back at any time, Valerie,' Fisher says, breaking the silence. As their eyes meet, their gaze lingers for a second or two.

I look across at Gray, trying to draw his attention. Jumping up, I begin stacking the plates on the tray. Valerie immediately rises up out of her seat, but Gray has got the message.

'You sit and relax for a bit, Valerie,' he insists. 'I'll give Immi a hand with the dishes.'

As the two of us slip inside I give Gray an appreciative smile.

'Thanks. It's the perfect opportunity for them to sit and chat for a while if we take our time. Will you ring your mum and suggest you collect her in the morning?'

Gray sidles up to me as I deposit the tray on the worktop. He spins me around and into his arms.

'Yes, I will. Now stop worrying. Everything is going to be fine. By the time we have all of this up tomorrow...' he casts his eye over the results of this morning's efforts '... it's going to look amazing.'

I'm itching to make a start, but I know it would be a mistake.

'We could put the tree up today, though, couldn't we? It was supposed to go up last weekend.'

The poor thing has been languishing in the shed, standing in a bucket of water.

'That's my next job. Then sort the lights.'

As I snuggle up closer to Gray, I can't resist taking a quick glance over his shoulder to peek at Valerie and Fisher. They're chatting away so comfortably together, it's a joy to see. I don't think either of them quite knows how to handle that awkward stage where you leave a casual friendship behind and move on to the next stage. They've both been on their own for a long while, but they'll figure it out when the time is right. Hopefully before the holidays are over, because I have a huge ball of mistletoe ready and waiting.

* * *

We both slip into a deep sleep, exhausted from the day. But just a few hours later I find myself in the darkness staring aimlessly out of the bedroom window, while Gray continues to sleep soundly.

I'm trying so hard to shake off the remnants of a disturbing dream, real enough to awaken me with a start.

As my eyes adjust to the dim greyness outside the window, the contours of the trees on the far side of the fields seem to step out of the shadows, like eerie sentinels keeping guard, and I begin to shiver.

Everything is going so well, that little voice inside my head speaks up reassuringly.

And it's true, so many people I care about seem to be edging towards their own happy-ever-afters, at last. And even Tollie is the most relaxed I've known him to be in a long while. It feels as if this Christmas is a turning point in so many ways, for so many people.

And you know what they say about endings, I tell myself firmly. *They signal the start of new beginnings.*

The image from my dream is still trying to replay in my head, as much as I'm trying to push it away. I keep seeing a magnificent tower made of wooden bricks, each one carefully positioned as it goes higher and higher. And then, suddenly, one brick is taken away and the tower comes crashing down to the floor. All that is left is a higgledy-piggledy pile of meaningless wooden blocks – the magnificence of the structure gone, as if it were merely a mirage.

My heart begins to race as that familiar sense of panic rises up within my chest. I had it the day before Dad died and many, many times since. Determined to pull myself together, I think about the conversation I had with Valerie. She said that loving someone means you face things together, no matter what happens, and she was right. That's all I need to remember now.

You're starting to hyperventilate, Immi, you know the signs. My inner voice sounds strangely calming as the blood begins to pound in my ears. *Slow your breathing down. You'll get through this – you know that for a fact. Good things happen all the time and now it's your turn.*

Holding onto the windowsill to steady myself, I take a slow, deep breath in and hold it for a couple of seconds before slowly releasing it.

One. *Do it again, Immi, you've got this.* Two. Three. Four. Five. Six. Seven. Eight. Nine. Ten.

My heart rate begins to slow, and the pounding sound starts to fade. *It's nerves, that's all,* I tell myself. *Getting engaged is a big commitment and finding your soul mate, the one man who makes you feel complete, is a blessing.*

'Hey, what's up?' A sleepy voice calls out in the darkness and I take one final deep breath in as I head back to bed.

'Nothing. It's all good,' I whisper as Gray throws back the covers so I can slip into bed. He proceeds to wrap himself around me to warm my chilled body.

It was just a dream, I reassure myself. As the cosy warmth of Gray's body banishes not just the chill, but the fears, I continue to stare up at the window and the half-open blinds.

'It's snowing,' I whisper. Gray's body shifts slightly, but his eyes remain closed.

'It'll be gone by morning. It wasn't forecast. Now close your eyes, Immi. It's going to be a long day and you need to get some rest. Sweet dreams, my darling. I love you.'

20

A DUSTING OF THE WHITE STUFF

Oh dear. Sitting eating breakfast, I gaze out at the layer of whiteness stretching as far as the eye can see. It's only a couple of inches, but no one was expecting it, so who knows whether the lane has been gritted? I suspect not as the temperature warmed overnight.

'Do you think it's possible to be weather sensitive?' I pose the question in between bites of honey-and-butter-covered toast.

'Weather sensitive?' Gray looks at me uncomprehendingly, before wiping a few crumbs from around his mouth.

'You know, emotionally. I felt a bit jittery last night and then when it started snowing everything changed and I settled back down.'

Now he's frowning at me.

'Well, some people say they get a headache when a storm is brewing, but it's something to do with falling air pressure rather than a premonition. I'm not sure a flurry of snow has the same sort of dramatic effect on the barometer, so I'd guess your broken sleep was probably due to eating late and going to bed on a full stomach.'

I pop the last piece of toast into my mouth and decide to let the subject drop. This morning I feel fine and it's probably best not to dwell on an unsettling dream. But now Gray is looking at me intently.

'You aren't having second thoughts about us, are you?'

My hand instinctively reaches out for his and our fingers entwine.

'No, of course not! I guess the truth is that I'm missing Dad. And Grandma. It doesn't feel right somehow, as if I'm waiting for them to turn up so the celebrations can really begin. I know how happy they would be for me, for us. It hurts that they aren't a part of it, and I can't get my head around them not being here.'

Gray wraps both of his hands around mine, drawing them together.

'That's perfectly understandable, Immi. I'd hoped that celebrating our engagement tomorrow would help lift your spirits this Christmas and make up for the disappointments of last year, but that was kind of naïve of me, wasn't it? You're bound to miss the people who should have been here. It will obviously play on your mind, so don't go fretting over the feelings it churns up.

'But can you do me a really big favour? Next time you wake up in the dead of night like that, dig me in the ribs, because I don't want you feeling alone, or lonely, ever. Once I'm out for the count, then I'm gone; it takes a lot to disturb me. I want to be there for you, though, whenever you need me, but I won't know unless you tell me. Fair deal?'

As he raises my fingertips to his lips I nod, tears beginning to blur my vision as I take in the concern reflected in his eyes. 'Yes,' I reply, my voice suddenly raspy.

'Hey, silly thing, it's Christmas Eve and you aren't allowed to get maudlin. We have garlands to hang and the tree to finish. Next year we'll get our act together a lot earlier, I promise. Anyway, are you a betting woman? Do you think the snow will be gone by the time I drop Mum off at Valerie's later this morning?'

Gray releases my hand and I swipe away a tear that's about to spill down over my cheek. Flashing him the brightest of smiles, I glance across at the patio doors once more to gaze out.

'Hmm. That's a very strange-looking grey sky. I'd wager a fiver that we're actually going to get a little more.'

'Are you saying that as an optimist, or a pessimist?' His eyes are teasing me, and I can't help but laugh. 'I think it'll turn to rain.'

'Well, as long as it doesn't stop our guests from getting here and we don't get a power cut before the turkey is cooked tomorrow morning, put me down as an optimist. It would be rather romantic.'

And then Gray starts singing, 'Let It Snow! Let It Snow! Let It Snow!'

His voice is soft and low as he pulls me to my feet and waltzes me around the kitchen.

'It's a big day for us tomorrow, my lovely Immi. I think the snow will melt away as quickly as the other day and the sun will come out to shine on us.'

I can't help but grin back at him as he looks at me with adoring eyes. A stray thought jumps into my head.

'Should I have organised an engagement cake, instead of the traditional Christmas desserts?'

His face falls. 'Cake? Christmas desserts? I was rather banking on a cheesecake.'

I slap my forehead dramatically with my hand as if I'd forgotten, then throw him a wicked smile.

'Third thing on my to-do list for today. I thought I'd make an extra big one, in case the others decide to sample it, too. But I'll only cut them thin slivers, I promise! Anyway, first things first. That huge pile of twinkly lights isn't going to sort itself. We don't want Santa driving on past us tonight, do we, if everything's in darkness?'

'Yes, boss. I'm on it,' Gray replies, giving me his best Captain Gray salute.

'I'll clear this lot away, if you get the ladder and start hanging the two ropes from the beams. I can then begin hooking on the bunches of greenery while you make a start on the lights.'

Gray immediately scurries away to get started and it doesn't take long to sort out the kitchen. As Gray returns with the ladder the doorbell rings.

'It's the farm shop,' I call over my shoulder as I walk out into the hallway. When I open the door, the guy in front of me has his arms firmly wrapped around a very large box.

'Morning, Immi. Where do you want the turkey? I also have another box for you. It's quite a trek back to the van, what with this snow.'

'Hi, Roger. Thanks. If you can pop it through here, that would be great.'

He follows me into the kitchen, placing it on the draining board as he looks up at Gray, who is now drilling and plugging the first fixing.

'Goodness, that's a job and a half you have on your hands there, Gray,' he reflects jovially.

'Anything to please my woman,' Gray replies, giving me a wink. 'What are the roads like?'

'Not too bad, at the moment. Right, second box on its way.'

As Roger disappears Gray stops what he's doing, nodding in my direction.

'Is that all turkey?'

I shrug my shoulders. 'Well, I'm assuming, hoping, that the meat is all in one box.'

Gray returns to his work and I go in search of my purse to give Roger a tip. Then the unpacking begins. I ordered a large joint of pork as my back-up plan, as suggested by Valerie, and I want to get it into the oven pretty sharpish. A couple of hours should do it and then I'll sort the cheesecake.

As I begin to unpack the box, to my dismay it's just the turkey and it's a struggle to lift it out.

'Immi, is that monster going to fit inside the oven?' Gray calls over, looking down at me from halfway up the ladder.

I'm thinking the same thing as I dump the shrink-wrapped bird down on the counter and go in search of the new roasting tin that I bought to accommodate it.

And it doesn't fit.

I'm conscious Gray is now laughing at my dilemma and as he clears his throat to speak, the long coil of rope slung over his shoulder suddenly slips. In his efforts to rescue it the drill slips out of his other hand and crashes to the floor. Nerves jangling, we stare at each other in a state of shock.

'Sorry, I didn't mean to make you jump. Are you okay?' he asks sheepishly.

At least his feet are still planted very firmly on the steps.

'Not the best start to the day, is it?' I murmur, glancing out to see that it's just started snowing again.

* * *

What is it they say about the best-laid plans? I give up scratching my head over the turkey and stick it back inside the box, then unpack the rest of the delivery.

'Right, I'm done securing these ropes, Immi. I might as well take the turkey and stick it in the utility room for now. It's cooler in there and you certainly won't get it in the fridge.'

Just the thought of how on earth I'm going to squash it into that tray is beginning to give me a headache.

With the joint of pork safely in the oven cooking, I climb the ladder to start hanging the bunches of greenery. My mood lifts with each little bundle I lovingly suspend with a bow of thin twine.

On his return, Gray looks up, impressed. 'That's awesome, Immi. There's only one set of lights I haven't managed to get working yet, but I think it's best that I fetch Mum now. It's not looking great out there, and the forecast isn't good. I'll sort them out as soon as I get back, though. Be careful up there and don't be tempted to over-reach.'

'Just drive carefully and don't you take any risks, either.' I lean down to accept his parting kiss, grabbing both sides of the ladder as I do so.

'I mean it. Think health and safety.' He tuts and waggles a finger at me as I go to lean a little further out, then change my mind and descend to reposition the ladder.

'That's my girl. Be safe.'

I'm glad that Gray has decided to go and fetch his mum a little earlier than planned, because the sudden change in the weather has caught everyone out. It's not exactly a blizzard, but the flakes are falling thick and fast.

On his way out, Gray puts on a Christmas CD and I find myself humming away to some of my favourite oldies. Music does lift the spirits and at least it stops me thinking about his journey and how awful the roads are likely to be.

Once I've finished the two long runs overhead, I grab a hammer and a nail ready to put up the mistletoe. It is a huge ball, but the ceilings in here are high and anything smaller would have been lost. The problem is where to put it, I wonder as I scan around. People are going to walk in, and most are going to be drawn to gaze out at the view. I can't reach the overhead beams, but I can reach the one above the patio doors. If I trim the back a bit so the ball sits flatter against the wall, hopefully it will hang there rather nicely.

When I'm finally able to put the ladders away, I'm very happy with how things are shaping up. Admittedly, the tree still needs trimming, but at least Gray managed to place one set of lights.

I can't put it off any longer – it's turkey time. Reluctantly approaching the sink unit in the utility room, knife in hand, I know this is going to call for drastic action but I'm not at all sure I'm up to the task.

Does a turkey have to be cooked whole? I wonder. I have no idea whether it affects the flavour, or how you adjust the cooking time if you do it in portions. I'm going to have to go online to check it out. People buy turkey crowns, though, so maybe Sarah was right and it's all about the basting. She stuffed her big bird and I've bought more than enough stuffing to fill even this hefty thing.

Lifting the wrapped bird out with great difficulty, I dump it rather unceremoniously into the sink.

One small slit allows me to peel the bag open. The feel of turkey skin beneath my fingers makes me grimace. At this moment I could cheerfully become a vegetarian, but I know I'd never stick to it and, besides, I have my guests to consider. Feeling a little uncomfortable wielding such a large knife, I grit my teeth and begin cutting. Off comes one leg and, after a lot of hacking and a bit of juggling, off comes the other. This is horrible. I feel like a murderer. Each massive leg looks obscenely large and rather purple. Never having seen a raw bird of this size up close before, I sincerely hope that's normal.

But already, my problem is looking a lot more manageable. Now I'm going to detach the breast from the carcass. With a bit of luck, it will all fit into the new roasting tin and if I cover it with foil, no one will be any the wiser. I will also be able to fit it into the fridge if I pull a few things out and ferry them across to the overspill fridge in the outhouse.

As I continue working away, I can't stop myself from wincing. I'm done with the thought of turkey before it's even touched the oven.

Luckily, just as I'm finally making room to slip the foil-covered tray into the fridge, Tollie appears.

'I let myself in thinkin' you'd be busy. How's it going, m'dear?'

'Good, thanks, Tollie. This lot will have to go into the other fridge, but the turkey is ready to pop into the oven early in the morning.'

'Them garlands look the business. Do you need a hand with finishin' off the tree? I could get the small stepladder out for you and pass up the baubles.'

'Gray is still sorting the lights, so there's nothing more to do until he gets back with Rona.'

We turn to stare at the eight-foot-high tree. It is a beautiful specimen and I love the smell of a blue spruce.

'Grandma would approve. Nice proportions, but then, knowing you, I bet you drove Martin mad makin' him stand them all up to check each and every one. You have an eye, Immi. Are you settin' up the table today?'

My shoulders sag a little. 'Yes, well, that's the intention. The turkey took a little longer to prepare than I expected, but it's all good. The next job is to whip up a cheesecake, then peel a lot of potatoes to part-boil them.'

'Just like Grandma did. Shake 'em around in the colander while they're hot and rough 'em up so they'll soak up the goose fat. Who can resist a crispy roast potato?'

Some memories instantly raise a smile and it's good to take a moment to reflect.

'Do you want to see if you can get that second set of lights working while I check on the pork joint and prepare Gray's must-have dessert?'

'It would be my pleasure, Immi, if you think Gray won't mind.'

'I'm pretty sure he'd be very grateful. Just between us, I suspect it wasn't so much the change in the weather conditions, as rising annoyance that he couldn't suss out the problem, that sent him scurrying off.'

I get busy in the kitchen area as Tollie sets to work unravelling the mass of wire and bulbs. It takes a while, but eventually it all starts to come together, and I wash my hands with a sense of relief and satisfaction.

'Two of the bulbs have blown. I'll just replace them and we're in business.' Tollie looks pleased with himself.

As I begin unpacking the boxes of baubles wrapped in tissue paper, Tollie retrieves the small stepladder from the cupboard.

'It hasn't stopped snowin' since just after eight this mornin'. It's not heavy, but it's definitely warmed up and that doesn't bode well.' Tollie chatters away as he snaps the steps into position and stands back.

'We'll work top down,' I say, passing the first box to him. 'The smaller ones at the top, then the medium size and the large ones at the bottom.'

It takes a while, as I have to keep moving the steps as we work around the tree in tiers. In between I keep glancing out of the window, wondering what on earth it's like in the long snaking lane that leads down from the main road. What if Gray can't get back to Aysbury? So many people will be travelling today and I daren't turn on the TV, because it will just send me into panic mode.

'I don't suppose you've been up to the shop for your paper today, have you?'

'Course, I walked up first thing. It was a bit slippery underfoot, but it wasn't too bad.'

'Were all the lights off in The Bullrush?'

'No. I'm not sure what time Kurt intended on leavin', but the car was still parked up. I took the shortcut over the bridge rather than trudge along the lane, otherwise I would have called in. They'll be well on their way by now.'

'So, the lane is still okay, you think?'

'If it weren't, I'm sure Gray would have let you know. Stop worryin' about everyone and don't overstretch. Tree's lookin' good, Immi.'

One glance outside confirms that in the last half an hour the flakes might not be any bigger, but the steady stream is now like a thick curtain. It's beginning to obscure the view outside. What was a two-inch covering is now probably five inches deep and I find myself absent-mindedly chewing on my lip; I shouldn't have let Gray go out in this. Rona wasn't going to come to any harm, safe at home, and she'd rather arrive a day late than risk an accident. I glance down at Tollie as I take yet another bauble from him, and he gives me a stern look.

'Let's just keep ploughin' on, m'dear, and they'll be here before you know it.'

21

OH, THE WEATHER OUTSIDE IS FRIGHTFUL

It's well past lunchtime, but neither Tollie nor I have an appetite. It doesn't help that visions of the turkey carve-up keep coming back to me. I check my phone yet again and just as I'm putting it down for what feels like the hundredth time, it kicks into life in my hands. I almost drop it with relief as I see it's Gray.

'Are you okay?' I blurt out, desperate to know what's happening. All I can see looking out now is an unbelievably thick wall of white bleakness.

'There's been a slight change of plan, but we're fine. We're going to have some extra company and I just wanted to alert you. I have to go. We'll be there in about an hour... ish. See you soon.'

Click.

Tollie is watching me closely.

'They're on their way. But something's wrong – I could tell by his voice and he cut me off quickly. He sounded like he was walking; he definitely wasn't in the car, that's for sure.'

We head over to the patio doors, peering out.

'Is this what they call a white-out?' I ask, thinking we don't get snowstorms like this in the UK. Even the snow on the patio table is now at least eight inches deep. Fortunately, there's no wind to whip it up into sculptured peaks, but everything is eerily quiet, wrapped in a thick white coat. It does look rather beautiful, but only if you aren't out in it. That is, either driving, or on foot. Gray surely isn't walking the last part with Rona – that would be sheer madness. Why did I think snow would make this Christmas more romantic? It's just turning it into a total disaster. You can't have a party without people. And if they can't get here, I reflect miserably, there'll be no Christmas dinner.

'It's unusual, but I've seen worse,' Tollie replies. 'You won't remember the really bad years when you were small, and then living down south it's generally milder towards the coastline. Gray wouldn't have said they were okay if they aren't, so there's no point in second-guessin' what's going on. They're going to be cold and hungry, no doubt, when they arrive – whoever Gray has managed to pick up along the way.'

'Thank goodness that joint of pork is cooling. At least I can make up a batch of sandwiches. Tollie, can you do the honours and carve? I'd only hack it about. I'm not good with knives.'

He smiles at me, affectionately. 'Leave it to me. I'll carve the turkey for you tomorrow as well if you like.'

Even the mention of the turkey sends a little shudder through me. I'm too ashamed to tell him about my poor, dismembered bird, sitting in the fridge. Everyone is going to expect a fine specimen on a platter in the middle of the table, as they show in Christmas films. Our turkey is going to look as if it's been run over by a lorry. Well, that's assuming there's anyone here to see it.

* * *

When the doorbell rings it takes me by surprise, as I can't imagine why Gray hasn't used his key. The moment I swing open the door I understand.

Four people are standing in a huddle, their faces obscured by hooded coats and scarves, as they dodge the now one-inch-sized snowflakes. The icy particles probably feel more like missiles than the soft, feathery little things we tend to imagine. Each of them is carrying a large plastic container, dusted with snow.

'Come in, come in.' I stand back, holding the door open wide as a shiver runs through me. Scrutinising the first person to step inside, I'm surprised to see it's Valerie.

'Hi, Immi. Sorry for the invasion, but there were no other options,' she explains as she yanks her scarf away from her face. 'We might not have been able to deliver these if we left it any longer. The walk is treacherous.'

She places a container on the stairs and sits down heavily as she begins to pull off her boots.

As I continue stepping backwards so everyone else can filter in, I'm almost through the doorway into the main room. The boxes are large and, together with four bodies, they fill the entire hallway.

'Pop your coats on the hooks and I'll take them into the utility room in a minute to hang them up to dry. I guessed it was bad, but... anyway, come on through.'

As they peel off their soggy outerwear, I let Tollie know we're catering for two extra people.

Valerie and Gray are the first to appear behind me.

'What a nightmare it is out there!' Valerie exclaims.

Gray looks tired, but he's making no attempt to take off his soggy padded jacket.

'It wasn't a good drive. Mum, come on through and stand by the radiator to warm up.'

Rona is standing in the doorway now partially obscuring my view of a young man I don't recognise. She stops for a moment, looking up at the ceiling in awe.

'Oh, how beautiful! And the tree – my goodness, this is a sight for the weary. I'm just relieved we made it in one piece, thanks to Gray's skilful driving.'

When I glance at the young man, he tilts his head by way of introduction, and I give him a welcoming smile. Rona walks over to the radiator to warm her hands and I follow on behind her.

'It's not good out there, Immi, to say the least,' Rona confirms, dancing her fingers against the heat. 'The main roads aren't too bad, but in a lot of places it's down to a single track. Some have had it heavier even than here. Most of the side roads haven't been touched and as for the lane, well, the snowploughs and gritters are struggling. It'll be a while until they can even think of little communities like this one. There's a milk tanker half in a ditch, the other half slewed across the lane, about a mile and a half down from the top road. We had to walk the rest of the way.'

Tollie and I are stunned. I can't believe they've walked several miles in these conditions. Gray continues.

'I'll head back with Liam to collect the things we couldn't carry on the first trip. We left Mum's bags and a small pile of things at Valerie's.'

Valerie casts me a nervous glance.

'Sorry, I should have introduced you already. This is my son, Liam. Liam, this is Immi and her grandfather, Tollie,' Valerie chimes in. 'I knew you'd be wondering about the starters and I wanted to make sure we could get them here. I assumed, rather naively, that it would be easy enough to walk back, but it's much worse out than I thought.'

Gray and Liam immediately turn to go and Tollie takes over, shepherding Valerie and Rona over to one of the sofas.

'Here, ladies, make yourself comfortable. I have a pot of tea brewing and we'll soon get you warmed up.'

They flop down, tired out and a little traumatised. It's hard not to begin firing questions at them, but Tollie shoots me a warning glance. He nods, indicating that I should take a seat as he has everything in hand.

Valerie turns to face Rona and they exchange a look of total disbelief.

'Have we been transported to Switzerland?' Valerie asks as she peers across to take in the view beyond the patio. 'I can't remember the last time I saw this much snow. It's caught everyone out, even the weather forecasters.'

'The tea is ready, but I wonder if anyone is up for a glass of wine, too?' Tollie enquires. Both Rona and Valerie raise their hands and I join them.

'How bad is it out there? That must have been a nightmare of a walk. Was it deserted?' I enquire gently.

Rona has virtually collapsed back into the cushions. 'Yes, it was once we got past the tanker. It's hard going walking even a short distance. Valerie could hardly believe her eyes when we knocked on her door, bedraggled and panting.'

Valerie takes over. 'When Gray told me to pack up everything Liam and I needed, as there's a chance we wouldn't be able to venture out tomorrow, I thought he was joking at first. I mean, it's what – two miles at most? It's taken us an hour and...' she glances at her wristwatch '... ten minutes to get here. I think Gray's right. No one is going anywhere tomorrow if this continues.'

'So, the lane is virtually impassable?' I can hardly take this in. A snowfall like this can't surely come as a total surprise to the people whose job it is to plan for emergencies when the weather turns bad. Don't the county councils have hotlines to the Met Office?

'At the moment it is. A Land Rover came up from Adler's farm and hopefully made it back with the tanker driver, so he could warm up. He was in shock but had managed to contact a recovery firm – who probably won't be able to get here, of course. Well, until they can plough the top part of the lane, that is, as it's just too dangerous to try right now. Aysbury is snowed in and no one is going anywhere in a hurry.'

Both Tollie and I sit listening to the story, sorry to hear what they'd been through.

'There's no point in venturing back out there until the worst of it is over. At least people will have stocked up with essentials for the holidays, which is a comfort of sorts, I suppose. Unless they were dining out, that is.' I'm thinking of our other guests.

Tollie deposits a loaded tray on the coffee table between the sofas and we all reach for the wine glasses first.

'Merry Christmas, everyone. According to the latest weather news on my phone it's now officially the second largest snowfall the Cotswolds have ever had on Christmas Eve,' Valerie informs us.

We raise our alcohol-filled glasses to toast a rather sobering statistic, as it begins to sink in that this is going to be a very cosy Christmas together, indeed.

* * *

'You did well today,' I whisper to Gray as we snuggle into each other after what turns out to have been an extremely eventful day.

'I didn't want to worry you unduly, but when we were brought to an abrupt halt by that tanker, to be frank with you, I didn't know if we'd make it back here. Even up to that point, I'd warned Mum to brace herself, as if I'd lost control and we'd slid, the road is so narrow the chances of not ending up in one of the ditches is slim to none. And they are dangerously deep in places.

'The tanker was at such an angle that the driver wasn't able to get himself out without help. I had real visions of losing control, but you get to a point where you are so committed there's nowhere to go other than forward. It wasn't much better once we began walking, as if either of us had fallen and broken a bone—' He stops abruptly, and I think a shiver runs through both of us at the thought. 'But we made it. So, luck was on our side.'

Winding my arms around his neck, I draw him even closer.

'When they say, "expect the unexpected" I doubt either of us would have envisioned this, would we?' I muse, attempting to lift our spirits.

Rona is settled into the very tired spare bedroom in Lock Keeper's Cottage after all, despite our best-laid plans. I thank my lucky stars at least I had a new set of bedding to make it feel a little bit special for her. Valerie and Liam have the two spare bedrooms here, so it's full houses all round.

'Everyone has a comfortable bed and we have plenty of food. I wish we'd had time to pop up and check on Abe and Ethel. And I'm assuming Kurt, Sarah and the girls eventually got away. I'm sure Martin will text me at some point, as he'll know I'll be concerned. That just leaves Fisher, Bernie and Yvonne. Tollie hasn't heard anything from either of the guys since this morning. What a mess this is all turning out to be.'

Gray chuckles softly and the bed starts to shake.

'How can you laugh about this?' I ask miserably. 'I wanted everything to be perfect. But the only thing that is are the decorations. The turkey... well, I can only hope it looks better once it's cooked and I don't let down Valerie and Rona's time slaving away in the kitchen. Those two were amazing today, taking over the rest of the food preparation while I sorted the sleeping arrangements.'

Even in the partial light from the unnaturally bright grey sky, I can see the fleeting smile pass over Gray's face. 'Be honest, you were relieved to hand it all over. It's not a criticism, as I wouldn't have had a clue about where to start, but a little experience goes a long way.'

Yes, and most people have a grandmother or a mother at their elbow for times like this. How I wish I'd taken more of an interest in what went on in the kitchen, rather than sitting back and just enjoying the results.

I give him a look of uncertainty, wondering what everyone will think when they see what I've done to the turkey. It's supposed to arrive at the table full of a generous helping of stuffing and looking golden brown from having been lovingly basted – as Sarah's bird did. Mine is going to look as if it's been run over by a car and someone threw the pieces into an oven tray to save wasting it.

'Well, maybe. But you have the most gorgeous New York baked cheesecake waiting for you in the fridge. I might not be a great cook, but that's the one thing I could never mess up. Then again, I have made a few since we first met.'

'You won't hear me complaining.'

As I lean over Gray to plant a soft kiss on his cheek, it's obvious sleep is beckoning him. He must be feeling exhausted from the stressful drive, let alone all that walking.

'In a couple of days Mum and I will be in LA. I can't even imagine that right now – it's surreal. I can only hope that the snow will have cleared by then, or our trip will be postponed. Mum's on edge and we need to get it over with.'

The lift in his voice at the end of his sentence tells me he's not upset about it, but he's anxious for her. Last night I was lying here stressing over a bad dream; tonight, I'm lying here too exhausted to even think about tomorrow. And then as I glance at the bedside clock, I realise it's here already.

'Sweet dreams, my lovely man, and happy Christmas. Thank you for being my rock. It was such fun, seeing everyone joining in and making do. And as for the karaoke session this evening... oh my, that was so funny! I swear I haven't laughed as much since I was a six-year-old and the cat pooed in the middle of Grandma's best rug.'

Whether Gray heard me, I don't know, but I prop myself up on my elbow and watch him sleeping for a few minutes before I lie back down.

Gray never complains. And he always rises to a challenge. He has this knack of knowing exactly what to do to keep everyone's spirits up, whenever the need arises. He is a natural entertainer because that's the way his mind works. I asked him once what went on inside his head whenever he hummed away, and he said it was like living in a commercial. But each day it was a different one and, even though he tried his best to keep a record of every little tune, so much ended up being lost because some thoughts slip away as quickly as they come. That's when I knew he was special and life with him would never be boring.

Softly, very softly, I find myself singing the words to 'Silent Night'. Grandma always sang that to me at Christmas and hearing the words as they wrap around me makes me feel she's close. I feel proud that I've chosen a man who is so caring and respectful of others. It isn't just my vocal cords that are singing, but also my heart.

* * *

It's early morning when I hear a noise downstairs. Rolling over onto my back, I hold my breath, waiting to see if I can hear it again. Gray is oblivious, snoring softly as I ease myself off the bed and grab my dressing gown. Descending the stairs, I hear the sound again, but this time it's a little louder and even through the obscure glass in the front door I can see a dim shadow.

The next knock is more insistent and very gingerly I turn the handle to peer outside.

'Immi, it's me – Kurt.' His voice is low.

I swing the door open wide and he steps inside. If it weren't for the sound of his voice, it could be anyone, as all I can see are his eyes, staring at me from behind one of those ski-mask-type balaclavas.

'Everyone is still asleep. I thought you left yesterday,' I whisper as he follows me on through and I shut the internal door noiselessly behind us.

'Jeez, it's flipping freezing out there.' Kurt's nose, when he pulls his thick navy-blue mask up over his face, is glowing a ghastly shade of reddish pink. He slips off his boots and it seems to take an inordinate amount of time. He must be frozen to the core. 'Oh, merry Christmas, Immi, although it doesn't feel very merry right now. It's lovely and warm in here, though.'

'The heating kicked in about an hour ago. Slip off your coat and take a seat. I'm just shocked to see you're still here.'

Glancing at the clock, I see it's just after six a.m. so I know something is very wrong. Kurt looks totally wiped out and simply lowers his hands, letting his thick padded jacket fall to the floor before sinking down with a sigh onto the sofa.

'Shortly before we were due to leave yesterday, we discovered one of the pipes on the ground floor had burst. It's my fault. The outside tap for watering the plants surrounding the car park spurs off the downstairs disabled cloakroom. I usually cover it up with lagging for the winter, but I forgot.'

'And it's next to the kitchen. Oh, Kurt, how bad is it?'

'Well, it didn't breach the steps up into the dining room, so that's something. The electrics shorted, but we can't tell what damage there might be until everything is dried out. It's unlikely we'll be able to get an electrician in to check it out until the roads are clear. That's assuming we're even lucky enough to find someone working between Christmas and New Year. I linked up a small generator to pump out the water through the night, but, with no heat and waking up to a freeze this morning, it's going to dry out very slowly indeed.'

He looks as gutted as he sounds.

'How are Sarah and the girls managing? What can we do to help?'

Kurt runs his hands over his eyes, and I look away, giving him a moment to compose himself.

'No one died and we have insurance. Sarah and the girls spent the night with Ethel on The Merry Robin. Abe gave me a hand, but I insisted he head back shortly after two this morning to get some sleep. I haven't spoken to any of them yet. I hope they're all asleep still, but space is tight onboard, and it probably meant sleeping bags on the floor. It would at least have been warm, and thank goodness for pot-bellied stoves, but it's not fair on Abe and Ethel. It's a four-berth, so trying to squeeze in six isn't going to be easy.'

'Well, you'll all come here, of course you will! These two sofas make up into double beds and the fridge and freezer are jam-packed with food, so there's plenty to go around. Put your feet up for a bit and I'll make you a coffee.'

He's so exhausted he can't even answer, and I move around as quietly as I can, placing the mug next to him on a side table before creeping back upstairs. It won't be long until his exhausted state drags him down into a deep sleep.

After closing the bedroom door quietly behind me, I tip-toe across the room.

'Gray, are you awake?' I know he isn't, but we're in need of an action plan.

'Mmm... morning, Immi. You look lovely.'

He rolls over onto his back, stretching out his shoulders even though he's still half asleep, and lets out a satisfied groan.

'Kurt is downstairs on the sofa and I left him snoring away. Sarah and the girls spent the night on The Merry Robin.'

'They what? Why are they still in Aysbury?'

'A pipe burst at The Bullrush and when they went downstairs

the kitchen and cloakrooms were flooded. Kurt worked all day yesterday and through the night. He hasn't been to bed. Abe helped him until the early hours. As soon as Sarah and the girls are awake, we need to bring them here and get them settled. I'll clear out the large cupboard in the utility for them to store some clothes and sort out some bedding for the sofa beds ready for tonight.'

Gray eases himself upright, a deep frown creasing his forehead as the information sinks in.

'Okay. I'll text Fisher. He was coming straight here about nine, but I'll throw on some clothes as I bet Tollie is awake and the three of us can meet up at The Merry Robin.'

'Should I wake Kurt? Unfortunately, I need to get the turkey in the oven and that's going to involve making a bit of noise. I daren't leave it until later in case anything goes wrong. I'm going to part-cook as much as I can in advance. The roast potatoes and the York-shire puddings alone will take up both shelves, so I figure I can reheat the rest in Tollie's oven. This is so stressful – I just wish my first attempt at pulling this off didn't put so many people's Christmas dinner in jeopardy!'

Gray gives me a reassuring smile.

'They'll understand, Immi. If Kurt sleeps through you moving around then leave him be. Sarah will probably have a set of keys for The Bullrush and they can pack a few things to tide them over. Well, it looks like the temperature dropped overnight, which isn't exactly going to help matters, but I really don't like the look of that sky. We'll know we're in trouble if it starts to warm up a little, as that could mean even more snow. But first thing the snow on the ground is going to be solid underfoot and slippery, so if anyone goes outside tell them to be careful. Anyway, I'd best jump in the shower and then alert Tollie and Fisher. Good luck in the kitchen, my Christmas chef. Guess we won't be doing presents until later.'

'At this rate, much later.'

22

Gently covering Kurt with a blanket, I move around as noiselessly as I can. Valerie is the first to surface and, thankfully, her entrance doesn't disturb him at all. I fill her in on what's happened and her face falls. We decide it's best to handle breakfast over in Tollie's kitchen, while I creep around organising the trays of veggies, in between basting duties.

'Rona will give me a hand,' she whispers. 'We still have the red cabbage and cauliflower cheese to sort out, but that's it. Anything else I can help with after cooking breakfast?'

Valerie is such a gem.

'No, thanks. I think I have everything under control here. Maybe we can ask Liam, when he's awake, if he can take some of the spare china and cutlery across to the cottage. At some point we'll have to figure out how we're going to accommodate everyone for lunch. The table just isn't going to be big enough to seat us all, as it's already a squash. I'm hoping to have everything ready for three o'clock, so there's plenty of time. I'm sure we can come up with a solution.'

Valerie stares down at her hands, interlacing her fingers.

'Thank you, Immi, for accommodating Liam. It's so typical for that son of mine to just turn up unannounced like that. He's a nomad really, and that's the lifestyle that suits him best as he gets bored very easily. Well, until he meets someone and falls in love, hopefully. He might consider putting down roots, then. The timing couldn't have been worse, though, and I feel bad that you and Gray are the ones who have been inconvenienced on your special day.'

She gives me an apologetic look, but I can tell from her demeanour that she's also pleased that Liam made the effort.

'After all the help you've given me, he's more than welcome, Valerie, and I mean that. I'm so glad for your sake, that he's here. It's a good sign.'

'I thought so, too,' she agrees. 'To be very honest with you it helps having other people around, as when he arrived it was awkward making conversation. We're starting to feel a little more at ease with each other, but mainly because we have no choice but to agree to disagree on a few things.'

'I haven't really had a chance to speak to him yet, but he seems like a very gentle man.'

Her expression softens as she nods her head, rather sadly.

'In many respects he is, but he's also a firm champion of the underdog. Sometimes he gets it a little out of perspective, I'm afraid, and he can't accept that things happen for a reason. As soon as the lane is safe, he'll be on his way and goodness knows when our paths will cross again, but it's good to see him looking so well. And happy.'

The door into the hallway swings open and Valerie suddenly springs across the kitchen in three or four strides to usher whoever it is back out. Before she exits, she leans around the door, her voice hushed.

'I'll put a sign on it, so that no one disturbs Kurt.'

I give her a wave of thanks, but the poor man hasn't stirred at all.

Grabbing a large bag of carrots and two hefty swedes, I start peeling. My head is still trying to process what's happened and I gaze across at the beautifully laid-out table. To squeeze a place-setting for ten into a standard six-seater was difficult enough and we'll be using some of the garden chairs. But to add another five is a real headache.

You can't have a jolly Christmas lunch if everyone won't fit around the same table. The open-plan arrangement means there's plenty of floor space, but this is going to take some organising.

Glancing at the clock, I see it's already time to do the first basting of the turkey. As I pull the tray out of the oven, I take great care as it's so heavy. Even heaving it up onto the stainless-steel trivet takes all my muscle power. But I'm grateful, as if I hadn't ordered such a monster of a bird, we wouldn't be able to feed everyone.

Without warning, out of the side of my eye I notice the door easing open very slowly and Liam slips inside, gently closing it behind him. He walks almost noiselessly across to me, the look on his face priceless as he keeps turning to check he isn't disturbing Kurt.

He comes very close, his voice a whisper.

'I carried one of those boxes over to the cottage. Mum said you could do with a hand in here. It's the least I can do as I feel bad that I've added to your workload. Timing has never been one of my strong points.' His grin is sheepish.

'Thank you, that's very kind. This lot will need slicing once it's all peeled, but I'm worried about the noise it's going to make.'

Liam gives me a thumbs-up. 'I got this,' he says softly, pulling out his phone. He stabs at the screen a few times and I prepare myself for an onslaught of sound, while continuing to baste.

Surprisingly, the volume is on low and the very soft and

relaxing sound of pan pipes carries on the air. He takes it up another notch, looking at me for approval.

'It's a meditation track,' he confirms in a hushed tone.

I give him a thumbs-up back and as I begin to pull on the oven gloves, he holds out his hands, indicating that he'll do it for me.

'Thank you,' I mouth at him.

My phone pings, and I grab it up, instantly muting it. It's a text from Martin to say happy Christmas and he hopes we're all fine. Well, at least he arrived safely at his in-laws and I quickly text back to let him know the lane is impassable. I promise I'll keep him updated, then wish them all a very merry Christmas and hope they have a great time.

Liam and I work in silence for a while and decide to up the volume a little before the chopping begins in earnest. In between, Liam makes us both a cup of coffee and I can't help wondering why he fell out with Valerie. They are both quiet people by nature, although Liam's natural reaction to strangers is to be very at ease, not aloof like his mother. I guess travelling around you have no choice but to strike up easy conversations with people from all backgrounds and beliefs. People whose paths you many never cross again.

'Are you hungry?' I put down the knife and place the palms of my hands on the island counter, my stomach starting to growl.

Liam shrugs. 'Hunger doesn't bother me; I often skip breakfast. I eat when there's food available.'

His casual attitude to everything is rather calming, that together with the soft music, which makes me want to curl up and relax on the sofa.

'I'll be back shortly. Merry Christmas, Liam. It's lovely that you could be here for your mum. I know she appreciates it.'

I turn on my heel, hoping he takes that in the spirit in which I meant it. Creeping out, I yank on my padded jacket and slip my feet into my snow boots; it's time to begin the trek across to the cottage. Everything is glistening and crunchy. The sun has already disappeared behind rolling white clouds, and it's bitingly cold. As I open the door to Tollie's kitchen what hits me first is the noise. There are people everywhere, milling around chatting, laughing and eating. The small kitchen is overflowing, and the sitting-room door is open. Looking through, I can see Jude and Jade sitting on the floor opening presents.

'Immi! How's it going? Is Liam making himself useful?' Valerie walks away from the hob, where she's turning sausages, to come across and give me a hug. 'I forgot to wish you a merry Christmas.'

'Me, too.' I laugh. 'Happy Christmas, everyone!' I yell out and heads turn, giving me a chorus of varying responses in return.

The atmosphere is jolly and as I walk into the sitting room to find Gray, it looks as if a coachload of people have just arrived. There is a pile of various bags stacked up in the hallway and one sofa is covered in pillows and duvets.

Sarah immediately jumps up out of Tollie's chair and hurries over to me.

'Oh, Immi. We can't thank you enough for accommodating us.' She scans around, taking in the huge smiles on her daughters' faces as they fiddle with their new tablets. 'You've saved our Christmas. Gray wouldn't let me come over to help. Is Kurt still asleep? He must be shattered, but, thanks to him and Abe, at least The Bullrush will begin to dry out and then we can assess the damage. We're gutted, if I'm honest. Kurt feels it's all his fault, but it's just one of those things.'

She looks pale and drawn, but she's trying her best to put a brave face on it. As she throws her arms around me, the tenseness in her body saddens me. What sort of a Christmas is this going to be for this wonderful, hard-working family?

'Don't worry, lovely friend. We're all here to help. As soon as

Kurt is awake everyone can come over to The Retreat. Thankfully there is plenty of room downstairs. The four of you can use the two sofa beds tonight, so you will be warm and comfortable. I just have one problem I need Gray to sort out for me.'

'Did I hear my name?'

As if by magic he appears and as Sarah releases me, I step into his arms.

'I knew you'd be missing me. What do you need? Because I'm your man; literally.'

Even in the midst of utter chaos, he manages to make me chuckle and I realise that no problem is insurmountable.

'A table to seat fifteen. That's doable, isn't it?'

As he presses his lips to mine his eyes are sparkling and he pulls away, looking in Tollie's direction.

'We can fix that, can't we, Tollie?' he asks.

Tollie nods. 'Only if you let go of my granddaughter and let me give her a Christmas hug, first.'

Tollie throws me a wink. He looks happy, overjoyed even, and it occurs to me that it's been a few years since the cottage was filled with so many people. Years ago, Grandma always invited everyone she bumped into and whenever Dad and I arrived we never knew who would be here. She was a natural gatherer of people and there were many years when people would end up staying over after an evening of partying. As long as there was enough floor space for the sleeping bags, no one ever complained.

'Immi, come and meet my Yvonne.'

Bernie steps forward, leading her by the hand. Yvonne is a rather shy-looking lady, but as she uncouples her hand and offers it to me her face breaks out into a wonderfully warm smile.

'Goodness, Yvonne, Immi is a hugger and you'll have to get used to that, my love,' he says as I bypass her hand and enclose her in a hug.

'It's wonderful to have you both here today, Yvonne. That's the biggest smile I've seen on Bernie's face in a long time. We've all missed having him around and you'll soon get to know us all. We're a friendly bunch and when we pull together even a snowstorm can't stop us having fun.'

'For a while there we thought we might have to turn back. You can't imagine how disappointed we would have been, but now we're here I do hope it eases up before we trudge back.'

Her eyes sparkle as she turns her gaze from me, back to Bernie.

'Bernie kept me going every step of the way. I'm so grateful to you all. I was nervous about meeting everyone, I will admit, but I've only been here for half an hour and I already feel at home. My house is so quiet, and I'd forgotten what it's like to... join in.'

'Well, it's going to be crazy and maybe a little disorganised today, but fun – I hope – and the more, the merrier. Aysbury welcomed me with open arms when I came to live with Tollie in 2006. And now there's nowhere else I'd rather be. So, I hope you get to feel the same way very quickly.'

As Gray seeks me out, Bernie turns to mouth 'Thank you, Immi,' before catching Yvonne's hand back up in his own and squeezing it.

'You haven't met Valerie yet, Yvonne. Let's head out to the kitchen.'

As I turn around, Tollie walks over to join Gray. They both insist I stay here as they head over to The Retreat to look at the issue of the table.

'I'm pretty sure I have a big piece of marine ply in the garage,' Tollie informs Gray. 'With a bit of luck, we can stabilise it on top of the table by fastening it underneath with a few blocks. That should add a couple of feet all round.'

'Hey, Immi. Merry Christmas.' Fisher appears, giving me a quick kiss on the cheek. 'That was a marathon trek, this morning.

My legs were telling me I'm not quite as fit as I thought. I'll give a hand, guys.'

They promise they'll creep around to ensure they don't disturb Kurt and will tell Liam that the best sausage sandwich he's ever likely to eat is ready and waiting for him.

Liam returns a few minutes later and as Valerie hands him a good, old-fashioned doorstop sandwich the look that passes between them warms my heart. Whatever has divided them in the past, it's obvious they want to reconcile and that's the first step towards changing their relationship for the better.

It doesn't take long to devour my breakfast sandwich and I laze back in Tollie's chair with my hands cupped around a mug of steaming hot chocolate. It's fun watching Jude and Jade, sitting on the rug in the centre of the small sitting room, oblivious to what's going on around them. The debris from the presents they've unwrapped is strewn around the floor, but no one cares. Everyone else is too busy chatting or eating.

The girls are playing an interactive game on their tablets and shrieking every time one of them goes up a place on the leader board.

'No-o-o-o!' Jude suddenly squeals. 'I fell off and that was my last life!'

It makes me giggle as I watch them, so engrossed they really aren't at all put out by the unexpected turn of events. Children are so adaptable, and, I reflect as I scan around, adults can be, too.

Sauntering back out to the kitchen with an empty plate and mug in hand, I walk up to Valerie, who is now washing up, aided by Ethel and Rona wielding tea towels. They'll soon have everything clean and tidy. It's lovely to hear them bantering between them- selves as they work like a well-practised team.

'You and Gray will have to extend this kitchen when the renovation work starts,' Abe's voice looms up from behind me. 'What do you think, ladies?'

They all nod in agreement. 'What it needs it a family-sized kitchen,' Valerie chimes in.

'I'll bear that in mind,' I reply as I pop my mug down on the side and make my excuses. 'Thanks, Valerie, that was amazing, and it hit the spot. But it's time to baste that turkey again, sorry, guys. When Kurt wakes up, I'll send him over and we'll move everyone across.'

Leaving them to it, I slip on my jacket, but, instead of heading straight for The Retreat, I take a little detour to gaze out over the fields, filling my lungs with the fresh, bracing air. It feels good to be outside. It isn't easy walking in what must now be more than a foot of snow, but it reminds me of a time when I was a small kid.

A crunching sound behind me makes me glance over my shoulder.

'I wanted to catch you to have a quick word. I'm not disturbing you, am I?'

Rona is all bundled up, as if she's going for a long walk.

'Not at all. I'm thinking about the Christmas Dad and I were here, when we had serious snow like this. I was probably about five years old at the time. Grandma and Tollie had Bessie, then, their Labrador. She had such a sweet nature. Dad and I took her out for a walk, and we had great fun. Bessie kept burrowing into the snow and didn't like how cold it made her, so she'd spring up in the air in a cloud of powdery white. Then she'd do it all over again. Daft dog.'

We continue on quite slowly, coming to a halt on the far side of the garden where it's bordered by low, ranch fencing. The fields beyond don't belong to the property, but when I'm standing here the openness is a reminder that nature belongs to everyone.

'I wanted to give you this. It's an engagement present.'

Rona thrusts a card into my hands.

'There's a cheque inside for five thousand pounds to help

towards doing up the cottage. Gray will make a fuss, but it's money I've saved over the years in the hope that I'd live to see this day. And now it's here I'm just so happy, although I wish the focus was a little more on the two of you. But, hazardous snowfalls aside, that doesn't make it any the less special and it makes me happy to be able to give this to you both.'

I'm speechless for a few moments and I lean in to kiss her cheek. It's too much, but how can I refuse her?

'Oh, Rona, that's so very generous and kind of you but it really isn't necessary.'

She puts up a gloved hand to stop me.

'Maybe not, but it's what I want to do.'

I swallow hard. This is a lot of money in anyone's book and even more to someone in Rona's position.

'It's very kind of you, Rona. We'll both be working hard to make this our forever home on a tight budget, so it will make a huge difference. Every penny of it will be most appreciated, you can be assured of that.'

'The two of you will make a great team and a mother couldn't ask for any more than that.' She looks, and sounds, a little choked-up. 'But it's time I thought about my own future and stopped relying on my boy so much. I, well, maybe I shouldn't say this and please don't repeat it to Gray, but I haven't stopped loving his father. We're both older and wiser. I fear my son won't understand and maybe when I meet Grayson face to face again, I'll feel differently. But there's a chance that I won't.'

Is Rona trying to tell me that she'd stay, if Gray's father asked her to?

'I love Gray with my heart and soul, you know that, Rona. I'll be by his side no matter what happens in the future. But you are right, and for your own peace of mind it is time to think about what's best for you.'

The look we exchange is one of total understanding. Life isn't easy, and difficult decisions can't be avoided. I shiver slightly as Rona heads back to the cottage and I make my way to The Retreat. I know that, in his heart, Gray will simply want his mother to be happy, but how accepting he will be if it involves his errant father, I have no idea. And what if she wants to move to the States?

Before I step back inside, I glance up at the sky. The sun's appearance was brief this morning and now I have to squint a little at the bright, light grey cloud that extends as far as the eye can see in all directions.

'That doesn't look good,' I mutter to myself. All around there is an eerie blanket of silence and then the snow starts to fall, once more.

You know that feeling when everything suddenly comes together, and you can stand back and let out a huge sigh of relief? Well, this is it.

'Mum, how many sprouts do I have to eat?' Jude stabs her fork into the tiniest one on her plate, turning up her nose in disgust.

'At least one,' Kurt confirms, as Sarah is still helping to dish up. 'They're good for you.'

As I carry two more plates across to the table, I notice that Tollie is sitting next to Liam and asking him about his travels.

'I guess my favourite place, because I keep going back whenever I can afford it, is the Seychelles. I did my PADI Open Water Diver course there earlier this year and I hope to go back again next year to do a Wreck Diver Speciality course.'

They stop talking for a moment to grab their plates.

Tollie gives me a wink. 'Thanks, m'dear. I've been looking forward to this all year.'

'This looks amazing, Immi.' Liam eyes the plate with delight.

'So, Liam,' Tollie continues, 'is there a bit of a treasure hunter in you, or is the diving itself the main attraction?'

I walk away to whisk a couple more plates off the side, delighted at how we've managed to seat fifteen people reasonably comfortably around the makeshift extended table. Albeit the assortment of chairs includes three stools and six plastic ones from the garden.

Fisher, I notice, is three seats away from Valerie and, while he looks happy enough, he keeps glancing her way surreptitiously. I so want those two to grow even closer, because they just seem to be a perfect fit.

'That's the lot,' Sarah informs me. 'I'll turn the oven down low and pop these back in covered in foil, as I'm sure a few will want seconds.'

'We did go a bit overboard on the roast potatoes,' I reply.

Sarah leans in, lowering her voice.

'What happened to the turkey? Did you have an accident?'

My lips twitch as I explain. 'It was huge. It wouldn't fit into the tray.'

She's trying very hard to keep a straight face.

'Well, you did a good job, all things considered, and I'm assuming you don't have a good set of knives. Which is just as well, as that's what we've bought you as a thank-you gift for helping out with the Christmas dinners.'

'Ah, that wasn't necessary. It did look a bit hacked about, didn't it? Was it hard to carve?'

Sarah gives me an encouraging smile. 'Tollie did a good job and I managed to make the slices look tidy on the plates. Anyway, you're a star to do that with the only sharp knife you seem to have.' She holds it up. 'You performed a miracle, Immi. This is a utility knife, mainly used for vegetables. The plan was to pop in with your present yesterday, before we left, as we thought you'd appreciate it. Anyway, it will make it much easier next year and they won't hack the flesh about quite so much.'

We both start laughing.

'What's funny?' Gray sidles up to me, on the hunt for some more paper napkins.

'We're talking turkey tales,' I answer. 'I think I'm going to get a few lessons from Sarah before I tackle my next one.'

'Turkey tails? Hmm, that sounds a little bizarre, but each to their own. Come on, don't let your dinners get cold.'

I pour on a little gravy and we're set to go.

'You rescued everyone's Christmas, Immi,' Abe says, clearing his throat as we join them. 'We're all very grateful to you, Tollie and Gray, for your hospitality. We've ended up descending on you en masse and now look at that, out there.'

As we all turn towards the patio doors, the view outside is totally obscured by a constant barrage of thick white flakes. I squint a little, dismayed at the lack of visibility beyond the immediate patio area.

'Gray, what's that big lump by the wall outside?'

Everyone stops talking.

'All will be revealed in a bit, Immi. Party hats on, everyone, and anyone else for more roasters?'

Hands go up and Gray strides across to the oven, as Sarah and I begin eating.

Both Gray and Tollie have been going on about buying a barbecue so I have my suspicions that I might know what my gift is. It's hardly a festive present, but they do say people buy the gifts they'd like to receive themselves. But that's certainly not the case with my Christmas present to Gray. He wanted an upgraded interface to extend his digital audio workstation. Well, at least that's what I hope is wrapped and waiting for him under the tree, but if the wrong thing was delivered in error, I wouldn't have had a clue. Tollie at least, was easier as I bought him a bigger tablet so he could keep up with his reading even as his eyes get weaker.

There's a cacophony of banter and laughter and reading of silly cracker jokes by Fisher, who has everyone groaning. Liam, I notice, has seconds and thirds of almost everything. Jude doesn't touch any of her sprouts, while Jade happily devours everything on her plate. With Gray's favourite CD of Christmas carols playing softly in the background on a loop, the lights on the tree twinkling away and the greenery overhead emitting a wonderfully evocative smell of pines and earthiness, I'm content. More than content. Valerie was right when I opened up to her. She had confidence in my ability to cope with whatever life was going to throw my way. It doesn't pay to get too far ahead of yourself and worry about things that might never happen.

Gray eventually taps his wine glass. 'I think it's time for the Christmas toast, so it's over to Tollie.'

As all eyes turn in Tollie's direction, he sits there twiddling the stem of his glass in his hands for a few moments before speaking. His head is bowed and he's deep in thought. When he looks up, he scans the faces around the table.

'Well, we have quite a gathering around the table and the first thing I want to say, on behalf of Immi, Gray, and myself, is how wonderful it is to have you all here with us today. It wouldn't have been as enjoyable without your company. Everyone is safe, we're all warm and my darling Immi, together with Valerie, Ethel, Rona and Sarah, have made this wonderful Christmas dinner happen, despite the drama going on outside.

'Immi, it has to be said, valiantly saved the day single-handedly, when the turkey turned out to be too big for the oven. Did that faze my granddaughter? No. As with everything in life, she rose to the challenge. And the next challenge will be bringing Lock Keeper's Cottage back to life. To do that she'll be calling upon her trusty partner, Gray, who, I believe, has a little speech of his own to make.'

There's an outpouring of laughter and handclapping, as I realise the 'turkey malarkey', as Gray is now referring to it, didn't go unnoticed. But sprouts aside, the plates were cleared and what it lacked in presentation didn't affect the overall enjoyment.

Gray stands and walks around to kneel down next to my chair. The hush in the room is filled with expectancy as he grasps my left hand and gazes into my eyes, somewhat nervously. I thought he was simply going to slip the ring on my finger to formalise his proposal the other day.

'My darling, Immi, the love of my life. You met this crazy man, the one who breaks into song at the most inappropriate moments, and let him into your heart. A man who struggles to keep his dream of a career alive and yet you support me every step of the way.' He pauses and we both swallow hard, exchanging a meaningful glance. 'The day you came into my life everything changed in an instant. And now, well, we're all rather taking it for granted you are going to say *yes*, and haven't had second thoughts. The question I put to you again is, Immi Tolli-man, you're the one I've been waiting for my whole life. Marry me... please.'

'Hmm. Decisions, decisions...' I string it out for a few moments. 'Okay. Hands up, everyone who thinks I should say *yes*.'

Hands fly up in the air. Most of the group holding up both hands, which is cheating.

'Did you offer bribes?' I level at Gray, as he exudes an air of smug satisfaction.

'Maybe. But you're worth it, Immi.'

I stand, pulling him up to meet me with my right hand, as he slips Grandma's ring on the finger of my other hand.

'Guess it's a *yes* then, by majority vote,' I concede.

We hug and everyone claps, accompanied by a few whistles and some tentative tapping on the table. Valerie and Rona immediately push back on their chairs and rush towards us. Rona is beaming as we hug, but when she releases me and turns to Gray, I see that

Valerie has tears in her eyes. She leans in to kiss my cheek and her voice is barely audible as she speaks.

'If ever two people were made for each other, Immi, it's you and Gray. I'm so very happy for you both.'

I'm touched by her words, as I can see they're heartfelt.

'Aww... Thank you, Valerie. Dad would have been thrilled and so would Grandma. I found my Mr Right and I know that sets Tollie's mind at rest for the future.' To my horror, my bottom lip begins to tremble now, and she throws her arms around me. 'Being alone, feeling lonely – even amongst friends – is a terrible thing and I wouldn't wish that on anyone.' It's hardly a whisper, but Valerie turns her face to look at me as our eyes well up.

'Always know you are loved, Immi, because you truly are a beautiful person inside and out. Life hasn't always been easy for you and you deserved better, so take heart. Nell will be wearing the biggest smile today.'

Suddenly, there's a jolt behind us that tips us slightly off balance and the spell of the moment is broken. Sucking in a deep breath, I look away as Valerie swipes her eyes with her hand. No one seems to have noticed us, as they are all too busy looking at Gray.

'Eek! Careful.' Tollie splays out his hands to steady the heavy, extended top, which has skewed a little as it sits balanced on the tabletop. Gray is on his hands and knees now, adjusting one of the blocks of wood beneath the table. 'We need to keep this thing stable as, I don't know about you, but I'm ready for dessert.'

There's a tinkle of laughter before Gray stands, pointing to Tollie, and then to the garden.

'Oh. Yes.' Tollie immediately jumps up. 'First things first. Feeling strong, Gray?'

In the background 'Good King Wenceslas' strikes up and I can see I'm not the only one who thinks this is a crazy idea. Gray goes off to grab their coats, as Tollie slides open the patio doors rather gingerly. The snow is now stacked up at least fifteen inches above floor level and, while hardly any of it moves, the wind gusts, knocking in several large clumps. That blast of chilly air cuts through the cosiness of the room like a knife.

'Guys, can't this wait until it warms up a little?'

Gray has already slipped on his coat and a beanie hat and is holding up Tollie's hooded jacket.

'By the look of it I think that could be quite a while. Shut the door behind us, but we'll need you to give us a little direction.'

I look at Gray as if he's gone mad and as I rush to slide the door back along the runners, everyone gathers round.

At the end of the decking area, under the edge of the over-hanging canopy, is what looks like a pile of blankets. We watch as Gray uncovers the handle of a trolley and the two men tilt it back but not without some difficulty. They begin pushing forward bit by bit until it's within three feet of the glass doors. That's way too close for a barbecue – what are they doing?

They untie the ropes securing the covers, and all of a sudden there he is in all his glory – it's Bert!

My hands fly up to my face in disbelief at what I'm seeing.

'What... how...?'

'We all chipped in,' Fisher informs me, placing his hand on my shoulder and giving it a tweak. 'And not only did Martin contribute, but he also did us a deal. The thing is, the guys want to know where you want him.'

Tears are prickling behind my eyelids again, but everyone is looking at me expectantly, so I plaster on a smile over my look of genuine surprise. 'This is too much, really. But I will admit, I was steeling myself for the day when Martin eventually sold Bert, because it would have broken my heart. Oh, guys – you are awesome and way too generous!'

Both Gray and Tollie are naturally growing impatient, stomping their feet to warm their toes, as they wait for me to indicate where to stand Bert. Gray points his hand, shrugging his shoulders and indicating first left and then right.

'He has to come inside.' I raise my voice as I slide the door back a little, because Gray is shaking his head, unable to hear me clearly. 'I know he's a statue, but I can't bear to think of him out in the snow.'

Tollie looks upwards at the heavens, but Gray thinks it's funny.

'Okay, it's your call. Stand back everyone.'

After a bit of head-scratching, Gray knocks the precarious ledge of snow back out onto the patio and then folds one of the blankets in four. He drapes it over the step up to the threshold of the doors.

Abe and Liam are closest, and they immediately rush forward to help.

'Count to three and you push, we'll pull,' Abe instructs.

'One, two, three.' There is a lot of groaning and I can't even imagine what Bert weighs.

But he's safely inside and no one strained a back, although the floor is wet and slippery now. I reach out to grab the other blanket sitting atop the mound of snow outside the door, then slide the door closed. I throw the woven tartan fabric down to sop up some of the melting snow; Gray and Tollie are now dripping all over everything.

Gazing at Bert, he seems very happy, standing as a statement silhouette against a backdrop of almost pure white. I pat his back and Gray slides his arm around my waist to give me a loving hug.

'You guys are mad, seriously mad,' I tell him, but we have matching smiles and I can see he's delighted with my response.

The temperature in here has dropped at least a couple of degrees and while Valerie and I mop the floor dry, everyone else is fixated on the garden. The wind is really beginning to whip up and it's now driving the piles of loose snow into drifts up against the fences and hedging. There's very little to see in the dim grey light as the visibility grows worse by the minute.

'Guess no one's going anywhere real soon,' Bernie mutters, mostly to himself. But Tollie and I hear him and I'm wondering how on earth we are going to accommodate everyone tonight. Abe and Ethel live closest, but that's a good mile plus, further along the towpath, and it simply isn't safe out there.

'Who's for charades after dessert? Let's clear the dinner plates away and get serving. Then we can move the chairs over in front of the patio doors,' I call out above the general background noise.

It's enough to get everyone moving.

The ladies all head off to the kitchen area, while the men clear the plates from the table. Gray lingers for a few moments, scooping me into his arms as I hold out my left hand, tilting my head to take in the detail on Grandma's ring.

'It is beautiful,' he remarks. 'I hope today hasn't disappointed you. Sharing the house and the cottage with thirteen of our closest family and friends, and someone we'd never met before today, wasn't quite how this was supposed to go. But I'm not at all unhappy and I hope you aren't, either.'

'Fourteen in total – you're forgetting Bert.'

'My sincere apologies, Bert. You love that chunk of metal, don't you?'

'I do. Almost as much as I love you, so be careful what you say.'

After a couple of hours of games, I realise I don't have enough bread defrosted to make sandwiches for everyone this evening.

'Hey, anyone up for a Christmas pizza?' I call out, and heads nod.

Valerie, Sarah and Gray follow me across to the kitchen as I turn on the oven.

'We're going to need to use Tollie's oven as well, or this will take forever. We can cut up the turkey legs for a festive topping. Gray and I will pop out to the freezer in the outhouse. Then we can figure out how we're going to carry the hot pizzas across once they're cooked.'

'I'll give you a few minutes, then I'll hang around by the front door.' Sarah looks at Valerie, who is already pulling out plates and piling them on the island.

'We'll get everything set up,' Valerie adds. 'Just be careful, you two. The last thing we want in this weather is for anyone to twist an ankle, or worse.'

Gray and I head into the utility room, which is now the temporary cloakroom. With a bobble hat pulled down to my eyebrows, the padded hood on my jacket pulled over the top, and my trusty snow boots, it's not exactly glamorous, but my fiancé still leans forward to kiss the end of my nose.

'You look so cute,' he murmurs.

'Cute? Seriously? Come on, fingers crossed Tollie's winter freezer delivery includes enough pizzas to feed everyone. We'll use up the last of that monster of a turkey, but at least there's still some leftover pork for tomorrow.'

Stepping outside, we quickly discover that the snow is several inches higher than our boots. Snow is supposed to be fun, but this is just cold and wet. It's difficult to see without constantly blinking, as the wind blows the hard, crystal flakes straight into our faces. It stings and it's relentless. The brick-built outhouse is only fifty yards away, but it's in the opposite direction to the cottage.

We trudge along in silence and it's slow going. Gray fumbles a little as he unlocks the hefty wooden door and when it finally releases, he stands back, encouraging me inside.

'Flip, that wind is cold,' I moan, glad at least of the shelter.

Scanning the shelf-lined walls, I take a mental inventory. If this weather doesn't break, at least we have lots of tinned soup and baked beans. All we are likely to run out of is milk, and maybe bread, after a few days.

Gray has already lifted the lid of the big chest freezer and is moving things around to get to the pizzas.

'How many do we need? They're pretty big. You could almost set up a shop with the stuff you have in here. I guess it's an advantage at times like this that you have to bulk buy to get a delivery,' he calls out over his shoulder.

'At least six. Yes. The delivery van driver has to trolley it down from The Bullrush Inn car park, so Tollie orders three months' worth of food at a time.'

After a little more foraging he begins handing out boxes to me.

'Might as well have them all as there are seven here, but two are pepperoni. How many loaves of bread?'

'Two. I know Tollie still has bread in the cottage. Can you grab a couple of packs of butter, while you're there?'

It's quite a pile and I sort around for two large cool bags and begin dividing up the goods. When we make our way back outside, the wet is beginning to soak up the legs of my jeans and my skin smarts a little as the seams rub as I walk.

'Give me the key for Tollie's and I'll see you in a bit,' I shout across to Gray. The wind does its best to drown out the sound of my words. He nods, throwing the keys up into the air. Miraculously, I manage to catch them, giving him a thumbs-up before we head off in different directions.

This isn't quite the romantic evening I've envisaged. I'd hoped that Gray and I would get a chance to have some alone time together, enjoying a long, carefree Christmas walk. I imagined us talking excitedly about the plans for the cottage as we basked in the joy of our special day. But here we are, worrying about having enough slices of pizza to fill everyone up.

By the time Gray returns, I'm unboxing pizzas and he hands me a parcel wrapped in silver foil.

'You're missing the festive bit.' He grins. 'Courtesy of Valerie.'

'She's been wonderful, hasn't she? I was so stressed about everything, but she sorted me out and calmed me down. We're coping and everyone seems to be in a fine festive mood.'

'We will need a bigger kitchen,' he reflects as I throw open the oven door to pop in the first pizza.

'Ah, well, yes. On that very subject, and don't get cross, but your mum has given us five thousand pounds as an engagement present.'

He stops, turning to look at me and shaking his head.

'It's her savings – that's utterly ridiculous. We have no idea whether she'll be left with enough equity to buy a place when the house is sold. I don't trust my father to do the honourable thing. And until I know what's happening with my own work situation, I might need to dip into my nest egg to help her out, anyway.' There's a tenseness in his voice that is hard to hear.

'Hey, it's just a quiet period. You know that. The work will pick up again and we'll manage. When Rona took me aside to give me the envelope my first reaction was to say no, too. But it means a lot to her, Gray, and you will offend her if you refuse. And before you say anything, put yourself in her position. She wants to do this for us, and it makes her feel good. We don't have to spend it – we could set it aside to help her out when she moves to Aysbury, but we don't need to tell her that.'

He begins to peel off his coat and we stand, looking at each other's soggy jeans. The water lines have now soaked up above our knees.

'Are your legs cold?' I ask.

'Frozen,' he declares, rather grimly.

'Slip off your jeans. I'll turn up the heating and we'll dry them off on the radiators. It's hardly likely anyone is going to interrupt us, is it?'

It turns out to be a task that is easier said than done, involving a lot of hopping around on one leg and pulling, then coaxing, but the relief is incredible.

'My teeth are literally chattering, and I can't seem to stop them,' I admit.

'Mine, too. Give those to me and I'll spread them out over the heat.'

'Do you fancy a glass of wine?'

Gray nods. 'Perfect. I'm enjoying this little spell of peace and quiet. Is that an awful thing to admit when everyone has been so generous? I would have bought you Bert as a present myself, but his price tag was a little on the hefty side.'

'I didn't actually want people to buy us presents. This was supposed to be low-key. Like our wedding.'

As we sit down, bare-legged, at the small Formica-covered table, we clink glasses.

'Here's to us, sitting together in what will be our new home! And grateful thanks for the people we have around us. And the fact that even in the middle of a blizzard we are blessed with the means to keep everyone fed. Let's not worry about money right now, Gray. Let's just be thankful for what we do have, beginning with each other.'

'Oh, Immi – the love of my life. You make my heart sing with notes my mind could never compose.'

And with that he begins humming, and nothing else matters, because everything is right in my little world as Gray leans in to kiss me.

* * *

'It might be my imagination, but is Fisher avoiding Valerie for some reason?' As Ethel helps me stack the dishwasher, she casts an eye in their direction.

'I think he's being careful, given that Liam arrived on her doorstep without warning.' She gives me a meaningful glance and I raise my eyebrows, as she realises what I'm referring to. Fisher is doing the right thing in giving Valerie some space. A strained relationship with an estranged son has to be managed carefully and now is not the time to introduce a third party.

'Of course! Well, thank goodness for that. It's all gone well, though, hasn't it?' Ethel gives me a little nod and a big smile. 'You've done us all proud, Immi. I can't remember the last time I had so much fun at Christmas. I don't think you're going to get away with a quiet little wedding, though, as today has been all about you doing the running around. Folk will want to make sure it's all about you two guys on the big day.'

I shrug it off. 'It's been the best Christmas I've had in a long time. I like the buzz, the chaos, and the fun. It makes me feel as if I'm finally living my life and reminds me that everything is about to change.'

'It's going to be a wonderful start to the new year. Are you keeping Bert inside permanently?'

I half turn to stare across at him.

'Of course. He's a member of the family now. He'll be moving into the cottage once the sitting room has been spruced up. Bert is going to stand in the corner, next to the fireplace.'

'Ah, lovely, Immi. You so deserve your happiness with Gray. What else can I do to help? Have you thought through tonight's sleeping arrangements?'

Suddenly there's a loud click and the lights go off, plunging the room into total darkness.

'Don't worry, everyone. Stay where you are. It's probably just a blip on the consumer panel and one of the circuit breakers has tripped.' Gray's voice rises up in the gloom.

One by one, out come the phones, acting like little torches to check everyone is okay. Tollie and Gray make their way out to the utility room. I run upstairs to glance out of the side window and there isn't a light to be seen. There's little doubt that this is a power cut.

'Everything is in darkness. It's not just us,' I call down over the bannister rail.

A flood of light appears at the bottom of the stairs and the outline of Gray's face peers up at me out of the shadows.

'Yep. Tollie, Fisher and I will head over to the outhouse to fire up the generator and see what we can power. Tollie is just digging out some storm lanterns.'

I groan, inwardly. 'I notice the heating's gone off, but we're on Calor gas, so we're good, aren't we?'

Gray screws up his face. 'Only if we can keep the pump running and that requires electricity.'

Oh no! Not to mention the fridge and the freezers. What next?

* * *

It's cold. And when I say cold, I mean the bone-chilling, teeth-chattering version. Before the power cut, Fisher said that, according to the news, fourteen inches of snow had fallen in our area and temperatures were due to plummet to minus seventeen degrees Celsius overnight.

By eight o'clock we've raided both attics for sleeping bags that haven't been used in a few years but, thankfully, proved to be a good investment. Together with three blow-up mattresses, which were Tollie's pride and joy in his camping days, every find is a treasure. It reminds me of summers sleeping in the back garden, with Grandma inside the cottage refusing to swap a sprung mattress for something filled with air. Tollie, Dad and I loved it on the occasions we were able to pack up the trailer and head off for a little trip.

In those days, the folding camper van was considered to be the best of both worlds, with two bedrooms and a living space. But more often than not, we'd put up his old tent in the garden and pretend we were camping somewhere, equally happy to pop back indoors to grab a snack and use the facilities.

Now we are cut off and who knows when the weather is going to improve? With no other options left, Fisher begins to inflate the mattresses with a hairdryer, and I take Kurt aside.

'We're out of space, I'm afraid. There's nowhere other than in here to fit the blow-up mattresses. I'm going to give Bernie and Yvonne mine and Gray's room and we'll take one of the doubles in here. Abe and Ethel will have to take the other double blow-up and we'll jiggle the furniture around in Tollie's sitting room for them. It's not ideal, but at least it's a little more private. Fisher will have to use the single in here, too. So, there'll be seven of us sleeping in this open-plan area tonight. Is that all right?'

'Listen, we're just grateful to be here. You do whatever you have to do to fit everyone in, Immi. This is no time to be making a drama out of a crisis.'

'Did you hear that?'

I tilt my head, calling out, 'Shush!'

The chatter quickly dies down.

'That was the pump, I'm sure of it.' I race over to place my fingers on the radiator by the door. It's stone cold and I shake my head but refuse to remove my hand. 'I heard it kick in, I swear.'

Everyone is swaddled in jumpers, duvets, or blankets, except for Jude and Jade, who grabbed two of the sleeping bags and are curled up on the floor playing snap.

'It's getting warm!' I yell, probably sounding more enthusiastic than if I'd just been told I've won the lottery. 'We will soon have some heat.'

The sound of heavy feet landing in the hallway sees me running towards the door to fling it open. Three very bedraggled and half-frozen men stare back at me.

'Well,' Tollie confirms, 'there's not enough power for the lighting. But the central-heating pump is up and running, and we can probably power the hob, oven, fridges and freezers without it tripping out.'

There's a hearty round of applause.

'I'll boil a pan of water and make some hot drinks.' Valerie jumps up. She's wearing two very thick winter jumpers. The top one is Gray's, the navy-blue, cable-knit sleeves falling well below her hands, but she looks toasty.

As I scan around, the battery-powered hurricane lamps cast a very pleasant glow. There isn't one miserable face among us. As Kurt asks the girls if they can help him make some room on the floor for the inflatable mattresses, they are both eager to help.

'It's like a village sleepover!' Jude yells at Jade, excitedly. They wriggle out of their sleeping bags to help Kurt and Sarah move the dining chairs and the table back against the wall.

The lights might not be illuminating our beautiful Christmas tree, but it still looks pretty, as the silver and gold tinsel reflects the light radiating out from the lanterns. The fact that the presents lying beneath it haven't yet been opened seems irrelevant.

Gray jumps up and begins singing 'I Wish It Could Be Christmas Every Day', made immortal by Roy Wood's iconic rock band, Wizzard. I seem to be the only one who finds this extremely funny, as I make my way upstairs to raid the airing cupboard for more pillows or cushions. But with each tread I mount, the sound behind me grows louder and it's amazing that everyone seems to know the words – even if it ends up sounding just a teeny bit out of tune.

* * *

I don't think I have ever laughed as much as I did this evening. Even in the darkness, wrapped in Gray's arms, as we share our sleeping quarters with three other adults and two thirteen-year-old girls, it's a hoot.

Jude and Jade have spent over an hour giggling and whispering and running back and forth to the window to check whether it has stopped snowing.

'Girls, that's enough now. We're trying to sleep,' Kurt keeps calling out with monotonous regularity, until eventually – despite the noise – he drifts off and promptly begins snoring.

The girls finally quieten down, and Fisher and I are the last ones awake. Gray has rolled over onto his side and is breathing heavily.

'You know who your friends truly are when you find yourselves sleeping together.' Fisher's voice rises up in a whisper from the other side of the kitchen island. 'I always wondered what this sleep-over thing was all about. Aren't we supposed to eat lots of midnight snacks, or something?'

'Mum won't let us when our friends stay over,' Jude bemoans in a hushed tone. 'She says we get hyped up enough and we don't need the added sugar to fuel us.'

I'm grinning in the darkness, my hands linked together behind my head to raise it up a little. Neither Gray nor I have pillows, but the mattress is more comfortable than it looks.

'Is everyone warm enough?' I ask, wondering what on earth it would be like if we didn't have the heating on.

'I'm good,' the three of them chorus.

Outside the glass doors everything is beginning to glisten as the snow finally stops falling. But it's glistening because the temperature has dropped, and the soft snow is beginning to harden.

25

The pinging of a text message awakens me at six a.m. and I shift position, suddenly remembering that I'm on an inflatable mattress. Gray is still asleep next to me and I suppress a giggle as I listen out and catch Kurt snoring softly. From here I can't see if the girls or Sarah are awake as the back of the nearest sofa is blocking my view. But the silence is only broken every few seconds by Kurt. I'm pretty sure it was Fisher's phone that disturbed me.

I lie quietly for a few moments, gazing around and allowing my eyes to adjust to the gloom. What looked rather cosy in the soft glow of the hurricane lamps late last night, in the slightly chilly greyness of a new day looks more like the after-effects of a party that got out of hand.

There's more pinging of phones in tandem now and Fisher, Kurt and Gray all rouse at the same time.

'Is that mine?' Gray asks, reaching out with his hand, his eyes still shut. They spring open when it dawns on him that there's no bedside table and he casts around on the floor to find it.

'Did you get that text, Gray and Fisher? Tollie just added you into the Aysbury adverse weather group, Gray, so you'll get updates throughout the day. It's run by Wes, the owner of Adler's farm,' Kurt calls out from the other side of the room.

'Thanks. Seems it's time for action. And the power is back on, apparently, so we can turn off the generator and get things back to normal,' Gray responds.

A very tired-looking Fisher suddenly looms up above the island, phone in hand.

'The messaging has been going on since about four-thirty. I spent a good hour in the utility room with Tollie, so as not to disturb you. The minute the snow stopped falling, Adler's farm started sending out updates. The ploughs have been out for a couple of hours now.'

'Ah, that was very thoughtful of you, Fisher, thanks. You must be exhausted, though. And those poor people who worked through a freezing night to get everything up and running; they are truly heroes.'

Sarah's voice appears out of nowhere as her dishevelled head rises up above the sofa cushions. 'Happy Boxing Day.' She waves out, and then promptly disappears out of view as the girls vault across from the sofa bed the other side of the coffee table.

The rest of us groan. This must be the worst start to a Boxing Day on record, surely?

However, it isn't long before everyone is up, because the whole of Aysbury has been mobilised. Updates keep pinging through, as news of the big dig-out plan, formulated in the wee hours in a flurry of texts between Tollie, Fisher and Wes, spreads.

I pop the kettle on, guessing that I'm probably not the only one in need of a little caffeine to get me started this morning. Tollie steps through the door.

'Morning, all.' He makes his way over to me, wrapping an arm around my shoulders and giving me a comforting squeeze.

'Don't worry about the state of the place, will you? Just fold everything up and deflate the mattresses. After breakfast, we're going to need everyone's help outside. Hopefully, Rona and Gray will be able to get the car out and drive back home tomorrow to pack.'

It had temporarily slipped my mind that they are on countdown to flying off to the almost unimaginable warmth of the Californian sunshine.

'Hey, m'dear, don't go frettin'. I'm sure the main roads and the motorways will be clear enough. Adler's farm is signed up to the Parish Response Scheme, so two of their JCBs have snowplough attachments. Wes's men have been out since about four this mornin', when the snow finally stopped fallin', and they know what they're doin'. He reckons a couple of hours and they will have cleared a single track all the way up to the top. If we can make a start on layin' some of the grit from the bins around The Bullrush Inn and the communal car park, then we can get people on the move. We also need to make the towpath safe. We don't want anyone endin' up in the water.'

Fisher joins us. 'I'll feel happier when I've been able to check on the canal boats moored a bit further up, just in case anyone has had any problems,' Fisher adds. 'I'll grab a quick coffee, if you don't mind, Immi. You know I'm fit for nothing at all until I've had my first one of the day.'

'You mean, two of the day,' I reply, laughing.

For a brief second it hits me that I won't be working with him any more. He's the one who picks me up on my grumpy Mondays and puts up with my annoying, over-excitement as the weekend looms. But not any longer. It's the end of another era in my life.

Tollie and Fisher are deep in conversation as I pass Fisher his coffee. He nods his head, appreciatively, but the two men are already running over today's action plan and I know it's best to leave them to it.

As I only have one more night here with Gray, I'm conscious that we've had zero quality time alone together. But there's no point dwelling on something I can't do anything about; we need to get the temporary beds put away and the dining table back in situ. I want everyone to at least have a seat to be able to enjoy their Boxing Day breakfast, before the shovelling begins.

I turn my head towards the patio doors; with the backdrop of an early morning sky getting lighter with every passing second, outside already bears no resemblance at all to that opaque, snow-laden greyness. It's a huge relief to think that, fingers crossed, tonight most of our guests could be sleeping in their own beds again.

Even though the snow drifts extend almost three feet high against the glass doors, there's a buzz of optimism that the worst of the bad weather is over. The reality of what lies ahead of us today is beginning to dawn on everyone, though. There's a lot to do.

Valerie and Liam join us ten minutes later and, together with Fisher, insist on taking command of the kitchen in The Retreat. It warms my heart to see them laughing and chattering away together as they get organised. Whether Liam knows Valerie and Fisher have a growing friendship, or that his mum will soon be working for Fisher permanently, I can't tell. Valerie keeps things very close to her chest by nature and, even though she's opened up considerably, there's still that cautious air about her. But maybe that's a good thing for now, as, although Liam seems easy-going, they haven't had much time alone together to talk since he arrived.

Kurt heads over to Tollie's, to offer his help to Ethel and Rona, while Sarah sorts out the girls. No one is going anywhere until they have been fuelled up for what promises to be a tiring day ahead.

With two kitchens working flat out to cook a hearty breakfast for fifteen people, it's all go. I wrap up warm, as I'm kept busy ferrying supplies between the two. At one point I lean so far into the big chest freezer in the outhouse, desperately hoping to get lucky and find some more part-baked bread rolls, that I almost fall inside. We always stock up for winter, but what feeds two for a couple of months doesn't last long when you have a houseful. Thank goodness I had that over-the-top shopping spree when I was in panic mode, as without it I don't know how we would have managed.

Everyone is in a jolly mood today, despite the task ahead, and every single person is helping in one way or another. Abe is busy sweeping the floors, while Jade and Jude are emptying the dish-washer – they are such thoughtful girls. Bernie and Yvonne do a grand job of packing away the bedding, then insist on laying the table.

By eight o'clock everything is looking a lot more organised, and I stand next to Bert for a few moments, surveying the garden. It does look amazing with a more encouraging backdrop. The bright blue of the wintry sky is a blessing, as the sun's rays filter through a few fluffy white clouds that are so wispy they are no threat whatsoever.

'I'm glad you're in here, Bert. Who wants to be out there, when you can be inside in the warm?'

He might be made of cast iron, but there's something in his expression that tells me he never was destined to rust away, battered by nature's extreme elements. Bert is a symbol, a symbol given with love. He holds his head proudly erect, his powerful shoulders reflecting his strength, and his stance is firm. He's setting an example and, no matter what else life throws at me from here on in, it's time to start believing Gray and I will be strong enough to cope with it.

The sooner Gray flies off, the sooner he will be back here by my side. I have nothing whatsoever to fear.

* * *

A little later, we all head out with scarves wrapped around our necks, hats firmly pulled down over our ears, and hands protected by gloves. Walking is laborious and laboured. With most of our party wearing several layers of clothes and thick coats, it isn't long before people are desperate to discard a few layers from all the exertion. Kurt and Sarah open up The Bullrush and it becomes operational HQ, although until the electrician arrives it's more of a dumping ground for discarded clothing. It is like a fridge in there at the moment, but it's not as damp as I thought it would be so at least that's positive.

'Are you doing okay?' Gray grins at me as I pull my rather charming snowflake jumper up over my head. I was hoping to wash my hair this morning but didn't like to take up too much time in the bathroom.

'I'm good. Just a little hot.' I sigh, thinking of the image I'd had in my head. The one where, if it snowed, Gray and I would be walking hand in hand, enjoying the beauty of the white landscape.

'That little bit of a glow suits you,' Gray comments playfully, his eyes sparkling. 'I love you even when you are hot and bothered and a little bit grumpy.'

'It's not like my girl to be grumpy.' Tollie walks up behind Gray, looking at me with a hint of concern on his wrinkled brow.

'It was supposed to be a beautiful setting but all it's done is cause chaos,' I moan. What I'm really annoyed about is the fact that the clock is ticking until I wave Gray off and there's a lot more snow on the ground than any of us could possibly have imagined. It's going to wipe out most of today, and tonight all we'll want to do is sleep, I suspect.

Last night I missed having some quiet time in bed, cuddling up with Gray and chatting before we drift off to sleep. Without a doubt, it's the favourite part of my day. It was the right thing to do to give our room to Bernie and Yvonne, but I slept fitfully, mindful of not disturbing the others.

'That's a sad face, Immi.' Gray tilts my chin with his finger to make me look up into his eyes. Pushing my sadness away, I give him the best smile I can muster. 'I know we were expecting a cosy, happy and relaxed celebration. Instead it's been hectic, and you haven't even had time to stop and catch your breath. Whatever happens, next Christmas we'll make sure everything is perfect. Even if you, me, Mum and Tollie end up heading off to a hotel for a few days so we can let someone else worry about the cooking. Anything to avoid putting you through another episode of turkey malarkey. What do you say to that, Tollie?'

Gray turns to look at Tollie, who turns to throw me a wink.

'You deserve a bit of pamperin', m'dear, and I think that's an excellent idea. Now, we'd best get out there and make a start. I'm just about to co-ordinate the various workin' parties.

'There is a bit of good news, though. To my complete surprise, it wasn't the manor's estate manager who rang me in the early hours after speaking to Wes, it was master Anthony, no less. He's going to send over a group of guys from the manor to lend a hand. Someone, maybe Fisher – or Wes himself – mentioned the fund-raising was going well. Anthony said he'd be delighted to make a donation and wanted to know where to send it.'

Stepping forward, I place an arm around my guys, drawing them into me in a group hug.

'Oh, my goodness! Some good can come out of something... well, not bad exactly, but testing. And now it's time for some hard work. Let's do this. It's just snow – it can't be that arduous a task, can it?'

They both shake their heads, laughing at my naivety.

'Hmm. You might discover a muscle, or two, that hasn't been

worked in a while. Let's just say that there will probably be a few of us in need of a soak in the tub tonight, laced with a generous helping of bath salts. Hopefully, everyone will be in their own homes, though.'

Kurt interrupts, bearing even more good news. 'It looks like we'll be able to switch the power back on within the hour. We'll soon get this place warmed up and the farm is going to get one of their dumper trucks down with a load of fresh supplies. Ethel and Rona have volunteered to take charge of the kitchen and will make sure hot drinks are available when people take breaks.'

At last, things are starting to look up and a real sense of relief is emanating from Kurt. With fridges and freezers full of food that will probably have to be thrown out, he simply wants to get things back to normal as quickly as possible.

Outside, however, it's another matter entirely. It's hot, sweaty work even though my nose, and toes, refuse to warm up. Ironically, the sky is now a stunning cornflower blue, and the sun is shining as if it's the middle of summer – it looks glorious, but the temperature is only a few degrees above freezing, so there's little sign of a significant melt. But at least it makes shovelling a bit easier, as we'd be sweltering otherwise.

I'm in a small party of six, with Valerie, Liam and three guys from the manor, who are very jovial.

Tollie is nowhere to be seen, but I bet he hasn't stopped. He waved out to me half an hour ago as he trudged off in the direction of the lane, phone pressed to his ear and deep in conversation. With JCBs and probably well over forty locals getting hands-on, this little community certainly knows how to pull together, but it's a lot to co-ordinate.

Gray has crept up behind me unseen and I jump as he suddenly leans in, making me turn around in surprise.

'We're nearly out of grit and we'll need someone to bring down a load from Adler's farm. I can't raise Tollie, so could you help me find him? His phone is permanently engaged, and Kurt and Sarah want me to let him know that the earliest they can serve lunch will be two-thirty.'

His voice is loud enough for everyone around us to hear and I'm grateful for an excuse to relinquish my shovel. My arms are already complaining and Gray was right, I seem to be using muscles I've never used before and they aren't happy.

'I'll be back in a bit, guys, promise!' I throw the words over my shoulder as I stride off in pursuit of Gray, who is already a few paces ahead.

When we reach the lane, he slows to allow me to catch up.

'I knew you'd feel awkward if I pulled you away, but you were giving it your all and you'll pay the price later, believe me, Immi.'

Out of sight of anyone, he catches my gloved hand in his, reassuringly.

'It's been hard work, but we've had a laugh, too. The dog walkers are out now it has warmed up a little and everyone has been calling out their thanks as they pass by.'

'Foot traffic helps break down the snow. And a track has been cleared down as far as the bridge over to the marina, but there's a long stretch to go to get down past the lock. There are a few hours of work ahead of us still.' I'm so relieved to see that Gray at least looks pleased with the progress so far. 'The real danger is more likely to be tomorrow if it freezes again overnight. We need to grit the footbridge and along the path by the permanent moorings. I'd hate to think of Abe, Ethel or any of them slipping and falling in.'

I feel rather guilty as the pace of my little group has slowed a little, even though a single track has been cleared and gritted, all the way around The Bullrush and back to the communal car park.

'Valerie was flagging a little, too.'

'Don't worry, I have it covered. Kurt is going to ask if she can help in the kitchen. Hopefully, Liam and the three guys will keep going for a bit after a round of coffee and some home-made chocolate brownies.'

I burst out laughing. 'Shame on you resorting to bribery, but I suspect it will work. Liam is getting on well with the other guys and asking a lot of questions about the manor. I can't imagine he's that interested, so I rather think he's grateful for their company. There's a little good-natured banter going on between them, as well as a bit of flexing of muscles. They've made it competitive, so none of them will want to be the first to give in. At least stopping for refreshments is a good excuse to allow them all to take a much-needed break.'

'I come in useful sometimes, then?' Gray quips, but I can see he has something else on his mind.

'Come on, you seem distracted; what's going on?'

'I worry about you, sometimes. When everyone descended upon us, I should have talked you out of doing the ring thing. You were supposed to be the centre of attention, not the hostess – what was I thinking? An engagement party should be memorable.'

'Trust me, it's a day I will never forget!'

We draw to a halt, standing two feet apart with our hands still clasped. I scan around, taking in the bare overhanging tree branches through which the blue sky and the glorious sunshine create an inviting vista.

'Okay, so it wasn't quite the cosy little dinner we'd envisaged. But it was lovely, for all sorts of reasons, not least because it reminded me of Grandma's Christmas dinners,' I continue. 'I won't make the same mistake with our wedding, though, I promise. You, me, Tollie and Rona will get our heads together and I'll listen to reason.'

Gray lets go of my hand and draws me into him; the look on his face tugs at my soul.

'I only intend on doing it the once, so it's important we get it right.'

Gray stares down at me, taking a long, slow drawing-in of his breath, and his happiness is very evident.

'Now let's make sure no one has an excuse not to make it home tonight, because I don't intend sleeping anywhere other than in our own bed. I want us to be able to enjoy our last night of the holidays together and I intend to make it a memorable one.'

26

FINALLY, THE SUN DELIVERS

After the delights of a mug of Sarah's hot chocolate, topped off with whipped cream and a dusting of cocoa powder, I'm ready for the last clearing session before a well-earned lunch. Fisher asked for two volunteers to give him a hand to clear a path from the marina's offices over to the footbridge.

As Fisher, Liam and I approach one of the sheds in the boat yard, the temperature is rising and off come the hats and the gloves.

'For the first time since we started this morning, I can feel the tips of my toes!' I exclaim.

'The forecast is for a gentle thaw and tomorrow it's supposed to warm up considerably. This shouldn't take us long. If I shift the snow, can you guys take control of the mini salt spreader and follow on behind? It's a pain having to refill it every few yards, so it's a bit stop and start, but it shouldn't take too long.'

Fisher unlocks the door and disappears inside, Liam close on his heels. I leave them to forage around and lean against the side wall of the offices, eyes closed and face upturned.

'Here you go, Immi.' Liam's voice breaks my reflective moment. 'This little baby is all yours.'

He wheels a compact, cherry-red machine in front of me that looks like a tub sitting on two bouncy tyres.

'I'll go and throw a few bags of grit into the wheelbarrow and load you up.'

Fisher exits the shed carrying the widest snow shovel I've ever seen.

'I've been itching to test this out. It's called a Mega Scoop and does the work of two people, allegedly.'

Men and their gadgets. Fisher is clearly excited as he lowers the beast to the ground. It's just a wide piece of polypropylene pushed along by a large steel handle covered in foam. As Fisher pushes against the frame, it seems to glide along with relative ease.

'Now that's what we need on the other side of the canal,' I enthuse, conceding that not all impulse buys turn out to be lemons.

There's no stopping Fisher, and Liam hurries over to shovel grit into the spreader.

'We're going to have to stop every couple of metres to top it up, but the upside is that it's not going to be too heavy for you to push, Immi, if Liam can do the shovelling.'

'A new set of muscles to test out, then,' I reply, smiling.

He's right and it's easy to follow in his wake. Even if there is a bit of a freeze overnight, this will do the trick.

'Mum was telling me that she's been working in the offices here.' Liam trundles along behind me, unfazed by the weight in the wheelbarrow. He's a strong guy and not afraid of hard work.

'Yes,' I call over my shoulder. 'It's been a great help in the run-up to Christmas, as I've had to do extra shifts at the Lockside Nurseries.'

'She said she's taking it on permanently after the holidays. It's a good job, then?'

Is he curious, or is he concerned about her? Either way, I'm glad they found time to have a proper conversation.

'Well, I've worked for Fisher for several years now and I've enjoyed it.'

'But you're moving on.'

I draw to a halt and Liam stops alongside me, to begin topping up the hopper. I unzip my coat, wondering if I should take it off.

'It's not possible for me to handle both jobs now and your mum and Fisher work well together.'

He finishes what he's doing, placing his shovel back on top of the barrow. Glancing ahead, we both watch Fisher for a few seconds and I'm pretty sure he's out of earshot. Clearly, Liam is thinking the same thing, but when he replies he still lowers his voice.

'He's okay, then? Trustworthy?'

'He's like a second dad to me and I'd trust him with my life.'

Liam nods, and I start pushing forward again.

'My mum has had a hard life.' Liam follows just a pace or two behind me.

'I'm sorry to hear that, Liam. She's a kind lady once you get to know her.'

'Yeah. She doesn't let people in readily. I'm like my dad. He's an open book. They drove each other mad and when things between them ended, he went off travelling. He teaches English at a school in Japan now.'

I turn around briefly, just to show him I'm listening.

'So, the travelling bug is in your genes, then?'

'I guess it is, or maybe the truth is that staying in one place has never really appealed to me, until now. I needed to see for myself that Mum really is all right before I make a commitment. I thought she was wrong coming back here in the first place. There was some talk about a link with the family in the manor house. Mum loves history but some things are best left alone.'

I don't know quite what to say to that, as he's assuming I am privy to whatever it is he's talking about.

'The thing is, I might not be able to afford to fly back again for another two years and it's easier to leave knowing there's someone around she can trust. At least we're back in touch properly now, so I won't be reliant upon updates from people she no longer sees on a regular basis.'

Something is telling me that maybe there's a girl involved and that's what's really behind this. Once he's settled, I wonder if he'll invite Valerie to visit at some point.

'You don't need to worry about her, you know. She has a good circle of friends and is a valued member of our community. Working at the marina has made a huge difference to her. Saint Nicholas's Well is a little off the beaten track, but, being around the marina on a regular basis, Valerie has begun taking part in more of the social side of things. We're all happy about that.'

'Thanks, that's helpful, as I'm heading off early tomorrow. She struggles to let go, you see. And that makes me feel guilty, like I've neglected her. But like my dad, I'm a free spirit.'

I stop again for Liam to refill the gritter and as he looks up at me I can see how much he cares about her. But there's clearly something he wants to get off his chest.

'It was my fault. I upped and left, and then didn't get in touch. The longer I left it, the harder it was to... well, I just can't have someone constantly looking over my shoulder, checking I'm all right every two minutes. She wanted me to have a plan, but I like to wing it. Life should be fun, after all.'

'Three more loads should do it, then we can head back for lunch,' Fisher calls out.

He's way in front of us now, so I slip off my coat and tie the arms around my waist. This last push is going to be hot work.

'Let's crack on, then,' Liam says enthusiastically. 'My stomach is telling me it's been a long time since breakfast.'

* * *

The Bullrush Inn is full. Sarah and Kurt are apologetic about the limited menu, but everyone is so hungry no one is about to complain. There's a hearty shepherd's pie, beef lasagne and a cheesy vegetable bake.

'The food is free,' Maggie informs me as I order my meal at the bar. 'You only need to pay for your drinks.'

It's a kind gesture by Sarah and Kurt, but people around here don't take advantage. The tip jar next to the point of sale is crammed full of ten- and twenty-pound notes and I have trouble stuffing mine in there.

'That's very kind,' Maggie says. 'They'll soon be back in service as normal and clearing the outside at least means customers can get in and out of the car park and around to the front safely. How's it looking over at the marina?'

'Good. And the sun is really warming up on that side of the canal, too. Mind you, another hour and the temperature will probably begin to drop rather quickly, but hopefully not too low.'

I carry a well-deserved glass of white wine across to find a seat. Gray waves out from a table in the far corner. It's for four, but there are five of them seated around it. As I approach, he jumps up.

'Good timing, Immi, you can take my seat. I'm off to give Abe a hand. We're going to begin clearing the snow off The Star Gazer for Fisher.'

He gives me a fleeting kiss, as Jade is heading in this direction with a plate of very hot food.

'Here you go, Immi. I made the sauce.' Her look is one of immense pride.

'Ah, it's going to be extra special, then. Thank you, gorgeous girl.'

She smiles back at me, shyly. 'Least we can do as you looked after us so well.'

Little does she know that it was her and her sister's bubbly laughter and excitement that helped to keep our spirits up and remind us what Christmas is all about.

'Hi, Rona, how are you doing?'

I slip into the empty seat next to her and she turns, giving me a contented smile.

'Good. And more than a little relieved, knowing the lane is almost clear. I was afraid we were going to be cut off for a while.'

The food in front of me is hot, but I'm so hungry I start nibbling away at the edges to load my fork.

'Are you anxious, or excited, about the trip?'

'I was anxious at first, but now I can't wait to see Grayson in person again. I've had several emails from him in the last twenty-four hours, as he was worried when he saw the awful weather we've been having. When we talk it's like turning back the clock and it reminds me that we both have a lot of good years ahead of us.'

Could this turn out to be the new lease of life that Rona needs right now to begin enjoying life again? Gray seems to be a lot more relaxed about her since he got his head around the trip, that's for sure, and I really can't see her pinning her hopes on retiring at fifty-five. When she's well, this woman has a lot of energy; I simply hadn't realised how much her health had declined since the first time I met her. But now she's bouncing back.

'So, it's all good, then?'

'It is and I'm feeling optimistic. That smells delicious.'

'This lasagne is hitting the spot, I must say, not least because I had no hand in the making of it. It's good to hear you sounding more like your old self.'

'Loneliness has a way of making you think about what matters most in life. Grayson is lonely and he's made that very clear. I couldn't have managed without my son being there every step of the way for me, but a serious illness is also a wake-up call. I'm a lot stronger than Gray thinks I am, but the truth is that I'm worried about his reaction. You know, if Grayson and I decide not to go through with the divorce.'

I put down my fork and stare at her. I always thought it was Rona who needed Gray. Was I wrong? We exchange a slightly worried look.

I eat in silence for a while, content to look around and glad that the water didn't breach the steps up into the restaurant area. Quirky old buildings sometimes have their advantages and it certainly stopped a nightmare from turning into a total disaster.

There's a pause in the conversation between Abe, Ethel and Bernie, and they turn their attention to me.

'We were just saying that this time yesterday, Immi, you were serving us up a turkey dinner. Best one I've ever had, I will admit.' I study his face, checking whether Bernie is pulling my leg. He looks serious.

'Well, hopefully it made up in taste what it lacked in presentation.'

Now they are laughing. 'Well, you did us proud. And it was a perfect way for Yvonne to get to know everyone, up close. In fact, Valerie and my lovely lady are down at yours right now doing a big clean through.'

My jaw drops. 'What?'

'After a stressful couple of days and all that physical exertion shovelling, you deserve to go back to a sparkling house. Tollie gave them the keys and by the time you, Gray and Tollie are ready to quit for the day it will all be sparkling.'

When the stomach is full it lets you know, and I'm done eating.

When the heart is full, that lets you know, too, and right now my heart is brimming over.

* * *

'Listen. Can you hear that?' Gray turns his head, first one way and then the other.

I strain my ears, shaking my head emphatically. 'No. What is it?'

All I'm conscious of at the moment is the wonderful smell of a freshly cleaned house, with a hint of lemon floor cleaner tickling my nose and threatening to make me sneeze.

'The sound of us, alone together – at last!'

It's hard not to smile at his enthusiasm as he spins me around in his arms, like dancers on a stage, as he hums softly under his breath.

'And Bert,' I add, looking across as he stands guard in front of the patio doors.

'So, you're adamant he's staying inside. Even during the summer?'

'Yep. And when we move into the cottage he's coming too, don't forget.'

Gray shakes his head at me, soberly.

'Some women need expensive clothes and flashy jewellery to keep them happy. My darling Immi, on the other hand, simply requires her grandmother's ring and a lump of cast iron to put a smile on her face. How am I ever going to figure out what to give you in the years to come? All those birthdays, anniversaries and Christmases?'

He's poking fun at me, humming in between.

'Shoo, shoo, shoo, shoo-be-doo, doo, doo, it's raining teardrops.'

I shoot him a quizzical look.

'Teardrops?'

'It's an ad for the prevention of dry eyes.'

Oh dear. I know Gray is up against it when his head is full of tracks for fifteen-second TV commercials, again.

'You haven't given up on finishing off that beautiful soundtrack you were working on, have you?'

He edges closer to the glass doors, feigning a sudden interest in whatever is beyond the immediate glow of the patio lights.

'No. It's just temporarily on ice for a while, until it's going somewhere.'

Does that mean he still hasn't heard back from the guy who, unfortunately, raised his hopes and hasn't even had the courtesy to put him out of his misery?

'I need to pay the bills and put my ego firmly in its place. It's a waste of life being a dreamer and it's time to focus on quantity, rather than quality. Hey, composing can still give me a reasonable income, although, I will admit, I've been offered a different job and I'm sorely tempted to consider taking that, instead.'

He sounds accepting of the situation, but I know he's not; not really. Gray is trying to side-line his creative spark and dismiss it as a foolish indulgence, but he has real talent and I believe in him. The musical track he's been working on is atmospheric, and at times menacing. It's edge-of-your-seat stuff, which is what the brief called for.

'You've heard nothing – not even a "thank you, but no, thank you"?'

'No. If Ollie was going to get back to me it would have been a few days before Christmas. He was flying out the day before Christmas Eve to spend the holidays with his family in Chamonix, skiing. I didn't get the gig… but I did get the girl!'

'You most certainly did get the girl. And she'll be counting down the hours until you're back with her, once more.'

It goes very quiet and I assume Gray has switched off when, out of nowhere, he says, 'Aha!'

'What?' I ask, wondering what on earth has popped into his head now.

'Give me a moment. I need to think this through.'

The seconds pass as I peer up at him.

'I think I've figured out how we're going to be able to move Bert safely across to the cottage. It took four of us to move him from the garage to the patio, and it was a nightmare over the uneven ground. The patio slabs out the back are fairly cheap to replace and perfectly flat, so it was a risk worth taking. But Tollie will never forgive me if I damage those wonderful old flagstones in the court-yard leading over to the cottage. Even if it is to please his beloved granddaughter. So, what we need to do is to build a flatbed trolley and then tip Bert on his side. It'll spread the weight more evenly and we'll be less likely to put anyone's back out in the process.'

'There you go, Bert, my genius of a fiancé has solved the prob-lem. Can we relax now, please? My arms and shoulders are killing me, and I need a massage before I slip into a hot bath.'

'Ah, my magic fingers are required. It will also give me a chance to run a few new tunes past you that have been whirling around inside my head all day. Dog food is sort of a new area for me and it has to be snappy.'

And as we make our way upstairs it's funny how quickly all thoughts of tiredness, aches and pains can fall away when your heart begins to race, and those endorphins begin to buzz around your body.

When, finally, it's time for bed and I fall into Gray's arms, a feeling of peace consumes me. He's the person who turns my half-empty glass into a glass half full. As the heat of his body begins to warm the chill on my skin, he starts to hum 'What A Wonderful World' – and it is.

27

THE SPIRIT OF CHRISTMAS HAS SUDDENLY... EVAPORATED

After a bitter-sweet night, conscious that we were both counting down our final hours together, yesterday was tough. Waving goodbye to Gray and Rona as they headed off home to pack, made it all gut-wrenchingly real. It's going to be the longest two weeks of my life. But today feels even tougher. I've gone from having a house crammed full of people, to being totally alone. I know Tollie is just across the way, but he has a couple of full days planned helping Bernie and Yvonne up at Turnpike Cottage.

This morning I feel empty and so achingly lonely. That awful feeling I remember only too well from my childhood. Times when I woke up in the middle of the night wondering why. Why me? When I was a child it was all very simple – I had clearly done something wrong; I was unlovable. That was the battle my dad fought, every single day – telling me over and over again, 'I love you, baby, and even though Mummy isn't with us, she loves you too.'

Did he believe that, or was he saying it to mend my broken heart? Every parting from someone I love drags up the familiar insecurities; not least the fear over whether I will ever see them again. As an adult I know it's illogical, but it's imprinted deep within me and at times I don't feel whole. A piece of me has always been missing.

Rona and Gray will be on their way up to Heathrow in a few hours' time. When we texted, earlier, I assured Gray I was fine and that I was going to begin sorting through the cupboards to declutter. When we swap over with Tollie, there's little point in moving stuff I haven't touched in a long while and I need to make room for Gray's things.

I was telling the truth, but the main reason was that I didn't want him to feel he had to keep texting or ringing me all the time. Rona will be both excited and nervous, I suspect, and deserves his full attention.

Sounding bright and cheerful, I told him to let me know when they were at the airport and then when they had landed. He seemed reassured. But thoughts of him never leave my mind and it's hard to get motivated.

Slumping down onto the sofa, I groan as every single joint in my body aches. Am I thinking myself into some sort of a depression? Compared to a lot of people I'm very lucky indeed. Am I such a wimp that I can't face being alone for a couple of weeks? It's pathetic, that's what it is – I'm pathetic when things are finally going so well.

The sound of the doorbell makes me reluctantly ease myself up onto my feet. It's probably the postman with a parcel Tollie asked me to look out for, as he was up and out early this morning.

However, when I swing open the door, it's Valerie I see standing before me with a bunch of roses in her hands.

'I thought it was a parcel for Tollie. Come in, Valerie.'

'I'm not disturbing you, am I?' she asks nervously.

'No. Not at all. Come through and slip off your coat.'

Her eyes flick over my face and she hesitates for a moment. As I open the door a little wider, she steps inside.

'These are for you, just to say thank you for making Christmas so special.'

I take them from her, lifting them up to my nose and breathing in their fragrance. The bouquet reminds me of summer and Tollie's profusion of climbing roses. 'You shouldn't have – it's very kind. I love roses.' Giving her a grateful smile, I notice that she looks rather unsettled. I hope nothing has gone wrong between her and Fisher.

Valerie hangs her coat on a peg in the hallway and then follows me over to the sofas.

'You were wonderful, coping with everything and everyone like that... disrupting your carefully made plans. And Liam went off with a smile on his face. I gather that's partly down to you. He didn't say very much, but he gave me a hug when he left and said he'd ring me in a few days' time.'

I indicate for her to take a seat, while I walk over to fill a jug with water. She seems content to sit and chat while I snip off the bottom of the stems and arrange the flowers.

'Liam told me the two of you had talked.'

She seems all right with that, but I think it's best to clarify I wasn't giving away any secrets.

'We only had a brief chat when we were gritting the path outside the marina's offices.'

Valerie shifts around in her seat, while I continue clipping and trimming leaves. I can sense that she wants to know more, but there's little to tell her.

'He questioned me about Jack, but I think you had already set his mind at rest on that front, Immi.'

I stop what I'm doing to look across at her.

'I told him that I'd worked very happily alongside Fisher for several years and that he's like a second dad to me. Liam just wanted to check you were safe and didn't feel lonely, I think.'

She looks startled, but I can't think why, because it's the truth.

Finishing up quickly and throwing the cellophane wrapper in the bin, I carry the vase of roses across to place them in the centre of the coffee table.

'There, don't they brighten the room? I, um... hope I didn't speak out of turn,' I offer, apologetically.

'No, no. Liam was simply looking for a little reassurance and you were kind enough to provide that. He seemed to get on well with Jack, the couple of times I saw them chatting. I'm not known for jumping into things and Liam was a little surprised about our friendship. And that's all it is, Immi, friendship.'

There's a firmness to her voice, but I don't feel it's aimed at me, more that she's trying to convince herself that's the case.

'But a friendship that might develop, I hope?' It's pointless either of us trying to pretend the connection between her and Fisher isn't getting stronger by the day.

'Well, I'm sure our working relationship will continue to grow, and I do appreciate having a job that takes me out away from the cottage. Working from home is a little isolating, I've come to find.'

She's being cautious and I wouldn't expect any different, but she sounds uneasy for some reason and I can't think why that should be.

'So, how are you doing, Immi?'

Now she's changing the subject.

It's a tough question to answer and my sense of emptiness is back, in a flash.

'It's quiet and I will admit that I really miss Gray. Which is silly, because I'm so used to him not being able to stay.'

Rather absent-mindedly I find myself twiddling with the ring on my finger.

'Yes, but this Christmas was special, and things have changed now. You're bound to miss him more now you're engaged.'

'I do, but I think I'm coming down with something too, so I'm wallowing a little – just ignore me.'

'Immi, I can't help thinking about the people who have let you down in the past. On Christmas Day when I said that you were a beautiful person inside and out, I really meant it. I saw how much it grieved you that your grandma and your dad weren't there to celebrate your engagement. I so vividly remember Nell wearing that ring and telling me with bright, shining eyes that one day some wonderful young man would place it on your finger. That was her wish and Tollie didn't forget.'

'Oh, Valerie. It never occurred to me to stop and think that staying here would dredge up old memories for you, too. You didn't just work here, you and Grandma were friends. And you continued looking after Tollie until I made everyone's life difficult and you left.'

'It was a joint decision between Tollie and me that I stopped coming here to help. We thought it was for the best. It wasn't your fault though, Immi. It's my fault and it's down to me to tell you the truth and suffer the consequences, because it's only right.'

Now I'm confused.

'I came back to the area as it was time I stopped running away from the past.'

'Is this to do with your mother's life here?' I enquire gently. 'Liam mentioned something about a link to the manor.'

'Oh dear, it's such a long story and it isn't really relevant. However, now he's mentioned it, I'd best explain. My grandmother had an affair with Henry Smythe, the man whose name you said rang a bell when you saw his photograph on the wall at the Linden Hotel. She was a nurse, looking after hospital patients who were sent home to recuperate.'

'But he was the person standing in the garden of Lock Keeper's

Cottage.' Why didn't Valerie mention this, that day when I went to tea with her?

'He was. His wife contracted tuberculosis and after a long spell in hospital they moved her into the cottage, which was on his family's estate. The day you sent me the photo it was the first time I'd ever seen his image. His wife eventually deteriorated and died in hospital some time later. Henry never moved back into the manor and there's no proof my grandmother ever told him she was pregnant.

'He continued to live there, alone, until his death, having no interest in the world outside his front door. Leaving no heirs, when he died everything he owned went to his brother, Joseph. No father's name was shown on my mother's birth certificate and it wasn't until we were clearing out my grandmother's things that we discovered a letter from Henry apologising for his "unforgivable actions". Judging by the tone of his letter, we realised what had probably happened.'

'That's incredible. What a story and how sad that the truth never came out.'

Valerie looks dismissive. 'It was 1936 and, as often happened in those days, my grandmother's pregnancy was kept hidden. She was sent away to stay with an aunt until Mum was born. Our lives had no connection to the way the Smythes lived and none of us would have been comfortable in that environment.

'The risk of a woman dying in childbirth in the nineteen thirties was high. It wasn't uncommon for families to take in a deceased relative's baby. People might have gossiped a little, but life goes on. My mother worked hard and as a headmistress ended up being well regarded in the community. Things are very different nowadays, thankfully, but in the past every family had secrets that were rarely brought to light. I'm very interested in it from a historical and a personal point of view, but I have no interest beyond that. But I will admit, I was hoping that among those old photographs there might have been one of him in the garden here, with his wife. And maybe the woman who nursed her.'

'I can understand your curiosity. It's a lovely way of looking at it, Valerie, and very respectful when you could so easily feel resentful for what must have been a tough time for your family to get through.'

'It's the reason Liam thinks I returned here, having overheard a part of a conversation I'd had with Mum, a long time ago. But a chance comment Liam made before he left made me break a pact I'd made with myself a long time ago and that's what brought me here to see you, today.'

'Um, Valerie, I'm having a bit of difficulty keeping up with this. Am I missing something, because I can't see what this has to do with me?'

'Liam assumed that's why I came back here. To see if I could find out what really happened, once and for all, and that suited me, but it wasn't the real reason. Oh dear, this is truly heartbreaking, Immi, because there's no easy way to say this. I'm the woman who walked away from her husband, Sean, and our darling little daughter all those years ago. Only Tollie and Bernie know the truth, now that Nell and Sean are no longer with us. Liam has no idea whatsoever that I have links of my own here.'

I'm too dazed to speak. How can that be? Wouldn't I know instinctively if I was sitting opposite my mother and not simply a neighbour who has become a friend?

'But you can't be.'

She wipes away a solitary tear that begins to trickle down her cheek.

'I know you deserve better, Immi.' Valerie's voice is hoarse with emotion as she anxiously twists her hands together, struggling to remain composed. 'When I bought Byre Cottage, I came to see Nell and Tollie, to beg their forgiveness and to explain. I was very young when I had you and it was several years after I left, before my condition was diagnosed. Then it was too late.'

My head is spinning. 'Condition? Too late for what?'

I watch as she swipes her hands across her eyes, then stares down at her lap.

'To try to redeem myself; to make contact with Sean and explain, but by then you were both settled in a place that wasn't a constant reminder for him of how I'd destroyed our life together. We'd been so happy, until without warning everything changed.'

'But my mother's name wasn't Valerie; that's not the name on my birth certificate.'

'I know, it's Alison. Alison James. I changed my name by deed poll a year before I met Jeffery Price.'

I stare at her, horrified as the words sink in.

'Why have a baby if you don't intend to love it and cherish it with every fibre of your being? There is no excuse, no reason on earth to forgive anyone for leaving their own child.'

'You're looking at me like I'm a monster and I deserve it.'

'But Liam is your son and you brought him up lovingly, because, as much as you might have fallen out, he cares about you. So why couldn't you love me?'

Valerie virtually collapses back against the cushions, her eyes flicker shut and for a moment I wonder whether she has fainted.

'Liam is my stepson. His birth mother died several years before I married his father, Jeffery.'

'So, if what you are saying is true, you left Dad and me and started over again, guilt-free. Then you managed to love and care for someone else's son while pushing away all thoughts of your own flesh and blood?' My words are full of the bitterness that begins to well up inside me. Valerie gave Liam all the love a child requires and doted on him. He never once referred to her as his stepmum, only his mum, and his only complaint was that he felt overprotected. 'And Liam obviously has no idea about our *connection*.' I can't bring myself to spell it out.

'No. And I appreciate how it might look, but I didn't take Liam away from his father. We had shared custody and Liam regularly stayed with Jeffery, but he wasn't a man who could cope with the constant needs of a child.'

'My father coped, and I had constant needs.'

I see Valerie flinch and I can tell how painful this is to hear. But why should I sit here feeling sorry for her?

Tears trickle down my face, but I want to hear what she has to say. Even though there's a numbness deep inside me.

'You deserve an explanation, Immi, at the very least. Almost immediately after Sean drove us home from the hospital, it was clear something was very wrong with me. The local doctor dismissed it as baby blues. For some women there is a condition that comes on quickly after the birth. It wasn't as talked about thirty years ago, or as well understood as it is now. It's a hormonal imbalance, which causes moods swings and, in my case, anxiety. But it didn't go away as it was supposed to do, and it got progressively worse. I was convinced you weren't safe in my hands and at one point was too afraid to even pick you up. I didn't trust myself, not that I would ever have harmed you – it wasn't like that. I loved you so very much, but I was petrified every time you cried. Was it something I was doing wrong, I wondered, or was I just a total failure as a mother not being able to soothe my own baby? To the extent that Sean insisted we move in with Nell and Tollie for a while, as he didn't know what else to do. He was working away a fair bit, at that point.

'I barely knew what time of the day it was, let alone how to cope with a fretful young baby who was picking up on my anxiety. Much later a psychologist explained that what I was probably suffering from was post-partum depression. It triggered a form of obsessive-compulsive disorder for a while and when it came to looking after my stepson, Sean, I couldn't let him out of my sight. There was no such thing as normal for me, given the level of guilt I carry for the suffering I caused.'

She pauses, not looking at me to register my reaction at all. This isn't something she's rehearsed, that's obvious.

'My dad was a good man, with a good heart. His life revolved around family and a job he loved doing. I know he wouldn't have given up on you, he wasn't like that. You gave up on us, Valerie, and that was your choice.'

She sighs and it comes from deep down within her. A cold, desperate sound.

'I wasn't me any more; there were times I didn't want to live, as I could see how I was hurting everyone around me. In pain, mentally, I was overwhelmed with guilt and feelings of abject failure. So, I ran away when you were three months old. Eventually, my mother tracked me down, just in time to save me from doing something stupid.'

My jaw drops a little as I stare at her.

'You thought about taking your own life?'

She doesn't acknowledge my question, as she continues.

'My mother was a very practical woman, thank God. I went to live with my parents in Dartmouth, until we had a proper diagnosis, and spent the next few years of my life as a waitress in their little tea shop. The nature of the illness I had is that I have little recollection of what happened. And no knowledge at all about the period shortly after I left. Tollie continues to honour his promise to Sean, to leave the past alone, and I respect him for that. Although I know it hasn't been easy for him. Perhaps my imaginings are worse, but I doubt it. I robbed you, my baby girl, of what you deserved – a loving mother to share the happiness and the tears, to be a constant in your world.

'I grieve, still, for the life that feels as if it was stolen from me and yet I did that, so I'm the only one to blame.'

I'm horrified as I listen to her rambling dialogue. It's as if Valerie is unaware that I'm here, and she's speaking only to herself.

How can they have kept this from me? Would I have done the same thing if I'd been in that situation?

'But Dad and I came to stay with Tollie and Grandma a couple of times every year. Why was nothing said after you'd moved back?'

'A part of the deal I made with Nell was that I stayed away whenever you were here. Our paths were not to cross – Sean made that very clear. He said you'd been through enough and that was his way of protecting you. I had forfeited any rights I had, and I knew that. But they could see that it was important to me to know you were doing well and there was no intention on my part to interfere. Just being here was enough.'

'Did Dad know the whole story?'

She nods her head and a sharp pain stabs at my chest.

'Yes. He wouldn't agree to a meeting, but I sat down with Nell and she told him everything.'

My mind is frantically trying to piece it all together, but there's little information to grasp onto. I remember what Liam said, that Valerie was constantly looking over his shoulder and checking on him. What she'd been through had left scars, as deep as my own.

'So why tell me this now?'

I realise I know nothing at all about the woman sitting in front of me, a person I'd trusted and grown close to in good faith, as a neighbour and friend. How can I trust anything she tells me now?

'I'm living a lie and I won't hurt you all over again. I had no idea this would happen, I swear, Immi, and I know that Tollie is beside himself, unsure of what to do for the best.'

Has he been living in fear of the day I discovered the truth?

'Jack is totally unaware of my real identity,' she continues. 'I know what his reaction will be when I tell him, but as I've grown closer to you I find I can't hold onto my secret any longer. Jack and I do have a special rapport, both feeling there is something missing from our lives. I know that telling you the truth will jeopardise that new friendship, but when I saw how much you were hurting on Christmas Day, I hated myself for my part in that, even more than I already do. I will never forgive myself and I have absolutely no right to plan any future happiness that could cause upset to you, Immi.

'You regard Jack as your second dad, and that role means so much to him. If I leave Aysbury now, Jack will get over it sooner, rather than later. I thought I could honour my promise to keep my distance from you, but Sean underestimated the size of your heart. Or your affinity with wounded souls.'

We sit quietly for a little while, motionless, and I'm not sure what to say, or do.

Valerie suddenly rises up from the sofa and before she makes her exit she pulls a small envelope from her pocket, placing it on the coffee table. Even after I hear the front door click shut behind her, I don't move.

I don't even know how I feel, or how to react to a story I could never have imagined. I've never felt as alone, or bewildered, as I do right now.

28

LOVE HAS THE POWER TO CHANGE EVERYTHING

It's late afternoon and Rona and Gray will have boarded their flight to the States by now. Gray rang a couple of hours' ago, trying his best to be cheerful, but the effort required for me to sound upbeat and pretend everything is fine here has taken a toll.

I stare at the clock. Fewer than ten minutes have elapsed since the last time I checked. Clock watching isn't going to make time speed up. They don't land until early evening US time but it will be the early hours of tomorrow morning, here in the UK. Gray's father is collecting them from the airport, so that will be a rather stressful journey. They will probably all go for a meal and then have an early night, as Rona and Gray will be shattered. Physically and emotionally, by that point, I shouldn't doubt.

I'm feeling miserable and lonely. And now I'm feeling unwell — coughing and unable to stop my nose from running. At first I thought it was from the tears I shed when Valerie was here, but I'm definitely coming down with a cold. There's little point lying on the sofa feeling sorry for myself. Sitting bolt upright, I ease myself up and head straight for the bathroom to find some eucalyptus oil to help me breathe more easily. The face staring back at me in the bathroom cabinet mirror is pale and blotchy. It's clear I'm running a temperature, even though I feel cold and clammy.

What I need is a cup of hot, sweet, tea.

'I'm glad you're here, Bert.' As I walk back into the open-plan area it has never seemed so vast and empty. But I'm not alone, Bert is on patrol and keeping an eye out.

'It's quiet without Gray here, isn't it?'

I have no idea why I phrased that as a question, and a sigh catches in my throat at how dejected I sound. However, the angle of his head as he stands watching over the garden is strangely reassuring.

I fill the kettle, then yank things out of the cupboards; eventually I carry a little tray across to the coffee table. I console myself with the thought that it's fine to spoil yourself when you're feeling poorly.

Bert looks as if he needs a pat, so I saunter over to him and we both gaze out. The snow is melting fast – only the huge mounds we made shovelling paths are taking their time to thaw.

All my life I longed to know who my mother was, to know what she looked like and to demand to know what reason she could possibly have had to walk away from Dad and me. This was right versus wrong and there are no excuses. There *were* no excuses. Or so I thought. The story Valerie told me was not the one I was expecting to hear, at all.

A key in the front door makes my heart sink. I told Tollie not to bother looking in on me after his busy day at Turnpike Cottage. Turning around, one hand leaning on Bert's sturdy back for support, I compose my face.

'Gray!'

The man I love more than life itself rushes over to me, sweeping me up into his arms and showering the top of my head with kisses. As he lowers me to the floor, surveying the tip of my bright red nose, which is smothered in moisturiser, he raises his eyebrows.

'You're poorly? Oh, my lovely Immi. Come on, sit down and drink your tea before you fall down.'

He's right, I'm clinging onto him as if my life depends upon it. He helps me over to the sofa and gently lowers me down. I open my mouth and the questions come out in a stream.

'What are you doing here? What went wrong? Was the flight cancelled? Is Rona okay?'

'Nothing is wrong,' he replies, sounding tired, but not anxious. 'I will need to grab a coffee first, though. It was quite a day and a long, wearisome journey back in heavy traffic.'

Picking up my mug and placing it firmly in my hands, he walks over to the kitchen and I sit sipping tea to help calm my nerves and ease my sore throat. I need the few minutes' silence to calm my racing thoughts.

Watching his back, I find it hard to believe I'm not imagining this, and I'm fearful of blinking my eyes in case he disappears. My brow is a little feverish, but he's definitely real.

'Waiting around meant Mum and I could have a good chat and she could see I'm not ready to meet up with my father yet. The timing isn't right because I just want to be with you. When I explained how I was feeling to Mum, she hugged me close and said, "Go. Be with Immi and take some time for yourselves – I'll be fine," and I knew she would be.'

Gray walks over to sit down next to me and we roll into each other, sinking back against the cushions.

'But your father...'

'He can wait a while longer. When I fly over, you will be by my side. In future we face our fears together.'

My heart sinks in my chest. Gray has no idea what's happened with Valerie. But he's here and he will never know quite how much I needed to see him today.

'Sometimes facing one's fears isn't quite as bad as we imagine it will be.' My voice sounds small in the cavernous hollow of the room.

Gray frowns. 'No? Well, that's encouraging. It did worry me a little when I texted you earlier on and didn't get a reply, I will say.'

I blink, looking sideways at him. 'But I responded. I was phone-watching,' I admit.

Gray stands, pulling his mobile from his pocket before lowering himself back down to sit on the edge of the sofa.

'Oh, the battery is dead. I'll drink this and dig out my lead. Now snuggle back and I'll put on a DVD. It's time someone waited on you, for a change.'

I shake my head at everything he holds up for approval, as I don't fancy a romantic comedy and I'm most definitely not in the mood for anything scary. My head is whirling, and I need time to gather my thoughts before I decide exactly what I'm going to tell Gray.

'Maybe a series, then. *Poldark*?' Gray jiggles the DVD box around, waving it temptingly in the air.

'Perfect.'

'Perfect?'

'Well, Aidan Turner is perfect.' I giggle; the joy of having Gray here changes everything. Even my cold doesn't feel quite so draining.

'Is he, now? I'm thinking maybe this is not quite the right programme for my fiancée, then.' As much as he's complaining, he still pops the disc into the slot, before covering me up with a throw.

'And here's a glass of water. You need to keep hydrated. I'll unpack my bag, but no fawning over that actor – I'll be keeping an eye on you.'

He casts me a stern look and I suck in my bottom lip, trying not to laugh as he teases me.

In the background, he hums as he places the mugs into the dishwasher and then I cosy up as he takes his bags upstairs to begin unpacking. As I blow my nose rather noisily, a trip to Cornwall seems like the perfect thing to calm my troubled mind.

It isn't long before I hear Gray shouting out at the top of his voice as he clatters, noisily, down the stairs. He rushes through the door with his phone in his hand and his eyes wide.

'My phone started pinging like mad the minute I plugged in the charger! Read this – start at the top and work down.' He forces his phone into my hands as I stare at him, rather puzzled.

There is a string of three texts from Oliver Harding, all sent this morning.

Hey Gray, my email keeps getting rejected, it says your inbox is full? Re-sending it now for the fifth time. You haven't committed to another project, have you?

I've left several voice mails. I really, really need to speak to you asap, Gray – you're the man for the job and I'm in trouble if I don't sign you up, mate.

Me again. Sorry for the garbled messages. Just phone me as soon as you can. Thanks, Gray.

'You got the job and the girl!'

I hand the phone back to him and he stands there looking at me as if he can't believe it. 'I spent some time while I was at the airport clearing my inbox of old messages. I had no idea it was full, though.'

'Well, ring the man, then, and put him out of his misery.'

The look that passes between us goes from shock to ecstasy in a split second and Gray starts punching the air.

'Whoop! I did it!'

* * *

Wrapping me in his arms, Gray pulls the duvet a little higher, then reaches over to tuck it neatly along the side of my body.

'You're going to catch my germs; you do know that?' I groan as he leans in to plant another kiss on my lips.

'What's yours is mine, germs and all. This commitment lark works both ways.'

I start laughing and he lies there, staring up at the ceiling and humming another of the endless tunes he has rolling around inside that head of his.

'I like that idea. And what's yours is mine... Mr Musical Composer for a sci-fi film who is about to earn a fortune.'

That makes us both chuckle. The first film may come with a modest cheque attached to it, but if all goes well it's goodbye doggy food ad jingles – my talented fiancé is spreading his wings and about to fly.

'One day I'll achieve my dream as a songwriter and a composer, but it all starts here, Immi.'

Gray rather dramatically holds up his hands in the darkness, spreading them out as if it's a screen, and begins to hum the opening bars to the piece that will accompany the film title and credits.

'*Dah, dah, dah-dah, da-da-da-da-da, d-a-h, d-a-h, d-a-h...*' It's thrilling to think that at some point we will be sitting in a cinema somewhere, watching in awe and checking the reaction on the faces of the people around us.

He lays on the tense atmosphere with staccato notes and then his voice softens as the lighter notes ripple up and down the scale.

'Imagine the blackness of outer space...' his words are low '...and then a craft comes into view. Inside, are ten people whose lives are about to change forever. They are going to discover something that will save the world.'

'Stop! Don't tell me how it ends. I want to savour that when I see the—' I let out the loudest explosive sneeze, only just managing to get a tissue out of my sleeve to catch it in the final second '—film in full, on the big screen.'

'Oh dear, you are suffering, aren't you? My poor darling.'

He rolls over to look at me and I hold my face away a little, not wanting to breathe on him.

'I really don't want you catching this, so please keep your distance.'

He looks at me, shaking his head.

'It's not just the cold, is it? What are you keeping from me? I can see it in your eyes. It comes and goes, so that means you're pushing it away. You haven't had second thoughts about going from a quiet wedding to a bit of a proper *do*, have you? I mean, everyone wants to be in on it, and we should be grateful about that. And now I'm not so worried about the money side of things, so let's make it memorable in a way that feels right for us.'

'It's not that. There's no easy way to say this because I'm still in shock – in fact it has left me feeling numb.' His brows knit together as he looks at me expectantly. 'I found out yesterday that Valerie is my mother; she is, or was, Alison James.'

Gray's jaw drops appreciably and his mouth gapes open in disbelief. He jerks upright, staring down at me.

'Did I hear that right? Valerie? Mrs Price? You didn't dream this, Immi, did you? I mean, your temperature keeps spiking and when someone is delirious their thoughts can sometimes seem very real.'

I ease myself upright as he wraps an arm around my shoulders, pulling me into him so tenderly. I can see that he thinks I'm getting sicker by the minute.

'It's true. There's no way she could know my mother's name. Tollie has no idea that Valerie has shared her secret with me and neither does Bernie.'

'Bernie? What's Bernie got to do with it?'

'Valerie was born and brought up in Middle Norton and that's how she met Dad. Bernie is Tollie's closest friend and they even went to school here together. Few of today's inhabitants will know what happened back then. But Bernie probably does.'

'How do you feel about that?' Gray's eyes search mine, hesitantly.

'Disappointed, I suppose, and overprotected in a way that leaves me feeling uncomfortable. I certainly didn't know Valerie until after I came to live with Tollie. And she didn't stay long before handing in her notice. I always believed it was because Tollie and I were constantly rowing over how messy I was and, well, selfish. But it turns out that wasn't the case. Grandma had asked Valerie to look after Tollie, thinking he'd be here on his own. No one could have foreseen that Dad wasn't going to be around by then, or that I would end up living here permanently, so I get that. Grandma must have believed Valerie's explanation, whilst honouring Dad's decision to let the past lie. Valerie may be able to take the blame for a lot of things, but what she went through was tough and hearing about it wasn't easy.'

As I tell him all about Valerie's illness, the poignancy I feel in repeating her words sends a chill to my core. His reaction indicates, like me, he's finding it difficult to process the information, let alone draw a conclusion from it.

'It's hard to take in. It's crazy, Immi. I'd imagined some heartless, selfish person, because she did the worst thing imaginable. Admittedly, Valerie is a very private woman and a bit of a loner at times, but her heart's in the right place. She's worked tirelessly for the community and on our Christmas project, and never asked for anything in return. And all the while she was keeping an eye on you, her daughter.'

I nod, forcing down a gulp as a lump suddenly rises up in my throat. 'She was. And Tollie said nothing, but she knew he was growing more and more concerned about the situation. Fisher is totally unaware of any of this and that's why she told me. Valerie said it wasn't fair on me, or Fisher, to think she can make a life here, given how things have developed. He is like my second dad; everyone knows that, and she believes he'll hate her when he finds out the truth because she doesn't deserve forgiveness.'

Gray hugs me even closer and I try not to sniffle.

'You believe her story, though?'

I sit quietly in his arms, trying hard to breathe over his shoulder and keep my germs at bay.

'I do. But that doesn't mean to say I know how to react to it.'

'Immi, you know that Tollie would do anything for you, don't you? He'd give his life for you.'

I nod and he feels the movement.

Gray's reaction mirrors my own. It had never occurred to me that at some point in my life I'd have to practise forgiveness for people who had always put me first.

'If I question him, he'll think he's failed me in some way, and he didn't. Dad had a right to decide what was best for me. Grandma and Tollie were simply falling in line with his decision. I think they all knew that I couldn't have coped with the truth back then and they were right. Getting to know Valerie as member of our community, I wasn't on my guard around her, or raking up feelings of bitterness about the past. I became friends with her because I sensed her pain and her regret, without even knowing we had any connection at all. I discovered the woman she really is and the sense of sadness that she has carried with her throughout her life. You can't blame someone when they're ill and their life suddenly falls apart around them – what she needed most at that time was help.'

Gray sighs. 'How ironic that you were the one who put Valerie and Fisher together.'

'I know and they're perfect for each other. But as for Valerie being my mother – I mean, my *mother* – it doesn't seem real, even though I heard the words from her own mouth. To me she's just Valerie. My mother is someone entirely different, some unknown woman whose face I could never quite conjure up.'

'You don't hate her, then?'

I loathe the word hate. I loathe it because I did for many years *hate* my mother. I hated her for leaving me motherless. For making me the odd one out. When other kids' parents divorced, at least they had two parents. It was Dad who did my hair and learned to paint my nails so I could be like the other girls. This six-foot-four giant of a man would often spend his Saturday mornings fussing with a five-year-old's hair, co-ordinating sparkly scrunchies with cute little dresses, before I went off on a play date. He was my father and my mother. And he always will be, no one can take that away from him. And that's why Tollie and Grandma honoured his decision that I didn't need to know the truth.

As for Valerie, well, I had started to see her as a friend. Now there is no easy slot for her to slide into, because three people took care of me during my formative years and she wasn't one of them.

'No. I don't hate her, but...'

'You can't change the past.'

I nod once more, unable to speak, but so relieved that Gray can understand exactly what I'm feeling.

'I like Valerie. She's a kind, thoughtful woman and I believe what she told you is the truth. The past only hurts if you can't move on. Maybe the best way to deal with it, Immi, is to judge her only on what she's done since your paths have crossed and what happens from here on in.'

It's a moment of complete clarity. I've been fretting over what to do, worrying about her expectations of me and how I should react. And Gray, just like that, has put it all into perspective.

'It's one day at a time, Immi. And I'm here to help you through it.'

Gray drifts off into a deep sleep and I'm left alone with my thoughts. I think about the envelope Valerie left on the coffee table and the tears I shed when I eventually got up the courage to open it. Inside was a photograph, just the one. It was a young Valerie cradling her baby daughter in her arms and on the back she'd written *'my darling Immi'*.

GRAY

HAPPINESS IS LEARNING WHEN TO FORGIVE

When I admitted to Mum at the airport that I wasn't ready to meet my father, the reaction I received was typically her.

'I'd come to the same conclusion, my son. I've been sitting here trying to find the right words. I didn't want you to think I was down-playing how important this trip is for us all, whatever the outcome. It's something that should have been addressed a long time ago and as parents we failed you, Gray. But there's a time and a place for everything and now simply isn't it. Your focus should be firmly on Immi and nothing else, at this time. So, first things, first. Don't worry about me. I'm a survivor and I've proved that. You kept me going through one of the toughest times in my life and both you and Immi put your future on hold for me. Gray, I feel truly blessed to have you as my son. Head back to Aysbury and see in the new year with your arms wrapped around my soon-to-be daughter-in-law, because nothing would make me happier.'

The look we exchanged was one of acceptance and I knew she'd be fine.

Immi is a survivor too, she's had to be, but she doesn't know when to stop battling. Or, when to let other people do things for her, for a change.

After Valerie's revelation, Immi continued to struggle to make sense of a past that had come out of the blue. Casting around for ideas to help, I asked Bernie to come to The Retreat, to have a heart-to-heart chat with Immi. She needed to talk to someone who at least had some knowledge of what had happened.

He explained how Tollie had vowed to honour his son's wishes and there was no way he would ever have broken that promise. I was pretty sure Immi would understand that. He single-handedly supported her during some very dark years, when she was angry and grieving the loss of two people who were most important in her life. For her it was a double blow served within just a few short years. But, somehow, Tollie pulled her through it all.

As for Immi's dad, well, even though he knew that Valerie was within walking distance, apparently his feet never trod that path. He had left it to Nell to make it clear to Valerie that she had to keep her distance. Too many years had gone by and Bernie told Immi that he often wondered whether her dad ended up leading the sort of life he always wanted. Free to be married to his work and have as his best friend and the focus of his life his wonderful, intelligent and capable daughter. Sometimes things happen for a reason, but it's only with hindsight it becomes apparent.

Immi admitted to me that she regretted the day she decided to stop asking her dad questions about her mother, for fear of hurting him. In hindsight, she wondered if that was why he made his decision not to hear Valerie's side of the story. But we talked it through, late one night, and agreed that it probably wouldn't have changed a thing. It was time to let it all go.

'Are you nearly ready?'

Tollie is looking very smart in his best suit, a white shirt and a badly tied dress tie.

'Um... I need a bit of help here, Gray. Immi normally does the honours. She has more patience than me.' He gazes at his reflection in the mirror, a deep frown puckering his forehead. 'It's been a few years since I've worn this tie, but the suit does me every time there's a weddin'.'

'And very fine you look, too. The plan is that Immi will jump in the taxi I ordered and head to the hotel at seven-thirty. Telling her that Kurt needed a hand in the cellar as an emergency made her roll her eyes a little, but you know what she's like. I told her he had a problem with his barrels. She looked at me blankly and I must have looked convincing, because she just shrugged and said, "Good luck with that," and I assured her I wouldn't be far behind. She thinks I'm walking Valerie down to join everyone at The Bullrush Inn and then heading over for our romantic dinner for two.'

Tollie shakes his head, giving a chuckle. 'That's my girl. Never moans if someone needs a hand, no matter how inconvenient it might be.'

I finish adjusting his tie and he checks himself out again; this time there's a twinkle in his eye.

'Takes me back a few years, to be sure, but it comes up a treat every time.'

'We need to get off a bit sharpish, just in case Immi decides to pop over to check on you before she slips into a relaxing bubble bath. If you're not here, she'll assume you left early, to help up at The Bullrush.'

Tollie looks a little uncertain. 'This is the right thing to do, Gray, isn't it? It won't be too much for her?'

'It'll be fine. She's trying to figure out how to deal with it all and not upset anyone.'

'Even I had my doubts about keepin' the truth from her, but my Sean did a grand job bringing Immi up and we respected his wishes. My darlin' Nell said that we should honour his decision, no matter what, and that's what I did.' He pauses for a moment, his face clouding over. 'Immi wouldn't have welcomed Valerie back just like that, and it would have ended badly. Instead, they reached out to each other in a way none of us expected. Deep down there was a link neither could ignore, but it happened naturally – it wasn't forced. And now I can relax, because I know it was the right decision after all.'

I place a hand very firmly on Tollie's shoulder.

'All Immi needs now is for us to act normally. She'll take it in her stride. Trust me.'

His hesitation is momentary and then he looks me firmly in the eye.

'I do, Gray, I trust you with my girl and that says it all.'

* * *

I don't know who is more nervous as we sit waiting for Immi to appear – me, Tollie or Valerie.

'When Immi arrives we are going to welcome her, ignoring the look of surprise on her face. Give her a hug and then sit back down, ready to enjoy a nice celebratory dinner to welcome in a new year.'

I'm talking to them both as if I'm the elder here, but I can't risk either of them bailing out now. This feels like the final hurdle, as we gather together as a family. In my heart I know it's what Immi longs to happen, but we're all treading carefully for fear of hurting her.

The moment Immi steps in through the door, I'm the first to look up and catch her eye – that gleam as she smiles back at me makes my heart leap in my chest. I rise up out of my chair and walk towards her.

Already her gaze is moving on over my shoulder and there's a moment of hesitation – then she straightens her back and walks forward with a smile fit to light up the entire room. It doesn't just come from her eyes, but from deep inside her.

'Tollie, Valerie – what a wonderful surprise!'

And the worst bit is over. For us all. Immi included.

Valerie and Immi will work out how their relationship is going to develop as they move forwards. They've made a good start and the bond they've formed over the last couple of months is real, based on nothing other than a genuine regard for each other. Anything that is born out of respect can only grow.

Valerie didn't step outside her door for a couple of days after her talk with Immi and we didn't quite know what to do about it. Then, one evening, Immi stood up and said she was going to see Fisher. The two of them spent an entire evening talking and I have no idea what was said, but the next day when we called into The Bullrush, Fisher and Valerie were sitting together at one of the tables.

I froze, but Immi whispered in my ear that everything was fine and, although we didn't go over to join them, she seemed content. There has been an awkwardness, though, which I suppose is only natural, so getting together to celebrate the new year is important. From here on in, we all need to look forward and not back.

We have a pleasant meal and spend a lot of the evening talking about the upcoming wedding. My suggestion of a wild west theme had them all falling about laughing when I described bales of hay for the guests to sit on. Valerie, I notice, took her lead from everyone else, but engaged in the conversation with a graceful ease.

There's a lot of Valerie in Immi; things I hadn't noticed, or connected, before because why would I? Especially that very private side that no one really gets to see, and which only appears whenever Immi and I are alone together.

'Fisher wondered whether a wedding cruise would be a fun thing,' Valerie throws in, as we languish over coffee and the last of the wine.

Immi's eyes immediately light up. As I sit back, watching the three of them looking relaxed and at ease, the interaction is lively, happy and full of light-hearted banter.

'Nice as it sounds, it won't work,' Tollie remarks, shaking his head. 'Even looking at the minimum numbers likely to be there, The Star Gazer just wouldn't be big enough.'

'It's a shame because it's a great idea,' I add.

'But what if you had the ceremony onboard? Floating down the river, with the vicar officiating. No more than twenty people in attendance, with something Gray has composed playing in the background. Maybe, stopping by the bridge across to the marina as you say your vows. I'm sure we could arrange that. If people happened to be standing on the bridge, they'd have a wonderful view of the service. Then, afterwards, maybe a marquee in one of the fields behind The Bullrush?'

All eyes are on Valerie, whose words came out in a rush of excitement and now she's sitting there, hesitantly.

'That sounds perfect,' Immi replies, giving her a genuine smile. 'What do you think, guys?'

Both Tollie and I look at each other.

'Wonderful.'

'Amazin' idea.'

'We have a plan, then,' I say, raising my glass. 'Immi, I think this calls for a little speech. Over to you.'

I almost spill the wine when Immi's foot suddenly finds mine beneath the table. As I look across at her, what I see is an amazing woman, who never fails to surprise or delight me.

'Sometimes the Christmas you get isn't quite the one you expect. As it turned out, we had the perfect Christmas and an even more perfect New Year's Eve.

'So, here's to a truly wonderful year ahead, full of happiness and laughter, shared with family and friends. It's time to count our blessings and make those dreams come true. Life doesn't get any better than this, does it?'

As our glasses chink together, Immi's eyes are twinkling, and she turns her head to gaze at me. Leaning in, she whispers: 'Thank you, my darling Gray.'

I feel that my heart is about to burst. It's the look of love that I see reflected in her eyes and a man can't ask for any more than that. The past is now just the past and a bright, new future beckons for all of us, born out of forgiveness and love.

ACKNOWLEDGMENTS

The launch of a new title is always a thrill and, for me, doubly so when it's a story that involves Christmas.

The author is just one link in the chain, though, and before I began writing I had no idea how many people were involved. Sarah Ritherdon, my awesome editor and publishing director, deserves a huge thank you for believing in me and the characters I create. Until the manuscript arrives in her inbox, she has no idea what the story is about, but, once she has her hands on it, it's a thrill to see it through her eyes. And her guidance ensures we end up with it in the best shape possible, ready for the wonderful line editors and proof readers to make it sparkle.

My agent, Sara Keane, is also very instrumental in the process and an incredible support. Knowing there is someone only a phone call away whenever you need to chat something through is a blessing.

And to the wider Boldwood team – a truly awesome group of inspiring women – I can't thank them enough for their amazing support and encouragement. The sheer enthusiasm of everyone involved is so appreciated.

I'd also like to thank my family and friends, who understand my erratic lifestyle as a compulsive writer. The person I am now is rather different from the person I was before I gave up the day job to write novels. It is hard to switch off when a story simply wants to be written and the characters fill one's head with constant chatter. I tend to disappear for long periods, coming up for a breather in between to catch up on what's been going on around me. Fortunately, my husband, Lawrence, is always there to keep the herbal teas coming and make me take frequent breaks.

As usual, no book is ever launched without there being an even longer list of people to thank for publicising it. The amazing kindness of my lovely author friends, readers and reviewers is truly humbling. You continue to delight, amaze and astound me with your generosity and support.

Without your kindness in spreading the word about my latest release and your wonderful reviews to entice people to click and download, I wouldn't be able to indulge myself in my guilty pleasure – writing.

Feeling blessed and sending much love to you all for your treasured support and friendship.

Lucy x

MORE FROM LUCY COLEMAN

We hope you enjoyed reading *Christmas at Lock Keeper's Cottage*. If you did, please leave a review.

If you'd like to gift a copy, this book is also available as an ebook, digital audio download and audiobook CD.

Sign up to Lucy Coleman's mailing list for news, competitions and updates on future books:

http://bit.ly/LucyColemanNewsletter

A Springtime to Remember, another glorious escapist read from Lucy Coleman, is available to order now.

ABOUT THE AUTHOR

Lucy Coleman is a #1 bestselling romance writer, whose recent novels include *Summer in Andalucia* and *The Villa of Dreams*. She also writes under the name Linn B. Halton. She won the 2013 UK Festival of Romance: Innovation in Romantic Fiction award and lives in the Welsh Valleys.

Visit Lucy's website: www.lucycolemanromance.com

Follow Lucy on social media:

facebook.com/LucyColemanAuthor

twitter.com/LucyColemanAuth

instagram.com/lucycolemanauthor

bookbub.com/authors/lucy-coleman

ABOUT BOLDWOOD BOOKS

Boldwood Books is a fiction publishing company seeking out the best stories from around the world.

Find out more at www.boldwoodbooks.com

Sign up to the Book and Tonic newsletter for news, offers and competitions from Boldwood Books!

http://www.bit.ly/bookandtonic

We'd love to hear from you, follow us on social media:

facebook.com/BookandTonic

twitter.com/BoldwoodBooks

instagram.com/BookandTonic